TE

NY

MA

SURG

BY

LYNNE MARSHALL

NYC ANGELS: AN EXPLOSIVE REUNION

BY

ALISON ROBERTS

MILLS & BOON

Step into the world of NYC Angels

Looking out over Central Park, the Angel Mendez Children's Hospital, affectionately known as Angel's, is famed throughout America for being at the forefront of paediatric medicine, with talented staff who always go that extra mile for their little patients. Their lives are full of highs, lows, drama and emotion.

In the city that never sleeps, the life-saving docs at Angel's Hospital work hard, play hard and love even harder. There's always time for some sizzling after-hours romance…

And striding the halls of the hospital, leaving a sea of fluttering hearts behind him, is the dangerously charismatic new head of neurosurgery Alejandro Rodriguez. But there's one woman, paediatrician Layla Woods, who's left an indelible mark on his no-go-area heart. Expect their reunion to be explosive!

NYC Angels

Children's doctors who work hard and love even harder…in the city that never sleeps!

NYC ANGELS: MAKING THE SURGEON SMILE

BY

LYNNE MARSHALL

Many thanks to Mills & Boon® for the opportunity to participate in this wonderful Medical Romance™ continuity. Special thanks to Flo Nicoll for creating Polly and John, two characters I grew to think of as friends by the end of this book.

First published in Great Britain 2013
by Mills & Boon, an imprint of Harlequin (UK) Limited.
Harlequin (UK) Limited, Eton House, 18-24 Paradise Road,
Richmond, Surrey TW9 1SR

Special thanks and acknowledgement are given to Lynne Marshall for her contribution to the *NYC Angels* series

ISBN: 978 0 263 89896 5

Harlequin (UK) policy is to use papers that are natural, renewable and recyclable products and made from wood grown in sustainable forests. The logging and manufacturing process conform to the legal environmental regulations of the country of origin.

Printed and bound in Spain
by Blackprint CPI, Barcelona

Dear Reader

Have you ever known a people-pleaser—someone who will do anything to keep others content? Perhaps you are one. If so, you know what a huge undertaking making everyone happy can be. Impossible, even. Yet Polly Seymour, RN, plods ahead with her challenging life, insisting upon sprinkling seeds of joy everywhere she goes, whether a person wants those seeds of joy tossed their way or not.

On the other hand, we might all also know the proverbial curmudgeon. A person who has been kicked in the teeth by life once too often—someone who has forgotten what it's like to be a part of the huddled masses, yearning for something better. Most observers would give up on him and his sour moods. But someone astute at reading people, like Polly, recognises a man with a big heart even if he doesn't want to admit it. Because any man whose day isn't complete until he's said goodnight to each of his hospitalised paediatric patients can't be all bad, right? Meet Dr John Griffin.

Throw these two most unlikely people together on a busy orthopaedic hospital ward, let them duke it out—her killing him softly with her charm, him coming off gruffer than he intends—and watch the sexual sparks fly. It just goes to show you never know which small gesture or innocent invitation might reach inside another person's heart and start the healing.

Now imagine running into someone your first day on a new job—someone who will change your life—but all you feel is annoyed. Imagine being the newest employee on the ward and still having the nerve to approach the head of the department with a grand idea. Imagine two damaged people, struggling to make it through each day, using completely different coping mechanisms. Meet Polly and John, two people I hope you'll root for as they stumble and fumble their way towards that often elusive prize—their very own happy-ever-after.

Welcome to **NYC Angels**—the hospital that won't turn anyone away.

Happy reading!

Lynne

Lynne Marshall loves to hear from readers. Visit www.lynnemarshall.com or 'friend' her on Facebook.

Lynne Marshall has been a Registered Nurse in a large California hospital for over twenty-five years. She has now taken the leap to writing full-time, but still volunteers at her local community hospital. After writing the book of her heart in 2000, she discovered the wonderful world of Mills & Boon® Medical Romance™, where she feels the freedom to write the stories she loves. She is happily married, has two fantastic grown children, and a socially challenged rescue dog. Besides her passion for writing Medical Romance™, she loves to travel and read. Thanks to the family dog, she takes long walks every day!

To find out more about Lynne, please visit her website: www.lynnemarshallweb.com

Recent titles by this author:

DR TALL, DARK...AND DANGEROUS?
THE CHRISTMAS BABY BUMP
THE HEART DOCTOR AND THE BABY
THE BOSS AND NURSE ALBRIGHT
TEMPORARY DOCTOR, SURPRISE FATHER

CHAPTER ONE

MONDAY MORNING POLLY SEYMOUR dashed into the sparkling marble-tiled lobby of New York's finest pediatric hospital, Angel's. The subway from the lower East Side to Central Park had taken longer today, and the last thing she wanted to do was be late on her first day as a staff RN on the orthopedic ward.

Opting to take the six flights of stairs instead of fight for a spot in one of the overcrowded elevators, she took two steps at a time until she reached her floor. As she climbed, she thought through everything she'd learned the prior week during general hospital orientation. Main factoid: Angel Mendez Children's Hospital never turned a child away.

That was a philosophy she could believe in.

Heck, they'd even accepted her, the girl whose aunts and uncles used to refer to as "Poor Polly". It used to make her feel like that homely vintage doll, Pitiful Pearl. But Angel's had welcomed her to their nursing staff with open arms.

Blasting through the door, completely out of breath, she barreled onwards, practically running down a man in a white doctor's coat. Built like a football player, the rugged man with close-cropped more-silver-than-brown hair hardly flinched. He caught her by the shoulders and helped her regain her balance.

"Careful, dumpling," he said, sounding like a Clint-Eastwood-style grizzled cowboy.

Mortified, her eyes shot wide open. Sucking in air, she could hardly speak. "Sorry, Dr.…" Her gaze shifted from his stern brown eyes to his name badge. "Dr. John Griffin." Oh, man, did that badge also say Orthopedic Department Director? He was her boss.

She knew the routine—first impressions were lasting impressions, and this one would be a doozy. Without giving him another chance to call her "dumpling"—did he think she was thirteen?—she pointed toward the hospital ward and took off, leaving one last "Sorry" floating in her wake.

At the nurses' station, she unwrapped her tightly wound sweater, removed her shoulder bag and plopped them both on the counter. "I'm Polly Seymour. This is my first day. Is Brooke Hawkins here?"

The nonchalant ward clerk with an abundance of tiny braids all pulled back into a ponytail lifted his huge chocolate-colored eyes, gave a forced smile and pointed across the ward. "The tall redhead," he said, barely breaking stride from the lab orders he was entering in the computer.

Gathering her stuff, and still out of breath, Polly made a beeline for the nursing supervisor. Brooke's welcome was warm and friendly, and included a wide smile, which helped settle the mass of butterflies winging through Polly's stomach.

Brooke glanced at her watch. "You must be Polly and you're early. I wasn't expecting you until seven."

"I didn't want to miss the change-of-shift report, and

I don't have a clue where to put my stuff or which phone to clock in on." Would she ever breathe normally again?

"Follow me," Brooke said, heading toward another door, closer to the doctor. "I see you already ran into our department director, Dr. Griffin. Literally," Brooke said, with playful eyes and a wink.

Polly put her hand to the side of her face, shielding her profile from the man several feet away and still watching her. "I think he thought I was a patient."

"Did he smile at you?"

"Yes."

"Then he definitely thought you were one of our patients. He doesn't smile for staff."

An hour later, completely engrossed in taking vital signs in a four-bed ward of squirming children wearing various-sized casts, splints and slings, Polly heard inconsolable crying. She glanced over her shoulder. "What is it, Karen?" The little girl had undergone femoral anteversion to relieve her toeing-in when walking, and was in a big and bulky double-leg cast with a metal bar between them keeping her feet in the exact position in which they needed to be to heal.

Polly rushed to the toddler's crib and lowered one of the side rails. "What is it, honey?"

With her face screwed up so tight her source of tears couldn't be seen, Karen wailed. Polly could have easily done a tonsil check while the child's mouth was wide open, but knew that wasn't the origin of Karen's frustration. She lifted the little one, who weighed a good ten pounds more than she normally would have because of the cast, from the bed and cooed at her then patted her back. "What is it, honey, hmm?"

Perhaps the change in position would be enough to help settle down the tiny patient. No such luck. Karen's cries increased in volume as she swatted at Polly, who sang a nursery rhyme to her to calm her down. "*Oh, the grand old Duke of York...*" Maybe distraction would work?

"Oh, look! Look!" Polly moved over to the window to gaze out over beautiful Central Park. "Pretty. See?" Praying she could distract Karen for a moment's reprieve, Polly pointed at the lush green trees, many with colorful white and pink blooms still hanging on though late June.

"No!" Karen shook her head and kept crying.

Polly bounced Karen on her hip, as best she could with the toddler's cast, and jaunted around the room with her. "Let's take a horsey ride. Come on. Bumpity, bumpity, bumpity, boom!"

"No boom!" Karen would have nothing to do with Polly's antics.

"I'm going to eat you!" Polly said, digging into Karen's shoulder and playfully nibbling away. "Rror rror rrr."

"No! No eat me."

Felicia, the five-year-old in the corner bed with a full arm cast began to fuss. "I want a horsey ride."

Polly danced over towards Felicia's crib-sized bed, which looked more like a cage for safety's sake. Factoid number two from orientation: hospital policy for anyone five or under. "See, Karen, Felicia wants a horsey ride."

Now both girls were crying, and all the goofy faces and silly songs Polly performed couldn't change the tide of sadness sweeping across the four-bed ward. Erin, in bed C, with her arm in a sling added to the three-part harmony. The only one sleeping was the little patient in bed D, who would surely be awakened by the fuss. What the heck should she do now?

"Hold on," a deep raspy voice said over her shoulder. "This calls for emergency measures."

Polly turned to find Dr. Griffin filling the doorway. He dug in his pocket and fished out a handful of colorful rubber and waved it around. Making a silly face at Karen, he crossed his eyes, stretching his lips and blowing out air that sounded like a distant elephant. Polly tried not to laugh. Quicker than a flash of rainbow he diverted the children's attention by inflating long yellow and green balloons and twisting them into a swan shape. Factoid number three: all balloons must be latex-free. How did he get them to stretch like that?

"Here you go, Karen. Now go and play with your new friend," Dr. Griffin said.

To Polly's amazement, Karen accepted the proffered gift with a smile, albeit a soggy smile in dire need of a tissue.

"Me next!" Felicia reached out her good arm, her fingers making a gimme-gimme gesture.

Dr. Griffin strolled over to her bedside and patted her hand. "What color do you want?"

"Red," she said, practically jumping up and down inside the caged crib while she held onto the safety bars.

"Do you want a fairy crown or a monkey?"

"Both!"

In another few seconds Felicia wore a red crown with a halo hovering above, and gave a squeaky balloon kiss to her new purple monkey friend.

Dr. Griffin glanced at Polly, with victory sparkling in his dark eyes. The charming glance sent a jet of surprise through her chest. Blowing up two more balloons and twisting them into playful objects, he handed one to the remaining child and left another on the sleeping girl's bed, then sauntered toward the door. *Was he confident or what?* He stopped beside Polly, who had just finished putting Karen back into her crib, and blew up one last balloon. It was a blue sword, and he handed it to her. "Use this the next time you need to save the day." He glanced around the room at the quietly contented children. "That's how it's done," he said.

Polly could have sworn he'd stopped just short of calling her dumpling again.

He left just as quickly as he'd entered and she paused in her tracks, feeling a bit silly holding her blue balloon sword. Outside she heard a child complaining to the nurse. "I'm sick of practicing walking."

Dr. Griffin joined right in. "I double-dog dare you to take ten more steps, Richie," he said. "In fact, I'll race you to that wall."

Was this really the man the staff said never smiled?

Humbled by the gruff doctor's gift with children, Polly went about her duties giving morning medications and giving bed baths to three of her four patients. At midmorning the play therapist made a visit, relieving her of both Karen and Felicia for an hour. Erin's mother had also arrived, which gave Polly one-on-one time with her sleeping princess, Angelica, the most challenging patient of all. She had type I osteogenesis imperfecta and had been admitted for pain control of her hyper-mobile joints. Her condition also caused partial hearing loss, which was probably why the three-year-old had slept through the ruckus earlier.

Thinking twice about waking the peacefully sleeping toddler, Polly gazed affectionately at her then drifted to the desk and computer outside the four-bed ward to catch up on her morning charting.

"How are things going?" Darren, a middle-aged nurse with prematurely white hair pulled back into a ponytail, asked. By the faded tattoo on his forearm, she knew he had once been in the navy.

"Pretty good. How about you?"

"Same as always. Work hard, help kids, make decent money, look forward to my days off."

So far Polly wasn't impressed with the general morale of the ward. Everyone seemed efficient enough, skilled in their orthopedic specialties, but, glancing around, there didn't seem to be any excess energy. Or joy. She found it hard to live around gloom, and had learned early on how to create her own joy, for survival's sake. Some way, somehow she'd think of something to lift the ward's spirit, or she wouldn't be able to keep her hard-earned title of professional people pleaser.

A physical therapist came by, assisting one of the teen patients who did battle with a walker. Polly gave a cheerful wave to both of them. The P.T. merely nodded, but the boy was concentrating so hard on his task that he didn't even notice.

Orientation factoid number four: Angel's is the friendliest place in town!

Really?

Polly turned back to Darren. "Can you show me how to work that Hoyer lift? I've got a special patient to be weighed, and I need to change her sheets, too."

"Sure."

"Sweet. Thanks!"

"Now?"

"There's no time like the present, I always say." Polly finished her charting and escorted Darren into her assigned room. Together they gently repositioned and lifted Angelica from the bed. The child stared listlessly at them, her pretty gray eyes accented by blue-tinged, instead of white, sclera. "Are you from New York, Darren?"

"Yeah, born and raised. Where're you from?"

"Dover, Pennsylvania." She smiled, thinking of her tiny home town. "Our biggest claim to fame was being occupied overnight by the Confederates during the civil war."

Darren smiled, and she saw a new, more relaxed side to his usual military style.

"Don't blink if you ever drive down Main Street, you might miss it." Self-deprecating humor had always paid off, in her experience.

He laughed along with her, and she felt she'd made progress as they finished their task. She could do this. She could whip this ward into shape. Hadn't that always been her specialty? Just give her enough time and maybe the staff would actually talk and joke with each other. She accompanied Darren to the door and sat at the small counter where the laptop was, and prepared for more charting.

"Yo. Whatever your name is." Rafael the ward clerk said, peering over his computer screen. "I've got some new labs for you."

After looking both ways for foot traffic, Polly scooted across the floor on the wheels of her chair instead of getting up. "Special delivery for me? Sweet. I love to get mail."

He cast an odd gaze at Polly, as if she were from another planet. When he found her lifting her brows and smiling widely, he quit resisting and, though it was half-hearted, offered a suspicious smile back. "Just for you," he said, handing her the pile of reports. "Don't lose 'em."

Brooke came by as Polly perused her patients' labs. "How're things going so far?"

"Great! I really like it here. Of course, it's ten times bigger than the community hospital where I worked the last four years."

"We call it controlled chaos, on good days. I won't tell you what we call it on bad days." The tall woman smiled.

Orientation factoid number five: Teamwork is the key to success at Angel's Hospital.

Hmm. Maybe the staff needed to go through orientation again?

"As long as we all help each other, we should survive, right? Teamwork."

Brooke glanced around the ward, with everyone busily working by themselves, and her mouth twisted. "Sometimes I think we've forgotten that word."

Which put a thought in Polly's mind. As soon as Brooke strolled away, she checked to make sure everything was okay in her assigned room, then went across the ward to a nurse who looked busy and flustered. "Can I help you with anything?"

The woman glanced up from calculating blood glucose on the monitor. "Um." Caught off guard, she had to think, as if no one had ever asked to help her before.

"Anyone need a bedpan or help to the bathroom? I've got some free time."

The woman's honey-colored eyes brightened. She pushed a few strands of black hair away from her face.

"As a matter of fact, why don't you ask my broken-pelvis patient in 604 if he needs a bedpan?"

"Sweet," Polly said, noticing a surprised and perplexed expression in the nurse's eyes before she dashed toward 604.

Polly took her lunch-break with two other nurses and a respiratory therapist in the employee lounge. They'd all brought food from home like she had. She'd have to count her pennies to survive living in New York City.

"Is your hair naturally curly?" One of the other young nurses asked, as they ate.

Polly slumped her shoulders. "Yes. Drives me nuts most days."

"Are you kidding? People pay big money to get waves like that."

"And people pay big money to have their hair straightened, too," the other nurse chimed in.

"Well, I can't pay big money for anything but rent," Polly said. The two nurses and R.T. all grinned and nodded in agreement. "That's why I stick to my hairband and hope for the best." She thought about her most uncooperative hair on the planet, and as if that wasn't curse enough, it was dull blonde. Dishwater blonde as her aunt used to call it. How many times had she wished she could afford flashy apricot highlights, or maybe platinum. Maybe get a high-fashion cut and style to make her look chic. Only in her dreams. The last thing she'd ever be described as was chic, and hair coloring was completely out of the question these days.

She took another bite of her sandwich and noticed everyone zoning out again. The silence was too reminiscent of her childhood, being shipped from one aunt and uncle to another, and how they'd merely tolerated her presence out of duty. The sad memories drove her to start yet another conversation.

"Do you guys ever go out for drinks after work? I mean, I know I just said I'm counting my pennies, but seeing that it's my first day on the ward and all, well, I'd kind of like to get to know everyone a little better. You know, in a more casual setting?"

She saw the familiar gaze of people once again thinking she'd arrived from another universe. "How expensive could a drink or two at happy hour be?" she said. "And wouldn't we miss the rush hour on the subway that way, too?"

"You know, I don't even remember the last time we went out for drinks," the first nurse said, forking a bite of enchilada into her mouth.

"Have we ever gone out for drinks?" the second nurse asked, sipping on a straw in her soft drink can.

"I think once in a while we organize potlucks, but..." The respiratory therapist with a hard-to-pronounce surname on his badge said, scratching his head. "I wouldn't mind a beer after work. What about you guys?"

"That's a great idea," Polly said, making it seem like the R.T. had thought up the plan. "Count me in."

"Where're we going?" Another nurse wandered into the lounge.

"To O'Malley's Pub, a block down the street," the first nurse said. "I hear they've got great chicken hot wings on Monday nights, too. Spread the word."

Well, what do you know, she'd pulled it off. One moment the room had been dead, now somehow she'd managed to infuse some excitement into her co-workers as they made plans to do something different. They smiled and chatted about their favorite beer and mixed drinks, and laughed with each other.

It always felt good to please people. It had been how she'd survived, growing up. She had a long history of perfecting her talent, too. A set of narrowing brown eyes and a raspy voice came to mind. "So who's going to invite Dr. Griffin?"

All went silent again. Polly glanced from face to face to face as they stared at her with varying expressions, all of which implied she'd lost her mind.

"What? You don't invite your department head for drinks?"

The first nurse cleared her throat. "Maybe one of the residents but, uh, he doesn't socialize with us."

"Yeah. He merely tolerates us, and only because he knows he needs us to take care of his patients," the second nurse said.

"But isn't he the guy who approves your raises?"

Three sets of lips pressed into straight lines as they all nodded.

"I dare you to ask him to come along," the nurse who'd just joined them said, as she finished heating her soup in the microwave. She laughed with the others at the ridiculous dare.

"Double-dog dare?" Polly had never heard that expression before Dr. Griffin had said it that morning, but figured now was the right time to use it.

"Triple-dog dare," the last nurse said, taking her place at the table and leaning forward with a clear challenge in her eyes.

Polly knew a set-up when she saw one. Let the new girl hang herself with the boss. Well, she'd seen a different side of him that morning and couldn't believe they'd never seen it too. "How bad can a person be who makes balloon animals for his little patients?"

The four other people in the room looked at each other rather than answer the question. That meant one thing. Polly, the diehard, would have to find out on her own.

As the afternoon stretched on, Polly was surprised by how energized the staff seemed since they'd made plans for after-work drinks.

Even Brooke approved. "This is just the injection of fun we've needed around here. I may have to nickname you Pollyanna."

Polly made her goofy face and shook her head. "Please, don't." Even though that was better by far than being called Poor Polly.

At four o'clock, the first shift of the day had ended and had handed over to the next team. Word had spread about everyone going for drinks at O'Malley's for happy hour, and more than half of the staff had signed on. Some of the evening shift wished they could go, too. Not bad for her first day.

Polly tied her sweater around her waist and licked her lips. "I'll see you all down there in a few minutes."

She'd promised to invite Dr. John Griffin, and she always kept her promises. She walked to the far side of the sixth-floor hospital wing. Staring down the hall at his closed office door, she took a deep breath and strode onward.

Someone knocked at the door. John made a face because it interrupted his train of thought, thoughts he'd been avoiding all day. Just one day. That's all he asked. One day not to remember images from twelve years ago. One day without memories sweeping over him, wrenching his gut. Was it too much to ask for? There was a second knock. "Who is it?"

All he could hear was some whispery childlike sound, but he couldn't make out a single word. Irritated, he raised his voice. "Come in. It's not locked." He tossed his pen across the desk blotter and leaned back in his chair.

Peering around the opening door were big blue eyes. *Those* big blue eyes. Son of a gun, it was dumpling, the young woman he'd mistaken for a teenage patient that morning. Damned if he was going to be the first to speak, he sat watching her enter his office. First her head and shoulders came round the door. Next one foot. Then the other foot cautiously followed suit. There she was, as large than life, except in her case that equaled a petite picture of youth and enthusiasm—the last thing on earth, and especially today, that he needed. When the hell had been the last time he'd actually felt enthusiastic about anything?

With one hand behind her back, she cleared her throat. "Hi, Dr. Griffin."

He sat as still as a boulder. Sure, he'd heard the rumblings about everyone going out for drinks after work that night, and little miss bright eyes being the instigator. Well, he wanted nothing to do with it. He didn't believe in fraternizing with his staff. It didn't set a good example. And even if he changed his mind, today would be the last day of any year he'd choose to break his hard and fast rule.

"Um…" Polly edged closer one tiny step at a time as he stared her down. "A bunch of us are going to O'Malley's for some hot wings and beer, and…" She scratched her nose, her eyes darting around the room to avoid meeting his stare. "Well, I was, um, I mean, *we* were hoping you'd join us."

"And why would I do that?" Even for him it came out gruffer than he'd meant.

She studied her feet. "To help raise your staff's morale?"

"Morale? What's that?"

"When people enjoy coming to work, and work better because of it?" She looked all of fifteen standing there, thick wavy dark blonde hair gathering on her shoulders, saucer-sized eyes, chewing her lower lip, hands behind her back, yet somehow seeming courageous.

Normally, he wasn't into torture, but she'd been the one to come to him. It might be twisted, but making her squirm also distracted him from those morbid thoughts looping over and over in his mind.

"Are you their sacrifice?" he said. She glanced up, looking perplexed. "Did they put you up for the fall, being the new girl and all?"

"No, sir. I *wanted* to invite you. It was my idea."

Her near opaque aqua eyes finally found their mark, and the sight of this young woman staring at him made the hairs on his arms rise. His wife had had eyes exactly like hers. Earlier today, they had been the first feature he'd noticed about the new nurse. Everything else about her physically was completely different from his wife, except those eyes. God, he missed Lisa.

But all the wishing in the world couldn't bring her back.

"Do they need their morale raised?" he said, sounding dead flat even to himself. Who the hell was going to raise his morale? "Don't they have lives to go home to every day? Doesn't that raise their spirits enough without me having to babysit them in a bar, too?"

"They don't need a babysitter. We'd all like to share a drink together, that's all." He saw the pink blush begin on her cheeks and spread rapidly to her neck and ears.

He wasn't a monster. He felt bad that he'd made her feel so uncomfortable, but someone should have warned her about trying to involve him in anything social. Brooke had clearly fallen down on her supervisory duties.

All he wanted to do was go home, hide in a dark room, and bury his sorrow in a glass of perfectly aged Scotch. The world didn't need to know that today would have been Lisa's thirty-sixth birthday. How the hell would it look to be chatting in a bar on a day like this?

"I can't." He stood to signal their meeting was over.

"I double-dog dare you." She grimaced.

He folded his arms and one eyebrow quirked. Was she serious?

With a look of desperation she whipped her arm from behind her back, revealing the silly blue balloon sword he'd made for her earlier. "It's just that I was hoping to buy a drink for the man who saved my day, today. You and that jar of latex-free balloons on your desk."

By the earnest expression on her face he knew it hadn't been easy for her to come into his office and beg him to meet with his staff at a pub. A staff he kept socially at an arm's length yet depended on, no, demanded they give his patients the best medical care in New York. He'd always assumed their paychecks were thanks enough. Maybe dumpling had the right idea.

He didn't have a clue, neither did he care, what would make her need to include him. But the employees were all probably at the bar having a good laugh at the new nurse's expense about how they'd managed to set her up for failure. What a dirty trick. Some nurses really did like to eat their young and this Polly was definitely that. Young. Innocent looking. Fresh. Sweet. Ah, hell, be honest—attractive. He gave a tentative smile. She instantly responded with a bright grin and raised brows, and he was a goner. How could he let someone down with a reputation on the line?

Surely Lisa would understand.

"Okay," he said.

"Sweet!"

"One beer and you're buying."

She nodded, triumph sparkling in her bright blue eyes. "Gladly, sir." She pointed the way to the door with the balloon sword.

"That stays here," he said as he passed her on his way out.

She stifled her giggle when he impaled her with his dead serious stare.

One thing she'd already proved to him. This girl… er…*woman* named Polly was fearless. He liked that.

John had to admit the tall glass of house draft tasted great and felt smooth going down. His newest nurse, in keeping with her promise, had fronted the money to buy it for him, which made it taste all the better. She really wanted him there. When was the last time he'd been wanted anywhere other than in the orthopedic operating room?

The look of surprise on the faces of the group of nurses and techs when he'd walked into the bar had been worth the effort. Everyone had gone quiet for an instant before slowly winding back up to their usual pub noise. He could only imagine what they thought about him showing up, and wondered if anyone had taken bets. He and Polly had shared a quiet but victorious glance.

Chatty Polly had burned his ears on the stroll over, too. She'd practically burst with excitement explaining how much coming to New York and landing a job at such a famous hospital as Angel's had meant to her.

Good for her. The world could use more idealistic nurses. Yet he craved the silence of his apartment, where he could sit in the dark and stare out over the neighborhood—remembering the vacancy where the twin towers used to be, nursing his Scotch, which could never fill the bottomless hole in his heart. Shifting his thoughts to the here and now, he took another drink of his beer and gazed at fresh-faced Polly to help banish the image.

She sat beside him on a barstool, sipping pale ale that left a hint of orange on her breath as she continued to chew his ear. "I wasn't always interested in orthopedics. I saw myself as an emergency nurse." Her eyes went wide. Even in the darkened bar they sparkled. "That is, until I worked my first shift on a busy night with a full moon." She covered her face with long fingers and clear-varnished nails, and shook her head, then quickly peeked up at him. "I thought I was going to die!"

Was everyone this animated, or had he quit noticing? He'd be dead between the ears if he didn't admit she was cute, and likeable. She shrugged out of her sweater and he realized she'd changed her nursing scrubs, which had baby koalas patterned over them, for a clingy pink top that dipped just enough to reveal a full-grown woman's cleavage.

How had he not noticed that all day?

He took another drink and tried his damnedest not to stare. She removed her hairband and put it inside her combination backpack-purse, and those light waves curtained her face in an alluring way, coming to rest on her shoulders…which led his eyes back to her breasts.

He certainly wasn't dead. Just severely inactive.

But this wasn't right, staring down her shirt. He needed to change his focus. "Bartender, the next round for this group is on me."

Everyone clapped and cheered, even a few people he'd never seen before in his life, and he took another drink of beer, feeling almost human again.

Polly wrapped her arm around his and squeezed. "Thank you!"

"You're welcome," he said, tensing, staring straight ahead, knowing his answer had come out clipped. He hadn't made contact with a woman like this in, well, longer than he cared to admit.

She must have sensed his tension and unwrapped her arm but moved closer on her stool. "So, Dr. Griffin, I've told you all about me, but I don't know where you come from."

The bartender delivered the drinks along the counter, and refilled the bowls with pretzels and mixed nuts.

"I'm a New York native."

"So your whole family is here, too?"

"My parents retired to Florida a few years back, and my sister lives in Rhode Island now."

"Are you married? Do you have any kids?"

If Lisa hadn't been killed he would have been a father of an eleven-year-old by now. But his world had officially ended the day he'd spent digging people out of debris as a first responder on 9/11. His always simmering emotions boiled and he snapped, "Look. I'm here for a drink, like you asked. My personal life is none of your business. You got that?"

A flash of hurt and humiliation accompanied her crumbling smile. One instant she'd been bubbling with life, the next he'd crushed it right out of her. Good going, Johnny. He had no business being around people.

She recovered just as quickly, though, straightening her shoulders and sticking out her chest, eyes narrowing, as if this routine was nothing new to her. "Sorry for crossing the line, Doctor." She slipped off the bar stool and gathered her things and the glass. "Thanks for the beer." Then she wandered over to a group of nurses a few stools away and joined in with their chatter.

He chugged down the last of his beer, not touching the second glass. "How much do I owe you?" he asked the bartender.

He knew he had no business pretending to be like everyone else. He should never have let the pretty little nurse talk him into it. He was only good for one thing, and that was fixing kids with broken bones.

As for the rest of his life, well, that had officially ended the day his newly pregnant wife had gone to work and died on the twenty-second floor of the twin towers.

CHAPTER TWO

POLLY HAD SPENT the entire subway ride home seething over Dr. Griffin's sour attitude. What had she done to turn him against her? After a little cajoling he'd smiled and agreed to go to the bar with his staff. They'd had a brisk and energizing walk to the pub, enjoying the late afternoon sun and moderate June weather. He'd allowed her to buy him a drink, and he'd even made a grand gesture of buying the next round for everyone else.

All had seemed to go according to plan in the people-pleasing biz.

Then she'd asked about his family and the vault door had clanged shut. It hadn't been mere irritation she'd seen flash in his dark, brooding eyes, it had been fury. Plain and simple.

As she prepared for bed in her tiny rented room on the Lower East Side, where the shared bathroom and kitchen were considered privileges in the five-story walk-up, she couldn't stop thinking how she'd messed up that night. Clearly, she'd overstepped her bounds with Dr. Griffin. But how? Didn't everyone love to talk about themselves and their families? That was, everyone except people like her who had miserable memories of feeling unwanted and unloved, like she'd had since her mother had died when Polly had been only six.

She put her head on the thin pillow and adjusted to the lumpy mattress. Of course! How could she be so blind? The man was miserable with his staff. He didn't like to socialize. She'd dragged him out of his comfort zone and asked him about something very personal—his family—then everything had backfired. Something horrible had happened to that man to make him the way he was. Surely, no one wanted to be that miserable without a good reason.

She had to quit assuming that she was the only person in the world with family issues and that everyone else lived hunky-dory lives. Obviously, Dr. Griffin wasn't happy about his family situation and she'd hit a nerve with her line of questioning. Maybe he'd gone through a messy divorce. Maybe his wife had cheated on him. Who knew? But he'd attacked with vengeance when she'd dared to get too personal.

She'd let down her guard, let him skewer her with his angry retort, then, wounded and hurt, she'd brushed him off and moved on. In her world it was called survival, but he'd seen a flash of her true self the instant before she'd covered it up, just as she'd seen his. Well, touché, Dr. Griffin.

Polly folded her hands behind her head and in the dim light stared at the cracked ceiling and chipped paint—what could she expect from an apartment built before World War I?—and thought harder. Maybe she'd inadvertently hurt him as much as he'd hurt her, and, man, she'd felt his anger slice right through her. John Griffin wasn't a person to be on the bad side of. Somehow she'd have to make up for it.

Her eyes grew heavy from the two beers she'd enjoyed at the pub, but one last thought held out until she acknowledged it so she could drift off to sleep with a good conscience. She owed Dr. John Griffin an apology, and first thing tomorrow morning she'd give it to him.

The next morning at work, Dr. Griffin was nowhere to be found. Polly realized during report that Tuesdays and Thursdays were his scheduled surgery days, and felt a mixture of relief and impatience about getting her apology over and done with. She'd never make the mistake of including her boss in any social event again, even though the staff was already talking about another pub night in two weeks. Something else she noticed today was that everyone smiled at her, which made her feel good and far more a part of the team than she had yesterday. At least she'd succeeded in pleasing some people around here.

Her patient assignment was heavy, and although she only had two patients, each needed a great deal of care. Charley was sixteen and in a private room after he'd taken a header on his skateboard, breaking several bones and his pelvis. Her second patient was in surgery and would arrive later in the day after a short stint in the recovery room. Fifteen-year-old Annabelle would also have a private room, having undergone an above-the-knee transfemoral amputation for localized Ewing sarcoma of the lower part of the right femur.

Polly's heart ached for her patient. She'd already been briefed that a team of social workers, psychologists, occupational and physical therapists, as well as wound-care specialists, would be participating in her recovery. Polly would take care of the nursing portion, and for today it would mostly be post-operative care—basic and important for pain control and maintaining strong vital signs. She'd guard against any post-op complications, such as bleeding or infection, to the best of her ability. Tomorrow the reality of being a teenager with a leg amputation would require help from each and every member of that specially organized medical team.

"Here, Charley." Polly handed a washcloth lathered with soap to her shattered-pelvis patient. "You wash your face, neck and chest. I'll help with your back when you're ready."

She believed in letting patients do as much for themselves as possible. Fortunately, Charley had one good arm, and with the overhead frame with trapeze he could lift himself enough to allow her to change the sheets and replace the sheepskin beneath his hips.

She kept a doubled sheet over his waist to give him privacy as they progressed with his bed bath. "Do you miss school?"

He gave a wry laugh. "I miss my friends."

"How are you going to keep up with your studies while you recover?"

He scrubbed his smooth face and chest with the cloth. "They're going to send out a tutor or something. School's almost out for summer break anyway. What really sucks is I was supposed to start driver's training next month."

"Do people even drive cars in New York?"

"I live in Riverdale."

Polly didn't have a clue where Riverdale was but assumed it was a suburb of the city. She'd never, ever want to attempt driving in New York, where being a pedestrian was risky enough.

She washed his back and changed the linen, keeping casual and friendly banter going. "Have you got a girlfriend?"

"Nah. We broke up."

Uh-oh, here she went again, venturing into personal information that might cause pain. Would she ever learn her lesson? At least he hadn't bitten her head off like Dr. Griffin had. "I'm sorry to hear that."

"It's okay. All she ever wanted was for me to buy her stuff, anyway."

Whew. "Sometimes teenage girls can be very superficial."

"Dude, tell me about it."

Polly gathered the soiled linen she'd heaped onto the floor and shoved it into the dirty-linen hamper just as the door swung open. "Well, look here, perfect timing. Lunch!"

The tall, bronze and buff dietary worker brought in Charley's lunch tray and placed it on the bedside table. Polly washed her hands and checked to make sure they'd delivered the right diet, with extra protein and calories for the growing and healing boy, then left him alone to eat with the TV on while she got his noontime medicine.

When she returned from her own lunch-break the ward clerk informed her that Annabelle was on her way up from Recovery. Polly rushed to the private room to make sure everything was in order then quickly checked up on Charley, who was fine and playing a video game. She explained she'd be busy for a while but made sure his call light and urinal were within reach in case he needed them.

Just as she exited the room she saw the orderly pull a gurney out of the elevator. At the other end was Dr. Griffin in OR scrubs. It was the first time she'd seen him that day and, taken by surprise, her stomach did a little clutch and jump. Would he still be furious with her?

Focused solely on the task, Dr. Griffin helped get Annabelle into her room. Polly jumped in. "I'll get this, Dr. Griffin."

He let her take the end of the gurney but followed her into the room. She'd pulled down the covers on the hospital bed and had already padded the bed with a layer of thin bath blanket, an absorbent pad and had topped both with a draw sheet in preparation for her patient. She checked to make sure the IV was in place and had plenty of fluid left in the IV bag. Annabelle was in a deep dream state, most of her right leg was missing and the stump was bandaged thickly and thoroughly.

"Careful," Dr. Griffin warned the orderly as he lowered the side rail on the gurney and prepared to transfer the patient to the bed.

Polly rushed to the other side of the bed, got on her knees on the mattress and leaned over to grab the pull-sheet underneath Annabelle toward her. To her surprise, Dr. Griffin came around to her side of the bed and helped out.

"On the count of three," Polly said, as the orderly prepared to pass the patient over from the gurney while they all tugged her onto the mattress. After she counted, they made a quick and smooth transfer. The patient moaned briefly and her eyes fluttered open, but she quickly went back to sleep.

As the orderly left the room Dr. Griffin gave a rundown of Annabelle's vital signs, a job the recovery nurse usually did over the phone, giving Polly the impression of how important the operation and follow-up care were to this orthopedic surgeon.

He ran down the list of antibiotics and pain-medication orders as Polly listened and adjusted the pillow under Annabelle's head. Next she placed the amputated stump on a pillow, checked the dressing for signs of bleeding or drainage, circling a quarter-sized area with her marker and noting the time, then made sure the Jackson-Pratt drain was in place and with proper suction before pulling up the covers.

Dr. Griffin ran his hand lightly over his patient's forehead, gently removing her OR cap and releasing a blanket of thick and shining brown hair. Such a tender gesture for an angry man.

"I'll check back later," he said, giving Annabelle one last, earnest glance before leaving the room. Polly almost expected him to kiss the girl's forehead from that sincere, loving parent-type look in his eyes.

How could she stay mad at a man like that?

"I'll take good care of her, Doctor," she whispered.

He looked over his shoulder and gave an appreciative nod.

Seeing him in his scrubs, OR cap in place, untied mask hanging around his neck, she realized how fit he was, and that his shoulders and arms were thick with muscle. Where he might look stocky in his doctor's coat, he really wasn't. He was just big and solid. For a man she suspected to be pushing forty, he was in terrific shape, and she allowed herself a second glance as he walked away.

"Hey, Doc G., you haven't signed my cast yet!" Charley called out from the next room.

"I'll sign all three, Charley, my boy," Dr. Griffin replied in a cheerful manner, changing his direction and somber attitude on a dime.

How could a man who was so great with kids be so lacking in people skills? It just didn't make sense.

Soon lost in the care of her newly received patient, and also checking periodically on Charley, the afternoon flew by. Before Polly knew it she was giving report to the next shift and preparing to go home. But she couldn't leave yet. Not before she apologized to Dr. Griffin. She'd promised herself she'd make amends today, and she always kept her promises.

Now that he was back from the OR, she knew where to find him and marched far down the hall toward his office as a new batch of butterflies lined up for duty in her stomach. Refusing to be timid this time, she tapped with firm knuckles on the glass of his office door.

"Come in."

Mustering every last nerve she owned, she entered far more assuredly than she had the previous evening, noting the irony in seeing a huge jar of colorful balloons on the desk of a generally grumpy man.

"Is everything okay with Annabelle?"

"She's doing very well, considering." Polly scratched the nervous tickle above her lip. "I medicated her for pain just before I ended my shift." She glanced around the room, with requisite diplomas and awards lining the gray-painted walls yet not revealing anything personal about the man, and took a long slow breath. "What I came for. Well, what I mean is I came here to, you know, after last night and how I upset you, I, uh, I just wanted to stop in and...well..."

"Apologize?" He'd changed back into his street clothes and white doctor's coat. His eyes were tight and unforgiving as they stared at her impatiently. Had she expected anything less?

"Uh, yes." Why did he make her so annoyingly tongue-tied? "As a matter of fact, I did want to apologize for whatever I did to make you angry last night." Heat flared on her cheeks. Frustrated by how uncomfortable he made her feel and how he offered nothing to ease her distress by sitting there just staring, she bit back the rest of her thoughts—*but you were a jerk about it, and anyone with half a brain could tell I didn't mean any harm by asking about your family. It's normal to want to know such things. Sheesh!*

Adjusting the neck of her scrub top, along with her attitude, and desperate for him to like her, she continued. "I overstepped the mark, practically forcing you to go out with the rest of us, then I thoughtlessly insisted you open up and tell me about your family." She held up her hand before he could growl or get angry with her all over again. "Which I understand, as the new girl on the ward, is none of my business. So, yes, I came to apologize. Profusely."

She sat on the edge of the chair across from his desk before her knees could give out. "And I hope you'll accept it, because I really want to be a part of this orthopedic team. I want to help you with special patients like Annabelle." She stopped short of wringing her hands, choosing to lace her fingers and hold tight instead. "I want to help make your job easier by you not having to worry about the level of care your patients receive. I want to be a top-notch nurse, Dr. Griffin. I want to be that for you, sir." Could she possibly grovel any more?

"Stop it already." He brushed off her apology with a wave of his hand. "I was needlessly sharp with you last night. I should be the one apologizing."

"But I started it, sir."

He gave an exasperated sigh. “Okay. I accept your apology. But knock off the ‘sir’ baloney and call me what my friends calls me. Johnny.”

Stunned by his instruction, she could hardly get her lips to move. “Johnny?” For such a simple name it sounded breathy and foreign, the way she repeated it. How could she call the head of the orthopedic department Johnny? Wasn’t that the shortened form for young boys named John? It seemed only families would continue to call a grown man Johnny, yet he said his friends called him that. Was he implying she was now a friend?

“Right. Johnny. Now get out of here. I’ve got work to do.” The terse words fell far short of carrying a punch, in fact they rolled off her back. Maybe she’d really gotten through to him.

“Sweet.” She didn’t mean to say that out loud and couldn’t stop the smile stretching across her lips. “Thank you, Doctor. Uh, I mean, *Johnny*.” She emphasized his name. “Thanks so much.” She stood to go, relieved beyond her wildest dreams. How had this mattered so much to her in such a short period of time? She shrugged. All she knew was that her apology and his acceptance of it did matter. “I’ll see you tomorrow.” *Johnny-boy.*

“Good, because I want you assigned to Annabelle for the rest of the week.”

“You do?” He trusted her nursing skills enough to ask her to take care of an extra-special patient. This was definitely progress on their ultra-rocky-start.

“Yes. Now would you please leave, or I’ll never get out of here tonight.”

Still smiling, she looked him in the eyes. His had softened the tiniest bit, but she could also see a slight change in attitude. Yes, she could. "Yes, sir." When she reached the door, calm washed over her and she turned round. "See you tomorrow, Johnny."

Already back at work, he nodded while writing, rather than look up. "Let's keep that name between you and me."

She'd accept that, too. This desperate need for him to like her would have to stop, but for now she was pretty darned glad she'd fumbled her way through the apology, and wondered how many other employees got to call their boss by their first name, even if only in secret?

John had to admit the sputtering woman on the other side of his desk had been strangely captivating. Perhaps it had to do with the fact that she was easy on the eye, energetic, full of life, and had a nice ass, too. When was the last time he'd noticed something like that? Her earnest and unrehearsed apology had done strange things to a few nerve endings in forgotten parts of his body. Not that he was into dominance and submission, but he really liked her baring it all, as it were, by nearly begging him to forgive her.

Hell, he should be the one apologizing to her. He'd treated her badly and had seen a flash of anger in her eyes, which she'd quickly covered up, and instead of calling him an ass, which he deserved, she'd taken the high road. She'd brushed off his remark with a mere flutter of her eyelashes and moved on.

That showed grit, and he liked grit in a woman.

He reached into a desk drawer, withdrew a bottle of water and took a long draw. Her Pollyanna attitude of be-nice-to-everyone was far from his own style, and probably a cover-up for her insecurities. A wry laugh escaped his lips. Who the hell was he to analyze anyone? His style was more make-nice-to-no-one because he didn't give a damn. But he had to admit she had a special way with kids. And his staff.

Remembering how she'd given a horsey hip-ride to Karen in her clunky cast yesterday morning made John smile. She'd been in way over her head with that group of toddlers so how could he not have gone to save the day? He knew his kids. Knew pediatrics. That was his comfort zone.

Adults were the issue for him. He didn't particularly like most adults, merely tolerated them. He had to get along with them if he wanted to continue to run the orthopedic department, and for the past twelve years his motto had been, Do what you have to do to survive, the kids need you.

How had he survived all these years without his Lisa? He pressed his lips together, allowing one little thought about Polly to slip inside his head. She oozed life, something he'd given up on, yet her vibrant approach to things really appealed to him. Maybe he wasn't as far gone as he'd thought.

Looking around the ward that afternoon, when he'd returned from surgery, he'd seen a more cohesive staff. They had been talking to each other and helping each other, even joking. He'd never seen them so happy.

The question was, had his sour attitude spilled over to his staff, and had this Polly from Pennsylvania saved the day?

Her big blue eyes and trembling lips came to mind. Why had he had the urge to run his thumb over her lips to test how soft they were? More importantly, what was with the impulse he'd had to wrap his hand around the back of her neck and drag her to him to test those lips on his?

When was the last time he'd given a woman permission to call him Johnny? What was up with that? What else might he get her to beg for so he could grant her permission? Most importantly, what in hell were these crazy sexy thoughts she'd planted in his head?

Maybe Pollyanna wasn't nearly as innocent as she let on. *Well, guess what, dumpling, neither am I.*

He guzzled more water and scratched his chest, surprised by his thumping heart. Antsy to finish his work and get the hell out of there, he veered his surprisingly sexed-up thoughts away from Pretty Polly and back to dictating his surgery reports for the day. Before he left he'd check on his kids, each and every one—like he did every day before he went home.

Maybe that was the reason he had been out of sorts yesterday at the bar. Maybe it hadn't been because she'd gotten too nosey, or had threatened his resolve never to feel again, or because he'd wanted to go home and brood, which he had to admit was beginning to get boring, even for him. He'd blame it on not saying goodnight to his kids, because he hadn't been ready to admit he was a man clinging so tightly to his past he'd forgotten how to socialize with the living.

Polly had rushed him away from work and he hadn't had a chance to tell all of his patients goodnight, and things just didn't seem right when he missed saying goodnight to his kids.

Yeah, he'd use that as the excuse for his behavior last night, otherwise he'd seem far too pitiful the next time he looked in the mirror.

CHAPTER THREE

THE NEXT MORNING Polly rode the hospital elevator up to her floor. A vibration in her pocket alerted her that a text message had come through her cell phone: *B in NY in 2 wks. Have dinner with me? Greg*

Rankled, since *Greg* had dumped her for another girl over a year ago, and she'd been heartbroken as well as angry at the time, she wrinkled her nose and shut off her phone with a harrumph.

"Bad news?" A familiar voice came from over her shoulder.

"Oh." She turned round. "Dr. Griffin, I didn't see you there." There were several people she didn't know in the overcrowded elevator but she hadn't noticed him mostly because she had been lost in her thoughts and hadn't been looking at anyone. Aching from her lumpy bed, already dragging from the daily rush to the subway, getting pushed and bumped the entire commute, and now hearing from an unwelcome voice from her past, she couldn't begin to paste on a cheery face today.

John edged closer to her. "You don't look happy."

She lifted a corner of her mouth. "I'm not. Old boyfriend just texted me." What did she care if he discovered that little miss Pollyanna from Pennsylvania was a sham, that her carefree moods were manufactured from hard work and years of practice.

"Sorry to hear that," he said, sounding curiously sincere.

"About the boyfriend or not being happy?"

"Both."

"Really?"

"Don't act so shocked." He gave her a John Griffin style smile, which meant it was hard to differentiate the smile between a grimace and/or gas.

"Do you actually notice things like people's moods?"

"No. Not usually."

What the heck did that mean? Had her self-deprecating plea last night in his office put her on his pity list? Maybe she'd overdone it.

"Well, thanks anyway," she said, lifting her brows and glancing toward the neon numbers indicating the floors, having run out of superficial things to talk about. The elevator stopped and several people got off.

He moved closer and whispered near her ear. "You know, you don't have to put on your forever-cheerful act for me."

Had he seen through her already? "Gee, thanks." She didn't mean to sound disrespectful, but he'd just given her permission to show her true feelings, hadn't he? She glanced to where he stood. There was that gassy grimace-style smile again and a playful glint in his eyes. Why did she find it cute?

Cute? John Griffin?

Maybe it was his mouth, the way the marginally off-center bottom lip curled out ever so slightly, making her want to take it between her teeth and nibble...just a little.

Come on, Polly, the guy is way too old for you. Prob-

ably pushing forty. And gruff as a bulldog. Who needs the aggravation? Besides, there was no way he'd ever be interested in her. Yet…that goofy attempt at a smile could only be described as cute. Charming, even.

The elevator came to a stop on the fifth floor and everyone else exited. Once the doors closed, John leaned his shoulder on the elevator wall and looked directly at Polly.

"Let's make a deal," he continued to whisper. "I'll show you mine if you show me yours."

She lifted her head from staring at her scuffed white clogs with the image of nibbling his lower lip fresh in her mind. "What in the world are you talking about?"

"Our moods." So he had seen through her carefully crafted façade.

"Well, no offense, Dr. Griffin, but I think I've already memorized your moods. Moody. Grumpy." She used her fingers to tick off the list. "Gruff. Did I say moody?"

What do you know, she'd coaxed out a real smile. "Yes. Smartass." He squinted graciously under fire, his dark eyes showing signs of renewed life. "Don't forget Bashful and Sleepy, if you're thinking of naming all of the seven dwarfs."

"And Doc. You definitely qualify for that one." She sighed, realizing that whatever this silly game was she was playing with *Johnny,* many of her cares had already evaporated in the stuffy elevator. By giving her the okay to be who she really was, warts and all, he'd liberated her from being Pollyanna. It felt pretty darned good. Hmm, had he said bashful? Him?

"Bashful? Not you," she said.

"Oh, yes, I am."

"I don't believe it."

"You'd be surprised."

The elevator door opened and they got out and headed their separate ways, she giving a genuinely bright smile, thanks to his lightening her mood, and he, well, still looking gassy but with an added spring to his step. That on-the-verge-of-flirting look he'd just sent her way was bound to stay in her mind and keep her smiling the rest of the day. The little fizzy feeling that look had given her hadn't been half-bad either.

Dr. John Griffin. Bashful? As in let the woman make the advance? Just what else might she be surprised about with him?

As Polly walked to the nurses' locker room, one more thought popped into her head. Johnny smelled good, too, like expensive aftershave and clean hair. Combine that with his rugged, all-man features and her new interest in the shape and angle of his mouth, thinking it looked all too kissable for a guy with salt-and-pepper hair, for a head of Pediatric Orthopedics, and she lost her step and tripped on the doorframe.

All things considered, Johnny Griffin had done a great job of lifting Polly's spirits that morning.

"How's my girl doing?" John asked Polly, entering the hospital room shortly after she'd taken Annabelle's midday vital signs.

"Great! Thanks," Polly said. "Annabelle's doing really well, too." She caught and enjoyed the quick confusion in his eyes before he got her joke.

"You've got a real smart aleck for a nurse, Annabelle." He took his patient's thin hand, and the gesture squeezed Polly's heart.

Annabelle gave a wan smile, and John lingered over

her bed like a fussing papa until she closed her eyes. Polly had given her pain medication through a shot into the hip a few short moments ago.

"The nurses told me she'd had a rough night, complaining about phantom pains, and when she started mentioning them again just now, well, I wanted to make sure she was extra-comfortable today."

He folded his arms across his broad chest. "Good. We'll give her some rest now, but by later this afternoon I want her out of bed and in a chair for at least an hour."

"Got it."

"Physical therapy will start tomorrow, and the wound-care specialist should pay a visit this evening when her parents are here to discuss dressing changes when she goes home."

"Yes, sir."

"You can knock that stuff off, too."

"You don't want me to follow your orders, sir?" Why did teasing her superior feel so delicious?

He took a deep breath, as if trying to suck in patience from the room air. "Are you trying to bug me?"

"Am I doing a good job…sir?"

"Very."

"Good," she said, straightening out the bedspread and double-checking the IV rate. She didn't dare look over her shoulder, but she sensed he was enjoying her feisty mood. Would any of his staff ever dare to give him a hard time?

"There's no excess drainage from the surgical site, and I emptied thirty ccs from the drain at the beginning of my shift," she said, all business.

He checked under the recently smoothed covers and found the Jackson-Pratt bulb was nearly empty. The quarter-sized marking on the post-op dressing hadn't gotten much bigger either, as he soon noticed.

"Good." He lingered at the bedside.

She'd decided, after her pitiful, stumbling apology, and especially their ride in the elevator, that he was a good guy, even if he didn't know it. He'd had the patience of a saint while she'd fumbled her way through her monologue, and he'd rewarded her by telling her to call him *Johnny.* Who else on the staff got to call him Johnny? Not that she ever would, at least not in front of anyone else, especially as he'd asked her to keep it to herself.

"Hey, Johnny." Another doctor entered the room.

So much for the short-lived "special person privilege" fantasy.

"Dave. Come to admire your work?"

"Sure did."

Polly surreptitiously read the other doctor's badge. David Winters. Vascular Surgery. Of course, with the amputation they'd have to make sure the stump had proper circulation, and who better to assist the orthopedic surgeon than a vascular surgeon?

"I was going to wait until later to change the dressing, but there's no time like the present. Polly, can you bring some gauze, dressings, four by fours and paper tape?"

"Sure. Would you like me to bring the Doppler too?"

"Great idea," Dave said.

She knew it was never too early to make sure there was proper circulation to the wound, and the Doppler would let them hear the blood flowing through Annabelle's vessels. A lot rested on every step of the recovery. In order to have Annabelle fit for a prosthetic device she'd need to have a strong and healthy stump. The post op-team, including Polly, would do everything in their power to make sure of Annabelle's success.

After dropping off the supplies, Polly took a quick look at Annabelle's surgical wound as John had already removed the dressing, and was surprised how clean and healthy the skin flap already looked. Cancer of the bone was a curse, but at least Annabelle would be able to wear one of the state-of-the-art prostheses being created these days. One day, when she was back on her feet and used to everything, wearing slacks or jeans, secure in her gait, no one would ever know that part of her leg was missing.

Later that day Polly took Charley his pills. She noticed the three signatures John Griffin had left on the teenager's casts, which made her grin. They were big, just like him, and colorful, hmm, and he had much nicer handwriting than she'd ever imagined any doctor could.

"What's so funny?" Charley asked.

"Nothing. I was just admiring your autographs from Dr. Griffin."

"He's cool."

"Really? He seems so stern all the time."

"Nah, he's funny. And he's the only person who hasn't given me a lecture about my skateboarding."

"Well, I guess accidents do happen, but maybe you should be more careful so as not to tempt the fates."

"Yeah, I get it. And I've heard that before, but yolo, you know?"

"Yolo?"

"You only live once."

So said a sixteen-year-old. "True, but preferably longer than shorter. Right?"

Charley blew her off with a toss of his long-hair. She

needed to change the subject back to something lighter, something more interesting for both of them.

"I never would have pegged Dr. Griffin as funny."

"No? You should see him do his Aquaman drowning imitation. And he can sing like that weird guy who got kicked off that TV *talent show* last season, too."

"Are we talking about the same doctor?"

"Definitely. He's a laugh all right."

"Never in a million years would I have thought Dr. Griffin was funny or talented. I mean, the man seems to take himself far too seriously, in my opinion." A second too late, she saw Charley's eyes go wide.

"Is that so?" Johnny Griffin's familiar voice flowed over her shoulder.

"Oh! Hey. We were just talking about you." Heat rushed to her cheeks.

"So I heard."

"I'm afraid you're going to have to do your Aquaman impersonation for me before I believe Charley here."

Charley smiled and, amazingly, so did Johnny-boy. A look passed between them like a secret handshake.

"Stop by my office after work and I'll be glad to give you the whole routine," he said, sounding as though he might be flirting. Really? In front of a patient?

She pointed at him. "I'm tempted to call your bluff on that, Doctor."

"I dare you," he said, a playful, sparkly glint in his otherwise dead-serious eyes. Eyes that were becoming more and more intriguing each time she dared to look into them.

The rock-steady gaze caused a response that zipped down her spine with a surprise destination. What was going on here?

She wasn't sure, but one thing she was positive about, she needed to leave the patient's room before Dr. Griffin got an inkling of how much he'd just excited her.

Polly's cell phone rang during lunch the next day and she was surprised to see who was calling. It was Greg. She hadn't responded to his text from yesterday. Why the persistence all of a sudden?

"What's up, Greg?" She tried to sound nonchalant.

"Did you get my text?"

"Oh, uh, I've been working a lot. I guess I missed it." She wasn't above lying to someone who'd lied to her. Repeatedly.

He went into his spiel about coming to New York in two weeks and how he hoped to take her out to dinner and maybe even to see a Broadway play. This couldn't be the Greg she'd once known. Would he actually want to take her to an expensive play on Broadway? Not likely. Unless he'd finally come to his senses about what a prize she was. Again, not likely. Maybe he thought he could come to New York on business and cheat on his girlfriend with *her* while he was here? As in letting history repeat itself.

She wouldn't put a sleazy plan like that past him.

One thing was sure—she wouldn't have to find out if she didn't accept his invitation.

"Can you give me a couple days to think this over, Greg?"

"Look, I understand I treated you pretty rotten last year, but I'd really like to see you again."

"Give me a couple days, okay?"

She hung up before he could say another word, desperate to talk over this invitation with someone else.

Her best friend back home worked the evening shift and Polly didn't feel comfortable yet about opening up to anyone on staff about her personal issues.

She ate her lunch in silence, deep in thought, then as she took a bite of her tuna fish sandwich she practically fell out of her chair when one person popped into her head. Johnny. He was the one person on staff she'd made a complete fool out of herself in front of. Now she'd advanced to being able to tell him exactly what she thought and how she felt, even in front of patients and other staff members, much to everyone's surprise. Hadn't he invited her to show him hers if he could show her his in the moody moods department?

She'd tested the waters and had had a great time being completely herself around him the last couple of days, and he had invited her to come to his office after work for the Aquaman imitation. She understood he had only put that invitation out there because of Charley listening in, but still.

Besides, the man had to be a good twelve or so years older than her twenty-seven, and there was no way on earth he'd ever be interested in her. So that wouldn't be an issue. Even if that look he'd given her yesterday had confused her and turned her on.

John seemed level-headed and world-weary. Why not run her dilemma by him? As a guy, he'd have good input for her. It might help her figure out Greg's true intentions, though she had her own strong suspicions. She'd bought herself two days before she had to get back to Greg.

Maybe Johnny could help her see things how they really were. Now, if she could only work up the nerve to approach him.

* * *

On Friday evening, for the third time in a week, a light tapping on John's office door interrupted his concentration on the computer. "Come in."

The best thing he'd seen all afternoon, well, since the last time he'd seen her anyway, which had been two days ago, walked in.

Polly wore black, straight-leg jeans and high wedge heeled shoes with open toes. Red toenails seemed to smile up at him. Her bright blue top clung to her body in soft folds and outlined her breasts and curves in an inviting way. Since when had he noticed what a woman wore, or how much he liked it?

"Finally came to see my Aquaman imitation, did you?" He pretended not to be distracted by how fantastic she looked.

She smiled, a look that spread like warm butter across her face. "Not really."

"What are you still doing here?" he asked.

"I was going to see a movie tonight, and needed to hang around until eight."

She brushed her bangs across her forehead. The rest of her hair hung loose and free, something he hadn't gotten to see while she was on duty or since the bar on Monday night. The waves and curls accentuated her features, big eyes, straight nose, those well-shaped lips, forcing him to realize she was pretty. Damn, she was pretty. "I was just going to pick up some pizza, wondered if you'd like me to bring you a piece, as you're obviously still here at six-thirty."

The thought of pizza did sound good, but if she expected him to join her in the employee lounge, she had another thought coming. "You deliver, too?"

"Sure, if that's what you want."

What he wanted. Well, the picture of youth and suppleness in front of him gave a whole new meaning to what he wanted. Polly had started a domino effect of interest, attraction, challenge, and all-out lust since her arrival this week. He'd spent more time in the last five days missing and thinking about the wonders of sex than he had in all the years since Lisa's death. It wasn't right, but he couldn't stop himself.

For whatever reason, Polly had the right combination of charm and good looks to make his body involuntarily take notice. The thought was wrong on so many levels yet he couldn't give it up. She worked for him, for crying out loud, and what about Lisa? Well, that was a whole other matter.

Maybe having a piece of pizza with the new nurse and having his little fantasy of making love to her might add some long-overdue entertainment. That wouldn't be such a bad way to spend an evening, would it? Compared to his usual Friday nights, a tasty slice of pie and a few naughty daydreams about the new nurse would be a welcomed change.

"You'd actually bring me a couple of slices of pizza, no strings attached?" He could think of a couple of strings he'd like to attach to a place or two on Polly, but that would be wrong on so many levels.

"Sure."

"You're too nice for your own damn good, Pollyanna."

"What goes around comes around, right?"

"That's only when the world makes sense, and most of the time there's no rhyme or reason about what's going on in the world." Especially now with these crazy thoughts about Polly, which seemed to be growing stronger by the minute. Man, he needed to get a grip.

"Are we talking pizza or philosophy?"

He smiled, letting her youthful beauty warm up his innards and tease at that other kind of appetite he couldn't shake. "Maybe a little of both." He sat back in his chair and put his hands behind his head. Was right now one of those life moments a guy was supposed to grab with gusto, or was he going off the deep end? "Can I ask you a question?"

"Of course."

"Why don't I scare you off like I do everyone else on the staff?"

She smiled, took a few more steps toward his desk, and perched on the edge of the chair. He liked the way she kept her knees together when she sat, all prim and uptight. He liked the scent of whatever she'd splashed on her skin after work, too. "It takes a lot to scare me off." She went silent for a moment. "You want the truth?"

Did he really want to find out how a needy people-pleaser like Polly had become that way? It could ruin this perfect storm of a fantasy brewing in his mind. He glanced at Polly, so appealing and open. He needed to quit thinking only about himself. "Nothing but the truth. Lay it on me."

"My mom died when I was six and my dad couldn't handle it. He took off without me. Later we heard he'd been killed in a car crash. After that I got shipped from one aunt or uncle to another. None of them really wanted me, though they pretended they did. Even a kid can tell when someone isn't being sincere, you know?" She gave a wry, lopsided and totally appealing smile. "So it takes a lot more than what you dish out to scare me off."

Her story snuck around his chest like a vine and tangled up his already confused feelings. It messed with those more basic thoughts floating around in his head, too. She'd been kicked in the teeth, and she'd gotten used to jerks like him giving everyone a hard time. It didn't settle well on his conscience that, in her world, he was one of the bad guys. Why did one person get kicked in the gut and become unbearable, while another learned to be sweetness and light. Exactly what kind of a heel had he turned into since 9/11?

He had a sudden need to make up for all the times he'd been an ass to her. As hard as it would be, he'd banish those sexual thoughts she kept stoking in his head and show Polly some long-overdue respect. "I've got an idea. Why don't you let me buy you dinner? I know a great Italian joint round the corner."

"Oh, I couldn't let you do that."

"But you will." He stood, took off and hung up his doctor's coat on the rack behind his desk, and walked towards Polly. "Let's go eat. I promise to have you back in time for your movie."

She stood and looked at her backpack and lunch container, and the small plastic bag with her soiled scrubs.

"Leave that stuff here," he said. "You can pick it up later. I promise to get you back in time for your movie. Besides, I've got to come back to say goodnight to the kids."

Her widened eyes showcasing those baby blues looked as though they were calculating a gazillion reasons why she shouldn't let him take over her dinner plans, yet she stood mute. If she'd had any clue how she turned him on, looking at him like that, she would run for cover.

Wondering how long he could keep his poker face, he took her elbow and nudged her along. "Come on, come on, let's go, I'm hungry." He'd use being gruff as his cover, because right now the feel of her skin beneath his fingers set off a whole new list of thoughts he hadn't dared to think in ages.

She lifted her brows higher, which seemed impossible, as if she'd felt something in his touch, too. "Okay, Johnny."

The Italian restaurant named Giovanni's was less than two blocks away, and though Polly's wedge heels weren't exactly made for walking—she'd planned to change into flats before heading for the subway home—she enjoyed the exercise. Being in a big, noisy, polluted city, surrounded by skyscrapers and cement—albeit with many well-kept neighborhood parks, not to mention Central Park to soften the blow—made her miss home. John looked after her as they juggled their way through the passing crowds, ignored crossing lights, and jaywalked to their destination.

Giovanni's was everything she'd hoped for in a restaurant—quaint, quiet, romantic, with tall, thin breadsticks waiting at each table and a handsome young waiter ready and willing to serve the diners. For a Friday night, the place was half-empty, and Polly wondered if it had anything to do with the food. Or if the time being only six-thirty in the city that never slept might have something to do with the small turnout.

Johnny knew the waiter by name and ordered a bottle of Chianti and a medium cheese pizza plus two dinner salads, without giving Polly a chance to change her mind about pizza for dinner. The list of pastas and seafood was impressive, but she had said she was going out for pizza, so she didn't fault him for that. She even kind of liked John's take-charge approach to all things in life.

While in his office she could have sworn there had been a flash or two of something in his eyes, after he'd ordered he gazed at Polly as if noticing her for the first time that day. That interesting curl of his lip stretched into a regular smile, like he was surprised and happy at what he'd found sitting across from him.

"I'm going to be straight with you and say I like your hair down," he said, shaking out his napkin and putting it on his lap, sounding more like he was reading the first order of business at an admin meeting than paying her a compliment.

"Thank you." A warm flush moved in a wave up her neck to her cheeks. Polly couldn't exactly say the sensation was unpleasant, and by the appreciative glint in his eyes he must have found her turning red appealing, which made her face heat up even more.

She'd noticed a few things about him on their walk over, too. Like the fact that he filled out his slacks really well and his broad back made even a man of his size look like he had narrow hips. He walked like a guy on a mission, too, which made it extra-hard to keep up, especially dodging traffic and crossing streets in her wedge-heeled shoes.

The Chianti came quickly, and after downing half a glass of her ice water Polly looked forward to sharing a glass of wine with her boss.

"So," he said, crossing his hands on the table top. "How did your first week at Angel's go?"

"Really well, thank you."

He nodded then took a long draw on his wine, all the

while staring into her eyes. He seemed to hold the wine in his mouth before swallowing, as if savoring the flavor and aroma. Oddly, his sensual care with the wine set off tingles across her shoulders. He soon diverted his stare over her shoulder and, she assumed, through the window to the busy street.

"I've got to say, I'm rusty with this sort of thing," he said.

"What sort of thing?"

"Taking a woman out to eat."

Dr. John Griffin didn't date? Even with his gruff shell, that surprised her. He was a good-looking man, a doctor with a gentle heart for his young patients, a… well, she wasn't sure what else he had to offer, but she'd figured he had a full life.

"Don't think twice about it. I practically forced you to do it, so…"

He hushed her by putting his hand on top of hers, and with a no-one-forces-me-to-do-anything look stared her down. "I wanted to."

His touch sent her reeling, and though she thought she might jump out of her seat, she settled and went all quiet, taking in the full significance of his message. Why would he want to spend time with her? She was a country bumpkin, a girl still searching for herself. Sometimes it was better to drop all the questions and just be polite. "Thank you, Doctor."

He shook his head. "Knock off the 'doctor' nonsense. We left that back at Angel's, okay?"

"Okay," she said, as she took her first sip of the strongly flavored wine. "Johnny."

That got an interesting look out of him, one that made her replay her earlier blush.

Midway into her second piece of pizza she'd finished her wine and let John pour her another glass. Another sip or two later, plus more pizza, and she remembered what had really been on her mind since earlier in the week, and why she'd gone to John Griffin's office in the first place.

"May I run something by you?" she said.

"Sure." His mouth was full of the best pizza Polly had tasted since she'd gotten to New York.

She took another drink of wine and placed the glass on the sparkling white tablecloth. "I'm in a dilemma about something and don't know what to do."

He, swallowed, looking very interested in her line of conversation. "Go on."

"I've had a bad history of men walking all over me and, well, last year I got dumped by a guy back home. I'd really had it with men after that, and part of the reason I moved to New York was to move on and start a whole new life."

She could read his body language. Shoulders hunched over the table, his chewing had slowed down. He squinted. This was not a topic of conversation he was interested in but she needed to discuss her options with someone, and tonight that someone was John Griffin.

"So, anyway, a couple of days ago I got a call from Greg, the guy who dumped me without warning last year. He's coming to town and wants to take me out to dinner. He doesn't mean anything to me any more, but I'm thinking he at least owes me a nice dinner, plus he mentioned something about taking me to a Broadway play, too. I know it may sound superficial of me, but I was thinking I deserved some kind of explanation and maybe he'd tell me what was up last year."

He sat perfectly still, hands fisted on the table for a few silent seconds, his expression impossible to read. "He wants to screw you," Johnny said curtly, before taking another drink of wine.

She winced from what felt like a slap in the face. "You don't think I should see him?"

"That depends if you want to get screwed or not." His irritated gaze delved into hers, sending a crazy mixed-up message right down her center. Had she just annoyed him? She sat straighter, using the table to help her balance. Did she want to have sex with her ex? Had she even thought about it in the last six months?

No.

Not until the last few days, that was…and Greg wasn't the face to come to mind when she did think about sex. Oh, cripes, could Dr. Griffin read her mind? Did he have any idea she had the hots for him?

"I'm sorry," she said, putting her napkin across her plate. "I should never have brought up the subject. It's just that I don't have anyone to talk things over with. The lady I rent a room from is probably eighty if she's a day, and my best friend works evenings in Pennsylvania, so it's not like I can pick up the phone after work and talk."

"You asked my opinion." He tugged on his earlobe. "I'm giving it to you straight," he said, his eyes darting around the room in an agitated way. "Unless you want to have sex with the jerk who dropped you last year, don't go near him." He looked at her as if she needed to have a psych referral.

"You're right. I was leaning in that direction, too," she said, mostly to her plate. "I won't even call him back or text him. Thanks for helping me see that more clearly."

Polly sensed a change in John's suddenly irritated mood when she spoke those last words. He inhaled subtly and took another drink from his wineglass, then glanced at his watch.

"We should probably get you back to the hospital to pick up your stuff so you'll have time to get to that movie," he said.

She lifted her chin and gave an exaggerated nod. "Right." She'd blown it. A perfectly lovely dinner with her boss. Until she'd opened her big mouth about some other guy. Could John be jealous? Of course not.

The walk back to the hospital was quiet between them, but the streets, which had come to life with people heading out for the Friday night, weren't. Across the way, Central Park looked hauntingly beautiful in the twilight. John strode on, not saying a word, hands in his pockets, a man on a mission. She did her best to keep up, but her feet were killing her.

"Thank you for buying dinner, Johnny," she said, the only words she could think of. Hoping to remind him he'd given her permission to call him that.

"Any time, dumpling."

That got a smile out of her. He was a paradox. She'd been around many gruff men in her life, but had never cared what they'd thought before. Staring at his profile in the dimming light, she saw a proud man, a talented surgeon, a man respected, if not liked by his peers, yet a man loved by his patients. A man she suspected hid something awful behind his gruff demeanor. Truth was, she found him more and more intriguing and attractive by the moment.

Beginning on Monday, she'd steer clear of him, especially after making a fool of herself by asking him for relationship advice. Whatever had made her think that was a good idea?

Since there was no way in hell she'd ever have a chance with a man like Johnny Griffin, what was the point of being around him? Because she liked him? Found him sexy? The thoughts caused her to pause on the pavement.

That's when he reached for her hand, wrapping his long, strong fingers around it, and pulled her brusquely along the crowded street toward Angel's.

CHAPTER FOUR

POLLY TAGGED ALONG behind John at a fast and challenging clip. They rushed through the hospital lobby towards the elevator, past the "welcome" clown pacing on stilts and the piano player, who was smack in the middle of "Old MacDonald". Diverse entertainment for visiting hours. He moved like a man with a single thought on his mind—how to dump his dinner date. Yet he never let go of her hand.

Still not saying a word on the crowded elevator trip to the sixth floor, he tugged her down the hall and, having left his office door unlocked, whisked it open, practically dragging her inside. Only then did he release his grip. She went directly for her bags and personal items, assuming he wanted her gone. Now.

Why had she thought that offering John Griffin pizza was a good ice-breaker in order to bring up her question about whether or not to go out with an old boyfriend? All she'd done had been to tick him off.

He stood off to the side, staring out the window, hands crammed into the pockets of his slacks, looking like he was doing battle with a slew of demons in his head. Had she done that to him?

"I feel like you're mad at me," she said, stating the unmistakable.

He turned abruptly. "I'm not mad at you, I'm angry about how you try to please everyone else and overlook yourself."

She bunched her hands into fists. "I've had a lifetime of practice. Old habits die hard, you know?"

He tugged his earlobe. "I know."

Relieved that he wasn't fuming at her but was more irritated at her situation, a wave of mismatched feelings swept deep, causing confusion in her mind and her eyes to water. She glanced away.

"If you don't mind—" her voice sounded congested "—I'll change out of these shoes for the subway first."

He turned and watched as she sat on the edge of a chair. "I thought you were going to the movies." The man had gone tighter than a stretched rubber band and the muscle at his jaw twitched as he blatantly ground his molars.

"It was a comedy, and I'm kind of not in the mood now."

He cleared his throat. "Sorry."

"It isn't because of you." She slipped off one shoe. "I guess I just realized how tired I am. It's been a long day." She stretched out her foot and toes. "A long week."

His gaze jumped all over her, from her face to her chest to her hips and legs and finally to her foot. His expression changed from indecision and caution to longing and oh-what-the-hell. Something had snapped in him, some decision Polly wasn't privileged to know, yet his change was as plain as the sudden jangled nerves in her stomach. He made an abrupt move, came in front of her and dropped to his knees. Without a word he handed her his handkerchief for her teary eyes then removed her other shoe. His warm, strong hands caressed her foot, sending shockwaves through her.

Polly stiffened as the idea registered of John Griffin giving her a foot massage. She inhaled raggedly while he gently worked the ball of her foot and the arch with amazingly talented fingers. Soothing sensations tiptoed up her calf, causing tingles behind her knee.

Oh, my God, what do I do?

A crazy answer popped into her mind as she wiped away the tears from her eyes with his monogramed handkerchief. *Enjoy it.*

He splayed her toes and worked each joint right out to the tips of her nails. She tensed and sighed, and felt his touch all the way up the insides of her thighs, though his hands never left her foot.

"The problem with women these days," he said, increasing the pressure on her heel, "is they mess up their feet with these super-sexy shoes. All men want to do is get them off." She looked down at his short-cropped, silver-salted hair, discovering a small endearing cowlick in the middle. His voice sounded hoarse, strained, like maybe he really *was* mad at her. Yet his hands told a completely different story. Was he turned on? "I say that as an orthopedic surgeon."

That made her smile, his rubbing her feet in such a sexy way yet trying to pull off a professional manner. He was looking out for her well-being, though, wasn't he? His ministrations were so amazing she couldn't help but sigh again, so he reached for her other foot. Call her easy, but her shoulders slumped and her head dropped back, savoring the heat of his hands on her totally susceptible skin.

"You're too kind to me," she whispered, shifting her gaze from the ceiling to his serious face as he concentrated on the task at hand—her foot. Her incredibly lucky foot. Her mind wandered to what it would be like if his hands touched her everywhere like that.

"This isn't about being 'kind' and you know it." He stopped his massage and delved into her eyes as if measuring the level of her understanding. She concentrated on his mouth and the hair-thin scar above his upper lip on the right. The growing warmth between her thighs weakened when he stopped touching her, but she'd read his message loud and clear.

He wanted her.

Just as much as she wanted him.

At some point, as he'd stood by that window, he'd made a decision. She'd sensed it then and felt it with every fiber now. Saw it in the serious dark eyes staring at her. Whatever he'd needed to overcome, he had, and now...he wanted her.

A deep desire to break out of her usual by-the-rules role and not to let this magical moment pass made her lean towards him, take his life-weary face between her hands and press a kiss to his irresistible mouth.

Surprisingly soft, his lips were warm and responsive, and he soon took over the advance, proving her hunch had been right. He needed her as much as she wanted him. His hands clamped around her waist, squeezing with urgency as he deepened their kiss.

She ran her fingers across his short, springy hair then down his powerful neck as she kissed him back. Solid. The man was solid. She smelled his lingering forest-scented cologne and enjoyed the end-of-day stubble of his beard. His tongue found hers and she let him have his will, matching exploration for exploration and tasting a hint of Chianti. The warmth pooling between her thighs quickly renewed as her pulse thrummed throughout her body.

A sharp knocking on the office door shocked her out of her dream about kissing her boss. Oh, wait, it was really happening.

"Environmental Services," a loud voice called. "Dr. Griffin, are you still in there?"

"Just leaving, Constantine, give me a couple of minutes." His voice sounded heavy and forced. Heat radiated from John's darkened eyes as he stared at her. "I know a place we can go. Will you come with me?"

The question of the day—will you come with me?

Overcome with his no-nonsense sex appeal, his smoldering gaze, and their incredible kiss, there was only one answer she could think of.

"Yes, Johnny," she whispered, banishing from her mind their age difference and concentrating on their total attraction to each other.

He hastily gathered her things as she used the back of her hand to wipe her already kiss-swollen lips, trying her best to recover from the mind-bending introduction to making out with Dr. John Griffin. She could barely wait for more as he grabbed his jacket and her hand and led the way out.

"Goodnight," he said in a clipped voice to the janitor as they passed, as if he dragged a woman from his office every night of the week and Housekeeping should think nothing of it.

Was the fact that she was barefoot a dead giveaway to what they'd been doing?

The janitor had his back to them, concentrating on

his cleaning cart, and she was grateful as John whisked her down the dark hall toward the stairs.

He led her through the back way and down a couple of flights to another deserted floor, then past half a dozen doors to an open on-call room. Rushing her inside, he hung up the "occupied" sign and closed the door behind them. Immediately, he dropped all of her bags and items into a chair and took her by the shoulders, walking her backwards against the wall.

"Where did we leave off?" he asked gruffly, digging his fingers into her hair before taking her mouth again.

His kisses were hot and wet and making her dizzy with desire. She bunched his shirt in tight fists, wanting him as much as he obviously wanted her. His hand wandered over her hip, skimming her waist and upwards until he found her breast. His other hand cupped her bottom and pulled her flush to his groin. She could already feel his arousal straining against her thigh. Knowing how she affected him excited her beyond any fantasy.

His kisses grew frantic and desperate, and his fingers found their way under her bra. Her breast was already tensed and peaked and he ran his thumb over the tip, which tightened her more. Tingles fanned across her chest, teasing her other breast. She angled the V of her thighs over his erection, and leaned hard into him, yearning for relief. He moaned and pulled her up, positioning her on top of his wedge. She slid over him, begging for more, hating the fact that they were still dressed.

Breaking apart only because she wanted to be without barriers, she raised her arms and he lifted her top over her head in record time. She reached behind and undid the catch on her bra as he unzipped his pants.

"Should we be doing this?" she asked, her eyes adjusting to the darkened room, seeing him stripping in front of her and realizing there was no turning back. Not for her, anyway.

"You started it." He kicked off his loafers and dropped his pants. Thickly muscled legs, like those of a Grecian god, made her gasp inwardly.

"I didn't think it would get this far." Impatient to be skin to skin with him, she moved fast and jerkily while her clothes refused to co-operate.

"It has." He helped her break free of the bra then moved her into a beam of slanting streetlight that had snuck into the room, and took the time to look at her topless and vulnerable, conveying with his eyes how much he liked what he saw.

Her nerves were quickly overcome by her desire, and after an eager glance at him she definitely liked what she saw, too. A combination of jitters and excitement flitted along her skin. He clamped his mouth on a breast, kissing and sucking, while he pushed on the waist of her pants.

On board with the total program, Polly understood this would be no-frills sex but long-overdue passion that could only be released in a flash and never fast enough. Ready for anything, everything, she squirmed out of her tight jeans and underpants while trying not to lose contact with his body.

Soon back to having her pressed to the wall, he sealed his lips tightly to hers and his heavy erection pressed into her belly. The rush and aroma of hot skin and stimulation made her squirm with need. His hand slid between her legs, fingers quickly discovering how ready she was. He positioned himself and she lifted her thigh and wrapped her calf around his waist so he could find her entrance.

Angling his full erection, he hesitated. “I don’t have a condom.”

“I’m on the Pill.”

Her answer seemed to satisfy him, and he launched into her, releasing a sizzling sensation that spread across her hips. A few more thrusts and she’d molded to his length and thickness, her moisture slickening him more with each move. The internal burning turned to smoldering and soon fire as he pushed into her over and over, setting off bells, whistles and alarms on every surface he touched.

It had been over a year since she’d made love with anyone, and her tightness intensified the sensations rolling through her pelvis and soon connecting with the shivers in her breasts. She ached for more as he drove into her again and again, thrilling her, making her beg he’d never stop.

Under the hold of his strong arms, her body banged against the wall. He emitted deep, throaty sounds as he continued to bury himself inside her hard and fast, seeming desperate to have all of her. As if humanly possible, he grew harder with each thrust. Though wanting to ride with him all the way to his climax, she couldn’t hold out. Her mounting thrill became too intense to control as crazy sensations spilled out and over her like demons storming through her body. She gasped and bit his shoulder as she came, helpless to stop the powerful release. His continued forceful rhythm extended her climax until she was as limp as a ragdoll against him.

With an “Ahh” he came and she felt his warmth spread inside. With spasm after spasm she adjusted her hips and drew him even deeper than he'd been as he crumpled against her. They stayed in that position, she limp, he holding her flush to the wall, locked tightly together until every last tingle and pulse from the top of her head to the tips of her breasts and all the way down to the soles of her feet completed their course.

Taking her chin in the V of his hand, he bussed her lightly on the lips. Near feral eyes burned into hers when he drew back. "I'm not through with you yet," he whispered.

Too numb to speak, she stared at him mesmerized, completely willing to be with him again, however he wanted it.

Still bound together, he carried her just as they were against the wall towards the small bed, as if she were a feather. With her legs still wrapped securely around his hips, he slowly and gently placed her beneath him on the mattress, careful not to lose their point of contact. Amazingly, he was still firm.

With a serious-as-hell gaze he lifted her arms above her head and clamped one hand tightly around her wrists, binding her to the bed. He bent and took a breast into his mouth and cupped the other with his free hand. Minutes passed with his soft, sexy torture of kisses here and nips there, his intensifying touch drawing her nearer and nearer to frenzy. When she squirmed and tried to free her hands he held her firm, completely in charge. Already on overdrive, every touch, nibble and kiss sent her reeling. She wanted more and more.

After a few more minutes he grew harder inside her and slowly began to move in and out, each thrust building force. Still a prisoner to his hold, she moved the only part she could, her hips. She matched his pace, adjusting her position to bring him closer, being rewarded with amazing sensations gathering and tightening in her core. Within a few more minutes he was back to full strength, and as he drove faster and deeper, her thrills intensified, coiling so tight she neared another release.

As if he could feel her mounting climax around him, still clamping her hands over her head, he broke contact with her breast, accelerated his thrusts, and smiled devilishly at her. "There's definitely an advantage to having sex with a people-pleaser," he said, quickly finishing her off.

Embarrassed by how easy she'd been to conquer, again, she laughed while she came, a complete first for her. He let go of her wrists and rolled onto his back, bringing her along. She straddled his waist and held tight, soon taking him right where she wanted him, helpless to resist her and completely at her mercy, just as she'd been with him only moments before.

After he'd come, she smiled down at him, kissed and licked the crease of his curled lips. "I'm not through with you yet," she said.

It was his turn to laugh. "So I *have* died and gone to heaven, huh?"

She rubbed her breasts across his chest and nestled into the crook of his neck, taking his earlobe between her teeth. "I haven't even known you for a week, Johnny," she whispered into his ear.

His hands cupped her bottom and squeezed tight, sparking new desire. "Crazy, isn't it?"

"Crazy good?"

"Definitely."

Before dawn, Polly woke up tangled up in John's arms and legs. The word "crazy" occurred to her again as she disengaged, used the shower, dressed and snuck out before John woke up. As it was her weekend off, she couldn't be seen sneaking out of the on-call room by any of her co-workers arriving on Saturday morning for the day shift without stirring questions. Fully dressed, hair damp and on her shoulders, she tiptoed outside, but not before glancing over her shoulder at John, who slept peacefully, then she quietly latched the door.

Lying there, listening to Polly shower and dress, John played possum when she left. Truth was he didn't know what to say to her. They'd amazed each other with great sex half the night, finally collapsing from exhaustion in each other's arms only a few short hours ago. He'd never let go so soon or so easily with anyone in his life until Polly the people-pleaser had arrived on his doorstep.

He scrubbed his face to help him wake up. What the hell should he do now? It was so out of character for him to screw an employee. The thought of running into her on the ward would be awkward as hell after everything they'd done to each other. How could he keep professional with her now?

He wasn't looking for a relationship. She was too damn young for him. Too sweet for her own good. Too wild and crazy in bed for a man still pining for his wife. He would be just as bad for her as that jerk she'd come to talk to him about. Why did the thought of Polly being with another man make his blood boil again, especially now that he'd made love to her? What right did he have to feel possessive of her? Wasn't he as bad as that guy after the way he'd brought her here to the on-call room for the sole purpose of making love until the burning she caused inside him finally stopped?

Thinking about her this morning, he realized the desire for her hadn't come close to burning out. But it had to. John Griffin didn't have gratuitous sex, especially with someone vulnerable like Polly. Or someone he worked with. He sat at the side of the bed, ran his fingers through his hair as he stood and headed for the shower. What about Lisa?

There were too many questions, but only one answer seemed to solve them all. He'd avoid Polly as much as possible, and once he worked out in his head just what the hell had happened last night and why, he'd explain to her that it was unethical and could never happen again. She'd have to understand.

That was his plan, and he'd have to stick to it, because he wasn't about to change his just-getting-by personal life for a flighty young thing like Polly Seymour.

Polly got on the subway heading for the Lower East Side. Not knowing what to say to him, she hadn't been able to get away from John fast enough. What had gotten into her? Granted, he'd taken her to the on-call room after giving her the most incredible foot massage of her life and, well, they'd taken the natural course from there. And wow. She hadn't held back, and neither had he. Never in her life had she done such a thing, had sex with a man she hardly knew. A man she worked for!

Sitting on the hard seat of the subway train, she wondered if everyone in the car, which was thankfully only a handful, could see her flush until her ears burned. She rested her head against the cold window and stared out at the quickly passing darkness. She wasn't about to act needy around Johnny Griffin. No. That would turn him off quicker than her kisses had turned him on. She'd have to ride out this awkward situation, see where John took it. As far as she was concerned, it was up to him to approach her. After the way she'd made love with him, the man at least owed her a thank you.

Allowing her mind to drift back to the night before and some of the amazing things that had occurred, she remembered that "thank you" swung both ways. Holy cow, did it ever.

On Monday morning Polly arrived at work with trepidation. Her palms tingled and her stomach clenched at the thought of facing the head of Orthopedics. Doubt upon doubt had cropped up over the weekend. Was having sex in the on-call room how Dr. Griffin initiated all the new nurses?

In her heart she knew that wasn't true. He loathed interacting with his staff, and after a week on the job she hadn't heard any rumors about his personal life… just that he was a loner who preferred the kids on the ortho ward to adult company.

Surprised to see that Annabelle had already been discharged, she took report on all new patients. Today she'd be nurse to four pre-teens in various sizes and shaped casts in a group ward.

In the middle of taking vital signs she heard John's voice outside. Nerves unfurled through her center, making her hands shake. Still unprepared to face him, she prayed he'd stay out in the nurses' station area and not come into her room.

The deep, masculine tone carried over the usual noise of the ward as he spoke to Brooke. "Tell your nurses to get their kids ready by nine."

Polly was still getting used to the non-stop activities of Angel's Children's Hospital. They even had an on-site radio show in the lobby, and often the kids were the subjects of interviews. The play therapists didn't allow the patients to zone out on video games or too much TV. They kept them interacting with other patients with games and challenges where everyone could participate. If a child was too sick to leave their room, they'd come to them.

Volunteer grandmothers and grandfatherly types regularly came for one-to-one bedside reading, and the children ate it up. Especially with the man who looked like Santa on his day off in a Hawaiian shirt and golf cap reading *Harry Potter* cover to cover.

Polly snuck a look outside her room just in time to see John turn and walk back toward his office on the far side of the hospital wing. Though not a tall man, his broad shoulders reminded her how strong he was. A quick flash of him naked and carrying her to the bed in the on-call room had her cheeks burning.

"Why're you red?" the girl with waist-length black hair and a full leg cast asked. "Do you have a fever or something?"

"No. I'm fine. Don't you ever blush?"

"Not unless I'm embarrassed. Are you embarrassed?" Her insightful, inquisitive eyes made Polly's skin crawl.

"Maybe a little."

"Why?"

Polly glanced around the brightly decorated four-bed ward, where stenciled sports equipment and swaths of primary colors made the white walls pop, as she searched for either a dodge or a believable answer. One thing she'd quickly learned working with kids was they could tell when someone wasn't being straight with them.

"I just remembered something I did over the weekend."

"Did you get hammered?" The young one's bright black eyes suddenly seemed far too mature for twelve.

"No. And how do you even know what 'hammered' means?"

"My sister goes to college." She tossed half of her hair over her shoulder, in a gesture that advertised she knew everything about being a grown up and drinking too much in college.

As if that explained and closed the topic, Polly let the subject drop, but not before she noticed John Griffin's signature on the girl's cast and she felt her cheeks flush again. Did the man sign every single cast on the ward?

As promised, at nine o'clock sharp a raucous brass quartet blustered onto the ward playing circus music, as if a parade would follow. Polly had gotten each of her patients into wheelchairs and rolled them to the center of the ward just in time. One of her girls wasn't the least bit interested in the music, instead staring at her cell phone, until the trombone player swung by and hit a low note by extending the slide right under her chin. It shocked and delighted her and Polly laughed along with the patient, especially when the girl glanced up and saw a good-looking college guy, and her eyes brightened.

In mid-laugh, Polly glanced up and caught John's gaze from across the room. It seemed a trapdoor had opened in her chest, and her heart skidded to her ankles. Maybe it was the circus music.

She couldn't inhale.

Attempting and falling far short of the mark, she gave some semblance of a smile, and in return he gave that half grimace, half smile he was so adept at then quickly looked away.

Could things get any more awkward?

By Wednesday afternoon, having great sex with John Griffin had started to seem more like a figment of Polly's imagination than fact. He'd drifted in and out of the hospital ward like a ghost leaving hints of things out of place, or the tell-tale scent of his woodsy aftershave, or an icy chill spiraling down her spine. Not once did he try to confront her, and she'd vowed to steer clear of his office no matter how much she wanted to chew him out for being so cold and inconsiderate for leaving her dangling and insecure since Friday night.

On Thursday morning the pet therapy Dalmatian made rounds, stopping beside Polly's toddler patient, Eugenia. The child had fallen from a two-story window and broken both arms, and had been taken into protective services after being admitted to Angel's. She was withdrawn and moody, and Polly didn't know how to reach her or make her comfortable. But Dotty the Dalmatian brightened the child's gray eyes with interest, and soon a smile crossed her lips as Dotty licked her fingertips.

Warmth washed through Polly's down mood, and she grinned at her young charge, then was rewarded with Eugenia smiling back. Simple things. Small steps. This was the way to put a life back together, as Polly only knew too well from her own childhood.

"May I talk to you?" From behind, the familiar voice made her eyes go wide. It was John. Adrenaline sprayed like scattershot throughout her chest. She schooled her expression before she turned.

"Sure," she said, acting as if nothing, especially her

ego, had been flipped sideways since they'd had mind-blowing sex.

Leaving her patient with Dotty and the pet therapy lady, she followed his long and purposeful strides toward the supply room.

When they arrived, he took a deep breath. "I don't want this to be offensive or anything," he said in a nearly inaudible voice, "but I think you should take some STD tests."

So this was all about medical business, about the messy little clean-up committee for being reckless with the new girl. He may not have wanted to offend her but pure insult made her send him a cutting glance. "Why, Doctor? Have you jeopardized me?"

"No!" he rasped. She could see the vein on the side of his neck pop out.

"But you worry I may have…"

"No," he said, in a strained whisper. "I'm just being practical."

She latched onto his eyes and stared him down. "For your information, I don't sleep around. I don't have any surprises to give you, so I'll skip. Thanks." She turned to walk away, trying her best to save what was left of her pride, but he caught her by the elbow and held her back.

"We were completely careless." He spoke quietly, directly into her ear. Even now, under the worst possible circumstances, the touch of his breath on her neck made her skin prickle. She looked up at him. His dark eyes peered into hers in warning. "As a doctor, I can't be negligent. I've ordered some tests for you."

"What about you?" she said, hackles fully raised and ready to fight.

He looked thoughtfully at his OR clogs. "I checked out okay."

"Then what's the point of me—?"

His flat expression warned she wasn't about to like his answer. "Because I'm not the one who can get pregnant, even if you're on birth control pills."

Stunned by reality, she swallowed around a dry knot. She'd already told him there wouldn't be a problem—didn't he believe her? Since he was being such a jerk about everything today, she wouldn't argue.

Desperate to save face, she shrugged free of his hold. "I'll handle the tests myself, thanks," she said as she walked away, trying her best to stand straight and look confident, while feeling anything but.

That night, still fuming, she stopped at the corner ma and pa grocery store and found a pregnancy test purporting to identify a pregnancy within seven to ten days after the missed period. But Polly hadn't missed her period, which wasn't due for another three days. Would she be able to hold tight and wait for three days then buy the test? The blood test John had ordered could tell much sooner than the urine test, but her pride had tripped her up and kept her from consenting. She was sure that just because John Griffin had ordered the test and the results would be sent to him, he wasn't going to be the first to know if, and that was a very big if, she was pregnant or not.

Of course she wasn't pregnant. She took her pills every night as directed.

For some illogical reason, that night when she prepared her dinner she made sure it was well balanced and nutritious as one short phrase whispered in her mind—

What if?—which was quickly followed by a heavy brick of panic landing in her stomach and replacing her appetite.

Monday morning, officially late for her period, Polly showed up at work withdrawn and anxious. Dread trickled down her spine as she remembered the antibiotics she'd taken a few weeks back for a sinus infection. It was a known fact that antibiotics could interfere with the potency of birth control pills for up to two weeks. It had been more than two weeks since she'd taken them, though, and that kept her hopeful all would be fine.

"Hey, Polly, how's it shakin'?" the ward clerk Rafael asked as she passed the nurses' station.

"Meh," she said, and walked on.

"What? If you're not in a good mood, how the heck am I supposed to be?"

She stopped in her tracks and saw honest surprise in his dark chocolate-colored eyes. "I guess you'll just have to work extra hard at it today, Rafe ol' buddy."

"That's cold, forcing a man to be in a good mood for no good reason all on his own." He laughed. "See, even in a bad mood you make me smile."

"What's this I hear about little Miss Sunshine being in a foul mood?" Brooke said, approaching Polly and putting her hand on Polly's shoulder. She rubbed back and forth. "You okay?"

Did her face have to be an open book?

"I've been better." She should have gotten her period on Saturday, but so far there wasn't even a hint that it was on the way. She had a question she wanted to ask Brooke, but didn't want to be blatant about how a person went about getting a pregnancy test done at Angel's, so she decided to wait for a better time under less obvious circumstances.

On Wednesday morning, Brooke assigned her once again to Eugenia, who was constantly being assessed and visited by social services, play therapists, speech therapists, and just about every doctor on staff. Polly looked forward to spending the day with a little girl who needed love as much as she did.

During Eugenia's bed bath, Polly tickled and teased the child to get her to laugh, which she did more easily this week than last.

"Mornin', peanut," a woman with a heavy Texan drawl said. "How's my girl today?"

Polly looked up to see the beautiful blonde Dr. Layla Woods. "Can you say good morning for Dr. Woods, Eugenia?"

"Mun."

Dr. Woods smiled at Polly, then at Eugenia. "That's very good."

Polly loved her accent. As Dr. Woods warmed the child up with a game of peek-a-boo and then delicately did a quick physical assessment of Eugenia, Polly studied her flawless complexion and gorgeous Texas-bluebell-colored eyes. She'd seen her before on the orthopedic floor several times making general medicine rounds, always smiling and gracious. Always approachable.

Polly had heard rumblings about Dr. Woods and the head of Neurosurgery, Dr. Alejandro Rodriguez, the most gorgeous man on the planet. Bar none. But she didn't want to get caught up in hospital gossip and had paid little attention to the stories.

She looked back at the doctor, who'd finished up her

examination of Eugenia with a tap on the tip of the toddler's nose. Dr. Woods could easily be a cover model or actress with her good looks, but there was an added ingredient, sort of like a secret sauce, that made the whole recipe of Layla Woods extra-special. Perhaps seasoned by her own life, the woman oozed compassion.

And that's when it hit her. No risk, no gain, right?

Polly cleared her throat and worked up the fortitude to ask the question of the day. "Dr. Woods, um, may I ask you a favor?"

"Sure, whatcha' need?"

"Could you order me a pregnancy test?" she mumbled, embarrassed.

"A pregnancy test?"

Polly wanted to shush her, but didn't have the nerve, instead lowering her lashes and staring at the floor. The perceptive doctor quickly caught on.

"Oh," she whispered, looking around. Thankfully no one else but the toddlers were in the two bed-ward. "Sorry. Certainly. I'll order that right now. You want a blood test, right?"

Polly nodded. "Thanks so much."

Dr. Woods winked, jotting down Polly's last name from her name badge, then Polly gave her medical record number.

"Your secret's safe with me. Good luck, whichever way you hope it turns out." She smiled and after pinching Eugenia's cheeks and kissing her forehead the lovely doctor left the room, heading for the nearby computer to input that order.

At the end of her shift Polly stopped at the lab to have her blood drawn. After a long day and a crowded subway ride home she was hot and exhausted and didn't look forward to taking those five flights of stairs up to her room. A room that didn't even have air-conditioning. If this was how it got in early July, how would she survive the rest of the summer?

While making a mental note to buy a big fan, she let herself into the apartment. Mrs. Goldman, her landlady, sat in the tiny, dim living room watching TV and didn't even look up, which Polly was glad about. The last thing she wanted to do was get sucked into one of her landlady's long and meandering stories tonight. After a snack she slipped into her room and took a nap.

A couple of hours later she decided to check her e-mails and saw the notice from Angel's hospital about her test results. Quickly accessing the hospital patient medical records program, she went into her account, eager to end this chapter in her book of life's mistakes. The sooner she knew all was clear, the faster she could close the door for good on John Griffin and move on. She'd sweep her regretful actions into a corner and forget about them, like she had so many other things in her life. Though forgetting her incredible night with John would take a lot of effort.

Opening up her lab test page, her hopeful attitude got hitched to gravity and plummeted into an abyss. Positive. The blood test was positive.

Prickles of fear stormed like a battalion across her skin as her entire body went hot.

She. Was. Pregnant.

CHAPTER FIVE

FRIDAY MORNING, JOHN sat at his desk on the computer finishing up the last of his administrative work, the thing he liked least about being a department head. If he had his way he'd do surgery every day, but he needed to play fair and share the admin duties with his orthopedic surgical staff.

Out of habit, he glanced at the spot on his desk he'd always looked when in doubt, but it was empty. He'd already forgotten that he'd put the framed photograph of his wife in the desk drawer the previous week. He hadn't been able to look at her picture without feeling guilty since he'd slept with Polly…even though it had been twelve years since Lisa had died.

He wasn't a saint, he'd been with a woman here or there over the years, but never had he gotten involved, and he liked it that way. That was, until Polly and this alien desire to get involved. Very involved.

He thought about her every day, relived their lovemaking in his head at the craziest moments, and even though he'd handled everything monumentally badly, he still smiled when he thought about her lively blue eyes, sexy grin, and perky young body.

Polly the people-pleaser extraordinaire.

At thirty-nine he was too young for a midlife crisis, wasn't he? With his elbow on the desk, he sank his chin into the palm of his hand and looked out the window. Damn, he'd become a moony teenager all over again.

Couldn't he just apologize to her for being so crass and start over?

Truth was he wanted to, and he'd never thought of himself as a coward…

The tap at the door yanked him from his thoughts. "Come in."

When Polly stepped into the room, looking tired and worried, something thick and cold dropped in his stomach and she got his full attention. Barely able to lift her eyes to his, she walked toward his desk.

He shot up from his chair. "Are you all right?"

She sighed and sat, finally lifting her gaze to meet his. "Yes, actually, I am."

He sat, not wanting to be a pushover. "Can you forgive me for being a jerk?" His mouth had gotten a jump on his cool-and-calm plan.

"That depends."

"On?"

"On how you react when I tell you something."

Another sinking feeling slithered down John's throat. What messy surprise was she going to spring on him? Would she tell him she never wanted to be with him again when he'd just realized how much he wanted to know her better? He sat perfectly still, keeping her in his line of vision, waiting for her big announcement. To cover his insecurity, he went the tough route.

"I'm a big boy. Don't worry about me." He thought about picking up his pen and pretending to continue to work on his papers, blowing her off, just to show her how absolutely fine he was with however she planned to dump him. Yes, he was a busy, busy man, who would hardly notice if she dropped out of his life.

Liar.

She put her fingertips over her mouth and watched him, as if gauging his true feelings. Shaking her head, she glanced at the floor then back up at him. “There’s no easy way to put this.”

He went still, sensing the heaviness in the room gather into a giant cloud directly over his head. This wasn’t the Polly he knew. This Polly seemed like she’d been steamrollered by life, not the bright young woman she’d been when she’d first arrived at Angel’s…before they’d made love.

Pretty lousy effect you have on women, Griffin.

Okay, he’d made a snap decision. He wouldn’t mess up her life one more day, no matter how badly he wanted to get involved. She didn’t deserve a moody old fart like him.

“I’m pregnant.”

He’d let her go, break it off clean— What?

“You’re pregnant?” He’d checked his lab reports every day and hadn’t seen her results. “And you know this how?”

“I asked Dr. Woods to order a blood test for me.” She raised her hand. “Before you say another word I want to tell you straight out that I will not end this pregnancy. And I don’t intend to give up the baby for adoption.” She looked into his eyes, hers shining from moisture. “I know how it feels not to be wanted…” her voice broke with emotion “…and I won’t let my baby go through that.” She swallowed and sat quietly, obviously trying to hold herself together.

He'd heard everything she'd said. He'd paid attention. Yet he needed to repeat the words, to make them real, and help them sink in. "You're pregnant."

"Yes."

With his hands on his desk, perfectly still, he leaned forward, trying to get his mouth to move so he could ask the question *What do we do now?* but nothing came out.

"And no matter what you say..." she stared at him out of those determined, teary eyes, having the same effect as reaching into his chest and wrenching out his heart "...I'm keeping this baby."

His baby. She was keeping his baby. He'd never thought he'd have a chance at a family again. A nugget of hope planted itself in his heart, filling a long-forgotten hole. He almost smiled at the absurdity of how he'd become a father at thirty-nine—from one amazing night in on-call.

Not since his wife had told him she was pregnant had he felt such a flash of joy.

A baby. A family.

But that had been long ago, and six weeks before 9/11. When he'd loved and lost both his wife and unborn child. When he would have gladly given his own life in exchange for theirs.

A jet of fear shot through his chest and strangled the breath out of him. He couldn't speak as a flashback of the hopeless feeling that had nearly ended his life—and had surely ended his wife and future child's life—played out in his head. The horror of that day. The frantic need to find her in the rubble. The sinking feeling as reality had put one foot in front of the other and stepped ever closer to ripping his life apart, as it had for so many others. The desperation when hope against all the odds had lost out and he'd found out she'd been killed. That he'd never kiss Lisa again, never hold her, never welcome their baby into his arms.

Oh, God, he couldn't do this again. He couldn't bear the pain if anything happened to this baby…or Polly. He'd used up an entire life's worth of pain and sadness already. He couldn't spare one more…

"Are you all right?"

Polly's gentle voice broke through his thoughts. Even when confessing her predicament, she'd put him first. Was he all right? What about *her*? Was *she* all right with him getting her pregnant? Of course not! Yet, trouper that she was, she'd come to tell him she was keeping their baby, whether he liked it or not.

He tried to unclench his fists, to act as if he hadn't just relived the worst day of his life. Unfortunately, his expression must have been a snapshot of his true feelings, and Polly was a solid people-reader. Perspiration moistened his upper lip. He rubbed it away.

"Yes, I'm all right." He took a deep breath, knowing it would be impossible to invest emotionally in this pregnancy. At least he could be a civilized man and offer financial support. Surely she couldn't do this on her own without his monetary help. He ground his molars and lifted his eyes to meet her steady and earnest gaze. "How much do you think you'll need?"

His hands shook so badly he wasn't even sure he'd be able to hold a pen if she agreed to let him write her a check. He held onto the desk rim to hide his shaking.

He may as well have slapped her face by the way she flinched at his words. "Pardon?" Anger, like an offshore squall, gathered in those luminescent blue eyes. Her face tensed, incensed. "You think I came here to ask for money?" Her voice quivered with barely controlled rage. "You want to pay me because you knocked me up?"

Of course she'd take it the wrong way. She didn't have a clue what he'd been through, and he sure as hell didn't have the strength to tell her now. He had to hold it together, to be the worst kind of bastard on earth in order to make it through this meeting. No matter what she thought of him, she at least deserved to be well taken care of.

He tugged his earlobe. "That's right." His jaw was so tightly locked the words had to squeeze themselves out.

Her obviously escalating fury forced her to stand. Her cheeks blushed red, her eyes looked wild. "You bastard!"

It was her turn to verbally slap *him*. "This pregnancy isn't some little problem you can clean up with cash. For me it's sacred!" She stormed out of the room and slammed the door, leaving the glass and walls shaking as much as his hands.

Ah, hell. He picked up his pen and tossed it across the desk. Could he have handled the situation any worse?

Almost a week later Polly helped her favorite LVN, Darren, start an IV he'd accidentally dislodged. She sat at the hospital bedside with her IV kit prepared and in reach. Children were always a challenge, and the little boy had started screaming the moment he'd realized what the "lady nurse" was going to do to him. Darren firmly held the six-year-old's arm to the bed, his other arm safely secured in a cast and sling. With Darren's free hand he pressed against the boy's knees to control the fidgeting legs.

Starting an IV on a child that was freaking out was

bad enough, but hitting a moving target was nearly impossible.

She wiped the skin with disinfectant and slipped on gloves. His wails escalated.

"Mikey, if you hold still for just a couple of seconds, this will go a lot quicker," Darren said. "Then I'll play *Battle Star* with you, I promise."

Fortunately, that morning the high school of performing arts had sent a troupe of street performers to their ward. A lanky kid in a fluorescent green shirt and a bright red beret appeared at the doorway, juggling neon yellow and blue bowling pins. He edged to the side of the bed, capturing the boy's attention.

The moment the child became distracted Polly slid the needle into the vein and anchored it with tape before Mikey's delayed protest made him squirm again. His mouth gaped as the juggler pretended, in an exaggerated way, to almost drop a pin.

"It's all over," Polly said. "Just need to tape it, Mikey." She wasn't even sure he was listening. "Then you can kick Darren's patootie in *Battle Star*, okay?"

The relieved child looked at his arm to make sure Polly hadn't lied, just as the juggler migrated to the next room.

Darren glanced at Polly, winked and smiled. She smiled back, then patted Mikey's shoulder. Teamwork. It was the only way to survive in a hospital.

Teamwork in a pregnancy was pretty darned important, too.

Leaving the room, she almost ran into John, who was holding a tiny patient and watching the juggler as he switched to multicolored balls. It had been a week since she'd told him she was pregnant and had stormed out of his office after he'd insulted her, and he hadn't lifted a finger to contact her since. She yanked herself back before they made physical contact, as her heart nearly hurtled out of her chest. "Oh, sorry," she said, by rote.

He handed the tiny patient to the nearby nurse then steadied Polly by holding her arms. "My fault. Wasn't watching where I was going."

She stared at his feet, rather than look at him, furious with him, the feel of his warm hands on her skin almost her undoing. What could she say that she hadn't already confessed in his office, and he'd frozen her out, tried to pay her off, leaving her hurt beyond comprehension? She'd calmed down since then for her baby's sake, and from now on her baby would be the only thing she cared about.

She stepped back, removing her arms from his grasp. The last thing she needed was for anyone on staff to become suspicious about them, or find out about their predicament. *Her* predicament, as he'd have nothing to do with it. The pregnancy would be apparent to everyone soon enough.

"How are you feeling?" he asked, under his breath.

"Fine. Thank you." She walked away, pretending her legs didn't feel like noodles, holding her head high. She felt his eyes on her, but refused to turn round.

"Dr. Griffin! Dr. Griffin!" a child's voice cried out. "Will you make me an elephant?"

"I'll make you two elephants, if you'll quit giving your physical therapist such a hard time, Nate."

Did he even give a damn about her?

The boy laughed, and Polly could practically see John messing his hair and pretending to punch him in the arm with the cast. The man was a natural with kids, yet he'd chosen to ignore his own child.

Later that day, when the opportunity came up to work a double shift, Polly jumped at the chance. She'd need to work lots of double shifts to earn as much money as possible while she could for her and the baby.

The evening staff had a whole different feel from the day crew. Gossip seemed to be their favorite pastime, and Polly got an earful from another RN named Janetta, a large woman with a loud voice. When Janetta spoke, everyone listened.

"You know that pretty new blonde doctor, Layla something or other?" Janetta said.

"Dr. Woods?" Polly asked.

"Mmm-hmm. That's the one. She talks weird."

"She's from Texas."

"That's right, honey. That's the one." Janetta leaned forward and looked around. "Guess who she's having an affair with."

Polly didn't have a clue, neither did she want to know, but something told her Janetta was about to tell her anyway.

"Dr. Dreamy himself. That hunk from Neuro, Dr. Rodriguez."

Come to think of it, Layla and Dr. Rodriguez would make a perfect couple, but Polly kept her thoughts to herself. "How do you know they're having an affair?"

"Everyone knows it. Where have you been? It's the talk of the hospital. Goes way back. I heard from a good source that it broke up Dr. Woods's marriage, too. It must be true, 'cos she's single."

The thought of her own and John's personal business

getting spread all over the hospital like poor Dr. Woods and Dr. Rodriguez made her skin prickle.

From the corner of her eye she noticed John entering room number one. "Goodnight, Chloe and Sandra. Sleep tight. See you in the morning light."

She'd never been here before for John's nightly ritual.

He zipped into the next room. "Jason and Brandon, don't give your nurses a hard time or you'll have to answer to me. Have a good night's sleep and I'll be back to check on you tomorrow."

How would John hold his head up at work if their affair became fodder for the hospital gossip mill?

As for herself, she couldn't wait to be a mother, single or not. Finally she'd have a baby to love and cherish and they'd be a family, just the two of them. She thought about Dr. Woods and wondered if she had a clue what was being said about her, and decided not to participate in this grapevine.

She thought about telling Janetta that unless she knew for sure about something, she shouldn't pass it along, but didn't want to get on Janetta's bad side. Instead, she nodded her head and let Janetta give her the rundown on several other people having affairs in the hospital, while listening to John enter each patient room and wishing the children a good night.

Soon enough her name would be added to the jilted-lover list.

Polly kept her thoughts to herself and to avoid John went back to caring for her patients, thankful that visiting hours made the floor busier and noisier than usual. The chaos still wasn't enough to keep her from thinking about her own situation, though.

She'd have to get used to the evening staff as she

planned to work at least two extra shifts a month from now until she went on maternity leave. She would have to in order to make ends meet, and there was no way she'd let John pay her for getting her pregnant. She'd never take his guilt money.

Thankfully, she'd get medical coverage through Angel's hospital after her probationary two months. She'd have to hold tight until then to have her first prenatal appointment. Since she didn't have a clue how to find a good obstetrician in town, she'd have to be discreet about getting a name without alerting the rest of the staff to her situation.

During her dinner break Janetta and someone Polly had never seen before joined her at the only table in the nurses' lounge.

"This here is Vickie. She's the receptionist up in hospital Administration offices."

Polly greeted her, but wondered what she was doing hanging around the hospital after hours. The look on Vickie's face made Polly think she was bursting with something to say.

"I thought we were going to be alone," Vickie said to Janetta.

"Oh, you can trust Polly. Now, spill. What's the big news you have for me?"

Vickie licked her lips as excitement widened her eyes. "You'll never believe what happened today."

"Go on, go on." Janetta practically rubbed her hands together with glee.

"Okay. Well, Dr. Woods got called up to the offices today. She showed up all solemn-faced and nervous. When they buzzed me and I told her to go inside, girl, she looked scared." Vickie took a big bite of bread and chewed quickly.

Janetta impatiently gobbled some of her dinner, as if not wanting to miss a single syllable. Polly wished she could disappear, but knew if she walked out Janetta would peg her as someone she couldn't trust with good old-fashioned gossip, which would make Polly an enemy, so she stayed in her chair, quietly nibbling at her meal.

Vickie's eyes brightened. "Okay, so a couple minutes after Dr. Woods is in the room, guess who comes barreling through the office doors?"

"Tell me, oh, tell me. Not…"

"Yes. Dr. R., and before the door can close I hear him say 'I insist Dr. Woods's name be cleared'."

"Cleared from what?" Janetta looked like she was sitting around a campfire hearing a famous urban legend being retold.

"I think this has to do with some surgery on a kid back in Los Angeles that they got sued for. But get this. I sort of got out of my chair and went over by the door so I could hear better. He says, 'She's a gifted doctor with much to offer our hospital, and she shouldn't have her name dragged through the media because of a surgery I agreed to perform'." Vickie put on a horrible accent, and Polly's stomach twisted with guilt, listening. "'I was the person who was charged in that malpractice suit, not Dr. Woods, and I was cleared.' He went on to say that he knew the surgery would be high risk, and if they wanted to lay the blame on anyone, it should be him."

"Oh, my God, this is something."

"Yeah, so next thing I know, Dr. Woods rushes out of the offices and out the door and Dr. Rodriguez keeps yelling at them. The last thing I heard was, '*No, you listen to me. The verdict was no malpractice. Make it public, then!*'"

Janetta was practically salivating over this news. Polly sat silent, watching the two women live vicariously through someone else's drama. It just didn't seem right.

Later, while exiting her patient's room, she noticed the nurses' station had gone quiet. She glanced up and spotted across the ward the very doctor Janetta and Vickie had been talking about at dinner. Polly waved and rushed to her side, not caring how it looked to her co-workers.

"Hi," Dr. Woods said with a genuine glad-to-see-you smile.

"Hi. I wanted to thank you for arranging my test, and ask another question if you don't mind?"

"Of course not. What's up?"

Polly guided Dr. Woods to a more private spot, noticing Janetta's eagle eyes watching. She lowered her voice. "I was wondering if you could recommend an obstetrician who is close by the hospital."

Layla raised a perfectly arched brow. "So the test was positive," she whispered.

Polly gave one solemn nod.

Layla patted her forearm. "Let me ask around, since I'm kind of new in town myself, and I'll get back to you, 'kay?"

"Thank you so much."

"Darlin', it's my pleasure. We girls gotta to stick together. You know?"

Overwhelmed by the doctor's care and genuine concern, once their hushed conversation had ended, Polly decided that regardless of the hospital gossip about Dr.

Woods having had an affair with the head of Neurosurgery while she was still married, Polly would be Layla Woods's number one fan.

Polly could barely breathe when on the following Thursday the case involving Dr. Woods and Rodriguez went public at Angel's. She read the memo addressed to the hospital staff about a boy named Jamie Kilpatrick and a high-risk neurosurgery that Dr. Woods had recommended to Dr. Rodriguez. One thing stood out beyond everything else: Dr. Rodriguez had valiantly taken full responsibility for the boy's death.

One major question crossed Polly's mind. Why would Dr. Rodriguez put his career and reputation on the line to protect Dr. Woods? She didn't need to think for long. The man was obviously in love with her, just like Janetta had said. Wow, what must it feel like to have someone love you that much?

That night Polly combed the aisles of her local market, hunting for healthy food. Her routine in the mornings had always been to buy a couple of pieces of fresh fruit from one of the street carts near the hospital. She'd bring a yogurt from home for morning break, then a sandwich for lunch, usually tuna, and eat the second piece of fruit. Now she worried she wasn't getting enough vitamins. She grabbed a bag of baby spinach, deciding to sauté it with oil and garlic and serve it for dinner over the chicken breast she'd just picked up. Eating for two was a big responsibility, and she wanted her baby to have the best opportunity possible at a healthy start.

Eyeing a package of her favorite cookies, she steered away. This pregnancy business would be harder than anything she'd done in her life, but she was determined to have a successful pregnancy.

The thought of a healthy baby brought back the need to see an obstetrician in the next couple of weeks. With fingers crossed that Dr. Woods would come through for her, she paid for her groceries and headed home.

John stood over his six-burner state-of-the-art stove, grilling salmon. He'd gutted the old-fashioned kitchen when his parents had sold him their condo at a steal before moving to Florida. Now he had a kitchen that connected to the flow of the house, instead of hidden behind a wall. The 56th Street, near Sutton Place address was perfectly situated for work, plus he had the East River within walking distance whenever he felt like taking a jog. With two bedrooms and baths, a living room, which he'd expanded by breaking down a small third bedroom wall, and the new roomier kitchen, he lived comfortably for a New York City bachelor.

Tri-colored squash sautéed in a small pan and the brown rice steamed in another. He loved to cook and wasn't shy about letting people know. While cooking, he wondered if Polly was taking good care of herself, and how she might enjoy this meal. Flipping the fish, he realized he didn't have a clue what she liked to eat beyond cheese pizza. For all he knew, she hated fish.

She was carrying his baby. Every time he thought about it, the breath squeezed from his lungs.

With everything under control dinner-wise, and Polly solidly implanted in his mind, he dug out his cell phone and called a forgotten friend. "Geoff, it's John."

The old medical school colleagues went through a required, though brief catch-up time, then John broached the true reason for his call. "I was wondering if you'd do me a favor. One of my ortho nurses just found out she's pregnant, and she needs a good OB guy. I told her I knew the best. Any chance you could squeeze her in?"

Geoff asked John to hold while he flipped through his calendar and, taking this opportunity, John checked the salmon and veggies, then opened his kitchen catch-all drawer, hunting for a pad of paper and a pen. Soon Geoff was back on the line with an appointment date and time.

"Fantastic. Thanks so much." He tugged his earlobe. "Oh, by the way, send me the bill."

By the brief silence on the other end before Geoff agreed, John figured he hadn't pulled the wool over his old classmate's eyes. Yes. John Griffin had knocked up a nurse. His nurse. Polly.

On Friday afternoon Polly was in the middle of hanging intravenous antibiotics for her newest post-op patient when John appeared at her side. Her hand trembled as she placed the small bottle of potent medicine on the hook and opened the drip regulator. She got mad at herself for letting him have that much power over her and hoped he hadn't noticed. He was in his OR scrubs, having followed the surgical patient back to the ward.

Having already received report from the OR recovery nurse, she knew Emanuel had been in a car accident, had broken his left leg, and needed to have a metal plate and pins to secure his bones back in place.

"I wanted you to have this." John handed her a small piece of paper.

She stared at it instead of reaching for it, thankful that Emanuel was completely out of it and in a private room so no one else would hear them talk. "What's that?"

"It's an appointment with the best OB guy in the city."

Hesitant to take anything from John, she shook her head. "That's okay. I've got someone else in mind."

John tugged his ear. "You need to let me be involved in this, too."

"Why, John? The other day you wanted nothing to do with me or our baby," she whispered spiritedly over Emanuel. "You wanted to pay me off." She wanted to sound indignant, but it came out hurt.

"Look, there's a lot to get used to for both of us. I'm just asking you to give me time."

She snatched the paper from his fingers. "You think I don't understand how much we both have to get used to? And as for time, well, you've got approximately eight months to work it out." She glanced at the appointment, next Thursday at four p.m. with a Geoffrey Bernstein. It was perfect for her work schedule, she'd give him that. Then she noticed the address. Park Avenue? "Forget it. I can't afford this guy."

"It's all taken care of."

It stalled her for a second, but she quickly recovered. "I don't want your guilt charity." She handed back the paper but he refused to take it and left, grinding his jaws, without another word.

That afternoon Layla Woods crossed the ward, heading directly for Polly, looking far less confident than usual. Up close, Polly could see she had dark circles under her eyes, as if she'd been on call and hadn't slept. "I've got some information for you."

"Great. Thank you so much." Polly glanced around to make sure no one was within hearing distance.

"I've been told this guy is the best OB doc in town.

The only problem is the wait list is long, and I think he's pretty pricey." She handed Polly the paper, and Polly opened it immediately. *Dr. Geoffrey Bernstein.*

Polly tried not to hide her disappointment because Dr. Woods had gone out of her way to help her out. "I can't thank you enough. I'll look into this right away."

They parted company and Polly watched the petite doctor walk away as a hollow, aching path burrowed through her stomach.

Round one had gone to John. Not only had he found her the most expensive doctor in town, he'd made an appointment for her, too. And he was paying.

As her least favorite Uncle Randolph used to say whenever Polly had resisted her cousin's baggy hand-me-down clothes: *Don't look a gift horse in the mouth.*

So be it. For the good of her baby she'd take the appointment John had made for her, and because she'd been raised right afterwards she'd swallow her pride and thank him for it.

Three nights later Polly worked her second double shift. It probably wasn't a wise move as she still hadn't recovered from the first sixteen-hour shift, even though she'd had the whole weekend to do it. Now she dragged through another.

The pregnancy had zapped most of her energy. She'd also become aware that other early signs of pregnancy were cropping up. Her breasts were tender, and she wanted to sleep more. And she was hungry. All the time. Maybe she'd be one of those lucky ladies who didn't get morning sickness, but it was still very early along.

For her dinner break, to avoid another gossip-infused lecture from Janetta, she decided to go outside and eat on a bench in the hospital garden. She walked to the elevator feeling more than fatigued, eager to breathe in some fresh air. With all of the gossip at the hospital and speculation about her own situation, she felt as though she had a brick on each shoulder. While she waited for the elevator she rolled her neck around and lifted her shoulders, hoping to release some stress from the stiff muscles.

The elevator pinged and opened to reveal Dr. Alex Rodriguez inside. Alone.

Polly had never seen the man up close before. She entered and tried not to stare at his handsome profile or notice the waves in his thick black hair as it curled along the collar of his shirt.

He stood stoically silent, deep in thought, hardly noticing she was there.

The elevator stopped at the next floor and Dr. Woods got on. Polly's heart tripled in beats. Layla nodded at Polly, looking noticeably riled, then turned to Dr. Rodriguez. "Hi," she said, sounding breathy and unconfident as she pressed the button for the lobby, which had already been pushed.

"Layla." His all-business attitude threw Polly in light of what she already knew about the memo and their supposed past, through Janetta.

"Listen, I wanted to thank you for what you did the other day," Layla said. "Sticking up for me in the board room and all."

"It needed to be done." Curt. Businesslike.

Had *she* become invisible?

"Well, I want to thank you for that, Alex. It meant a lot to—"

With a quick gesture, he brushed her off. "It was

nothing." He wouldn't look her in the eyes, and that must have bothered Dr. Woods. It sure would have if Polly had been in the doctor's shoes.

Layla punched the button for the second floor, obviously upset. "Both of us getting out of the elevator together in the lobby would only fuel the fire of the gossip around here." She tossed her hair over her shoulder and the moment the doors opened she started to get out, but Dr. Rodriguez stepped around her and exited first.

Holy cow. Polly hoped and prayed that Layla didn't think she had participated in the rampant gossip around the hospital. Especially after all she'd done for her.

Dr. Woods let him leave, watched him go, staring, even though the elevator doors had closed again. Polly didn't know what to do so she kept quiet, hoping maybe she really had become invisible. They continued downwards in silence, Dr. Woods deep in thought, until the doors opened to the lobby.

Straightening her shoulders, she glanced at Polly, the first sign that the doctor had remembered she was there. "He may think this is finished between us, but it isn't. Not by a long shot." With that, Dr. Layla Woods, looking determined and undeterred, exited the elevator.

Polly stood frozen to the spot, her mind swirling with what she'd just witnessed. It wasn't hatred or anger that fueled them, it was passion. Pure and simple. Those two were meant to be together, and somehow, some way, they'd both have to figure it out. Just before the doors closed Polly rushed out of the elevator and toward the garden exit.

As she ate her dinner, she made a vow. No way would anyone hear a hint of what had gone on in that elevator. Their secret was safe with her, and she hoped Layla was right, that whatever they had going wasn't over by a long shot.

At the end of her shift, completely exhausted, she went to the bathroom to splash some water on her face, hoping to pep herself up for the long subway ride home. Afterwards, she gathered up her belongings from the employee locker room and headed toward the elevator, the last person to leave from the late shift.

A lone silhouette stood at the other end of the hall. White doctor's coat, broad shoulders, short-cropped hair, unmistakably John. Her heart fluttered at the thought of facing him after several days. He met her at the elevator door.

"What are you still doing here?" he asked.

"Did a double shift."

"Should you be doing that?"

She yawned, and covered her mouth. "No choice these days."

She noticed he festered over that response. He blinked and turned his head as if he had a thing or two to say to her, but had maybe thought better of it.

He looked at his watch. "I don't like the idea of you taking the subway home at this time of night."

"It really isn't about what you like or don't like, now, is it, *Johnny*." Yes, she could be a brat when she wanted to, make that *needed* to. Being pregnant had put her in a whole new frame of mind. Her baby came first, and John wasn't on board with her being pregnant. End of story.

"Let me give you a ride home."

"No way." But, man, oh, man, her feet were tired, and the thought of walking the required blocks just to get to the subway station did seem daunting at almost midnight.

"Look, I had early surgery today so I drove my car. I'm parked next door. Don't be stubborn *and* foolish."

Stubborn? Look who was calling whom stubborn. "Do you have any idea how big the gossip mill is at Angel's? People would have a field day if they saw us leave together." *And then found out soon enough I'm pregnant.*

"Look, dumpling, I don't give a rat's ass what other people think. Right now, all I want to do is give you a ride home."

"Don't call me dumpling."

"Sorry."

If, and that was a big if, she decided to let John give her a ride home, it wouldn't be because she was giving in to him. No. It would be because she really didn't want to face that long subway ride to the Lower East Side. It had been almost two a.m. before she'd gotten in bed the last time she'd worked a double shift and, being honest, she worried she might fall asleep on the subway and miss her exit.

"Okay."

"Okay you accept my apology or okay you'll let me give you a ride home?"

"I'll take the ride."

He looked surprised, as if she hadn't put up nearly as big a fight as he'd expected.

Ten minutes later she slid onto the smoothest kid leather seat she'd ever seen in a fancy sedan like his. It was soft and cushy, too, and, oh, the headrest was adjusted perfectly to her neck. She touched the button to lower the head of the seat, making it like a lounge chair, and snuggled in after clicking her seat belt.

John didn't say a word, but she could see his cheek lift in that unbalanced smile of his. He'd won. He knew it.

But she was reaping the benefits.

Before he'd even exited the parking structure, she closed her eyes and drifted off to a sweet dream about being curled up on the softest sofa in the world, while the sexiest guy she'd ever met touched her knee and talked to her softly.

CHAPTER SIX

JOHN PARKED THE car, walked around to the other side, opened the passenger door and lifted Polly up and out. She slept sounder than his mother's cat, and only stirred when he pulled her to his chest.

"Shh, go back to sleep," he whispered in her ear, as he motioned with his head to the doorman of his building to let them in.

Marco the doorman gave a deeply inquisitive look but followed orders. John had been a resident in the building for three years now and had never brought a woman home in this condition.

"Drunk," John mouthed to Marco, who gave an affirmative *Aha* nod.

"Park the car in your usual spot?" Marco whispered.

John nodded, knowing his car keys would be left in the parking-garage office where he paid a hefty monthly fee for the privilege of driving and parking in New York City.

He punched the elevator button with his elbow and hoped Polly didn't wake up until he was ready. He'd driven the long way home around Central Park to make sure she'd fallen asleep deeply enough once he'd decided to bring her here.

As he rode the elevator to the ninth floor, he took the liberty to study her close up—flawless skin, though maybe a little pale, ash-blonde hair with waves that made him want to dig his fingers in every time he saw her. Her thick brown lashes fluttered the tiniest bit under his scrutiny and her nostrils twitched as she breathed softly. She was sweet and tender, and he felt the urge to kiss her.

The elevator door opened, and though it was a bit tricky to unlock his door with one hand while holding Polly with the other, he balanced her on his thigh and succeeded, and had them inside in no time at all. Before anyone on his floor had a chance to wonder what in the world he was doing with a woman in his arms on a Monday night at this late hour. He chuckled inwardly, thinking how they'd never probably even seen him with a woman before, had probably assumed he was gay or celibate.

The condo was dark, but he knew his way around by heart and took her immediately to the guest bedroom, where he carefully laid her on the double bed. She stirred but only to reposition herself on her side. Not wanting to freak her out in case she woke up, which surprisingly she still hadn't, he laid a comforter over her, left the door ajar and went to the kitchen. There, he turned on the light and rummaged around the refrigerator for something to eat.

Three bites into a turkey and Cheddar sandwich he heard the gasp. "Where am I?"

He rushed down the hall to the bedroom. "Don't worry, you're at my place."

"Why am I here?" She came to the door looking

groggy and very appealing with mussed-up hair and heavy-lidded eyes.

"You didn't tell me where you lived before you fell asleep, and you looked so comfortable I didn't have the heart to wake you."

"So you thought you'd make me a prisoner at your house?"

"You're not a prisoner."

"Then you'll take me home?"

"If you insist."

She stood staring, obviously considering his offer. Maybe she needed some convincing.

"Look, I was thinking of your best interests. I've got the guest bedroom and you'll get a good night's sleep, then I'll take you home in the morning."

"I don't have to work tomorrow because I did the double shift."

"That's fine."

"Don't you have to be at work?"

"Not until nine. It's my clinic day."

"So you'll take me home before you go to work?"

He nodded.

She leaned against the doorframe looking drowsy and too tired to put up a fight. "Where's your bathroom, please?"

He gestured with his forehead towards the door down the hall, then took another bite of sandwich.

On her way back to the guest room she slowed down by the kitchen and gave him a suspicious glance. "Don't get any ideas about sneaking into that room tonight." She pointed to the guest room.

"I won't."

"Because what we did was a one-time deal."

He didn't bother to swallow his bite of sandwich. "By my count, that was a three-time deal."

Obviously too tired to put up a fight, she tossed him an aggravated look then went inside the guest room and closed the door. At least she didn't lock it. He took the last bite of sandwich and decided he'd got a kick out of riling her. Come to think of it, there was a lot about Polly he got a kick out of. Now, if there was only a way to get her back into his life on much better terms.

Early the next morning, John had a full breakfast prepared by the time he tapped on her door and woke her up. She rolled out of the room, stretching and yawning and looking even more inviting than she had the night before.

"What time is it?" she asked.

"Seven. Have some coffee. It's decaf," he said, before she could protest. Somehow he knew she'd take good care of the pregnancy. "I've scrambled some eggs and there's fresh OJ over there. Do you like wheat or sourdough toast?"

"Wheat," she said, before closing the bathroom door.

The fact that she didn't throw a hissy fit or make a major protest about getting home right this minute gave him hope, and that notion made him smile. Maybe she was back to being that people-pleaser he liked so much, though the feisty version of Polly definitely had its merits. He smiled and pushed some perfectly scrambled eggs onto a second plate then sprinkled some finely grated Cheddar cheese on top.

They sat on bar stools in companionable silence while they ate at his granite counter.

"Tastes good," she said, eating a second piece of toast slathered with blackberry jam.

"You're eating for two now, right?"

He'd named the elephant in the room, and she took her time to respond. "I don't need you to remind me." Her gaze was brief and filled with icy-blue warning.

"I want to be a part of this pregnancy, Polly."

"That's not the impression I got when I told you about it."

"I was in shock."

"You wanted nothing to do with me or this pregnancy. You tried to pay me off, as if I'd go away and never mention another word about it."

He reached for her hand and squeezed. "I didn't mean it to come off that way. I wanted you to know you weren't in it alone, and that you didn't have to worry about money. That's all."

She dropped her gaze toward her lap. "We're not for sale."

If that was the metaphor she wanted to run with, he'd play along. "Look at it from my perspective." He pointed to her stomach. "There's prime real estate inside there, and though you may be the landlord, I own half of it."

She made a face at him. "Have you always been this romantic?"

He shrugged. "It's a gift."

"You don't have the right to make it all neat and tidy like that. Like a business deal." Polly shoved another bite of egg into her mouth and stared straight ahead. Once she'd swallowed, she leveled a serious gaze at him. "I don't have a clue what your issues are, but since I believe you do need to be there for this baby I'll generously consider whatever part of 'being there for this pregnancy' you think you can handle."

He grinned. That was the people-pleasing Polly he

knew. "Good. For starters, I intend to go to all obstetric appointments with you."

Her eyebrows dropped and furrowed. "That's a very private thing."

"And one doesn't wind up pregnant by not doing a few *very private* things with the father of the baby, does one?"

She sighed. "Okay, you can come to the OB appointments."

"And you should let me cook for you at least twice a week."

"You cook?"

"What do you call these scrambled eggs?"

"A six-year-old can scramble eggs, Johnny."

She'd called him Johnny again, and he'd consider it progress. "I happen to be a good cook, and I want to make sure you get a balanced diet."

"Look, I may have gotten knocked up with little effort but I am not an idiot. I know how to eat healthily."

"There was a *lot* of effort involved in you getting pregnant, as I recall, and for the record you didn't get 'knocked up', as you so poetically put it, on your own."

Silence stretched on for a few seconds while he regrouped. How long would he have to keep pointing out to her that she didn't have to be in this alone? If he didn't handle things right this time, he could blow it all for good.

"I was on birth-control pills," she said. "I swear I was, but I'd taken antibiotics a few weeks back for a sinus infection."

"I see." He understood perfectly what she was getting at, she didn't want him to think she'd set him up. Antibiotics could interfere with birth control pills' potency and effect for a couple of weeks after use, enough to make a woman potentially vulnerable to pregnancy. Under the circumstances, and without added protection, which they'd completely blown off that night, pregnancy wasn't out of the question. Polly and her baby onboard were living proof.

John ate the remainder of his breakfast vigorously. The real question was, though, why hadn't she thought about that when they'd made love? Ah, hell, why hadn't *he* thought about anything but how much he'd wanted her that night? There was no point in making this a blame game. What was done was done. They'd had sex, hot sex, and made a baby.

Though there was no way on earth he could invest emotionally in the pregnancy, or be a proper father, he could at least be an ally for Polly during a time when she would definitely need a friend. As for after the pregnancy? He downed the last of his orange juice. Well, he was content to take it one step at a time for now, and she'd just have to understand.

"So I'll wait for you at the hospital parking lot on Thursday when you get off work, and take you to your appointment."

"Okay." She sounded like a teenager who'd given up on getting out of a major book report. "But can you take me home now? I'd really like to shower."

"Of course."

On Thursday, Polly ran a little late after change-of-shift report and had to run-walk to meet John at the car. He'd had the car brought up to the entrance and leaned against his silver sedan, checking his watch as she jogged his way.

"Sorry! We had some late admits and I couldn't just dump and run."

"I've already called the doctor's office and let them know we may be a little late. I'll drop you off in front then park."

"Great. Thanks." She fixed the flying strands of hair around her face, knowing her skin was probably shiny from working hard all day and that her colored lip gloss had long ago been chewed off. "I really appreciate it."

"It's the least I can do."

The least he could do, was that how he looked at it? Was he only trying to get away with doing the bare minimum so as not to come off as a deadbeat? Boy, had she been there and done that with her aunts and uncles after her mother had died. Every part of that equation made her skin crawl, yet here she was, riding in John Griffin's fancy car on her way to the doctor's appointment he'd arranged. She was sick of people going through the motions on her behalf, but that seemed to be the repetitious hand life had dealt her. Resigned, she'd just have to make the best of it this time, not for her but for her baby's sake.

Dr. Bernstein's nurse was ready for her the minute she walked in and whisked her into one of the examination rooms in the glamorous medical suite. She had no intention of letting John in on the actual examination.

The doctor looked to be around John's age and had gentle hands and an affable personality. He looked intently into her eyes as she explained her side of the pregnancy, and she believed him when he promised to keep her and the baby healthy and happy for the next eight and a half months.

"You can get dressed then meet me in my office,"

he said on his way out the door after the thorough examination.

Polly suffered a surprise when she entered Dr. Bernstein's office only to find John already sitting there, chatting amicably with "Geoff", as he called him. The moment Polly stepped inside the conversation stopped and John shot up. He reached over and pulled out the chair next to him so she could sit. She'd give him points for always being a gentleman.

"Polly," Dr. "Geoff" started right in, "you are a healthy young woman, and at this early stage in the process I'd say you're going to do well. Your uterus and cervix look good, the pregnancy is implanted securely in your uterus lining, and your pelvic cradle should handle the body changes just fine. I want to get some baseline lab work done for you and start you on prenatal vitamins. In a couple of weeks we'll do an ultrasound." He scribbled on a prescription pad, ripped it off and handed it to her, then sat back in his chair and steepled his fingers. "Do you have any questions?"

"My due date?"

"Right. My calculations show March twenty-eighth, give or take a day or two."

The skin on her shoulders and arms prickled. Somehow, this actual date of birth made everything come into focus. It was real. She'd have a baby and be a mom beginning March twenty-eighth. John must have noticed her emotional reaction when he put his arm around her shoulders and tugged her close. She couldn't help the brimming tears. She was going to be a mother in eight short months from now. Only because the long and stressful day had caught up with her, and she needed it right this moment, she accepted John's comfort as she buried her weeping eyes on his shoulder.

Back at the car, John grinned at her as he let her in the passenger side. "You agreed to let me fix you dinner twice a week, and I thought tonight would be a good time to get that routine rolling."

"You don't even know if I have food allergies or anything." She'd recovered from the emotional high in the doctor's office and had pulled up her guard again.

"Chicken tetrazzini with wholegrain noodles and a garden salad."

Her mouth watered at the description. "I hate onions. Does it have onions?"

"Not now. I hope you like garlic, though."

She bobbed her head as she slid inside the car. Hating having to hold back all her excitement about being pregnant, she tightened her jaw and ground her teeth for most of the ride back to John's condo.

Marco the doorman gave her and John a knowing nod when they walked inside, and it made her pause. Had she ever seen him before? The small but tasteful lobby gave her the impression that well-off, long-time New Yorkers lived in the building. What a difference from her turn-of-the-century walk-up.

Though John had overall masculine flair in his taste in interior design, a maroon leather couch and chair with glass and chrome tables got her attention, and across the room a surprising floral-upholstered overstuffed chair and ottoman looked beyond inviting.

"Have a seat," he said, gesturing to the living room that flowed naturally into his kitchen. "You need to rest as often as you can." He tossed her the newspaper he'd just sorted out of his pile of mail. "Read this while I get cooking."

"Don't be so bossy." At a little after five o'clock she was hungry and more than ready to eat, and decided not to give him a hard time, so she did what she was told and put her feet up, shaking out the newspaper and reading the headlines of the day, all of which were depressing.

She surreptitiously kept track of him while he cooked. He wore khaki slacks that fit in all the right places and a pale blue shirt. He'd removed the tie while he'd shuffled through his mail, and the open-collar look held her interest longer than she'd wanted. But most of all what kept her riveted to watching John was how he genuinely seemed to enjoy cooking. She liked discovering that about him.

He ran a tidy kitchen and was very comfortable in it, like cooking was a less sterile version of surgery. She thought of her living arrangement and the tiny outdated appliances she shared. What she'd give to have such a gorgeous modern kitchen at her fingertips. The comfort of the chair and the simple dream of living in a place like John's soon had her closing her suddenly weary eyes…

"Dinner's ready!"

Polly sat bolt upright. What time was it? She glanced at her watch. Six o'clock. She'd taken a forty-minute nap. The hint of garlic, chicken and freshly drained pasta weaving their way from the kitchen and up her nostrils was heavenly. "Give me a sec to wash up, okay?"

"Of course." He whistled while he set plates and flatware on the bistro-sized table in the corner of the kitchen, and she stopped a couple of moments to enjoy the sight.

The food smelled fantastic and her taste buds went

into overdrive, looking forward to the meal as she hurried down the hall to wash her hands.

He hadn't lied. John Griffin was a darned fine cook. Every mouthful sent jets of pleasure through her gastronomic senses. She could get used to these twice-a-week meals, maybe bargain for a third as time went on. Piecemeal, really, since that was all he was offering in the way of getting involved in the pregnancy. Far be it from her to want to ruin a delicious dinner, but really was that the best the man could offer? She continued to eat with a disappointed outlook.

After a few bites John put his fork down and cast a pressing gaze at her. She wasn't about to stop eating, but the daunting stare did slow her down a bit.

"I want you to know that I liked you right off. You know, that first week you came to Angel's. I, or we, did something crazy and out of character, and now we've been thrown together in some pretty astounding circumstances."

She wanted to ask him how long he'd practiced the speech, but decided, as he was finally opening up, not to be a smart-aleck.

He cleared his throat. "What I'm getting at is I know you're disappointed in me. I'm only skirting around the perimeter of our predicament."

She started to protest his calling her pregnancy a predicament, but when she opened her mouth he raised his voice a pre-emptive notch. "I don't think any guy would know how to handle it perfectly, but I'm not making excuses for myself. I'm just being honest with you, because I think you deserve it."

He got up, refilled his water glass, took a long draw and sat back down. "There's something you need to know about me. Maybe it will explain why I'm not all balloons and bubbles over your pregnancy."

Sensing his earnestness, she put her fork down and gave him her total attention. "Go ahead, John."

As if the words strangled and fought in his throat, John's pained expression made Polly brace for what he was about to say.

"I don't even know if I told you that I used to be married. Happily married for two years. My wife, Lisa, was a financial adviser." His voice clogged and he stopped every sentence or two to clear it. "Anyway, we were happy because she'd just found out she was pregnant."

The heavy foreshadowing made the gourmet meal in Polly's stomach suddenly feel like a large lump of paper maché. John talked to the table rather than engage her eyes.

"We'd stayed up late, planning, all excited about our baby, how our lives would change." He had to clear that stubborn lump in his throat again. His nose ran and he wiped it with his paper napkin. Instinctively, the hair on Polly's arms rose and John's profile grew blurry.

"We were going to tell my parents over dinner that night. I kissed her goodbye that morning and she went to work on the twenty-second floor of the World Trade Center on September eleventh."

Chills rolled over Polly's skin. Tears broke free from her eyes and she realized the implication of that fateful day. She'd been a high-school student at the time, eating breakfast and listening to the kitchen radio when she'd heard the news report. She grabbed John's knotted fist and squeezed tight. Oh, God, he didn't need to say one more word. She understood. He'd lost everything he loved and held dear on one historic day.

Polly got up from her seat and circled around John, banding her arms around his chest as she cuddled him from behind. He sat stoic, like the rock of Gibraltar he'd tricked himself into becoming—for survival's sake, she was sure, she understood that now. Bleeding emotionally for his loss, she stayed with him wrapped in her arms for several long moments as she mulled over their circumstances. She was willing to give him a pass for now, for not committing to their child beyond the neat and tidy logistics of appointments, well-prepared dinners, and finances.

Slowly, as she stood hunched over, holding him, a tiny thought wiggled and snaked its way clear of her emotional landslide on John's behalf. The thought gained power and implanted itself in the center of her head. *That was twelve years ago.* Was John determined to keep his life stagnant and take the loss to his grave? More importantly, would Lisa want that for him?

They may have made love under unusual circumstances, but something bigger than both of them had come out of it. They'd made a baby. He could never get his wife or child back, but she and John had made a little life that was growing inside her. A baby with a birth date. March twenty-eighth.

It was Polly's turn to clear her thickened throat. "John, please don't get me wrong, I realize how horrific your loss was. But twelve years have passed, and that's no excuse for abandoning your responsibility to *this* child." She stood straight and placed her hand on her currently flat abdomen, one hand anchored to his shoulder. "This baby needs you now. You're the father."

He sat staring at his plate rather than acknowledge

her, and when she'd given up on him answering she dropped her hands from his shoulder and her stomach and cleared the dishes from the table.

"I'll take care of that," he said, belatedly.

"No, this is my way of thanking you for a great meal." As long as he held onto the past, she'd never have a chance to really get to know him.

John removed the remaining dishes and joined her at the sink. Together they worked in silence, cleaning the kitchen.

"Can you take me home now, please?" she asked, once everything was done.

"Sure."

Noncommittal seemed to be all the man could offer, and his history explained why, but that definitely wasn't something she'd settle for, and John really did need to let go of the past.

John watched Polly from across the kitchen. Her petite frame looked good in anything she wore, which happened to be hospital scrubs. She was right about so many years having gone by, he knew. He couldn't argue with the logic of being held captive by a time capsule, but the habit had become so deeply rooted into his being that he couldn't seem to break free. He'd been one of the first responders at the scene and to this day he had flashbacks of treating the injured and mangled, of staring into the faces of the dead, while desperate to find his wife. He'd taken risks amongst the falling debris and rubble searching for Lisa, but it had all been fruitless. She'd died and taken most of him with her. To this day he questioned why he'd lived and she hadn't.

When Polly had gathered her things, he got his keys and they headed for the elevator.

An hour later, due to heavy traffic conditions, when John dropped Polly off at her century-old building on the Lower East Side, a crazy idea popped into his head. She was the one accusing him of abandoning his responsibility to the child. She'd probably never agree to it but, what the hell, when the time was right, he'd make his pitch.

He'd double-parked and watched while she climbed the stoop stairs and buzzed herself into the building. The thought of her surviving during the long hot summer while being pregnant and living in the ancient brownstone walk-up didn't sit well. He couldn't offer his heart to a stranger, but he owed her the common decency of making sure she was comfortable and cared for.

Patience, John, give her some time to realize how hard things will get on her own, then you can make her the offer she can't refuse.

CHAPTER SEVEN

FRIDAY MORNING POLLY was measuring out liquid antibiotics at the medicine station for the three-year-old toddler in Room Twelve B when John appeared in her peripheral vision.

He pushed a small brown bag her way. "Here."

"What's this?"

"Your lunch," he said, already walking away.

"I made my own lunch."

"Save it for tomorrow. You'll like this better."

"How do you know that? Maybe I've been craving peanut butter and jelly all day. Maybe I've been dreaming about my home-made lunch since breakfast." When had she reverted to being a contrary teenager again? Could it be the hormones?

He stopped, turned and flashed that slanting smile, his dark eyes reminding her of milk-chocolate chips. Beneath his knee-length doctor's coat he wore a white shirt and blue silk tie, looking dressier than usual. She inhaled, the savory scent coming from the bag already making her mouth water. Something warm and spicy awaited her, thanks to Dr. Griffin, the father of her baby.

He'd gone out of his way to bring this to her so the least she could do was be grateful.

She mouthed, "Thank you". He dipped his head and walked away. Truth was, she could easily get used to him catering for her, and wondered how abruptly it would end once she had the baby. She glanced around, noticing Brooke and Rafael giving her odd looks. Oh, man, what must they think? The last thing she needed was to get picked up for the gossip grapevine like that poor Dr. Woods and the neurosurgeon, Dr. Rodriguez. Thank goodness Janetta didn't work the day shift.

After finishing the obviously home-made minestrone soup with spinach and chicken meatballs, Polly found at the bottom of the lunch bag a large peanut-butter cookie with a note hidden behind it.

Meet me for an early dinner at Giovanni's tonight? See you there at five.

How could he be so confident she'd come running just because he'd told her to? She went back to work determined to blow him off. Let him sit there and wait for her to show up. She may be pregnant, but she was darned sure not to be taken for granted because of it.

As the afternoon wore on, she prepared a teenage soccer player for surgery on his left knee and right shoulder. She'd given him his pre-op medicine and shot and stayed close by until the transportation clerk could take him to the operating room. As his eyelids grew heavy and he dozed off, she thought about John and his sexy blue silk tie and that off-balance but charming smile. Did she really want to play games with him? He'd asked her to dinner, had seemed sincere enough, and she had no reason not to go, so why stand him up?

The man had been to hell and back over the past

twelve years. Here he was getting a little sparkle in his eyes again, and the last thing she should do was give him a hard time. It wasn't in her nature to play games with men anyway. Besides, in her dating life the guys had always been much better at game-playing than she could ever compete with.

No, after work she'd take her time and freshen up then walk over to Giovanni's for another dinner with John. Memories of what had happened after the last time they'd eaten there made her lose her step but not stumble. She'd make sure it didn't happen again, and maybe she'd ask him to drive her home, just to make sure. Besides, lately the fumes in the subway made her feel nauseous.

To her surprise, John was already there, waiting, when she arrived. He'd ordered bottled water instead of Chianti, too, which was sitting on the table. He stood when he saw her, and the smile he gave was definitely genuine. So was the warm feeling inside when she smiled back at him. Without his doctor's jacket she could see his solid, football-player physique, and it spawned a quick flash of being naked in his arms and near bliss.

"If you like shrimp, I recommend the scampi," he said, sitting down after she'd shaken the sexy thought from her mind and taken her seat.

"So much for idle conversation. You say dinner. You mean dinner." She picked up the menu and scanned the specials.

"I'm sorry, is there something you'd like to talk about?"

She screwed up her face. "No. It's just, well, customary when meeting someone for dinner to start off with small talk like 'Hi, how was your day?' or something before getting right down to ordering."

"Sorry. I have an administrative meeting at seven."

"On a Friday night?" There went her chance for a ride home. "So why'd you invite me here, then?" If he wanted to get right down to business, so could she.

He poured both of them a glass of the sparkling bottled water then took a drink of his. "I want you to move in with me."

She almost spit her water right into his face, but instead she swallowed it wrong and coughed. He patted her back, looking concerned. She coughed and hacked for several more seconds, eyes bugging out, feeling embarrassed about how she must look. He looked on, earnestly trying to figure out how to help her. After she settled down she said, "You what?"

"You heard me right. I've been thinking about this and as we're having this baby together, it's the least I can do."

That warm something or other she'd felt momentarily when she'd first walked in and seen him smiling at her turned to ice. "The least you can do? Well, how kind of you, sir. Thank you for the magnanimous crumb." She stood, fully intending to leave. "As far as I'm concerned, you can take that crumb and shove it!" With the room melting down to nothing as her anger overtook every cell in her body, she stomped towards the exit. Before she made it to the street, a big, strong hand grabbed her arm.

"Hold on, hothead."

She yanked back her arm and kept moving, now outside the restaurant. He followed close behind. "Leave me alone. You're a jerk."

He managed to get in front of her, planted both hands on her arms and forced her to stop and look at him. "I know I'm a jerk. I can't figure out how not to be a jerk *or* how to handle this thing. Give me a break, will you? I'm trying. I want to do what's right, okay?"

The fury rumbling through her chest lost strength with each of his sentences. The man was being painfully honest, how refreshing, and she could see it in his tense yet imploring eyes. She blinked then glanced at the darkening sky. She'd made a point to never depend on anyone after the day she'd turned eighteen. Being a child at the mercy of uninterested aunts and uncles had been the most painful part of her life. She couldn't allow herself to depend on John, though she sure could use his help for a while.

Was it wise to get more deeply involved with someone she barely knew? No. Especially since she'd had a fierce crush on John until everything had gone to hell in a handbasket with this surprise pregnancy.

"Well?" John said, confusion with a touch of impatience in his stare.

"I'm thinking. Can't you give me a minute?" She glanced at him, reinforcing his jerk status, then went back to staring at the sky. She didn't know what the heck she wanted from John, yet he was offering to open his home to her. It wasn't all about herself any more. Nope. She had a baby to think about. Was there anything wrong with testing the waters where John was concerned? She wouldn't dare get her hopes up or anything, but maybe for a while staying with John in a strictly platonic way could be useful for both her and her baby.

"Okay."

He lightened his hold. “Okay what? You’ll give me a break?”

“I’ll move in.” Why mess around with pretenses. She was knocked up. He was the father. She hated where she lived, and he’d just offered her a room in his homey condo—a beautiful apartment in a gorgeous part of the city. Why be coy?

“Just like that, you change your mind. You’re ready to move in?”

“Yes. I’ll try it out for a week, see how things go. It will depend on whether or not we’re compatible. In a strictly platonic way. Got it?”

His shocked expression quickly turned to happy, then ricocheted to suspicious. “Whatever you say, dumpling.”

She slowly shook her head. Even if it was a crumb, he’d offered to help, and though she’d been prepared to make it through this pregnancy on her own, she appreciated his gesture, knowing it was way out of his comfort zone. How often in her life had she been invited into a home? Why not take advantage of a win-win situation? A nice place to live. Good food prepared in a kitchen without grease stains everywhere. A roomy bathroom without leaky faucets, mildew, and cracked tile. She could walk to work. Take walks by the East River in the evenings. If she got sick there’d be a doctor in the house.

He tugged on his earlobe, a combination of relief and shock registering on his face. “Okay, then. It’s settled. One week with the option to make it longer, okay?”

“Sweet.”

“Now will you have the scampi?”

Against her will a laugh escaped her lips. “Sure, why not?” He guided her back into the restaurant. “It isn’t every day a girl gets a proposition she can't refuse, *plus* a shrimp dinner."

He ran his hand over his short hair. "Yeah, well, it didn't come out the way I'd practiced."

She sputtered another laugh. "You practiced that?"

"Like I said…" He pulled out the chair so she could sit back down.

It did her heart good to see a grown man and skilled orthopedic surgeon, department head like John Griffin fumble and stumble over his words and actions because of her. Maybe she and the baby did mean something to him. *Don't let yourself go there. He's got a lot of proving to do first.*

She sat down and took another sip of water. There was only one way to find out if the man cared about her or not, and under these challenging and unusual circumstances she'd made a snap decision to find out.

By moving in for a week.

Saturday afternoon, John helped Polly move out of her tiny rented room and managed to fit everything in the trunk and back seat of his car. She'd decided to bring everything so she wouldn't have to keep running back to the old place for this or that as the need arose. Besides, there wasn't that much and why leave anything for Mrs. Goldman to snoop through while she was gone?

When she assessed all her worldly belongings, it made her heart feel a little heavier in her chest. The only precious item was a small cherry-wood jewelry box that had belonged to her mother. In it was a delicate gold locket with an enameled cover. It was heart shaped and opened to her mother's picture on one side and Polly's on the other. Thinking about her single cherished item from twenty-one years ago made her wonder what object John still treasured from Lisa.

Back at the apartment, she would set the boundaries right off—she intended to stay in his guest room rather than share his bed. Until he could move on from his past, there was no point in trying for a real relationship with John. It kind of hurt her feelings when he didn't put up a fight about their sleeping arrangements, but she let those thoughts pass.

For a reputed grumpy old department head, John had been polite and helpful the whole weekend, and she began to see the balloon-twisting, cast-signing side of him. The man all the kids on the orthopedic ward adored. He made coffee in the morning and breakfast after that. Before she could offer to make lunch, he beat her to it. Being in his home, he was more relaxed and extremely considerate about making her feel welcome. If only the rest of the staff could see through his shield, but children seemed to have that special gift of looking into the true heart of a person. As for her, she was happy for the new glimpse of him.

On Sunday afternoon John took her on a walking tour of his neighborhood, which was another way of making her feel welcome. Delighted to find a yarn shop, she talked him into letting her go inside. Not in the least bit interested, he waited outside, chatting with a neighbor he'd run into, and she made her purchase quickly, embarrassed to let him see what she'd bought. It was silly, she knew, but she hadn't knitted in a long time and, well, she was pregnant! She kept the items in a brown bag and his lack of interest made it easy to drop the subject so on they walked through the amazing and upscale neighbourhood of Sutton Place.

They ended the tour on a bench at a small park overlooking the East River. How different this part of town was from the Lower East Side. From a money standpoint, John lived a charmed life, but she knew the whole story—he was alone and hurting. Terribly alone. Even though it seemed he was the one with all the advantages, she knew she could bring something sorely missing into his life. Maybe, with this pregnancy, she could help him experience joy again.

As she stared at the Queensboro Bridge arching across the river, she hoped for any tiny miracle that could open John's heart again. If an unexpected pregnancy was what it would take to shake some life back into him, so be it.

Deep in thought, she jumped when he took her hand. "What do you say we head for home?"

Home? Did she really and finally have a home?

"I thought I'd make pasta for dinner tonight."

So far he'd cooked all the meals. "Why don't you let me cook tonight?"

"Let me take care of you."

Polly couldn't let herself dream too much. All the years she'd never let herself get too comfortable wherever she was staying had trained her to take nothing for granted. If she got swept up in this little fantasy of having a home, it would hurt that much more when reality kicked in, and in her life reality always stepped in.

"Besides, you're my guest. It's my job to make you feel at home."

So she was just a guest. She really needed to keep that in mind. She may as well let him wait on her, and while he made the spaghetti sauce she'd start her knitting project.

By Monday, Polly didn't know how the hospital radar had picked it up so fast but she'd noticed odd glances and hushed conversations that stopped abruptly whenever she got near. It wasn't in her nature to be paranoid, but she was beginning to wonder if someone had been spying on her and John over the weekend.

During lunch, while eating another carefully prepared meal by John, she cornered Darren and grilled him. "Is something going on I don't know about?"

"I think I should be asking you that," he said, taking a huge bite of an Italian lunchmeat sandwich.

"What's everyone whispering about?" She decided to continue to play dumb.

"We're all wondering exactly when you and Dr. Griffin found the time to become a couple. That's all."

"We're not a couple."

"You're not. A couple."

She thinned her lips and shook her head.

"Who made that lunch for you?" He used his sandwich to point at her wholewheat bread, sliced chicken with avocado and sprouts sandwich.

She thought about lying but that wasn't in her nature. "John—I mean Dr. Griffin did." She didn't want to come clean until she cleared it with John.

"And who'd you walk into work with this morning?

In a month or two it would be apparent enough that she was pregnant, but until then why rush to tell everyone? "I got kicked out of my apartment and Dr. Griffin said I could use his guest room until I found something else." Okay, it was a half-lie, but she didn't have to spill the beans about being pregnant just yet.

Darren leveled her with a you-can't-fool-me glare. "His guest room. Uh-huh."

She leaned forward and got in his face. "Yes, uh-huh, his guest room. And I'd appreciate it if you kept everything I've told you to yourself, Darren."

He stared into her eyes, as if assessing how serious she was, then seemed to make his decision. "My lips are sealed," he said, immediately taking another huge bite of sandwich.

Realizing her personal business would sooner or later become a juicy story for workplace gossip made her feel queasy. She'd only managed to eat half of her own sandwich but had already lost her appetite.

The next morning Polly moaned over the bathroom toilet, experiencing her first full-fledged bout of morning sickness. Lord, how would she be able to go to work feeling as though she stood on the ledge of losing it all, just waiting for someone or something to nudge her over?

"Breakfast is ready!" John called from the kitchen.

Oh, God, that was all it took. She hurled.

"I'm not hungry." She'd come up for air and managed to call back between bouts.

A few seconds later determined footsteps down the hardwood hallway grew closer. He tapped on the bathroom door. "You okay?"

"If you call being sick to your stomach okay, then I'm peachy."

"Morning sickness?"

She moaned instead of replied.

He waited outside while she cleaned up, rinsed out her mouth and opened the bathroom door. "I think if you eat some dry cereal or saltine crackers before you get out of bed tomorrow, it might help."

The thought of eating anything made her stomach clench in preparation for losing more of its contents. She twitched her nose and put her hand over her mouth. "I'm sorry, but your cologne is making me more nauseous."

"I'll wash it off," he said, without giving it a second thought.

A few minutes later he was at her bedroom door with a plastic bag in his hand. "You might think this is crazy, but it used to help Lisa." He handed her the bag filled with lemon slices. "It helps to smell citrus or suck on peppermint if odors set off your nausea." He handed her a roll of peppermints. "You can squeeze the lemon into water, too. Oh, and I can get some bottled fruit juice and make popsicles for you to suck on so you won't get dehydrated."

She wanted more than anything to be grateful for the sweet gesture, but everything he said had to do with eating, and her nausea grew worse and worse. She walked backwards toward the bathroom, listening to him and bobbing her head, then quickly closed the door.

"I'll tell Brooke you're not coming in today. You can't go to work like this."

"I don't have sick leave yet. I won't get paid."

"That's the last thing you need to worry about. I'll handle it," he said, walking way.

And handle it he did. From the bathroom she could hear him all the way down the hall.

"Brooke? It's Dr. Griffin. Listen, Polly is having morning sickness and needs to miss work today. How do I know?"

Obviously, John hadn't thought through all the ramifications of him calling in sick on Polly's behalf. Now what would he do?

"Well, uh. Listen, this is strictly confidential. She's staying with me for now. Just keep that between you and me, okay?"

Polly moaned. Didn't he have a clue? The effect of his innocent honesty showed how out of touch he was with his own staff, and the phone call, coupled with what she'd already let slip with Darren, was nothing short of a department-wide gossip memo announcing they now lived together and she was pregnant with his baby.

So much for keeping the cat in the bag a bit longer.

As if feeling sick to her stomach wasn't enough, the realization that soon everyone at work would know her personal business sent her head right back into the bowl.

John wasn't sure he'd ever get used to the quick glances and whispers whenever he did rounds on the orthopedic ward, so he chose to ignore them. He did, however, have to admit that never in a million years would he expect his name to be linked to a sweet small-town girl like Polly Seymour.

Having her living with him hadn't taken nearly as much getting used to as he'd assumed he'd need. She was quiet and calm, and sometimes he barely knew she was there, especially when she went to her room and did whatever she did after dinner until she went to bed. He wished she'd come out of her room more often and spend time with him.

He sensed she didn't want to be any more of an imposition than she assumed she was. Truth was, she wasn't an imposition at all. He liked having her there, having someone to cook for and look after. Someone to talk things over with. He liked her gentle, sunny nature, too.

He even got a kick out of the twangy country music she liked to listen to on the radio in her room.

His apartment had never seemed more like a home.

John walked toward a fourteen-year-old boy's room to talk with the mother about Thursday's scheduled knee and ankle repair. The young teen, named Eric Caldera, had injured it playing in the dark at summer camp in Maine. It would be a long procedure and involve pins and plates and possibly even a bone graft. He wouldn't know exactly how extensive the repair would be until he started surgery.

Eric's parents were estranged, making all consultations tricky. The father had visitation rights with Eric, but the mother preferred never to be in the same room with him. Cases like these at Angel's required social services to step in to work out the details so all involved, especially the patient, could have their wishes met. After seeing the mother, who wouldn't leave her son's bedside, he'd give a call to the father and repeat everything he'd said to the mother. It might be double work, but he believed both parents deserved to be informed.

On his way into the room his gaze met and held Polly's. Something odd fizzed through his chest, and he winked at her. Her sky-blue eyes got wide and she covered with her hand the smile threatening to burst free. He liked taking her by surprise…like that night they'd made love.

She looked cute in her brightly colored top covered in cartoon angels on clouds and those bright pink scrub pants. Pretty in pink. Yeah, his new roommate was pretty in pink.

Entering the patient room, his smile was wide. Well, wide by John Griffin's standards, anyway, because he had something special to look forward to. Later today he'd accompany Polly for her first ultrasound at Geoff's office.

Standing beside the procedure table in the darkened ultrasonographer's room, John was as interested as Polly in seeing the first view of their baby. An ultrasound this early in the game wasn't called for, but more than anything John wanted to make sure the pregnancy was well implanted.

Having followed the preparation orders to a T, Polly had been dancing around the waiting room, swearing she'd wet herself if they didn't take her in soon. He'd laughed at her antics, wishing he could help her get comfortable some way, but knew this was totally out of his realm of expertise.

Polly lay on the table with a sheet over her abdomen, looking excited yet in pain from her extra-full bladder. When the tech pulled back the sheet and squirted the cold conducting gel on her belly, she glanced at him, raised her shoulders and grimaced, letting out a tiny squeal. How could that flat abdomen possibly house a baby? John wondered. He hadn't seen her smooth ivory skin since the night they'd been together, and his reaction of longing to touch her surprised him. But now was not the time or place to get hot for his live-in nurse.

He'd pulled strings to have the ultrasound this early along in the pregnancy. After all, it had been barely five weeks since she'd gotten pregnant, the baby's heart wouldn't even be completely formed or beating yet, but Geoff was more than happy to accommodate them.

"We'll only be able to see the gestational sac," the

sonographer said as she moved the transducer back and forth over Polly's taut skin.

Polly reached out and on reflex John took her hand. She squeezed, and he mindlessly ran his thumb back and forth over her icy fingers. He wanted to kiss her, right there in front of the tech. He didn't give a damn. He wanted to kiss her.

But he didn't, choosing instead to squeeze back on her hand when the fan-shaped image of Polly's uterus first appeared on the monitor.

"There it is," the tech said. "That's the gestational sac. Oh, and see that tiny thing? About the size of an orange seed? That's the embryo."

John had to squint to see it, but it was there. Their baby. The hair on his arms rose as assorted feelings of awe and joy along with an ancient ache rolled through him. He was definitely going to be a father, and he remembered exactly how he'd felt when Lisa had told him the news all those years ago.

"Oh, my gosh, look at that, Johnny," Polly said on gust of breath.

Warmth enveloped him, reaching through layers of protection to the deepest part of his heart as he glanced first at the screen then into the face of an angel. His angel, who'd brought life back into his lonely existence.

"Looks like we're really having a baby, dumpling."

The look she returned, full of wonder, joy, and excitement, was worth every single one of those twelve barren years.

John took Polly to a restaurant in Central Park for dinner on the balmy August evening. Outside on the deck they watched swans and ducks, rowboats, and even a gondola drift by as she sipped lemonade. She ordered hazelnut-crusted East Coast halibut with asparagus, cherry tomatoes, mushrooms and some kind of divine vinaigrette, grateful her morning sickness always seemed to wane by early afternoons. He went for a curry with shrimp and scallops.

As they ate, things loosened up between them. Even more incredibly, John opened up to her about his family without Polly prodding him first.

"My sister Dana is going to be floored when she finds out I'm going to be a father."

"Is she close by?"

He shook his head. "She lives in Rhode Island. She's been on my butt to get married again for years." His eyes drifted away momentarily and Polly wondered what he was thinking. Certainly he wasn't thinking about marrying her.

"Uh, Johnny, we hardly know each other. Aren't we going to just wait and see how things work out?"

He pulled back from his brief mental absence. "Oh, of course. I was just thinking back to when I lost Lisa and how important Dana was in helping me get by. My mom and dad were as devastated as I was and, well Dana was this rock for all of us."

"She sounds like a great sister. I always wished I'd had a sister or brother."

"We hated each other growing up, but now we're like this." He crossed his fingers. "First thing every summer I give her and her husband, Jerome, a break by taking my nephews camping."

"That sounds fun. Where did you go this year?"

"Maine. Acadia National Park."

"I've never been."

"You've got to go. It's beautiful."

There were so many places she'd never seen. Dare she dream of having someone to travel with and share special moments? Her mind drifted far away to the land of dreams come true, and she hadn't a clue how long she stayed there but most of her dinner had been eaten and John was talking about his parents when she checked back in.

"My parents eat dinner at four-thirty every day in Florida. They drive around in these electric carts like everyone else in the retirement community, it's the funniest thing. I took my life in my hands when I visited last year and insisted on walking around the place. They need some kind of signage that says *'Pedestrians Beware'!* I nearly got sideswiped twice." He gave that genuine cockeyed smile she'd come to adore.

Polly laughed, imagining John dodging electric carts in some distant retirement community.

When dessert came, she ventured into uncharted waters. "Do you think it's too early to think about names?"

"Mort," he said. "I like Mort." When John let down his guard he had natural deadpan humor. At least, she hoped he was being funny about this name business.

She threw a leftover piece of bread at him. "No way, dude." The impish expression on his face gave him away.

"Hey, my favorite uncle was named Mortimer." Such a tease John was.

"What do you think about Sterling?"

"It's okay, but only if I can call him Mort for short."

She rolled her eyes and glanced at the full moon hanging in the sky. Mr. Sterling had been her favorite teacher in high school, the one who had encouraged her to pursue the sciences. She'd always thought his last name would make a great first name.

"How about Caledonia for a girl? We could call her Callie."

Polly couldn't read John's face on this one. Was he kidding or…? Actually, Callie wasn't such a bad name. "Sweet. I like it."

"You do?" His brows tented together. "It was my grandmother's name." He tugged his earlobe then drank the last of his after-dinner coffee and leaned back in his chair. The night air and hint of jasmine helped engrave this more-than-fine moment in her mind. Because she didn't own a camera, she'd have to take a mental picture to remember for the rest of her life. Had she ever dreamed about casually tossing baby names around with a man before?

He'd also been by her side for the day's exciting test. Not because he'd made the appointment but because he'd wanted to be. They'd seen their baby together for the first time and celebrated with this romantic yet playful dinner by the Central Park Lake.

"I guess I'm a traditionalist at heart," he said, with that adorable half-lifted smile.

At that moment affection and something more flooded her heart for John, almost making it hard to breathe. She wanted this. So. Much.

"Why are you looking at me all funny like that?" he asked.

"I'm not looking at you funny."

"Yes you are. It's sort of like this." He imitated a goofy I'm-in-love-with-a-dove look and she burst out laughing.

"I've never made a look like that in my life!" She feigned offense.

He repeated the silly expression and they laughed together while he paid the bill and continued all the way out of the restaurant to the car.

Arriving back at his apartment, they strolled toward the doorman, holding hands. Marco greeted them with a broad and telling grin.

"Beautiful night," Marco said.

"It is," John said, lightly squeezing her hand.

All afternoon and into the evening Polly had thought she'd fallen through the looking glass into a parallel world filled with bright colors, good will, and dreams come true. John was by her side. He wouldn't desert her over the pregnancy, as she'd feared. He'd promised and she believed him.

Marco opened the door and Polly snuggled into John's shoulder as they got into the elevator, feeling like half of a real couple. The fact he'd called her dumpling earlier hadn't escaped her. He smiled down at her and brushed his fingertips across her cheek. She saw the look, the same one he'd let slip several times during dinner. He wanted her. Badly.

As he unlocked the apartment door, the only question left on Polly's mind was who would make the first move.

Before he switched on the lights he stopped her by the front door, brought his lips down to hers and kissed her tenderly. She'd missed kissing him and savored his smooth, soft lips surrounded by end-of-day stubble. He broke free from the kiss first and flipped the light switch. Under the entryway light, he cupped her face in his palms and looked deeply into her eyes with his hazel stare. She couldn't help but notice the tiny gold flecks around the pupils. They were kind eyes, and right now expressed desire. For her.

"Things will be different this time. I promise," he said.

She went up on tiptoe to reach his lips. "I liked it last time just fine." He enfolded her in his strong arms and kissed her thoroughly. She'd never felt sexier or safer in her life.

Once he'd kissed her into a mindless state where all senses vibrated on alert, he took her hand and led her down the hall, bypassing her room and heading straight for his bedroom.

She'd peeked into both his office and bedroom several times over the last week, but had never stepped inside either room. Never considered being in his bedroom again before now. It was a strongly masculine room, like him, with big, dark wood furniture and deep blue covers over the king-sized bed. The walls were pale gray and peaceful. Though peace was the last thought on her mind at the moment.

Her breathing quickened as he stepped toward her, removing her shoulder bag and unbuttoning her top. She'd brought a change of clothes to work, knowing they had a doctor's appointment and not wanting to wear work scrubs there. She started to help him with her blouse.

He stilled her hands. "Let me." Always in charge.

The thought of letting him have his way with her sent a second wave of heat across her skin and a subtle coiling in her core. She knew what letting go with John in control meant. As he unbuttoned more, the tiny raised bumps didn't go unnoticed by him, and one corner of his mouth lifted in appreciation as he delicately traced his fingertips across her clavicle. That set her nerve endings to humming all the way down to her waist.

With her top opened, he pushed it over her shoulders and kissed the side of her neck. The single kiss sprinkled more tingles across her chest, this time dipping down to her center. With nipples tight and tender, she couldn't wait for him to remove the bra she could barely squeeze into any more. He did.

One raised brow signaled he'd noticed the change in size, too. He took the weight of her breasts into his hands, gently lifting and massaging then kissing each one.

How much more could she take standing up?

He must have read her mind because he bent over and scooped her up behind the knees, carrying her to his huge bed. He pulled back the covers and lowered her then undid his buckle and removed his belt. She took the cue to take off her slacks.

"Uh-uh," he said, stopping her in mid-zip. "Let me do it."

He crawled over her on the bed, kissed her breasts again, taking longer this time, making her gasp with pleasure, then unzipped and peeled back her pants. He quickly unbuttoned his shirt and removed it then his undershirt, all the while looking at her with hungry eyes. Heat engulfed every surface of her skin in anticipation of what would follow.

She loved the sight of his body, thick muscles and broad shoulders, a wide patch of brown hair across his chest. Not the kind of man you'd see in a model's magazine but a man's man, solid, all testosterone and heat. Boy, could she feel the heat.

First taking a full and firm feel of one hip and cheek,

he removed her French-cut underwear in record time. The man broke bones and realigned them for a living, his grip didn't go unnoticed. She glanced into his eyes and could tell that even now he was practicing restraint. In the next second his slacks were gone along with his briefs, and seeing him completely naked she remembered how he'd brought her to climax over and over their first night together.

She reached for his arousal but he intercepted her hand, giving her a firm look. He was taking control. Again. Fine by her. If he wanted to devour her, she'd let him.

As he dropped kisses across her chest and stomach, she arched and writhed in order to keep her hands to herself. When he reached the top of her thigh, gliding his tongue towards her center, she couldn't help herself and grasped his head, holding on for dear life as he kissed and licked her most sensitive parts. Unrelenting, he continued, and shivers rained across her flesh, exquisite sensations folding deep inside her, until she gasped and clenched her muscles uncontrollably, the release strong enough to make her buck against his mouth. He didn't let up, staying with her until she'd ridden the mind-blowing waves to the very end.

He came up smiling as she crossed her arms over her eyes and let out a long breath. "I won't survive if you keep that up."

"I'm a doctor, I know how to resuscitate." He scooped her up and began to roll onto his back, planting both hands firmly on her hips. She rolled with him, reaching for his face, kissing him, tasting herself on his lips. That deep hip and bottom massage continued seeding her desire as she lay on top of him, and she could feel his firm length beneath her belly. Before she knew it he'd hoisted her hip up and over his erection with one hand, guiding himself inside with the other. She straddled him as he slid along every sensitive spot she owned all the way inside.

"No need for a condom this time," he said, as he began to move inside her. Their gazes met and melded together in understanding.

She adjusted her hips so they fit closer together. As if it were possible, the early pregnancy made her even more sensitive to his touch, and she wondered if he felt the change, too. His powerful hips thrust upward, the strength of his thighs lifting her off the bed. She balanced herself by placing her hands on his chest, leaning into him for added pleasure. His hands cupped and squeezed her hips and soon the lazy lifts and rolls weren't enough and they turned to rocking. Faster. Firmer. Desperately penetrating.

He stopped abruptly, and in one quick move flipped her onto her back so he could drive deeper and faster yet. Jets of pleasure rocked through her with each surge. She was gone before he'd barely gotten started, the powerful grip of her muscles sending shockwaves to every part of her body. "Johnny!"

Dissolving into his determined rhythm, she wrapped her legs around his hips, urging him deeper, encouraging his release. Bucking together for several more minutes, he reawakened her need. His strength built fiercely inside as he slid in and out at a frantic pace, until he groaned and she gasped and he erupted with a growl, sharing the bliss with her one more time.

CHAPTER EIGHT

POLLY AND JOHN lay folded together in bed for several minutes. He kissed her forehead and lightly rubbed her back while he rested his eyes. She snuggled into his chest, cushioning her head on his well-padded, muscular shoulder, enjoying the thump-thump-thump of his heart.

"From now on you sleep here with me." He didn't ask, just stated how it would be.

He'd tugged his earlobe when he'd said it, the gesture she'd come to recognize whenever he spoke from his heart. Whenever he spoke the truth.

"I'd like that," she said, embracing the magnitude of his statement. Maybe it was the ultrasound, seeing their baby together, but Polly had felt the change in John tonight. He'd let down that wall between them and finally invited her inside.

He rolled her onto his chest and had a good look at her as if for the first time, playing with her chaotic hair, brushing it out of her face and hooking it behind her ears. "I can't get enough of you, Polly." His hands drifted downwards and he cupped her bottom. "It's like I've been dead and now that you woke me up, all I want is you."

With her heart swooning over this man who wanted

to be with her, wanted her to live with him, to sleep with him, to have their baby, she kissed him long and heartfelt. Afterwards their gazes met and held—his as dreamy as she knew hers must be. Was this love? Her legs came together over his, and she discovered he was a man of his word, he really couldn't get enough of her. She cuddled his building erection with the insides of her thighs, and soon he'd slipped into her again. They stared at each other as their easily coaxed passion mounted slowly but steadily.

"I've been waiting for you a long time," he said, his voice husky with desire.

"I never knew I could be so lucky," she said, wanting nothing more than to please him for the rest of her life.

After making love again, just before they finally settled down for the night John popped out of bed and padded down the hall to the kitchen. He came right back with half a dozen saltine crackers and a glass of lemon water, placing them on Polly's bedside table.

"How thoughtful," she said, tiny prickles of contentment breaking over her. "Thank you." The small gesture meant the world to her. No one since her mother had shown they cared by doing little things. He made her lunch each day, fixed dinner more often than she did, and always asked if she'd taken her prenatal vitamins and folic acid. It might not seem like a lot, but to her his thoughtfulness was everything.

"I've got to look out for you and our baby," he said, cuddling next to her, tucking the covers around them.

Polly drifted off to sleep that night grinning, happier than she could ever remember and thinking she knew for sure who the true people-pleaser was of the two of them.

* * *

The surgery on Eric Caldera had been long and difficult, but after four hours John was satisfied he'd repaired everything to the best of his ability. Twice the anesthesiologist warned that the vital signs, especially the heart rate, had increased and a small dose of beta blocker had fixed it. Eric had been watched closely after extubation to make sure all was well. Once it was established he was breathing on his own and his vitals were stable, they sent him to the recovery room.

John left the OR and yanked off his mask, leaving patient recovery to his nurses. His first order of business was to call the father in one waiting room and the mother in another. With everything having been carefully planned by social services prior to the operation, Eric's parents had agreed to wait in separate locations. That afternoon, he'd inform each of them that surgery had been a success. Their boy would be back playing whatever sport he wanted after several months of recovery and physical therapy. The mother would be first at Eric's bedside when he returned to his room and, though unhappy about playing second fiddle, the estranged father agreed to wait an extra hour before seeing his son.

Polly took report for Eric Caldera from the recovery-room nurse. "Vital signs are stable. No sign of bleeding. Unremarkable recovery."

Polly first jotted down her notes then awaited the arrival of her patient by tending to two little girls in a double room.

"I want Dr. Griffin to make me a monkey next time." The little one with red hair held her bright pink balloon princess crown from yesterday and smiled.

"I want a monkey," the second girl said. Both her legs were in casts, one suspended above the bed in a sling. Polly noticed John had already signed both casts and added a goofy-looking happy face next to each signature.

"Dr. Griffin will be glad to make whatever kind of balloon figure you want, as long as you both take your medicine, okay?" She wasn't above making a good bargain, especially with some of the sour-tasting pills having been an issue for these two girls over the last couple of days.

"Okay," they replied in unison sing-song fashion. Sweet, it worked!

Darren stuck his head in the room. "Your post-op just arrived."

"Thanks, Dare. Could you ask Raphael to let his mother know?" With that Polly said goodbye to the girls and trotted over to Eric's room.

Still completely out of it, Eric merely moaned when Polly, Darren and the transportation clerk slid him from the gurney to the bed she'd prepared for him. In the middle of her initial assessment Eric's mother entered the room with a huge bouquet of flowers accentuated with half a dozen bright balloons.

"How's my baby doing?" Mrs. Caldera had either used extra body splash today or the star jasmine in the bouquet was emitting a particularly strong scent.

Mostly asleep, but responsive to touch, Eric crinkled up his nose as if he didn't care for the smell. His blood pressure and pulse were low, but that was to be expected with a sedated patient, and Polly remembered the recovery nurse mentioning something about beta blockers having been given to lower his heart rate during surgery. Placing the oxygen monitor on his finger, she waited for a reading.

"He seems to be doing fine." The news smoothed the deep crease between Mrs. Caldera's brows. The oxygen saturation was at the low end of normal but holding. Polly put a nasal cannula in his nostrils and turned on the wall oxygen at two liters.

After making sure Eric was comfortable, that the site of the surgery wasn't oozing blood, the IV was intact and flowing, and checking there was good circulation to his toes, she headed out to input his medication orders into the computer. On her way she spotted John heading her way, still in OR garb, looking downright sexy and authoritative. Working to control her reaction, she grinned at him then waved.

With the blue OR cap still on his head, he gave her the smile that crinkled the corners of his dark eyes, and never failed to send her heart beating double time. Also on a mission, he headed for Eric's room.

Polly set out for the medicine room to get afternoon meds for the two little girls in her other assigned room. Now that she'd bargained with them, she expected them to co-operate. In the middle of her getting the medicine, another nurse entered and she got into a conversation about a memo going around regarding blood-sugar testing and new finger-stick protocol. When the conversation ended and she'd finished pouring her meds, she heard a code blue over the loudspeaker.

"Code blue. Room 614. code blue. Room 614."

Eric's room! She rushed back to the ward only to find a crowd gathered around the door of her patient. What could have gone wrong in the few minutes she'd been away? Peering inside, she saw John was at the helm of the code in progress, calling out orders while working to re-intubate the teen. The ambu bag was in readiness in the nearby respiratory therapist's hands.

One of the medical aides assisted the mother out of the room. The woman was crying and visibly shaken. "One minute he was fine, the next he stopped breathing. What happened to my baby?"

Knowing the code team was there in full force, Polly rushed to Mrs. Caldera's side to offer support. "He's in good hands. If he's having trouble breathing, they'll fix him right up. Has your son ever been diagnosed with asthma?"

"No. When he was a baby one doctor said he had twitchy lungs, but he's never had a problem."

Could the boy have asthma and not know it? Could the sharp scent of those flowers have set him off? Or perhaps the latex in the balloons? She searched her memory for "latex allergy" on his chart, but was positive she hadn't seen any allergies noted. Latex was such a common allergy these days that John's balloons were all latex free, and the hospital had been a latex-free zone from the beginning, but who knew about florist displays? Polly was surprised Mrs. Caldera had gotten that bouquet past the hospital entrance.

Oh, God, Eric had been given a beta blocker in surgery for his elevated vital signs, if he was having an asthma attack that drug would make the effect much worse and would block the antidote. She knew John was well aware of all the medications given during the surgery, and the code team was top-notch, so she settled for worrying her lower lip with her teeth along with Mrs. Caldera.

Five minutes. She held the mother's hand and promised all would be well. Ten minutes. The rush and chaos inside the room continued in a tunnel of noise.

"We need more epi," a resident hollered from the doorway.

Leaving Mrs. Caldera with the medical aide, Polly shot across the ward to the med room to retrieve more medicine, wondering who'd been assigned to restock the crash cart that day. How could they run out of epi during a respiratory arrest? If they *had* gone through that much epi, it couldn't bode well for poor Eric.

With shaky hands Polly got the medicine and rushed to the entrance of Eric's room.

"All clear," John called out, holding the defibrillator paddles in place on the boy's chest and torso. He zapped Eric with enough joules to start a horse's heart. All eyes went to the heart monitor. No change. Flat line.

Polly delivered the epinephrine and went back to Mrs. Caldera, positioned close enough for Polly to peer through the door. They defibrillated Eric again with the same outcome.

The mood in the patient room had changed drastically. John stood sullenly at the head of the bed, head down, staring at his patient with deep remorse in his eyes. No matter that the respiratory therapist squeezed the ambu bag to force breathing, the flat-lined bedside monitor squawking its continual alarm told the full story. A young teenager had had a respiratory arrest, which had led to a full code, and he had died after surgery.

Never could anyone have foretold this outcome for a routine surgery on an otherwise healthy child, yet sometimes it happened. Truth was, surgeries were never routine.

With terror in her eyes Eric's mother sensed the change. "My baby. Is it all over? Is my baby all right?" She tore away from Polly and the medical aide and lurched for the hospital room.

Polly intercepted her but the mother's weight pushed her off balance. Polly stood firm, held her in a hug. "Give us a second, Mrs. Caldera. Please."

In a desperate move the mother broke away. "I want to see my boy."

John stepped into the hallway just as she reached the threshold. He braced her by both shoulders, a grief-stricken look in his eyes. "I'm so sorry, Mrs. Caldera. He stopped breathing then his heart stopped. We did everything in our power to save him."

Her scream reverberated off the ward walls.

John held her tight and let her cry. He glanced over her shoulder at Polly with a grim expression. "Go and find the father in OR waiting room two and let him know what's happened. I'll explain everything to him when he gets here."

Dreading having to face a parent and tell them their child had just died, something she'd never had to do before and which wasn't normally an RN's job, she bit her lower lip and nodded solemnly, wanting some way, somehow to help John through this tragedy. Oh, God, what would she say to the father? How would she tell him the boy had been alive one minute and dead the next?

Rather than wait for the elevator, she hustled down the stairs, her legs shaky from the adrenaline pouring throughout her system. Arriving on the third floor, thinking her heart might just jump right out of her chest, she found waiting room number two. A tall, overweight, swarthy-looking man in a business suit paced the floor. The instant she arrived he looked up. "Are you Eric's nurse? Can I see him now?"

Her heart practically burst. How was she supposed to tell him? "There's been a problem, Mr. Caldera. Dr. Griffin will explain everything to you—"

He stopped in his tracks. "What do you mean there's been a problem?"

"Eric stopped breathing and—"

He grabbed her by both arms and squeezed to the point of pain. "You'd better not be telling me what I think…"

"I'm so sorry, Mr. Cal—"

He shoved her aside, exiting the room, and she bumped against the doorframe.

Rubbing her elbow, focused solely on her task, she followed him down the hall. "Mr. Caldera, it will be quicker if you take the stairs. Follow me."

With fury in his eyes, his jaw set, he came at her. She opened the door to the stairwell and he followed her inside. "It's three flights up," she said, stepping back for him to go first, "but much faster than the elevator."

"You killed him. You killed my son!" He glanced up the stairwell. "Are you trying to kill me, too?" Three steps above her, with a contorted, out-of-control, grief-stricken expression on his face, he kicked out at her, the leather sole of his shoe landing solidly on her solar plexus. It knocked the wind from her lungs and sent her hurtling down the lower flight of stairs.

Head over heels she tumbled, arms flailing, searching for purchase, enduring sharp pangs of pain as first her shoulder, then her head, then her back and bottom hit cement, all the way to the lower landing.

She couldn't breathe and clutched at the point of greatest pain, her stomach, as Eric's father raced out of the stairwell. If she could inhale she'd call for help, and warn John what was coming his way.

Trying her hardest to get to her feet, still unable to catch her breath, the dim stairway light faded to black.

Polly worked to open her eyes. Everything hurt. She wasn't at the bottom of the stairs. No, she was on a thin mattress. Cracking one eye open, the bright lights of the emergency department had her immediately snapping it shut. But not before she saw John, and felt the warmth of his hand over hers.

"How are you feeling, dumpling?" he asked, obvious concern in his voice.

"Like I got kicked down a flight of stairs."

"God, I'm so, so sorry." He leaned close, held her hand between both of his, lifting it to his mouth where he kissed her fingers. "Forgive me."

"I'll be okay." She tried an achy smile, which quickly turned into a grimace. She did a quick test—her arms moved, her ankles rotated, her knees bent, her neck twisted just fine. Of course it hurt like heck to do any of the movements, but she could move. That was a start. "I'll get over all these bangs and bruises in no time."

The rows of lines in his forehead and wary dark gaze told a different story. "I shouldn't have sent you to do my job," he said.

"John, you had your hands full with the mother. You'd just coded your patient. If the parents could get along they would have been there together. You can't do everything."

He shook his head, biting his lower lip. "I should have sent the resident to tell Mr. Caldera."

"You were in shock from the failed resuscitation. Your resident was busy with the clean-up." She reached up to hold him, and his desperate need to hold her tight warned something more was at stake. "I'm okay, I swear. I'm okay, John."

He pulled back, shaking his head. *She wasn't okay?* The only thing she saw in his eyes was pain. "You're bleeding, sweetheart. The baby..." His voice cracked on the word. He shook his head again.

Her pregnancy was in jeopardy? Little Callie? "Did I miscarry?" Her eyes welled up as she said the word.

He shook his head—a world of weariness in his gaze. "No. They're keeping you for observation for now." One tear slid down the outer part of his left eye, soon followed by another on the right. "I'm so sorry."

She believed with all of her heart that he was sorry. But she was bleeding. Her hands covered her face as the deep emptiness of possibly losing her pregnancy took hold. Soon her hands were covered in tears as she rocked forward and back, unleashing the dammed-up tears of a lifetime filled with disappointment.

John held her and moaned. She used his shoulder to brace her forehead as she bawled until there was nothing left. The brightest spot in her life, her pregnancy, was in jeopardy.

CHAPTER NINE

IN THE CRAMPED and drab ER cubicle, John held Polly until she was ready to let go. Until she'd digested the awful news. She'd had the life nearly kicked out of her womb, and he'd been responsible for sending her to do his job. She could have been killed falling down those stairs.

The words "guilt" and "anger" didn't come close to how he judged himself.

"Can you help me to the bathroom?" she said.

"Of course." He hopped to her side and dragged the IV machine along with them. She felt so vulnerable under his care that it made his heart wrench. Against all odds he hoped this pregnancy would survive. They'd have a new start, get their chance to be parents. Hell, he'd even marry her before the baby was born. Yeah, that's what he'd do.

Would the Big Guy hear his prayer and promise?

If our baby survives, to make things up to Polly, I'll marry her and be the best damn father on the planet. If only you'll let our baby make it. Not for me, for her. No. That's a lie. For me, too. I want this. I really do.

Helping Polly into the bathroom, he closed the door and waited outside.

Soon her moan carried through the thin wall loud and clear.

"What's wrong, sweetheart?" He rushed inside to find her sitting on the toilet, dejected and bereft. "Are you okay?"

"I just miscarried." She whimpered the phrase so softly he didn't understand what she'd meant at first. As the words sank in, he dropped to his knees in front of her and put his forehead to hers. Was this some cruel joke? How many times was he supposed to lose everything dear to him? He ground his molars.

"Oh, baby, I'm so sorry. So, so sorry." Rather than call for the nurse, he helped clean her up and walked her back to the bed. He put on the call light for the nurse, then made Polly comfortable, but there was no way on earth anything he could do would take away her loss or her pain. She'd lost the baby. Their baby. Her tears ran without effort down her cheeks. So did his as sorrow wrapped around his chest and squeezed the last of his feelings from him.

When the nurse arrived he told her what had happened.

"We'll need to schedule a D&C," he said, knowing the routine protocol for such things.

"I'll get right on that, Doctor," the nurse said on the way out the door.

John held Polly's fragile body until she fell asleep. Pacing the tiny ER cubicle, thoughts stabbed at his conscience. He hadn't been able to protect his wife and future child before, and look at him now—he'd sent Polly into the eye of the storm. He hadn't been there for Lisa and now he hadn't been there when Polly had needed him most. Hell, it was his job to tell parents when their children died, yet distracted by the failed code, in partial denial, and concentrating on Mrs. Caldara he'd taken the easy way out and sent Polly to fetch the father.

She could have been killed! Now she'd lost her baby.

What kind of man was he?

A man who didn't deserve to be loved by Polly or anyone else on earth.

Her lids fluttered and cracked open. He sat straighter. "You need anything?"

She studied him for several seconds with reflective eyes, as if she could read his thoughts, then shook her head soberly and went back to napping. He reached for her hand out of obligation, his fingers nearly as numb as his heart had become over the last few hours, and he stayed by her side for the remainder of the afternoon. In limbo. Lost, without a tether. Prayers unanswered. His heart cracked apart. He had nothing left to offer.

"They're ready for her in the procedure room," the nurse said at the cubicle entrance.

John jumped to his feet, prepared to go along with Polly.

As if she'd sensed his rote response, she looked at him. "I'll be fine. You don't have to come along."

"Are you sure?" He didn't even put up a fight.

"Positive." She squeezed his dull grip and he kissed her forehead, though his lips were numb, too.

"See you later, then," he said, watching the gurney roll down the corridor, not sure he recognized his own flat and distant voice.

Polly put her stained work clothes in the plastic bag provided by the hospital. She'd changed into the clothes

John had brought from home. "I'm ready," she said that evening.

"Okay." He stood, his eyes drifting everywhere but to hers. "I'll bring the car round and meet you at the ER entrance."

The transportation clerk waited nearby with a wheelchair. Protocol was protocol, and Polly felt too weak and achy to fight it.

When she met him at the curbside of the hospital exit, John hopped out of the car ready to assist her from the wheelchair, seeming robotic and acting out of duty. Yet he was here, she reminded herself, attempting to hold onto the positive. At least he hadn't run away from their depressing mess.

His hand felt chilly to the touch when he helped her stand. Again, his eyes avoided hers and she curled her lower lip and chewed on it just to have something else to concentrate on.

Unable to think of a single thing to say, Polly remained quiet on the drive on Central Park South toward Sutton Place, choosing instead to watch the tree-lined streets they passed. Once they were back in the apartment, he helped her to the guest room, where he'd already pulled back the covers in readiness. He must have planned making the change from lover to guest when he'd come back earlier to get her change of clothes and the car.

"I thought you'd be more comfortable in here," he said when she'd sent him a questioning glance. The ball of emotion swelling in her chest sank to her stomach when she noticed how detached he seemed. Cold even.

Too weak and bumped up to protest, she got under the covers and let him tuck her in.

Every considerate thing he did felt distant and done out of obligation as the evening wore on. He brought her a tray with soup and crackers, helped her to the bathroom when she wanted to get ready to turn in for the night, and assisted her back to bed as if she were a fragile ninety-year-old woman. Making her feel nothing like the woman he'd made love to.

Polly had hoped to curl into his protective embrace tonight. To sleep next to him and feel his heat radiate over her, healing her. Together they could get through this by clinging close and comforting one another. She'd hoped to regain the strength that had hemorrhaged out during the course of this incredibly long day by being by his side. But John had sent her back to the guest room without even asking her, as if without the pregnancy he no longer had reason to make her a part of his life.

What they'd made together was no more.

She was plumb out of tears as she lay in the darkness, staring at the white ceiling.

Today she'd been kicked down the stairs, she'd lost her baby, and somehow during the horrific series of events she may as well have been kicked in the gut again, because now she'd lost John, too.

Three days later Polly insisted on going back to work. She couldn't bear the thought of being a prisoner in John's apartment another day, and longed for the distraction of a busy orthopedic ward. They'd hardly spoken since the miscarriage and she felt more like an obligation than a lover and a grieving partner.

At times he'd pulled so deeply inside himself that she'd felt like an invasive war lord, demanding attention whenever she'd tried to engage him in the simplest things.

"Want to help make a salad?" she'd said the previous night, insisting making her own dinner.

"You go ahead," he said. "I'm not hungry."

She ate alone while he sequestered himself in his study. They hadn't taken one meal together since the miscarriage.

At work, word traveled fast. During the Monday morning report Polly accepted each and every hug from her friends and fellow staff. It felt good to be back. At least in Darren's and Brooke's eyes she saw genuine sadness, something missing from John's. When she looked into his eyes, the unfathomable detachment made it seem like he wasn't there. As if he'd checked out for good.

Piling the pain of losing John on top of the heartache of her miscarriage, she could barely stand up straight. The house had become heavy with silence, washed in colorless depression. At night she'd hole up in her room working on a bitter-sweet but necessary project.

Warm hands rested on her shoulders. For an instant Polly imagined John had walked up behind her. He'd barely touched her since she'd lost the baby. Maybe there was still hope? Maybe all could be well again? She turned to find Raphael, his kind eyes probing hers, and she tried not to look disappointed. "You've got a phone call," he said.

"Oh, thanks." Shaken out of her thoughts, she forced a shift in her attitude. She was at work and needed to give it her full concentration. She punched the blinking light and picked up the receiver. "This is Polly."

"Ms. Seymour, it's Mrs. Goldman." Her landlady. "I

have someone interested in taking your room. I know you paid me for an extra month, but…"

"No. Please, Mrs. Goldman, I'd like to keep that room a little while longer. I'm paid up through August and September. If you'd like, I'll pay for October now, too."

Agreeing on a compromise, Polly hung up the phone feeling less helpless in her current living situation by having another option.

"Who in the blazes messed with the bed traction in Room Twelve?" John sounded like an ornery bear as he headed toward Brooke at the nurses' station. His rugged, masculine appeal had vanished along with his civil mood.

"P.T. was in there earlier," Brooke said, straightening her shoulders and making her taller-than-average frame seem even taller.

"Get them up here, now!" he growled, and stormed off to the next room.

Brooke glanced at Polly, alarm in her eyes. How quickly they'd forgotten how difficult John could be. No longer an avowed people-pleaser, Polly shrugged, realizing she'd also lost her magic touch where John was concerned, and went seeking solace in her assigned patient room. A teeny-bopper with bright eyes and a lively attitude was just the distraction she needed. *Sweet.* And thank heavens for small favors.

"Who forgot to put Brandon Seamus in the CPM machine today?" John's baritone carried all the way across the ward.

Darren popped his head up as Brandon was his patient. "Last week we had an in-service from P.T. that said the continuous passive motion device didn't make a difference by six weeks post-surgery."

"Did I DC the order?"

"No, sir."

"Then get off your duff and put his knee in the machine. Now!"

Polly came out of her patient room, shaken and embarrassed for John. "There's no reason to speak to Darren like that. He was following the recommendation of Physical Therapy."

"Did I ask your opinion?"

"I don't care if you asked it or not. You don't have the right to talk to your staff like that."

He looked at her as if he hated her and everyone else in the world, harrumphed and walked away. "I'll have a little talk with P.T. about going over my head and disregarding my orders," he said when he passed Brooke.

Knowing deep in her heart the pros and cons of using a CPM machine after knee procedures wasn't the issue, Polly felt queasy for John. She wished she could find a way to reach him before he quarantined himself completely from the world of the living.

That evening John cooked again. Maybe it was his way of apologizing? After having a well-prepared but tasteless meal in silence, Polly finished putting the dishes in the dishwasher. "I think I'll go for a walk to the park." There were two parks nearby and the one she had in mind overlooked the East River.

"I'll go with you."

She'd known he'd say that. Not because he wanted to be with her but because he wanted to protect her. From what? She'd walk to a beautiful park in a well-to-do neighborhood. It was still only early August, and it wasn't even dark out yet. But she'd depended on his twisted sense of obligation to accompany her, to open up the opportunity to talk. Maybe, while they walked and enjoyed the evening, she could crack that ever-hardening shell he was doing such a fine job of constructing.

The night air was still thick and humid. Polly chose a brisk pace and John had no problem keeping up. If anything, she had to widen her stride to match his.

"So, what's been going on?" she asked.

"What do you mean?" He gave her a look as if she'd just landed from planet crazy.

"You've been very bristly."

"I've bent over backwards to give you space, to help you heal."

Silence doesn't heal anything. She didn't want to go there right now. She wanted to intervene on her coworkers' behalf, before John drove them to resign one by one by one. The orthopedic kids didn't need to deal with constant staff turnover along with all their other ailments.

"I'm talking about work, about how you're chewing everyone's heads off, like before I came..." Her voice drifted off. She didn't want to suggest she'd had anything to do with his turnaround in attitude at work... before everything had gone to hell in a handbasket.

"Nurses are tough. They can take me. Always have." End of subject.

They entered the park lined with red bricks and bushes. She found an empty bench facing the river and sat. Inhaling, she realized the air was nothing like the sea. This humongous East River by the huge city smelled like life itself—of car exhausts, hot cement, hordes of people—yet the pewter-colored water overcame it all and offered a hint of refreshment. Polly needed to be refreshed. Living on this side of town with John, however briefly, this view had become one of her favorites in the city.

A jogger passed by. A hundred yards behind a woman with a stroller walked her baby. Polly had to look away, choosing to focus on the long steel sculpture of the Queensboro Bridge rather than lost possibilities.

"People can take all kinds of things, but they shouldn't have to. Your berating everyone wears skin thin." She reached for his hand, a gesture she'd given up on since he'd brought her home from the hospital. "You're hurting, John, and you're taking it out on the people around you."

It wasn't obvious, but she felt his hand recoil the tiniest bit. "Look, you handle things your way, and I'll handle them mine." She let go of his hand just as the woman with the stroller came by.

They sat for several more minutes staring at the river, thousands of necessary words going unspoken. How could she get through to John in his emotionally shut-down state, where the only feeling allowed to appear was anger?

"You ready to go back?" he said. "I've got an early surgery tomorrow."

With that, they walked back to his apartment in silence, Polly feeling as though she had cement bricks chained to her ankles.

By the end of the second day back at work and after several more outbursts from John towards the staff, Polly dreaded going home with him again. How much could she take of his foul mood while she grieved? And yet at home he'd become docile, so docile, in fact, she'd begun to suspect he was no longer alive.

"I think I'll walk home," she said, at his office door that Tuesday evening.

He stood and came around his desk. For the first time in days she saw an expression besides anger on his face, but she couldn't make out exactly what it meant. "But you're too weak to walk all the way home." With brows lowered, looking gruff, his words didn't match.

"I managed working all day yesterday and today without problems. I'll be fine."

"Only two days back at work, five since the miscarriage. All the more reason to let me drive you."

Obligation. Pure obligation. Though it was the first time he'd mentioned her miscarriage since the day it'd happened, and that struck Polly as progress. But not enough to want to spend another painful night in his presence, longing to crack his hardened shell, to get back to that wonderful man she'd known so briefly. John wouldn't allow it.

"So we'll have more time to sit in that dead apartment of yours and stare at each other?"

His brows shot up. Surprise tinted his brown stare. "I thought you'd appreciate some peace and quiet."

"More like rest in peace, you mean? Just bury me and get it over with, why don't you?"

He folded his arms. "I've done everything I possibly can to make you comfortable."

"Including shutting me out."

"I didn't think we needed to talk about our loss just yet."

"You banished me from your room, John."

With the topic becoming personal, he strode around her and closed his office door. "You can't stand the sight of me."

"What in heaven's name gave you that impression?"

"It's my fault you lost the baby. Why would you want to be anywhere near me, let alone sleep in the same bed?"

She shook her head. "You don't know me at all, do you?" With that, she swung open the door. Didn't the man know the meaning of comfort, both giving and getting, by sharing sadness? "I'll be home later, don't wait up," she said, and took off down the hall determined to find something to do to keep her busy until it was time to go to bed. Maybe she'd stop at the bookstore the next block over and read until she couldn't keep her eyes open. Oh, wait, there was that letter she needed to write, she shouldn't put it off another day. She could write the letter at the bookstore.

Anything not to have to face the man who'd checked out on her when she'd needed him most.

CHAPTER TEN

TWO MORE DAYS of living with John had drained the flow of energy from Polly's core. She could barely lift her head off the pillow. Would this be the story of her life? Drifting from person to person, never really cared for, ever to be seen as an obligation and nothing more?

She sat bolt upright. No. She wouldn't settle for that. She deserved more. She was young, she could get pregnant again if she ever found the right man. Melancholy thoughts about what she'd almost had with John, how he could be "the right man", how her dreams of having her own family had been just within reach but had been snatched away at the last moment invaded her thinking. A cruel joke.

Getting out of bed, she grabbed her robe and headed for the shower. Passing the kitchen, she smelled fresh coffee brewing, piquing her senses. Now that she could drink coffee again, she'd pour herself a cup and enjoy it. She was damned if she intended to live the rest of her life like a ghost, the way John had chosen to do. In his case, an angry, bitter ghost.

She got into the shower and scrubbed herself to near shining, ready to take on the world again. But this time she wasn't going to fall back into her old ways. Nope.

From now on the only person she intended to please was herself. This would be the summer and fall of Polly, and she wouldn't let an out-of-touch-with-his-own-feelings sad-sack like John drag her down one more inch.

As she toweled off and combed out her hair, she made plans. She'd ask Darren to help her move out over the weekend and she'd go back to Mrs. Goldman's and put this sad episode of her life behind her. Little Caledonia would forever have a special place in her heart, and she'd honor her miscarried baby by living each day, not merely existing as John had chosen to do. She couldn't be around negative people any more. She just couldn't.

The John she had glimpsed and fallen in love with was long gone. How could she possibly tie herself to a man who wasn't even able to tell her how sad he was after the miscarriage? He'd cried half a dozen tears at the ER, but since then an iron wall had been erected, and she could waste a lifetime trying to scale it but never succeeding.

No. There was nothing here for her at the 56th Street apartment. Striding down the hall, she came to an abrupt stop when she saw John in the kitchen, eating a bowl of cereal, and was perplexed by the pop of feelings in her chest. When he saw her there was a sheepish quality to his glance. Surely he knew—how could he not?—he'd become unbearable at work and to live with. Yet what was up with that tiny circle of softening in her chest? She had to ignore it, harden up like he had, or she'd never get away.

"Good morning, John," she said, as if she'd walked into a business meeting.

"Polly." He kept spooning the cereal to his mouth yet watched her move around the kitchen.

She poured herself a cup of coffee, spilled in some creamer, took a sip and smiled. “Hmm, I’ve really missed this stuff.”

His lips quirked but not enough to call it a smile.

“I’ve decided to walk to work today.”

He’d finished his cereal and dropped the bowl into the sink. “It’s supposed to get really hot, you may want a ride home.”

“No, thanks.” She rummaged through the cupboard to find a bowl and poured herself some cereal, too. They liked the same brand, just as they liked so many other similar things.

Didn’t matter. That was the past. This was her future. The new Polly only lived for Polly now, regardless of a guy’s taste in cereal.

“I’ve got surgery in an hour, so if you’re sure you don’t want a ride…”

“I’m sure.”

He stopped before he left the kitchen, gray suit slacks fitting perfectly, white dress shirt tucked in over a flat stomach, his muscular arms apparent through the sleeves. She didn’t want to notice any of it, but couldn’t help herself. He turned round and studied her, as if seeing her for the first time. Maybe he was wondering what he was doing, letting a stranger share his home. Or maybe he sensed the new, determined Polly, the one eager to take life by the horns again. She honestly couldn’t tell from the gaze he gave her. Neither did she care.

“I’ll try not to make any scenes at work today.”

Well, that was something anyway. She cocked her head and tossed him an it’s-about-time look. “Good, because that stuff gets old, fast.” Then took another drink of coffee, rather than let her heart soften one tiny bit more.

He twitched a sad smile with resigned eyes, and left.

She heard the front door click closed, and she ate the rest of her cereal feeling curiously alone. It didn't matter. She wouldn't be living here much longer.

Before she left for work, she ventured down the hall to John's study, deciding to check it out just this once. At first glance it was a typical office with dark wood desk, blotter, computer and printer. Piles of medical journals covered one section.

Something on the book case against the wall caught her eye. A small glass orb sitting on a solid gold holder with the inscription "Forever", and inside the orb two wedding rings lay overlapped. Not only did Lisa live on in his heart, she lived real as life itself in his office. Polly had wondered what precious object John had kept from Lisa. It turned out he'd kept the whole marriage. His vows had gone beyond "till death do us part." Evidently they extended for ever. She had never stood a chance.

"Darren," she said later that morning at work, "is there any way you can help me move this weekend?"

"That bad, huh?" The ex-navy man may have let his body go, but his posture was always erect. He turned to look into her eyes. "Are you sure it's the right thing to do? I mean, you just moved in."

"It's a long story, Dare. I just need to get away. I don't have much stuff. All I need is one car trip to the Lower East Side, otherwise I'll have to make a dozen trips on the subway."

He put his hand on top of hers. "I'll help you. Does he know?"

"Here's the deal. I want my moving out to have some

impact. If I come out and tell him, he'll just say…whatever, and I need him to feel something. Other than anger, he's forgotten how to feel."

She folded her arms and chewed her lower lip. "I probably don't mean anything to him any more, but I want him to be hit by my not being there." She shook her head, giving a brief exhalation through her nose. "He probably won't even notice I'm gone."

Darren leveled a serious look at her. "You don't see it, but I do. That guy is crazy mad in love with you. Men don't process stuff the same way women do. Maybe you should be patient."

"I've been patient all my life, Dare. I'm done. All I've ever done was tag along, grateful to have a place to live, grateful for whatever crumbs I got. I need more than that now. I deserve it."

"We all deserve things. Life doesn't always cooperate, that's all. Take Dr. Rodriguez and Dr. Woods that everyone has been talking about these last several weeks. They were supposed to be in love and some lawsuit got in the way. Here's a little surprise for you—everyone has them broken up for good, but not me. Everyone say's they've got too much to overcome and they're both too stubborn, but not me. I see how he watches her whenever they're both on our ward. She acts all 'oh, he doesn't know I exist' but he's totally aware of her.

"That's how it is with Dr. Griffin and you. Polly, the man has lost everything in his life, now you're leaving him, too. I'm your friend and I'm asking you to think about not moving out. Maybe just give it some more time."

Surprised by how observant Darren had been, she stared at him and considered his caution.

"I don't have any more time. I'm a shadow in John's house and I need to be so much more than that. Until he snaps out of it, I may as well be a ghost." She put her hand on Darren's arm. "I can't be a ghost any more. Thank you for being my friend and helping me move."

"Sure, kid. Someone's got to look out for a small-town girl like you in the Big Apple."

She hugged him and they spent the rest of their lunch hour working out the details. Polly knew John liked to go to his athletic club on Sunday afternoons for racketball, and she planned to be gone by the time he got home.

On Monday morning John waited for Polly to get up, but didn't hear a thing. He'd gotten home late last night as after racketball he'd gone out to dinner with Carl, his friend since childhood, had laid the whole sorry tale at the guy's feet and had gotten some insight on what a jackass he'd been. Most importantly, Carl had given him some solid advice. This morning John put his wedding rings inside a box and packed them away in the office closet. Lisa was gone. She was never coming back. Polly was here. Alive.

Her door had been closed when he'd come home last night, and he hadn't wanted to disturb her, even though he'd had some major apologies to make and had found it hard to wait to get them off his chest. Regardless, he'd gone directly to bed.

Why did the place feel so deadly quiet this morning? The hairs on his arms rose. He knocked and jiggled the doorhandle. "Polly?"

He opened the door to an empty room. Every breath

of life she'd brought into his world had dissipated. The effect of negative air sucked the wind from his lungs.

She'd left him. After the total ass he'd been lately, why should he be surprised?

Entering her room, a pang of loneliness dug so deep it may as well have taken him by the lapels and thrown him against the wall. She was gone. Had left without saying goodbye.

He walked around the room, inhaling the tell-tale scent of Polly. Lemon water and flowery bath gel, and the bouquet of her gloriously wavy hair on the pillow. God, he missed her. He'd played his hand so incompetently he didn't deserve to have her back. But how could he go on without her?

He searched the room. Circling the bed, he found the table drawer ajar. Inside, something pink caught his eye. He pulled open the drawer and discovered a pair of tiny booties. One pink. One blue.

The air went out of his lungs again as he realized the significance, as his heart squeezed with anguish. With eyes stinging, the whisper of what John had lost became reality. Their baby was gone. He'd lost another part of himself to tragedy.

How much more could he bear?

Tears tracked down his cheeks as he sat on the bed and fingered the tiny slippers, perfectly knit by Polly. How long would he punish himself for his mistakes? Something crackled inside the pink slipper and he put his index finger inside, practically filling the entire bootie, and found a small folded piece of tissue-thin paper.

Opening it, he had to squint several times to clear the burning tears blurring his vision.

Dear Caledonia (Callie) or Sterling (Mort)

Oh, God, how was he supposed to be able to read the note? His heartache deflated and oozed out onto his skin, making him fragile and achy.

Polly had written a letter to their miscarried baby. He swallowed, unsuccessfully, the knot of anguish in his throat and continued to read.

I know it's foolish to write you this letter, but I needed to tell you how happy I was when I found out you were growing inside me. I've never been so lucky in my life. For once I would have somebody to love with all of my heart, someone who would look up to me and love me back.

I remember my mother, and I know how important a mother is. I miss her as much as I miss you. I'm so sorry I didn't get to know you, or to be your mommy. We would have been so happy...

Pain tore at John's throat and down his chest. He could hardly breathe it hurt so much. She'd taken the words he'd buried inside and put them on paper. He wanted to be a father more than anything, but had been afraid to admit it. He'd substituted his young patients for his lost child. How could such a young woman as Polly be so much wiser than him?

John clenched his jaws and cried silently over all he'd lost. Soon the intensity of his grief and loss overcame him. Foreign, keening sounds emitted from his throat over everything gone or dead in his life. Finally, he let it all out. He hadn't sobbed this much since 9/11.

Oh, God. But Polly was alive. He'd practically ignored her and now he'd let the best thing to happen to him in over a decade slip away. What a fool he was.

Polly was the most honest person he'd ever met. She'd been kicked in the gut by life yet had refused to lie down. She was optimism and energy and sweetness in the flesh. Instead of burying her feelings the way he had, she'd put them on paper and written to her unborn child. She'd suffered terribly, losing the baby, and when she'd needed him most, what had he done? He'd pulled inward, sent her to the guest room, as if turning his back on her.

How stupid could a guy get?

Maybe it was time for him to quit kicking himself. Sure, he'd screwed up plenty, but Polly was living proof that a life could change. He wanted to change for her.

He'd made so many mistakes—too many to count—but he couldn't let Polly be one of them. He loved her. Absolutely. He did. There was no doubt in his mind. And he missed her, with all the enthusiasm and spirit she'd brought to his dull life. He craved her, the desire and lust she'd reawakened in him. She'd made his life so much better on countless levels.

But more than anything, he needed her back.

She'd never felt wanted since her mother had died, and he couldn't change that, but he sure as hell could change her not feeling wanted by him! She deserved to know without a doubt that she was loved, and cherished, and would be for the rest of her life if she'd just give him a second chance.

There was only one way to get his point across. In person. He picked up the phone, called work, spoke to Brooke and made sure Polly was there.

He ran down the hall and splashed some water in his

face, then did everything in his power to make himself look presentable. He wanted to look good the next time he faced the love for the rest of his life.

Polly flushed the line in the IV piggyback after delivering the antibiotics to four-year-old Jeffrey Pomeroy the third. The adorable little boy slept soundly even though he was inside a body cast that defied the word "comfort".

When she'd disposed of the syringe she noticed Dr. Woods across the ward, looking at a computer. Not more than fifteen feet away stood Dr. Rodriguez, pretending to read a report, but he was watching her. How could the woman not feel that smoldering gaze? Before long, Dr. Woods's pretty blonde head lifted and her gaze drifted towards and locked with Dr. Rodriguez's dark and mesmerizing stare. Quicker than a hummingbird, her eyes flitted away, but it was undeniably there, that one intense second had said it all—they definitely weren't over by a long shot. Polly shook her head and smiled to herself. That Darren knew a lot more than he let on.

She went back into the patient room and prepared to give her second patient a bed bath. All the while she thought about Dr. Woods and Dr. Rodriguez, and the one person she couldn't get out of her head or heart, John.

"Polly Seymour?" She heard John's distinct voice echo off the walls. "Polly. Get out here!" He'd promised to behave after last Friday's outburst. Oh, God, had he lost it altogether? Would someone be calling Security and taking him away soon?

Sheepishly peeking around the threshold first, she ventured out of the patient room. Anything to quiet him down until Security could arrive. The poor patients and their families didn't need to be subjected to his unpredictable and escalating mood swings. The constant ache in her heart since she'd left him panged deeper.

Of course a crowd had assembled to watch the poor man's demise. Brooke and Rafael, Darren, not looking the least bit alarmed, and all the other nurses and technicians she'd grown to know and enjoy from working with them. Even Dr. Woods and Dr. Rodriguez were there, still exchanging quick passionate glances, while lingering on the fringes of the group, most likely wondering what was going on with their colleague. Everyone huddled around the nurses' station, watching John, who looked amazingly dashing for a man on the verge of professional suicide.

"Polly." He spoke the word now, softened the tone of his voice, as if her appearance had taken the edge off. He smiled an honest-to-God, no mistaking expression of his happiness at seeing her.

Though shaking inside, she hoped beyond hope that if she played it cool and calculated she could de-escalate his impending meltdown. Polly schooled her voice. "Yes, John?" She could humor him until the hospital security squad arrived.

"You forgot something."

She stood cemented to the spot, her heart rapping a wild rhythm all the way up to her ears, watching as he pulled out the booties from the pocket of his doctor's jacket. Heat started at her clavicles and traveled to her neck, soon invading her cheeks. He'd found them. He'd discovered she'd let herself get so carried away with loving and longing for her baby that she'd knitted booties. Booties for a baby who would never be born.

Did he think she was pitiful?

"I need you to finish these," he said. "No. That's not

entirely true." His voice was now low enough for only those in the front row of the crowd to hear. Others got on tiptoe and leaned in towards the spectacle of their department chief confronting the newest staff nurse. "What I need…is you. You, Polly. The thing is, I finally realize I can't live without you."

He came toward her, took her hand, and that tender look he'd had after each time they'd made love was back in his eyes.

"I love you, Polly. You belong with me. You've got to finish these booties because we're going to need them. After you marry me and…"

Applause broke out. Time stopped. With her heart reeling, she quickly glanced around the room, catching Dr. Woods and Dr. Rodriguez smiling at each other. Beside them, Darren grinned first at the lovebird doctors then at her.

"I told you so," Darren mouthed.

Real time snapped back in, ungluing Polly from the spot, and she grabbed John by the elbow and whisked him away to the consultation room at the far end of the ward. She closed the door. What she had to say needed to be said in private.

"What makes you think I *want* to marry you?"

He wore a goofy grin and dreamy eyes, and she could tell there would be no reasoning with him. "Because you're a smart girl, and I love you, and I want you in my life." His fingertips traced the length of her jaw.

She dropped her head back and stared at the ceiling for guidance. No one had ever wanted her before, but that was no reason to let him seduce her with words.

He grasped her neck, brought her head up straight in line with his lips and delivered a tender, sincere kiss.

Nothing fancy, just his warm lips to her startled ones, and she felt his touch all the way down to the tips of her toes.

"I was a total jerk after the miscarriage, but I've come to my senses." He dangled the booties before her eyes as if to hypnotize her. "You did this on purpose, didn't you? Left these behind."

She glanced at his delving, dark eyes and quickly studied a speck on his white doctor's coat. "Maybe."

He took both of her hands in his. "I know you've never really felt like you belonged anywhere, honey, but I'm the guy to end it. The buck stops with me. I'm your man. The one who loves you. I'm the man who wants to spend the rest of his life with you." He looked so deeply into her eyes she was positive he could read her brainwaves, which were dancing around erratically and happily over his proposal. "So I guess the question of the day is, do you love me?"

Tiny pins stabbed behind her eyes as tears that she'd sworn she'd never cry again for John Griffin materialized. "I couldn't bear it if you ever shut me out again, John. You have to promise me you'll always talk to me no matter how hard or how horrible your feelings are."

He held her arms and kept her steady. Steady as his warm brown gaze. "I promise to love and honor you, to share the good, the bad, and the ugly, whether you want to hear it or not." His lopsided smile appeared. "How's that for opening up?"

How could she not adore a face like that? A tiny laugh escaped her trembling lips.

"I do love you, Johnny."

His smile morphed into a huge grin and spread from jaw to jaw as he took her into his arms. "So it's settled, then." He grew serious and kissed her again, this time with much more gusto, enough to spread warmth across her chest and make her toes curl in her clogs. After several more seconds of deeply attentive kisses dazzling enough to make her head swim and her heart believe he truly wanted and loved her, he stopped.

"Then let's blow this joint and get married, dumpling. Do you like the sound of that? The married part, I mean?"

Staring into the eyes of the man she'd fallen head over heels in love with on short notice, the man she'd run the gamut of any other long-term relationship in her life, but this time on hyper-speed, she could only think of one succinct yet most appropriate answer.

"I do."

EPILOGUE

Eleven months later...

"BE CAREFUL!" JOHN SAID, jumping up to help Polly walk across the living room.

"I'm fine, Johnny, seriously." She held her swollen belly as if it might fall off her body if she didn't, and wobbled toward the kitchen.

John tagged along behind her. "How's the back?"

"Achy," she said, looking into the face of the man she loved and trusted more than anyone on earth, "but I'll survive."

"I've got your suitcase packed and ready to go, just like the midwife instructed," he said, hovering like a penguin on a newborn. "Say the word and we'll go to the hospital."

Polly put her hands on her back, the habit she'd developed during the last few months of her pregnancy, and smiled at John. "It's not quite time yet, honey-bunches, but thanks."

Once in the kitchen, she opened a cupboard and started to reach for a glass. John jumped between her and the glassware and got one down for her. "Water?"

"Yes, please."

"Sit. I'll bring it to you." He pointed toward the table and she obeyed.

Since she'd been on maternity leave for the last two weeks, with twenty-four hours a day of intense attention from John and a uterus that felt ready to explode, no one was more anxious to deliver the babies than she. Babies. Yes. Two. A boy and a girl. She pinched herself. It wasn't a dream. Polly liked to blame those pink and blue booties for the twins. Maybe if she'd stuck to one color she wouldn't feel as if she had a small crowd inside her. But with John's loving care, the four of them had been getting along beautifully over the past nine months.

If she didn't count the constant acid reflux and a diaphragm so under pressure that taking deep breaths was almost impossible, she'd say life was perfect.

Polly sat on the kitchen chair, and John was quick to pull out another so she could elevate her feet, then he handed her the water. Just as she swallowed her first sip, Callie and Sterling decided to take a run around the indoor gym and pool.

"Oh!" She quickly set the glass on the table and sat straighter.

"What is it?" John jumped to his feet again then dropped to one knee in front of her. The poor man hadn't had a moment's rest since she'd announced with pride he'd made her pregnant again. And Polly had never felt more wanted and cared for.

She couldn't talk as pain escalated like she'd never experienced before. Her eyes bugged out and she held her breath.

"Don't forget to breathe, dumpling, remember what the birthing coach told you." John looked at his watch. These days she really did feel like a dumpling.

The labor pain began to let up and she relaxed into the chair. "How far apart are we now?"

"Four minutes. Are you ready to go to the hospital yet?"

She shook her head. "Let's walk a little bit first, okay?"

She loved her evening walks along the East River, even though it was hotter than usual this July. The last thing she wanted to do was show up at Labor and Delivery when she hadn't even begun to dilate, and a walk by the river might just be the ticket to moving her labor along. Dr. Bernstein was thrilled she'd carried the pregnancy the whole nine months, but with John's tender loving care she wasn't the least bit surprised.

John didn't look convinced that a walk during early labor was such a great idea but, as with almost everything else in their life together, he wanted to please her. "Okay, then, let's go." He helped her to her feet and they headed for the door.

By the time they'd reached the street, Polly was having another contraction. She stood perfectly still and tried to breathe. John rubbed her shoulders and lower back as she did.

"This time it was three minutes," he said. "Change your mind about going to the hospital yet?"

The contraction had lasted longer and felt more intense, and even though John was a doctor she wanted to be around the trained midwife and OB nurses when she delivered. She nodded. "Okay, call the hospital and let them know we're coming in."

John's eyes went wide as he dug out his cell phone and pushed autodial. "It's really happening?" He squeezed her hand, excitement and fear registering in his gaze.

"Yes. Maybe you should get my suitcase."

"And leave you alone?"

"Marco can watch me until you get back."

John hesitated, but when Marco got a chair for Polly to sit on while she waited, he dashed back into the building, heading for the elevator.

Ten hours later…

John watched his wife snuggle with their newborns. Her hair had grown thicker and curlier with the pregnancy, and the sight of her holding the twins, well, she was never more beautiful. In awe, he looked on. The babies had tiny fingers and toes, and nostrils that couldn't possibly pass enough air to keep them alive. Amazing. Nothing short of a miracle.

His kids. His wife.

If he'd performed back-to-back hip replacements, he couldn't have been more exhausted, yet being with his new family energized him. Polly had worked like a trouper during labor, and he'd been by her side every step of the way. The sight of Caledonia entering the world had brought tears to his eyes and when he got to hold Sterling seconds after his birth, he'd thought he might pass out for fear of dropping or injuring his son.

What a team they'd been, Polly in mid-contraction breathing and pushing, John holding her hand, cheering her on. *You can do it. Don't give up.* Like a fearless warrior she'd gone through labor fighting her way to victory, eager to get to the prize. Now, watching his children with their mother, the abundance of love and blessings welling in his heart made his eyes go bleary. Nothing could ever match this most special moment in time.

"We did it," Polly said. "We made beautiful babies."

He cupped her face and saw his children squirm in Polly's arms. "With me as their father they only had a fifty-fifty chance of that beautiful part, you know."

She grinned and shook her head. "They'll be strong and smart because of you."

"And they'll always know they're loved."

"Yes. Just like I do."

After all the losses John had experienced in his forty years on the planet, through Polly he'd learned to trust that life could still bestow wonders and joy, too. She'd complained he was way too protective of her, but she'd slowly gotten used to it. She'd had no choice.

"Now I'll be on triple duty, watching over all of you," he said, pride ringing from each word.

"You poor man, you're bound to wear out!" She feigned worry, but he knew she was delighted he'd promised to always be there for his family.

"Never."

He snapped a picture with his phone and sent it to Brooke to share with the hospital staff.

"We're going to have to work as a team with these little dumplings," she said.

He'd been warned by younger colleagues that nothing was more difficult than being a parent.

"We'll be the perfect team," he said. "You. Me. Callie and Sterling."

John gazed at his family in the hospital bed while reeling with ever-expanding love in his heart. Since meeting and opening his life and love to Polly, becoming a husband and now a father, he knew one thing deeper and better than anything else in the world.

No matter how many curve balls life threw at him, as long as Polly and the kids were by his side he would survive anything.

* * * * *

NYC ANGELS: AN EXPLOSIVE REUNION

BY

ALISON ROBERTS

First published in Great Britain 2013
by Mills & Boon, an imprint of Harlequin (UK) Limited.
Harlequin (UK) Limited, Eton House, 18-24 Paradise Road,
Richmond, Surrey TW9 1SR

Special thanks and acknowledgement are given to Alison Roberts for her contribution to the *NYC Angels* series

ISBN: 978 0 263 89896 5

Harlequin (UK) policy is to use papers that are natural, renewable and recyclable products and made from wood grown in sustainable forests. The logging and manufacturing process conform to the legal environmental regulations of the country of origin.

Printed and bound in Spain
by Blackprint CPI, Barcelona

Dear Reader

Visiting New York City is pretty high on my bucket list of things I want to do.

When I was six years old I had a year living in Bethesda, Maryland. I went to school there, and had all the fun of big, big snow in the winter and a 'real' Halloween. I still have a major fondness for both events.

I just loved doing the research for this **NYC Angels** continuity book. Not only did I get to include Halloween, but I was also obliged to spend many hours learning about a magic city that I fully intend to see in the not so distant future. I've fallen in love with Central Park already, because it's very close to the Angel Mendez Children's Hospital and snuck into my story.

Even better, I had a feisty Texan heroine, a gorgeous hero, and a past conflict between them that was *huge*. My Alex and Layla had a lot of growing to do and stuff to sort out before they could get anywhere near a happy ending.

I loved getting so close to them on their journey to really discover each other. Hope you do too!

Lots of love and happy reading!

Alison xxx

NYC Angels

Children's doctors who work hard and love even harder…
in the city that never sleeps!

Step into the world of NYC Angels and enjoy two new stories a month

In March New York's most notoriously sinful bachelor Jack Carter found a woman he wanted to spend more than just one night with in
NYC ANGELS: REDEEMING THE PLAYBOY
by Carol Marinelli

And reluctant socialite Eleanor Aston made the gossip headlines when the paparazzi discovered her baby bombshell
NYC ANGELS: HEIRESS'S BABY SCANDAL
by Janice Lynn

In April cheery physiotherapist Molly Shriver melted the icy barricades around hotshot surgeon Dan Morris's damaged heart in
NYC ANGELS: UNMASKING DR SERIOUS
by Laura Iding

And Lucy Edwards was finally tempted to let neurosurgeon Ryan O'Doherty in. But their fragile relationship had to survive her most difficult revelation yet…
NYC ANGELS: THE WALLFLOWER'S SECRET
by Susan Carlisle

In May, newly single (and strictly off-limits!) Chloe Jenkins made it very difficult for drop-dead-gorgeous Brad Davis to resist temptation…!
NYC ANGELS: FLIRTING WITH DANGER
by Tina Beckett

And after meeting single dad Lewis Jackson, tough-cookie Head Nurse Scarlet Miller wondered if she'd finally met her match…
NYC ANGELS: TEMPTING NURSE SCARLET
by Wendy S. Marcus

Finally join us now, in June, as bubbly new nurse Polly Seymour is the ray of sunshine that brooding doc Johnny Griffin needs in
NYC ANGELS: MAKING THE SURGEON SMILE
by Lynne Marshall

And Alex Rodriguez and Layla Woods come back into each other's orbit, trying to fool the buzzing hospital grapevine that the spark between them has died. But can they convince each other?
NYC ANGELS: AN EXPLOSIVE REUNION
by Alison Roberts

Be captivated by NYC Angels in this new eight-book continuity from Mills & Boon® Medical Romance™

These books are also available in eBook format from www.millsandboon.co.uk

CHAPTER ONE

'No.'

The single word was as dramatic as the way the man had stormed into Layla Woods's office and slammed a piece of paper onto her desk.

As dramatic as the man himself.

Alex Rodriguez was clearly furious. The waves of his thick, jet-black hair looked rumpled—as if he'd pushed angry fingers through it. Eyes that were nearly as dark glared down at Layla.

A long way down. Layla had to fight the urge to leap to her feet so that she could feel taller. Braver. But that would be a dead giveaway that she was rattled, wouldn't it? And she couldn't afford to let Alex know the effect he was still capable of having on her.

With a satisfyingly steady hand, she reached for the piece of paper. The memo she had sent out that morning to all the senior staff members here at the Angel Mendez Children's Hospital.

'This is the agenda for the next monthly report meeting.'

'And you've put me down as being the first presenter.' Alex folded his arms. 'The answer's no. I decline the invitation.'

'It's not an "invitation",' Layla flashed back. 'It's the case I've chosen to open the meeting. I'm sorry if it's inconvenient but it's your patient, Alex, therefore you present the case. End of story.'

The head of paediatric neurosurgery made an exasperated sound, turning as if he intended to storm out of her office in the same way he'd entered. Instead, he stopped beside the large window, with the backdrop of a bright blue October morning. Was he taking in the fabulous view of New York's Central Park that this prestigious top-floor office had to offer?

An office befitting Layla's position as the new chief of paediatrics at this famous hospital. Her dream job. A position that had been in jeopardy a few short weeks ago until Alex had stepped in to protect her.

'What the hell are you playing at, Layla?'

The angry tone of Alex's voice must have carried because Layla's secretary appeared at the open door. Layla gave her a tight smile.

'Hold my calls, please, Monica.' The tilt of her head conveyed the message that she wanted more than her calls held to deal with this. The door was tactfully closed as her secretary retreated.

'Well?' Alex turned back to face her and this time Layla got to her feet.

Slowly.

She walked to the other side of her desk but couldn't go any closer to Alex. The huge can of worms that represented their shared history was blocking the way.

Or maybe it was the memory of what had happened the first time they'd confronted each other since they'd both been working here at Angel's. When they'd been close enough for the flames of a sexual chemistry that had clearly never died completely to flare into that scorching kiss.

It couldn't happen again.

Their past had been precisely what had put her new job in jeopardy. Had she really been naïve enough to think that it had been so long ago it couldn't affect her life any more? That she could take a high-profile position like this and it wouldn't matter that she hadn't disclosed her involvement in the malpractice suit that had nearly destroyed Alex's career five years ago?

Somehow they had to move past this. Learn to work together.

'I had intended discussing the agenda with you. You declined the appointment I tried to set up last week.'

'I was busy.' Alex held her gaze. 'As you would have noticed if you'd bothered checking my electronic calendar.'

Layla kept her expression carefully neutral. She *had* checked his calendar but he could have easily suggested another time. They both knew the real truth. He had been avoiding her.

Since that kiss.

He hadn't even let her voice her thanks for the way he'd stepped in and defended her at the board meeting when her integrity had been under examination and it had been highly likely that they would decide she was not the right person to oversee the talented staff that Angel's was so proud of.

Being thwarted in expressing her appreciation had been a putdown but Layla's aggravation went deeper than that.

Good manners had been drummed into Layla Woods since she'd been knee high to a grasshopper and saying thank you to someone who'd done her such a huge favour wasn't just about maintaining a good appearance.

It was the right thing to do.

The idea of using the monthly report meeting had been a brainwave. OK, choosing a time she'd known Alex was busy to offer a chance to discuss the agenda could be deemed unprofessional, but Layla had had enough. She was taking control.

She hadn't expected it to backfire quite so instantly. Why hadn't Alex simply continued to avoid her? He could have asked his deputy head of neurosurgery, Ryan O'Doherty, to present the case on his behalf.

'It's not a current case,' Alex added. 'And it was successful.'

Of course it was. Layla would hardly have picked a case that was presenting a current dilemma or, worse, one that had had a bad result.

The last thing either of them would want would be to go over *that* old ground. To the case of the toddler, Jamie Kirkpatrick, that had brought them together in the first place. To the cutting-edge surgery for a complicated brain tumour that had fallen disastrously short of being successful. Jamie had died. Alex had been sued by a distraught family looking for someone to blame. He'd been cleared but Layla hadn't been there to help him celebrate, had she? She'd ended their affair the night before Jamie's surgery.

She nodded at Alex's terse summary. 'That's precisely why I chose it. We don't just put up a current, complicated issue to get the benefit of input from different specialties. Or to dissect what went wrong in a case that wasn't successful. Sometimes it's a good thing to reflect on a triumph. And Matthew *was* a triumph.'

'There are plenty of other cases you could have chosen.'

'Not one that so many people are so interested in.'

The brain tumour in the nine-year-old boy had been so rare and complicated that surgeons all over the state had refused to touch it. Until the little boy's desperate parents had brought him to Angel's as a last resort and begged Dr Rodriguez to use his legendary skills to give their son a chance to survive. And that was why it wouldn't make any difference if Ryan presented the case. Everybody already knew who the real hero was.

'The criterion for picking a case to report is that it's out of the ordinary,' Layla continued. 'From what I've heard, this one was all that everybody talked about at the time and the staff involved in the recent follow-up appointment were thrilled by Matthew's progress. I also heard that you're writing the case up for a top journal. I thought it would be nice to share that.' The occasional triumph shared at the meeting was good for everybody. A counterbalance for the heart-breaking cases.

'Shine the spotlight on someone else, Layla,' Alex growled. 'Somebody's going to wonder why you picked on me and I've been talked about more than I'm comfortable with around here lately.' Alex turned to look out of the window again as he spoke but then his gaze swerved back to Layla. 'Gossip about the Kirkpatrick case was bad enough. What happens when people start talking about the fact that I was having an affair with a married woman at the time? How do you think that's going to help my reputation?'

The glare Layla received would have intimidated anyone.

Layla straightened her spine.

'I came to Angel's for a fresh start,' Alex ground out. 'I won't allow you to drag my name through the mud.'

Oh…Lord…

OK. The plan had been to make this a public gesture of thanks, whether Alex liked it or not. She knew that this case would earn him even more respect from those colleagues who didn't know all the details of the case, even though it had been breaking news on the grapevine in the months before she'd come to Angel's. She had also known that it would be a public statement of her own faith in his abilities.

But it was a huge leap to go from not wanting her gratitude or public support to accusing her of being prepared to damage his reputation. The attack was unjustified. Unfair.

'You're not the only one who's come here for a fresh start,' Layla snapped. 'And I'm sure you haven't forgotten but I *was* the married woman. I don't want that being common knowledge any more than you do.'

'So stay away from me, then.'

Layla let out an incredulous huff. 'You're the one who came storming into *my* office.'

'Because this needed to be dealt with.'

'What needs "to be dealt with",' Layla responded, 'is the fact that we find ourselves working in the same hospital. Again.' She took a deep breath. 'It's unfortunate, I agree, but you had your chance to get rid of me. You could have let me get fired.'

'I didn't do it to protect your job and keep you here, if that's what you're thinking.'

No. That idea had been farfetched enough for Layla to have dismissed it at the time.

Almost.

'So why *did* you do it?' she asked quietly.

'Because I'm not going to let my past dictate my future. The Kirkpatrick case did enough damage already. I stood up for you because…because it was the right thing to do.'

Thanking him had seemed like the right thing to do, too, but he wouldn't let her. Now Layla wasn't even sure she wanted to thank him. Had he just been facing his own demons? Making them a part of a past that didn't matter any more?

She had to look away. 'Well…we're going to have to work together. I'm not about to leave a job I've only just started.'

'Neither am I.'

He was still angry. Layla could feel the waves of it reaching her across the distance she'd been careful to maintain between them. She could also feel other currents mixed in with the anger. Like his determination to succeed and the fierce intelligence with which he was assessing his options. And beneath all of that she could feel his raw magnetism and power. The charisma that Alex Rodriguez wore like a second skin.

There seemed to be nothing left to say.

They were at an impasse. Both of them struggling to

take control of their present by focussing on the future and dismissing the past.

Could it be that easy?

Layla had to make an effort to swallow. 'Fine. Then let's start as we mean to go on from now on. I've set the agenda for the meeting. I'll look forward to hearing your presentation, Dr Rodriguez.'

Alex said nothing. With no more than another searing glance, he turned and left her office.

Two days later and people were filing into the small lecture theatre tucked away on an upper floor, along with the operating theatres. Some were carrying Styrofoam cups of coffee and paper bags containing sandwiches and some were reading messages on their pagers. All of them would have a notebook and pen available.

Fellow Texan, neonatal doctor Tyler Donaldson came in, protectively ushering his now very pregnant fiancée, Eleanor, into a front-row seat where she would have plenty of room. Eleanor smiled at Layla.

'Don't mind me if I have to sneak out to the bathroom,' she said. 'My bladder capacity is shrinking by the day.'

'Yeah…' Tyler beamed proudly. 'And that little rodeo rider in there likes to work out and use it for a punching bag.'

Layla returned the smile but said nothing. She wasn't in the mood for baby talk and Tyler might be an old friend but it wasn't exactly professional to sit there holding hands with Eleanor, was it?

There was a quiet buzz of conversation going on and seats were being filled but there was still no sign of Alex. Layla gave Ryan a questioning look, her head tilted towards the door. As Alex's second-in-command, surely he would know where the senior neurosurgeon was? But Ryan merely shrugged and then turned to his companion, a smile on his face as he responded to some comment. The atmosphere in here was relaxed and why wouldn't it be?

There was no blame, no shame for unsuccessful cases but the discussion could get robust. What could have been done differently? What *would* be done differently next time? Hindsight was a wonderful thing when it could be used for a good purpose. You could never say they didn't learn from mistakes around these parts.

Could Layla say that about herself?

Professionally, of course she could.

Personally? Layla suddenly became aware that she was tapping her foot impatiently. How long had she been doing that? Had anyone noticed? Her foot stilled.

Of course she could say that she learned from personal mistakes.

She hadn't got married again, had she?

She had challenged Alex, though. She hadn't heard a peep out of him since that tense exchange in her office and she'd been left wondering if he would back down and appear to present his case. Surely he would guess that a non-appearance would start people talking even more than if he'd shown up as her star turn of the day?

There was an air of expectancy in the room now. These were busy people. They only had an hour to spare and they were all giving up their lunch-breaks to attend. There were a few empty seats but that was normal. Some people couldn't make it on the day, even if they were rostered to present a case, but that was OK, too, because they always had more cases lined up than they ended up having time to discuss.

She'd give Alex exactly one more minute to show up.

'Aren't you supposed to be at Monthly Report?'

'Yep.' Alex Rodriguez was facing his half-brother, Cade. Both men were semi-crouched and already sweating in the midday September sunshine that bathed the small area out the back of the ambulance bay where a basketball hoop was attached to the wall.

Alex had control of the ball right now, bouncing it in sharp movements as his body wove from side to side, looking for an opening to get closer to the hoop.

'So why aren't you?'

'Could ask you the same question.'

'Hey, I was only going to listen. Aren't you supposed to be presenting a case?'

Alex ignored the question. With a lunge, he dived sideways, scooping up the ball and firing it at the hoop. With a resounding thump it hit the backboard and went through the net.

'*Yes…*'

Both men went for the ball as it bounced on the tarmac. This time Cade made contact first and gleefully took control.

'You may as well give up, bro. Go and have a shower and make Layla happy.'

'What the hell is that supposed to mean?'

'*Whoa…*' Cade caught the ball instead of bouncing it and spun it on his hand. 'Who put the burr under your saddle?'

Using Layla's Texan drawl, along with a phrase

they'd both heard her use, was like rubbing salt into the wound. With a move Cade didn't see coming Alex knocked the ball from his hand and took off across the court, scoring another goal.

Cade laughed. Game on. For several minutes they played hard, ignoring the heat and the sweat and how out of breath they were getting.

No way was Alex going to go to that meeting and *make Layla happy.* It wasn't so much that this was obviously a public pat on the back for a case that had gone so well, it was the string-pulling that he could sense going on behind it.

OK, he'd done Layla a favour but he'd done it in order to face his own demons, not to protect her. He didn't want her thanks.

Hell, no…

Because if she got close enough to thank him properly, he knew exactly what could happen. Had already happened. That chemistry between them would explode and they'd end up in a clinch, kissing like there was no tomorrow.

And, God help him, he was not going to let it happen again.

Who the hell did Layla think she was that she could pull a string or two and have people dancing to her tune?

He'd told her that he didn't want to present. She'd had plenty of time to back down and change the agenda and she hadn't done so despite knowing that it could kick off a fresh wave of gossip. Well…he wasn't even going to put in an apology for the meeting.

He just wasn't going to show up. They might have to

work together again but was going to do it on his terms, thank you very much.

She could deal with that. By herself.

This was getting borderline embarrassing.

From her position on the podium Layla nodded at the group. It was time to begin. Her heels sounded loud on the podium, rapping smartly on the wood as she moved to the microphone attached to the lectern. She tapped it gently to check it was on.

'Howdy, folks. Glad y'all could make it.' Her smile was bright. Along with good manners, Layla Woods had grown up knowing exactly how to present the perfect public face, no matter what was going on inside her head.

Or her heart, for that matter.

'Looks like our first presenter is missing in action,' she continued, 'so let's get the ball rolling with our second case. Dr Donaldson is going to share one of our neonatal department's case histories.'

'Thanks, darlin'…' Tyler reluctantly let go of Eleanor's hand and strolled up to the podium. He winked at Layla as he inserted a memory stick into the data projector.

Layla kept her smile in place with difficulty. She knew what that wink was about just as clearly as she could sense the significant looks being passed between the people seated in the tiered rows in here. They all knew that Alex's name was on the top of the agenda. Now they were all wondering if he really had an emergency keeping him away or if there was something else going on. Were some of those rumours circulating about a romantic involvement between Alex and Layla true?

'Meet Madeline,' Tyler Donaldson announced, as a photograph of a tiny, premature baby almost hidden by wires and tubes came up on the screen. 'Born at a gestation of twenty-five weeks, this li'l gal weighed in at six hundred and eighty grams and measured thirty-two centimetres. She was intubated immediately after birth and given positive pressure ventilation due to her prematurity.'

To outward appearances, Layla was listening attentively to the presentation of all the complications this baby had had but in reality she was trying to unravel the knot of anger forming in her gut.

He could have put in an apology for the meeting. Or arranged for Ryan to present the case. They could have both kept their dignity intact and made a fresh start by putting their professional lives onto some kind of an even keel. The gossip would be fuelled by his non-appearance with no explanation. Layla didn't like being the subject of gossip. She didn't like the ashes of the past being raked over. Would she ever get away from the mistake she'd made in getting involved with Alex in the first place?

Don't you mean get over *him*?

That tiny voice in the back of her mind got ruthlessly silenced. Layla glared at Tyler.

This was all his fault, wasn't it? They'd known each other practically their whole lives. Ty knew how badly her marriage had ended and how strained her relationship with her family was. OK, maybe he hadn't known about the affair that had spelt the end of that marriage, or that Alex had been the man she'd had an affair with, but it had been Ty who'd persuaded her to apply for the job here at Angel's.

The job that meant she and Alex were working at the same hospital.

Again.

Layla took a deep breath and tried to tune in to what Tyler was saying about the complex surgery baby Madeline had had to go through. The fleeting thought that his specialty had to be harder now that his fiancée was pregnant with his own baby only led Layla straight back to her own personal issues.

Like how she was going to deal with the tension between Alex and herself. It wasn't just about avoiding damage to their reputations, was it? There was still something there. Something powerful. That kiss had been more than enough to make it obvious. And, despite what Alex had said, she didn't believe that doing the right thing had been the only motive for defending her against the management board.

Did he care about her on some level?

Did she care about him?

Not like that. Layla may have fallen in love with him the first time around but the disaster the affair had created in her life had been enough for those emotions to morph into simmering resentment at how thoroughly her life had been derailed. Whatever was still hanging around was about lust, not love. But, man, that sexual chemistry hadn't lost any of its power, had it?

She just needed to learn to control it.

Like she tried to control everything else in her life?

Good grief, that little voice was annoying. A control

freak? Her? Well…Layla had to admit she'd engineered what had been supposed to have happened today but look how well that had worked.

She was already planning how to get around it, though, wasn't she? To take control some other way. Instead of thanking him now, part of her wanted to let Alex know just how aggravated she was with the way he had dropped her into covering for his absence and fielding the ensuing curiosity.

She wanted to demonstrate that she was able to stand up for herself.

Like she had when he'd put her aside just before little Jamie's operation?

When she hadn't been prepared to stand aside quietly and she'd taken control and told him it was all over?

Why had she chosen the night before the surgery to take her stand? She could have contributed to why Jamie's case hadn't turned out to be the kind of miracle that the case she'd asked Alex to present today was.

The guilt was still there, wasn't it? Not just that she'd been cheating on her husband but that she might have made a difference to Alex's performance that day.

And maybe *that* was why it had seemed so important that she got the chance to thank Alex.

And why he didn't want to hear it.

Why did it matter so much, anyway? It had been years and years ago. They'd both moved on.

Or had they?

Impossible not to remember that kiss…

It had been the last thing she had expected.

No. Maybe the *last* thing she had expected had been the way she'd responded to it. To have stepped so far back in time to when her desire for this man had made her throw her caution to the winds, along with too many of the values she'd grown up believing she held. They'd been fried in the heat that one touch from Alex could generate. Even now, Layla could feel a flicker of that heat, deep in her belly.

Was she blushing? Was that why there was this sudden silence all around her and why everybody seemed to be looking at her?

No. On an inward groan Layla realised that Tyler had finished his presentation. They were waiting for her, as the meeting's chairperson, to move things along.

Her smile was bright. 'Sorry, folks… Such an interesting case, I got lost in my thoughts. Anyone want to ask a question or add something?'

Several hands were raised and heart surgeon Molly Shriver got the nod.

'Can you talk us through your choice of antibiotic to deal with the pneumonia? And did you consider a blood transfusion immediately after the first surgery?'

Layla couldn't help looking past Molly, up into the dimmer corners of the lecture theatre where someone could have arrived unnoticed during Tyler's presentation by using the back stairs.

Not that she really needed the visual confirmation that Alex wasn't present. She could feel it. Like a shadow blocking the sun.

Forced to stop the hard physical activity due to exhaustion, Alex bent over, palms on his thighs, fighting to catch his breath again. Cade mirrored his action.

'It's working,' Cade panted. 'Think I've pulled the burr out from *my* saddle, anyway. How 'bout you?'

Again, Alex ignored the query. 'So what was your beef?'

'I'm fed up,' Cade growled. 'I was in charge of my department back in L.A. I don't like being told what to do like I'm just an intern. Getting squeezed out of the best cases. Having my decisions second-guessed.'

'You knew you were going to be second-in-charge when you took this job.'

'Yeah...I just didn't know how much I wouldn't like it. I'm beginning to think I should have followed your example and tried the other side of the world to escape. Australia is looking pretty damned attractive right now.'

'You didn't have something big enough to get away from.'

'Wanna bet?' Cade had caught his breath. He was moving again. His expression suggested he needed to blow off a bit more steam. He certainly didn't want to expand on that cryptic comment.

Alex tucked it away. He'd find out. He knew better than to push his half-brother to reveal more than he was ready to. It was too fragile, this newly re-formed relationship they'd managed to forge in the wake of the recent trouble.

Cade scored another goal. He was well ahead of Alex now.

'Anyway...' he panted, letting Alex get the ball again. 'It's all sorted, isn't it? The whole deal with that malpractice suit. You know I'm sorry for letting the cat out of the bag but we're good now, aren't we?'

'Yeah...' Alex was standing still, taking aim at the

basket. Better than he could have hoped they'd ever be, that was for sure, given their history.

'And it's all out in the open and they're not going to fire you. Any more than they're going to fire Layla after you stood up for her.'

Alex missed the hoop and swore softly. He grabbed the ball as it bounced and took aim again.

He just couldn't get away from it, could he?

Away from Layla.

Away from the memories.

The demons he'd tried to deal with by running away after the malpractice suit that had followed the Jamie Kirkpatrick case were only part of the story.

Cade was trying to distract him from shooting the goal. Standing in front of him and waving his arms. He was grinning. He didn't know that Layla was another demon.

He'd heard she was divorced now. Well…no surprises there. Alex could feel sorry for the mug she'd conned into marrying her in the first place. Had she just dumped him—the way she'd dumped *him* when she'd got bored with their affair?

Affair.

Nasty little word but there was no getting away from the facts. He'd had an affair with a married woman. He wasn't proud of it and he certainly didn't want people to start talking about it. Had Cade been getting away from something that bad?

Now wasn't the time to find out. It was too hot for this and they both needed to go and shower and cool off.

Alex took another shot at the basket and the ball went through without even touching the backboard.

'Nobody's getting fired,' he finally agreed. 'And the whole mess taught me something very valuable.'

'Oh?' By tacit agreement, both men were calling it a draw and finishing the match. They high-fived each other and started walking back into the hospital.

'You don't beat demons by running away from them,' Alex told his younger brother. 'You can only beat them by confronting them.'

The sound Cade made was dismissive and Alex couldn't blame him for his disbelief.

He wasn't exactly confronting the demons that Layla represented, was he? He'd been avoiding her like the plague ever since she'd tried to thank him for standing up for her and saving her job. And then he'd marched into her office and told her to stay away from him. How was that supposed to sort anything out? And had he been entirely truthful? He'd told her that he'd gone to that board meeting to defend her because the Kirkpatrick case had done enough damage and it should be left in the past, but weren't the feelings Layla stirred part and parcel of the whole Jamie Kirkpatrick business anyway?

It had been so hard to put her aside so he could focus on that little boy's surgery. And he still suspected, deep in his heart, that the body blow of getting dumped the night before that high-profile operation had been why he hadn't been completely on top of his game that day. Yes, the demons were so intertwined they were impossible to separate.

Which meant he hadn't really confronted anything, despite letting the whole thing get aired in public again. Maybe he'd made it worse by giving Layla a reason to be grateful to him. He certainly hadn't helped his cause by giving her something to be angry about today.

Deliberately avoiding her hadn't done the trick. Fronting up and warning her hadn't achieved much either. And Layla was right about one thing. If they both wanted to keep their jobs here, they had to find a way of being able to work in the same hospital.

A corner of Alex's mouth lifted in a wry smile. Maybe he'd subconsciously realised that what he needed was to have Layla avoid him. The way she had after Jamie's death when she wouldn't even acknowledge him. All that was needed was a good push to get her started and what better way than a public refusal to let her jerk his strings?

Alex stood under the cool shower, letting the sweat sluice away. Be nice if the demons could get washed away as easily but he'd soon find out if he'd made life any easier for himself by what he'd just done. Monthly Report would be well and truly over by the time he was dressed again.

The discussion about Tyler's case was taking off now. They might finish a few minutes early but there certainly wouldn't be time for another case.

The gap left by the unpresented case would probably be old news by the time everybody headed back to their normal routines. They would all move on with ease.

The way Layla and Alex needed to if they were both going to keep their jobs and work together.

Maybe what was stopping them was that it was unfinished business.

And if there was something that bothered Layla more

than being the subject of gossip it was having unfinished business hanging over her.

Mulling it over as she headed back to her office, Layla realised that dealing with this particular business would be dangerous. The tingle that kissed her skin as if she could still feel Alex's presence in this private room was enough of a warning. The way the memory of that kiss was lingering rang an even louder alarm.

But facing something dangerous…and winning…was kind of an attractive challenge.

And Dr Layla Woods had always found a challenge irresistible.

Besides, it could be good for both of them. She had a responsibility to try and ensure that the senior staff members could work together on good terms, didn't she?

Of course she did.

Layla took a moment to enjoy the view from her window. Plan B was beginning to shape up rather nicely.

CHAPTER TWO

EVERYBODY WAS WAITING.

Expecting Alex Rodriguez to be taken to task by the chief of paediatrics for failing to put in an appearance or even the courtesy of an apology for the monthly report meeting.

Alex had caught more than one oddly expectant glance from people over the course of the afternoon following that meeting. When his path crossed again with that of Layla for the first time he was in the cafeteria for lunch the next day, and the air of anticipation around him was palpable. A public arena and an attentive audience to witness a senior staff member being told off was gold for feeding a grapevine.

Alex gritted his teeth and waited for the kind of acerbic comment that would let him know by how far he'd missed the mark in his professional responsibilities.

Instead, he was treated, along with everybody else snatching a quick meal, to one of those thousand-watt smiles that Layla was so good at.

'Good to see you're finding time to eat,' she said, with that husky Southern edge to her voice that always made her sound vaguely amused about something. 'I hear you're busier than a one-armed paper-hanger over there in Neurology.'

He waited for the kicker. The jibe about being so busy that he couldn't have found the good manners to let her know he couldn't make the meeting. But that smile didn't dim. With a flick of those tousled, shoulder-length blonde waves, Layla continued moving towards the food counter, leaving nothing but a faint scent of something deliciously fresh in her wake. Apples?

Realising that he was sitting there with his mouth half-open, trying to identify what flavour shampoo Layla used, was enough to make Alex aware of the unpleasant burn of embarrassment, but he needn't have worried. Everyone around him was still watching Layla. Especially the men. And the collective gaze was laced with admiration.

Definitely apples, he decided the next day when Layla brushed past him in the recovery room to visit with a small patient of hers who'd just undergone open heart surgery.

He knew it was a coincidence that had placed her patient right next to the little girl he'd just operated on to correct a spinal abnormality but did she have to stand on his side of the bed? Did she really have to be here at all?

'I've been so worried about this wee man,' he heard her say to the nurse. 'I just had to come and have a peek.'

'He's doing just fine,' the nurse reassured her. 'We'll be transferring him to PICU any time now.'

Recovery was an extension of the operating theatre suite. Alex's turf. As Chief of Paediatrics, Layla often got involved with the more serious cases that came into Angel's and he'd often seen her in places like the paediatric intensive care unit. Even when she was sticking to her own specialty of paediatric cardiology, she would often have small patients who spent time in there when their condition deteriorated or after they'd had surgery. But he'd never come across her in the actual recovery area and it felt like more than a professional coincidence.

Was he getting paranoid or was Layla trying to get in his face at every possible opportunity and…and *enjoying* it?

'Don't tell me…' Alex didn't try and erase the sardonic lilt to his words as the nurse sped off to attend to another patient arriving from Theatre. 'You're regretting your choice not to become a surgeon.'

'Not at all.' Layla's glance flicked the whole length of his body and Alex instantly felt at a disadvantage.

Underdressed, standing here in his loose-fitting scrubs. He still had a theatre cap on his head and he'd only broken the top strings on his mask so it was hanging around his neck like a bib. Layla was wearing a smart, close-fitting pencil skirt and a crisply ironed blouse under her spotless white coat. And she had her trademark high heels on. Alex was wearing white, plastic gumboots.

'I adore cardiology,' Layla continued. 'I get to make the diagnosis and I get to enjoy the follow-up and see the way lives improve after surgery. I don't have to do the messy, in-between bit of adjusting the internal plumbing.' Her gaze seemed to intensify. 'My surgical rotation back when I was an intern showed me that it wasn't where I wanted to be.'

That rotation had been when they'd met. When Layla had become little Jamie's champion and she'd persuaded him to take on the toddler's complex surgery.

When they'd been together as far, far more than professional colleagues. Was that what Layla was really referring to here? Maybe he didn't want to find out. He backed down.

'I've just never seen you hanging around Recovery before,' he muttered. 'That's all.'

She knew, dammit. She knew exactly how uncomfortable he was with her presence in what had previously been a sacrosanct area for him.

We're colleagues. Her raised eyebrows managed to convey even more to the message. *We work in the same hospital. We are mature, professional people who are passionate about our careers. Deal with it.*

Fine. Alex *would* deal with it. He tilted his head towards the tiny patient in the bed.

'What was the procedure?'

'Just an ASD closure. But it was a big one and little Josh here is a real cutie. One of triplets.'

Triplets? Good grief… Why was nothing about Layla…*ordinary*?

Even this unusual visit was vaguely disturbing.

Any other doctor would be looking at the monitors or reading the recovery notes. Or at least quizzing the nurse. But not Layla. She was leaning over the tiny, unconscious boy. Finding a patch of skin that wasn't covered by an electrode for monitoring or tape that was holding an intravenous line in place. Stroking that skin with such a gentle touch that Alex couldn't look away.

'Hear what that nurse told me, honey?' he heard her murmur. 'You're doing just fine. You keep it up now. Your momma and daddy aren't far away and they can't wait to see you.'

Alex forced his attention back to the monitors attached to his own patient but he couldn't ignore the knot in his gut. It tightened when he glanced back in time to see Layla on the point of leaving. She had two fingertips against her pursed lips and, having turned her head to check that the nurse wasn't watching, she took that tiny kiss and transferred it to the forehead of the unconscious toddler.

A tiny moment in time. A very personal moment. If Layla hadn't turned in his direction again as she'd straightened, she would never have known that she had been observed. Alex was busted. He wasn't going to pretend he hadn't been staring so he held her gaze steadily and it was gratifying to see the flush of colour that painted Layla's cheeks.

But she didn't look away. Her chin came up and the spark in her eyes was one of defiance.

So I get emotionally involved with my patients, the spark said. *Deal with that, too. I happen to think it makes me a better doctor.*

'See you later, Alex.'

'Yeah…I'm sure you will.'

The high heels of Layla's shoes beat a sharp tattoo as she exited the recovery room and, despite himself, Alex knew he was watching her leave with the same kind of expression that every male in the cafeteria had had the day before.

You had to hand it to her. Layla Woods had very decided opinions and more courage than you could shake a stick at to defend them. And that feistiness, wrapped up in such an attractive package, was the kind of challenge any red-blooded man would get drawn to.

Look at him. He knew the deadly consequences of rising to that challenge and he was still finding it difficult not to get sucked in all over again.

Alex looked down at his small patient. He had done the best he could for her with the surgery to correct the spinal malformation and he was confident that it had been a success. This little girl would soon be able to sit up and walk and catch up with the developmental milestones she had missed. Her parents were going to be thrilled and he would take a great deal of pleasure in following up on her progress.

He cared about her. A lot. But he wasn't going to start cuddling and kissing his patients. He'd learned long ago how dangerous emotional entanglements could be. Probably even before his mother had died.

Alex hadn't needed the gut-wrenching confirmation of that lesson represented by the disastrous notion that Layla might have been different enough to deserve his trust. And he wasn't going to lay himself open to the kind of heartache that came with losing a small patient that you'd got too attached to. He knew how to keep just the right amount of distance to make sure he stayed at the top of his game.

He just had to apply the same wisdom to his professional relationship with Layla, never mind how many times he found himself close to her. Or how many personal things he happened to notice.

Personal things like the kind of shoes she wore or shampoo she used were superficial and easily ignored. The personal detail he discovered about Layla a few days later nearly did his head in.

Plan B seemed to be going slightly astray.

The idea had been to show Alex that the past was well and truly behind them. That they could enjoy a professional relationship and put any lingering attraction behind them as well. Tuck it away, along with the malpractice suit and the way both their lives had been derailed.

But it seemed to be taking on a life of its own now.

Alex didn't like it that she was invading his space. Layla could feel the 'Oh, God, not *again*' vibe whenever she just happened to be in the same place at the same time. Like the cafeteria or Recovery or the intensive care unit or one of the wards. She was getting so good at this she didn't need to check his electronic calendar to guess where he might be next. Often her instinct put her in the right place. Or maybe fate was helping because her path seemed to be crossing with that of Alex far more often as she fulfilled her own professional duties.

Well, Alex had only himself to blame. The effect of her subtle campaign was magnified considerably by how successful Alex had been in trying to avoid her in the run-up to that meeting he'd stupidly decided to miss. This could have all blown over by now. She would have given Alex his moment in the limelight, taken the opportunity to say thank you in a heartfelt manner and they could have agreed that this was a fresh start for both of them.

Bygones could have been bygones.

But no… Alex had taken a stand and presented a challenge and she knew perfectly well that he would have been expecting her to front up and tear a strip or two off him because everybody knew that she didn't hang back from necessary confrontation. The perfect opportunity had presented itself the very next day, in fact, in the staff cafeteria, with the bonus of a built-in audience.

What a stroke of brilliance it had been, doing the complete opposite of what they had all been expecting. Her ultra-friendly smile and the way she had simply ignored the whole issue had thrown Alex off guard completely. He was still suspicious of her motives and she couldn't blame him for not liking what was happening. She was in control here.

The problem was that she was enjoying herself. A bit too much perhaps. She was quite confident of how aware of her Alex was. She could sense the way he watched her, like that time in Recovery. She could feel the intensity of that gaze like a touch on her skin.

No. The real problem was the flip side of that particular coin.

She was equally aware of him.

Just how unhelpful this awareness was became strikingly obvious a few days later after Layla had been called to the emergency department to consult on a 'blue baby' case that had been rushed in by ambulance. The mother had had almost no prenatal care so the baby's cardiac abnormalities had not been picked up prior to birth and, to complicate matters, the young mother had gone into labour and had given birth at home. With the baby safely intubated and stabilised and now under the care of the neonatal surgeons, Layla was free to leave the department to carry on with the rest of her duties when she spotted Alex.

He was standing just outside one of the resuscitation rooms where the more serious cases were assessed and stabilised. Right next door to the one she had been in. That small thrill of excitement and the way her heart rate picked up was due purely to the stroke of luck crossing his path in such an unexpected place. Neither of them had much to do with the emergency department so what were the odds of them both being here at the same time? That this would annoy Alex no end might be a kind of a bonus.

Except that he didn't even seem to be aware of her standing so close by. His attention was focussed on the woman he was with. White-faced and sobbing, she looked barely more than a teenager. She had long, dark, wildly curly hair and she was talking fast and loudly. In Spanish.

Alex was looking stunned. As though he had no idea how to handle the situation.

Layla had never seen him look like this.

She'd seen him in charge of emergency situations in Theatre. Running a resuscitation scenario in the intensive care unit. Dealing with distraught parents. But never once had she seen him look as if he wasn't in complete control.

Looking…vulnerable?

Well…she had once. When things had gone so disastrously wrong at the end of Jamie Kirkpatrick's surgery. She'd had to stand back and watch helplessly then.

She didn't have to now.

Layla moved swiftly towards them. 'Can I help you?' she said to the young woman. *'Te puedo ayudar? Digame lo que pasa...'*

Her Spanish was fluent. The woman grabbed her arm in relief and sobbed out her story. Alex looked, if anything, even more stunned when Layla turned back to him.

'Ramona says you're treating her baby. Felix?'

His nod was terse. 'He's got a skull fracture. I was hoping to get to the bottom of the story but the language barrier's suddenly got a lot worse.'

Layla asked Ramona a question and then translated the response. 'His brother hit him with a toy brick.'

She could see the total disbelief in Alex's face. 'I'm talking about a fracture here. A *broken* skull. An *unconscious* child.' His voice was so tense it cracked.

Layla's brain sent out the kind of alert signal that any Chief of Paediatrics would be wise to pay attention to. It had been known to happen, hadn't it? She'd read of more than one case where parents had had children taken away from them by social services and had been prosecuted for child abuse.

One sprang to mind immediately, of an eight-month-old boy whose sibling had hit him with a toy aeroplane and caused a fracture. And what about the Tommy Jenner case a few months ago when the child-abuse screen had been started and then they'd found that Tommy had actually been injuring himself because of the seizures caused by his brain lesion?

Alex needed to be careful of what he was saying here but Layla found that she was thinking of something else entirely as she stared at him. Had she really not noticed before how those glimmers of grey had crept into his jet-black hair? The way those lines at the corners of his eyes had deepened over the years they hadn't seen each other? Had she really forgotten the way those chocolate-brown eyes could darken when something emotionally intense was going on, like anger or…physical passion? Heavens…they looked positively black at the moment.

Ramona had picked up the tone of Alex's voice. Looking terrified, she made a huge effort to pull herself together and change languages.

'No…don't say those words. No person hurt my baby. I…I *love* him.'

The anguish in her eyes and broken words was heart-breaking. Alex put his hand on the young woman's shoulder.

'Try and calm down, Ramona. I won't ask any more questions now. We've got Felix stabilised and we'll be taking him up to surgery in a few minutes.'

'*Què*? I…no understand…'

Layla translated but she couldn't look away from where Alex's hand was still resting on Ramona's shoulder. She could feel that hand herself.

'Ask her if her husband's on the way,' Alex ordered.

But Ramona understood that.

'Not husband. Boy…friend. I was…' With an impatient head shake and hand movements she reverted to rapid Spanish and Layla had to relay the information.

'She was already pregnant with Felix when she met

him. He's bringing in her older son. She's scared that you're going to call the police and she doesn't want to get into trouble.' It was quite possible there was an issue concerning illegal immigration here. Layla bit her lip, wondering if this was another alert signal her new position meant she should be worrying about.

The hand had dropped now. Layla watched as Alex's fingers curled into a fist but that was the only sign that something was disturbing him very deeply. That and the sense of raw power he was exuding. Right now that power was all about anger on behalf of a defenceless small child. Did he know for sure that his little patient's head injury had not been accidental? Layla wouldn't want to be standing in his way if he was planning to do something about such a conviction.

When he looked at Layla, she knew he was barely aware of her.

'Tell her that my only concern is treating her son.'

Alex left the impression of power in his wake and it stayed with Layla long after leaving Ramona with one of the nurses. She was left with a whole kaleidoscope of impressions whirling around her head, in fact.

The tension in Alex's face. The image of his hand on Ramona's shoulder. The way those dark, dark eyes had seemed to look right through her.

Memories... That first time they'd made love in the wake of her being so wound up after a blazing row with Luke. The urgency and the mind-blowing *heat* of that encounter. The unbelievable bliss in which it had culminated...

The feel of his lips against hers, which she'd experienced again not very long ago. The sheer wanting that it could conjure up every single time…

Oh, yes. It was just as well Alex was nowhere near where he might be able to see what was whizzing through her head because any control Layla felt she'd had in following this fool plan of hers had just gone out the window.

Concentrating on what she had to do for the rest of her day was quite a tall order. Layla was still feeling out of kilter by the time she got to the end of her list, long after most staff members had finished their days and gone home for dinner. She always liked to pop into all the intensive care units before she went home, to make sure she was in touch with how all Angel's most seriously unwell children were doing.

Her little 'blue' baby was in the cardiac unit, having had surgery to correct the abnormality she had been born with. All was well in NICU, the neonatal intensive care unit. PICU was her last stop. Maybe because she was a little nervous at crossing paths again with Alex today?

A little nervous? Judging by the way she actually jumped when she heard the sound of his voice even before she saw him, she was as jumpy as spit on a hot skillet.

'For God's sake…a skull fracture with acute subdural and epidural bleeding. You can't tell me a two-year-old kid can throw a wooden brick hard enough to cause that kind of an injury.'

'Are there any other potential signs of abuse?'

Another male voice. And they were both talking quietly, probably confident that their intense conversation was private. Had they left the unit for precisely that reason?

Layla stopped in her tracks, unsure of whether to round the corner where she'd have to walk past them to get to the locked door of the intensive care unit. The indecisiveness was an alien sensation and she didn't like it at all. She shifted her weight from one foot to the other, fingering her security badge, which would allow her access through that locked door.

'I don't know.' Alex's voice was a growl. 'I haven't had a chance to check him over properly yet. I've been too busy trying to save the poor little tyke's life. My suspicions are more than enough to base a report on and it needs to be filed within thirty-six hours of admission.'

'You need to be careful. Do you remember the first time I went to the monthly report meeting? Who was that kid you presented the case on? The one who's been on chemo for months and you're going to think about operating on soon?'

'Tommy Jenner.' Alex sounded impatient now. He didn't want to change the subject.

'You presented that case as a warning, didn't you? Not to make assumptions that just might be wrong. The *last* thing you need is another malpractice suit on your hands.'

'Are you telling me to stand back and say nothing? You, of all people, should know better than that, Cade. We *both* know the kind of damage that can do, don't we?'

'Yeah, yeah...point taken. But that's exactly why you need to tread carefully, man. You're too wired to see the worst-case scenario. You know too much.'

Layla was standing very still now, her eyes wide. What on earth was all that supposed to mean?

'You're following protocol,' Cade continued. 'Treating the child is number one. You can order a child-abuse screen and do the other tests you need, like X-rays to look for old fractures. The kid's safe and you've got some time up your sleeve. You need to cool down.'

Having Layla appear around the corner probably wouldn't help Alex to cool down. She found herself backing away. Turning, ready to leave, only to find herself face to face with a man who had a small boy with him. The child was about two or three years old and he was a reluctant companion. The man had a grip above the boy's elbow and was half pulling, half shoving him along. With long, greasy-looking hair and the skin of his arms beneath his T-shirt barely visible between tattoos, the man looked distinctly menacing.

'Get a move on,' he snarled down at the child, ignoring Layla. 'We're going to find your mother and then I'm outta here. I'm done with babysitting someone else's snivelling brat.'

He swept past Layla and around the corner. He practically banged into Alex and Cade.

Layla was hot on the man's heels. She didn't need the strong whiff of alcohol that reached her nostrils to know that a very volatile situation was forming.

'Whoa…' It was Cade who held up a hand to ward off a collision. 'Take it easy.'

'I'm in a hurry,' the man responded. He ignored Alex and walked past Cade. 'What…is that door *locked*? What kind of a joint is this? I thought it was a hospital, not a bloody prison.'

Layla was watching Alex. She could see he had assessed what was going on with the speed and intelligence she had learned to expect from him long ago. He was also putting two and two together as fast as she had. A young man arriving at the intensive care unit with a small boy. His patient's mother was inside the unit with her son. The baby had an older brother who had, supposedly, caused his severe head injury.

Alex caught her gaze and she felt that tingle of connection. Of knowing they were on exactly the same wavelength.

But there was more to this than a surgeon worried about his patient or a doctor who found treating a case of child abuse appalling. The shadows she could see in Alex's gaze created a flood of questions. She'd always been aware of that dark side to him, hadn't she? She'd never had the chance to find out how it had got there. She'd been happy to just let it add to the frisson of danger that had gone with getting close to this man. The excitement of the illicit affair.

And, right now, it was more than just wanting answers to those questions…she wanted to defuse this situation. Or was it more than that even? That squeezing sensation in her chest suggested that she wanted to… make it better somehow. For Alex.

As if he read something of that in her face, his gaze jerked away from her to the stranger.

'You're Ramona's boyfriend, aren't you?' Alex sounded calm. Dangerously so.

'Who wants to know?'

'I'm Alex Rodriguez. Felix's neurosurgeon. I'm the person who's been operating on Felix this afternoon.

Getting some of the blood out of his skull before it did too much damage to his brain.'

'Good for you.' The man eyed Alex up and down. More up than down. Both Alex and his brother towered over this stranger by at least six or seven inches. Layla could see that he was practised in assessing another man's strength but if he was intimidated by his male company he didn't show it. He stepped closer to Alex. 'If you're a doctor, you can let me in through that door. I've got a right to see Ramona.'

Alex was taking a breath. Layla could see the way his eyes narrowed as he smelt the alcohol. 'I'd like a word with you first, if you don't mind.'

'I do mind.' Layla saw the way the man shoved the little boy to one side and then curled his fists.

The little boy staggered sideways and bumped into Cade, who caught him as he started sobbing. 'You're OK, buddy,' he said.

'Shut up, Cody, or you'll be sorry,' the man warned.

'Like Felix was?' Alex's query was almost conversational.

'Alex…' Cade's tone was a warning.

The men were squaring off at each other. Layla could feel the fury of Alex's stare even though it was fastened firmly on the man directly in front of him. The tension was indescribable. Any second now and all hell would break loose. Alex would flatten Ramona's low-life boyfriend and then what? She wouldn't be trying to thank him for saving *her* job. She'd be fighting a losing battle trying to save his.

Not going to happen.

Without pausing to think about what she was doing,

Layla stepped in between the two men just as both men raised their fists.

The vicious shove she received from behind was meant to get her out of the way but, in fact, it slammed her against Alex's rigid body. He had no choice but to lower his fists to catch hold of her before she fell sideways. It still felt like she was falling but she was encased in an astonishingly powerful grip.

From the corner of her eye she saw the fist aimed at Alex, which would have connected with the side of her head if Alex hadn't hauled her out of harm's way.

He only held Layla long enough for her to feel that strength and all that leashed power. To feel the pounding of his heart against her own for no more than a second. And then he let go of her and moved so swiftly the attacker didn't have a chance.

'That's *enough.*' Alex grabbed the raised arm of the attacker and then twisted it behind the man's back.

'*Ow*...lemme go,' the man snarled. The words turned into a whimper of pain as Alex clearly tightened his grip.

Layla, Cade and little Cody were all staring, wide eyed.

'Call Security,' Alex told Cade. 'Layla, take Cody in to find his mother.'

Layla did as she was told. She held out her hand. 'Come on, honey. I'll just bet your momma is going to be so happy to see you.'

Behind her, she could hear Cade talking urgently to Alex. 'I'll sit on him till Security gets here. You need to go and cool down before you talk to them. I'll tell them you got paged.'

'No way…' The refusal was almost drowned by a stream of obscenities and threats from Ramona's boyfriend.

Layla used her swipe card to gain entry to the unit. As the doors closed behind Cody and herself she could only hope that Alex could control his fury. It didn't matter what the man was guilty of—a member of staff in an altercation with a parent figure would be a dismissible offence.

She found a staff member to take care of Cody and filled them in on what had happened. She even spoke briefly to Ramona and learned that Felix had come through his surgery with flying colours and everybody was very pleased with how he was doing. It was only a few minutes before she could head back to see what was happening on the other side of the door. With a curious mix of both relief and disappointment she found Alex was nowhere to be seen. Ramona's boyfriend was also gone from the scene and the security guard talking to Cade had finished whatever he needed to do.

'I'll go and have a word with the boy's mother,' he said. 'And I'll catch up with Dr Rodriguez when he's done with that emergency.'

Layla pinned Cade with a look that told him she wasn't leaving without some answers.

'Where's Alex?'

Cade shrugged. 'Gone. I thought he should cool off a bit before he started talking to the cops.'

There was a moment's silence as they stared at each other. Cade looked…defensive? As if he was challenging Layla to criticise Alex for coming on too strong. She weighed her words.

'I heard you guys talking,' she said carefully. 'What did you mean by Alex knowing too much?'

She could see the shutters come down. Cade shrugged again, a gesture that told her this was between brothers and none of her business. And then his eyebrow rose.

'Is it true what I've heard around here? That there's something going on between you and Alex?'

Was this a case of attack being the best form of defence? Or was it a brother looking after a brother? If Layla wanted an honest answer from Cade, maybe he deserved the truth first.

'Not now,' she told him. 'There's…history. We were together way back. At the time of the Kirkpatrick case. You'd know about that.'

A sharp nod from Cade. 'It's what made me get in touch with Alex after not seeing him for years. Not that I got much of a chance to spend time with him before he took off to Brisbane.'

'It messed up a lot of things,' Layla agreed. 'But what's important right now is that I owe my job to Alex and I'm not going to let him get into trouble over what just happened here if I can help it.'

Cade's nod was relieved. 'Just as well. The creep's telling everybody that Alex started it. Just laid into him without any provocation.'

'I'll sort it,' Layla promised. But she wasn't letting Cade off the hook just yet. '*After* I've talked to Alex, that is. Now, are you going to tell me where he is so I can do that before the cops start looking for me?'

Cade sighed. 'He didn't say where he was going but

I'd guess he's where he always is when he wants to burn off some steam. Where we both go.'

'Which is?'

'The hoop-shooting court out the back of the ambulance bay.'

CHAPTER THREE

THE SLAP OF the ball against the palm of his hand was hard enough to be causing pain.

Firing the ball towards the hoop with such aggression before he'd warmed up properly had ripped a bit of muscle, too, so that every subsequent attempt at a goal sent a stabbing sensation through his shoulder. On top of that, Alex had been going hard enough to be out of breath enough to make his lungs burn and create a satisfyingly deep ache in his chest every time he tried to suck in some more oxygen.

But he wasn't ready to stop yet. No way.

This felt like a fight to the death.

OK, he'd been wrong about Tommy but he'd known in his gut that Felix had been the victim of abuse from the moment he'd seen him. He should have had the cops there waiting for that creep of a father figure to turn up.

He'd wanted to kill the guy. Or at least hurt him enough to make him stop and think about what he'd done to an innocent child. Felix was a *baby*, for God's sake. He had no chance to defend himself in any way. He'd still feel the pain, though, wouldn't he? And the shock of such a betrayal from a person he had to trust because his survival depended on it.

His breath coming in ragged gasps, Alex did another circuit of the court at high speed, hammering the ball on the tarmac with every step, getting back to the point where he could make another leap and fire the ball at the hoop as fast as he could.

He'd been luckier than Felix. Ten years old and big for his age before the abuse from his stepfather had really started. Big enough to be fiercely determined to protect his little brother. Strong enough to stand up to a man who'd made it very clear he didn't give a damn about his dead wife's kid.

He hated this part of his job. Hated the memories that came with cases like this. Felt consumed with anger that his time and skills had to be used to fight something that should never, ever have happened in the first place. In a perfect world he could devote his life to being the absolute best in dealing with the kind of things that weren't preventable. The kind of complicated lesions that came out of nowhere and threatened to blow a loving, *real* family apart.

Everybody knew he was well on the way to being the best. What they didn't know was that he was driven to it by the mix of guilt and determination that he had to live with for ever. Guilt over what had happened in the little Jamie Kirkpatrick case. Determination that it would never, ever happen again. That nothing, and nobody, would ever put him off his game.

And that was under threat.

It wasn't just the anger about child abuse in general that Alex was trying to burn off here. Or the fury and disgust at coming face to face with the perpetrator in a single case. Part of what was pushing him on and on despite the pain right now was fear. This threat was huge.

Because of the guilt that had spurred his determination in the first place.

Because the reason he hadn't been on top of his game for little Jamie was back in his life again.

And because the pull of it was unbearable.

It had been bad enough earlier today when he'd heard her speaking *Spanish*, for God's sake…

He could probably have conversed with Ramona himself except that he'd shut the door so successfully on the language he'd heard so much of in his earliest years. The Rodriguez family had kept close ties with their culture but his mother had refused to speak Spanish after his father had died. Phrases had slipped out in emotional times, though, on the occasions she'd got cross. More often when she'd been happy, like when she'd been giving him a cuddle and kiss to say goodnight.

It was a language that touched something very deep inside Alex. It had roots in a happy time that was so long ago it was only a fairy-tale. Hearing Layla speaking it so fluently had given him a chill down his spine. Made him realise that there was more connecting him to this woman that he'd thought.

Pulling him back.

But he hadn't realised the terrifying power of that pull until a few minutes ago. When he'd been so consumed with that anger towards Ramona's boyfriend that he might have ignored Cade's warning about what the consequences might be until…until Layla had stepped between them and everything had changed in a heartbeat.

The need to protect her had come with the same kind of automatic speed that he'd practised as a kid, making sure that Cade wasn't going to get in the way of his father's fists. And *that* had become more important than anything else.

And then that low-life had pushed her and she'd slammed up against his body and, as inconceivable as it should have been given the circumstances, the awareness of her warmth and softness and…just that she was *Layla* had messed with his head completely.

The desire to hurt the creep had been diluted by the relief that Layla was safe. The memories were jangled and confused. Cade had been right. He'd needed to get away to cool off and clear his head.

Was he succeeding?

It didn't feel like it. Another circuit of the court and the muscles in his legs were burning now. Every pore was releasing sweat in a vain attempt to cool him down and he felt light-headed for a moment because he wasn't getting enough oxygen.

But he still kept going. The anger may have worn off but he still had too many other emotions curdling his blood.

He had to fight the threat. Find a way through it. He wasn't going to let his life get derailed again. He'd learned his lessons.

Not instantly, of course. He'd gone from his disastrous fling with a married woman to falling into bed with Callie Richards, one of his new colleagues in Brisbane. The lust had burned off fast enough, though, and he'd been left with a friendship he knew they'd have for ever. Callie was just like him. Burned by love to the same extent and determined that it would never interfere with her life again.

She'd tell him to do whatever it took to forget and then move on.

Like they had, after their fling had fizzled out. They'd been able to salvage a true friendship and work together without this gut-wrenching tension he was trying to get past now.

It was so hard fighting the past here. Especially now. The memories of Jamie. And Tommy. And now Felix.

And not just the *memories* of Layla. He had to deal with the *reality* of her. Every day. Every minute of the day it had started to feel like. That kiss. The feel of her body against his so recently upstairs. That disturbing, automatic need to protect her.

He had to deal with it. Or he'd have all his demons snapping at his heels for the rest of his life and he'd never find peace.

Alex was finally forced to stop moving and catch his breath.

Exhausted now, he could start to push everything out of his head. Except for the knowledge that he had to find a way through this and that he had no idea where to start.

Give him a case that was complicated enough to scare anyone else off and he was fine. He could make a plan. Step by step. A thorough investigation and then treatment with the goal of a cure lighting the path.

Work was great like that. But personal stuff?

Callie might know what he needed to do. She was a touchstone for advice.

Maybe Cade could help. He'd lived with the same

background of violence and he'd only been protected until Alex had abandoned him and walked out when he'd been sixteen. Cade had been justifiably angry but they were sorting out that emotional minefield now. They were brothers again and that was thanks to Cade making the first move so maybe he would have a clue where you got started on a journey to make peace with the past and move on.

He certainly needed to talk to someone. If he didn't find an outlet for the emotions he couldn't suppress, he'd go crazy.

Things weren't hurting quite so much now. A few more minutes of this over-the-top physical activity and he could go and have a shower. With a bit of luck he'd be too tired to even think after that.

Layla had gone through the emergency department and out the automatic doors that led to the ambulance bay. There was a crew unloading a young patient who appeared to be having a severe asthma attack. He was sitting bolt upright on the stretcher, clutching a nebuliser mask to his face. His anxious parents gave Layla a hopeful look as if the stethoscope around her neck and perhaps the seniority her white coat advertised meant she would pause on her way and put things right, but all she could offer was a sympathetic smile.

She'd never been around the back of the ambulance bay before. As far as she knew, this was where all the rubbish skips were lined up ready for collection so there'd never been a reason to go there. Tucked into the corner, however, and brightly lit by the powerful security lights, was a good-sized patch of tarmac. The backboard and hoop were securely attached to one of Angel's walls.

Alex had clearly been working out without a pause since she'd last seen him. He was wearing nothing more than some shorts, a singlet and trainers, and his exposed skin gleamed with sweat.

And, oh, man…there was a lot of exposed skin.

Standing at the end of the line of rubbish skips and not directly under a light, Layla knew she was probably invisible. Alex was so focussed on his lonely game that he probably wouldn't have noticed her anyway, even if she was out in the open. She should call out or something because it felt suddenly as if she was seeing something private but when she opened her mouth Layla found it was inexplicably dry and no sound emerged.

Even if the overhead lights weren't picking Alex out from the surrounding darkness like spotlights, it would have been impossible to look away. This was the image of a very well-built, very fit man. There wasn't an ounce of fat on Alex Rodriguez. Muscles rippled and tendons appeared like ropes on his thighs and arms as he ran and twisted, changing direction and gathering speed before firing a shot at the goal. Layla found herself holding her breath every time, waiting for the crack of the ball against the backboard and the satisfying slide of it going through the net.

There wasn't a woman alive who wouldn't be impressed by Alex's body even when he was fully clothed and standing absolutely still. To watch him display this level of fitness and physical acuity was mesmerising. Erotic, in fact. She could hear the rasp of Alex's ragged breathing and the occasional grunt of effort. She could almost feel the body heat coming at her in waves and smell the salty tang of his sweat.

Her mouth might be dry but there was another part of Layla that most certainly wasn't. Her breathing rate had picked up as well and her knees were actually feeling weak, like those of some swooning heroine from a story like *Gone With The Wind* or something.

When Alex finally stopped to catch his breath, Layla ordered herself to get a grip and focus on what she'd come here for.

Which was what, exactly?

To talk about what had just happened outside the intensive care unit, of course. So that they could make sure they were singing from the same hymn book and that, if necessary, she could use her position to make sure Alex didn't get into any trouble over this.

And…if that went well enough, maybe she'd push him just a little bit and try and find out what Cade had meant about Alex knowing too much. What it was that had made him shut her out so convincingly.

Layla didn't like being shut out.

She pulled herself together enough to think she could manage to start this conversation but by then Alex had started running again. Not nearly as fast and furiously as he had been when she'd arrived. The anger he'd been burning off must be spent and that was a good thing. He probably wouldn't mind being interrupted now. Swallowing hard, Layla walked away from the rubbish skip and out into the open where he couldn't fail to see her when he started a new circuit after the next goal.

It wasn't so good that she'd have to talk to him while he was more than half-naked and dripping with sweat, given the ache of raw desire she could still feel pulsing in her belly, but Layla already had a plan in place. She'd tell him to have a quick shower and then they'd grab a coffee. She'd wait outside the door of wherever he was going to have a shower to make sure that she got to talk to him first.

The clock was ticking. The police were probably paging him already.

Alex became aware of Layla's presence the moment she stepped into the periphery of his visual field but he totally ignored her while he did another circuit of the court.

He could guess why she'd come looking for him. Well…she could stand there for another minute or two. The fact that the few items of clothing he was wearing were now dripping wet and clinging to his body didn't bother him at all. The physical activity and his success in burning off that anger made him feel powerful. In control. Layla, standing there with her pretty skirt and her hair getting ruffled by the warm evening breeze, looked feminine and fragile. Definitely on the back foot.

The final goal was accompanied by a snort of something close to laughter from Alex.

Layla *fragile*? Not in this lifetime.

With a final bounce Alex caught the ball. He turned and walked decisively to where Layla was standing. He couldn't miss the way her eyes widened as he got closer. Or the way her breath hitched, allowing just a tantalising glimpse of cleavage to peep over the scooped neckline of her blouse. She even averted her gaze when he got within touching distance.

Oh, yeah…Layla wasn't very comfortable right now.

'We need to talk,' she said.

Alex let one corner of his mouth curl upwards. 'Sure. Unless you'd prefer me to shower first?'

'That...would probably be a good idea. I...um... wouldn't want you to catch a chill or something.'

'I'll only be a minute.' Alex tilted his head towards the rarely used facility built into one corner of the ambulance bay. 'We often use the shower in the decontamination room over there.'

'Fine. I'll wait out here.'

The decontamination room was big enough to allow a stretcher to get wheeled in. It was designed to deal with a situation like people or equipment being in contact with a toxic chemical or potential infection. Completely tiled, there were overhead showers as well as hand-held sprays over a tilted floor with large drains. There were also big tubs and shelves that held stacks of clean towels and other items that might be needed, like gowns, gloves and masks.

Alex stripped off and got under the shower, pumping some soap from the container attached to the wall. He scrubbed some lather through his hair and then sluiced it off, letting the water rain on his face and onto his chest. He shook his head when he turned the water off but still had rivulets running over his skin as he stepped off the tilted floor to reach for a towel.

He felt the cool touch of the breeze on his back and knew the door had opened behind him. With a corner of the towel dangling from one hand, he turned to see Layla closing and locking the door behind her.

'What the *hell* do you think you're doing?'

She was leaning against the door now, facing him but with her eyes closed.

'There's a cop out there. The squad car's parked in the last ambulance slot. I didn't want them to see me yet. Or find you yet. I…couldn't think what else to do.' Layla opened her eyes. 'Sorry.'

Alex was trying to process this. She was hiding from the police? Because she had some misguided notion that she could protect *him*? Why did she want to do that?

In the time it took for the thoughts to take their turn Alex was also processing the way Layla's gaze dropped. Slowly. Travelling down his body and then up again. The way her pupils dilated. The way the very tip of her tongue appeared to moisten her lips.

Oh…God… What was it about the chemistry between them? This was way more intense than the atmosphere had been before that kiss. Alex could feel the oxygen being sucked out of the air around them. That final plunge before the electricity exploded. If he didn't do something…anything…right *now*, they would both be consumed by the flames and there would be no turning back.

But it was too hard to even think, let alone move.

He was as naked as a jaybird. With his hair all spiky and drops of water caught on the damp whorls of hair on his chest. Hair that arrowed down to where his fist was holding the edge of the towel.

She knew what was barely concealed by that drape of towelling. She knew what that hand was capable of doing when it wasn't busy holding something. Maybe if every cell in her body wasn't screaming for more than the memory of that touch she could have handled this. But then Layla's gaze dragged itself upwards until it snagged with Alex's mouth and she knew she was completely lost.

She couldn't look away. The only thing her brain was capable of was willing those lips to come closer. To touch her own.

A pager sounded. Hers? Maybe Alex's, coming from the pile of his clothing that was on the bench. They were both off duty so it was most likely to be something connected to the incident upstairs. Something that should have been enough to break the unbearable sexual tension in this small, clinical space.

It certainly broke the impasse but not in the way Layla had expected. With a muttered curse Alex moved.

Not to look for his pager.

Towards Layla.

His fingers caught in her hair as they curled around her neck. She closed her eyes, instinctively tipping her head back. Exposing her neck to him. Parting her lips. Waiting for *that* moment…The touch of his lips…his hands…his tongue. The moment when nothing else in the world mattered.

And when it came, it was better than she could have imagined. That unexpected kiss, weeks ago now, had erased the first shock of their bodies meeting again. This time it was all about what they knew they could give each other. What they craved like an addict denied his fix for too long.

How was it that the passion could be so white hot and desperately urgent and yet it could feel gentle at the same time? That buttons could come undone and not ping onto the tiles like bullets?

The sounds echoed around them. The fast breathing. The groans of pleasure so intense it was painful. Did the sound come from her own throat when Alex's hand cupped her breast, his thumb pulling the lace of her bra aside so that his lips could find her nipple?

Of course it did. But it was matched by the low growl that came from Alex. Her cry was much louder moments later when her skirt was hitched up and she was touched where she wanted it most.

It wasn't enough. Layla could feel the hard tiles against her back. She had the hardness of Alex's body against her breasts and her belly. Her own hands sought the hardness she knew she would find. That she couldn't live without for another heartbeat.

This was wild. Irresponsible and totally, absolutely irresistible.

Layla felt her panties being dragged down.

Yes…

She felt herself being lifted. She wrapped her arms around Alex's neck and her legs around his hips. It would only be a matter of seconds before she got tipped off the world into paradise and maybe the bliss wouldn't last nearly long enough but…oh, *God*…nothing was this good and never could be.

For a long, long minute there was nothing but the sound of them both trying to catch their breath.

Not a word was spoken as they finally peeled apart. Layla fixed her clothing while Alex got dressed.

He checked his pager.

'Cade's looking for me.' Alex had to clear his throat. 'He's talking to the cops.'

'We still need to talk.' Heavens, her voice had come out all husky too, from the aftermath of passion.

'We'll do it on the way. Come with me?'

A bubble of wild laughter threatened to escape from Layla. *I just did*, she thought. And then the realisation hit her. Of what had just happened. How huge it was—to her, at any rate. Of how weird it was not to be saying anything about it. Of how enormous the new problem had just been created. What did it mean and, more importantly, what on earth were they going to do about this?

Maybe it was too big to know what to say yet. Layla stared at Alex and he held her gaze. She could see the kind of peace that only came from ultimate physical satisfaction. But she could also see confusion there. Regret, maybe? She didn't want to hear him say anything to confirm that.

'And, yeah…I reckon we do need to talk.' Alex still hadn't broken eye contact. 'We'll do that real soon.'

With a nod Layla followed him to where they needed to be now.

The promise was enough. Alex was a man of his word. They *would* talk soon and somehow, between them, they would be able to sort everything.

The tension between them had been resoundingly broken, that was for sure. Plan B had succeeded in a most unexpected way. Now all they needed was a new plan. One that would enable them to find a way forward.

A plan that Layla couldn't begin to formulate because it was going to be very different. And it required input from both of them.

CHAPTER FOUR

'You didn't…' A gasp was followed by an echo of incredulous femininc laughter over the international phone line. 'Oh, my God, Alex. You *idiot*.'

'Hey…I rang you for some advice, Callie Richards. Not a character assassination.'

'OK. Sorry, mate. But…but *Layla*? Wasn't she the final straw that drove you over to this side of the world?'

'Yeah…I *know*…' Alex scrubbed his fingers through his hair as he stood, clad only in his boxer shorts, beside the open windows of his Manhattan apartment, trying to catch a hint of breeze in the middle of this sultry Indian-summer night. He sighed heavily. 'I *am* an idiot. I thought I could handle it, you know? Stay the hell away from her, even though we're working in the same place. But there she was…'

'You were at *work*. Even *we* never did anything that crazy.'

Being ashamed of himself was a very alien sensation for Alex. He tried to ignore the unpleasant squirm in his gut.

'I hope some of your brain cells were still active and that you used a…'

Alex had to cut her off. Callie may be an ex-lover

and his best friend but there were limits to how candid he wanted this conversation to be. 'No,' he snapped. 'They're not something I generally have on hand when I'm at work.'

There was a moment's shocked silence on the line. She didn't need to tell him how stupid he'd been. How irresponsible. That he was thirty-eight years old, not eighteen, and he should have known better.

'It just happened, Cal. I can't undo the past, no matter how recent. What I'm trying to figure out here is what the hell am I going to do about it *now*?'

Callie's voice had a sharper edge. 'What did Layla have to say about it?'

'That we need to talk.' Alex wasn't about to admit it, even to the woman he considered to be the closest friend he'd ever had in his life, but the prospect was terrifying. He didn't want to have that conversation with Layla. Didn't want to be that close to her again until he was absolutely confident he could handle it. And his level of confidence in that situation had been badly shaken. Destroyed?

'She's right,' Callie told him.

'I *am* talking,' Alex growled. 'To *you*.'

Callie's voice softened. 'And it's great to hear you, mate. I miss having you around.'

There was another short silence that seemed to contain a sigh of regret. Of them being a world away from each other? Sadness that their brief fling when Alex had first gone to Brisbane had burned itself out so convincingly that nothing more than the chance of friendship was left in its wake? Not that the friendship wasn't wonderful. They were so alike they could have easily come from the same genetic pool. Callie was a soul mate in the way a sister could have been.

'You've hardly called since you moved to the Big Apple,' Callie added. 'Not good enough.'

'I know. I'm sorry. It's been hectic.'

'Yeah, yeah…I know what you're like, Alex. But being a workaholic to escape personal stuff might not be the whole answer.'

It was Alex's turn to let a snort of laughter escape. 'That's the pot calling the kettle black.'

'So? I'm an expert.' Callie was unrepentant. 'I know what I'm talking about and I'm better at it than you.'

'OK. If you're such an expert, tell me what I'm supposed to do about this. I don't want to get tangled up with Layla Woods again. With anyone, for that matter.'

'That might have been your first mistake,' Callie said seriously. 'If you hadn't taken that vow of celibacy after our…after we…' She cleared her throat. 'Anyway…you're not cut out to be a monk, Alex Rodriguez. If you'd just had some fun now and then, it wouldn't have been all bottled up and ready to explode like that.'

'I didn't take a vow of celibacy. I just haven't met anybody else that…that spun my wheels enough.'

Because nobody had come close to being like Layla?

No. That was ridiculous. The world was full of gorgeous women. He just hadn't wanted the complications that came with even a brief entanglement. Work had been the answer. Satisfying enough, anyway.

Until now?

'Layla still spins them, then, I take it?' There was an odd note in Callie's voice. Wistful? No. More like resignation. This was more a sisterly thing. As though she was wanting to protect him from someone she knew had hurt him so much in the past.

'Obviously.' Alex's response was dry enough to evaporate instantly.

'Hmm. Well, at least it was just a quick shag in the shower. Nobody could say that was romantic.'

'No. I guess not.' Unbidden, images of Layla in a more romantic setting flashed into his head.

A big bed with rumpled sheets.

A soft rug in front of a crackling, open fire.

A candlelit dinner by a moon-touched sea.

Oh...God... It didn't matter that the images were so fleeting they almost hadn't touched his consciousness. They still left a drag of something way too close to longing in their wake.

He *didn't* want any of that. No way.

'And you didn't have a heart-to-heart and trot down memory lane?'

'We didn't get a chance to talk. The cops were waiting for us.'

'What? That was fast. How did they know what you'd been up to?'

Alex laughed and instantly felt better. Trust Callie to be able to break the tension like that. He filled her in on the incident with Ramona's boyfriend, which they'd managed to defuse completely with the solid wall of evidence from Cade, Layla and himself to refute the creep's claims that Alex had attacked him.

'And then I got caught up checking on Felix and by the time I'd finished, Layla had gone home so Cade and I went to O'Malley's for a drink.'

'Who's O'Malley?'

'It's an Irish pub. Close to Angel's so it gets used a lot. You'd love it. Irish pubs are the same the world over. Could have been in O'Reilly's in Brisbane. Felt kind of like home, anyway.'

Except he didn't have a real home, did he? Never had. Maybe he never would. A shaft of a very melancholy shadow made him fall silent suddenly.

Callie didn't notice. 'And a good brotherly chat? You've really patched things up between you?'

'Yeah… Seems like it.' The shadow lifted. Maybe home was really about people, not places.

'So what did Cade have to say about you and Layla hooking up?'

'I…didn't get round to telling him about that.'

Callie made an impatient sound. '*Men.* What is with you and talking about personal stuff?'

'We talked about plenty of personal stuff.'

'Oh, yeah? Like what?'

'Cade's stuff.'

'Worse than yours?'

'Maybe.' Alex pressed his lips together. He wasn't about to break a confidence. And Cade's stuff had made him think his own worries were insignificant.

The worst that had happened to him had been that a girl he'd been crazy about had dumped him. She hadn't tried to trap him by getting pregnant and then punished him for not responding in the way she'd planned. Cade had had to deal with the guilt of this girl taking an overdose and then having a miscarriage.

'Anyway…' Callie had given up waiting for him to say anything more about the conversation. 'You working tomorrow?'

'It's Saturday and I'm not on call. I'll do a ward round in the morning and was planning to catch up on paperwork after that.'

'Talk to Layla,' Callie ordered. 'If nothing else, you need to find out if she's on the Pill. Or whether you need to get screened for an STD or something.'

A curl of anger came from nowhere and was bright enough to make the night seem even hotter. 'Layla's not like that,' he snapped.

Why was the urge to protect her so automatic? What did he know about Layla these days? How on earth could he be so sure that he hadn't been put at risk despite doing something so irresponsible?

His rebuke had hit home. Callie sounded wary now. 'You still need to talk to her. Tomorrow. The longer you leave it, the harder it's going to be, and if you avoid her, you'll just be setting yourself up for another…um… shall we say, inappropriate means of dealing with the tension?'

A repeat of what had happened in the shower room? Oh…*yeah…*

Alex gave himself a firm mental shake. 'You're right. I'll catch her tomorrow and we'll talk about it. I'm sure she's as horrified as I am that it happened at all. Between us, we'll be able to figure out a way of making sure it doesn't happen again.'

'And…be careful, Alex.'

'How do you mean?'

'I'm not saying that Layla's not trustworthy or anything. Don't get me wrong, any woman that's managed to get under your skin the way she has must have a lot going for her. I'm just saying that maybe there's some merit in the whole "once bitten, twice shy" approach.'

Meaning he could get hurt. Again. As if he didn't know that.

'I get it,' he said softly. 'Thanks for caring, Cal.'

'No worries. Now, you need to get some sleep. What time is it over there?'

'Three a.m.' But Alex didn't want to end the call. Not while Callie was still sounding hurt by his defence of Layla's reputation. 'But I want to know how *you* are, Cal. How's it going at Gold Coast General?'

'Well…seeing as you've asked, I'm overworked and stressed out. If I don't get a new prenatal surgeon who's up to my impossibly high standards very soon, I will go stark raving mad.'

'Hmm.' Alex was only too happy to get completely distracted from his personal issues. He was also keen to do something to cheer Callie up. 'You know what? I might just be able to help you out there.'

'You're a neurosurgeon, Alex, not a prenatal surgeon.'

'True, but I might know one who could be interested.'

'Who? He'd have to be good.'

'He is. And I'm not just saying that because he's my brother.'

'You mean Cade? I thought he'd only just started at Angel's.'

'He has but he's finding it a bit frustrating. And I have to agree that he's too good to be second in charge. Funnily enough, he said something just the other day about thinking I had the right idea in going off to start a new life in Australia.'

With the benefit of hindsight, he could tell Cade that running away from some things didn't work. They could lie in wait for you and the ambush could be unexpected and very disturbing. He might be better to stay here and face his demons head on, if he had any. Except that maybe it *was* the answer for Cade.

Callie had picked up on his train of thought with her customary level of intuition.

'What's he running away from? If it's just his position on the ladder, there's nothing stopping him from finding a different hospital in the States.'

'Maybe he just needs to stretch his wings and see a bit of the world. He's young. Brilliant. Frustrated.'

'OK.' Callie was sounding much happier now. 'Tell me more, then. Just in case I need to talk to him.'

Finally, a puff of deliciously cool air came through the windows. Alex settled himself on the window sill. This was a conversation he was more than happy to have.

The one he would have to have tomorrow, with Layla?

Not so much. To put it mildly.

'Layla… Hey, wait up…'

'Chloe.'

The two women hugged each other in greeting. A paediatric nurse, Chloe Jenkins—no, Chloe Davis now that she'd married Brad—had been the first real friend Layla had made after arriving at Angel's.

'What's up?' Chloe pulled away to give Layla a questioning glance. 'You don't look like you're feeling great.'

'I'm just a bit tired.' Layla forced a smile. 'It was so hard to sleep last night with that heat. I need to ask my landlord to look at the air-conditioning unit.' She needed to change the subject quickly in case Chloe guessed she was trying to hide something. 'What are you doing in here on a Saturday morning when you're not on? I thought you and Brad were grabbing every chance you could get to go house hunting?'

'We are, but didn't you hear? Eleanor Aston had her baby last night.'

'Oh, wow…isn't that a bit early?'

'Yes, but they're both fine. Little girl. Tyler's over the moon.'

'I'll bet. What have they called her?'

Chloe laughed. 'I don't think they've decided. Right now, she's either "Peanut" or "Honey".'

'So Tyler's a daddy…' Layla shook her head. 'Astonishing.'

'Oh, that's right… You two go way back, don't you?'

'Since we were knee high to grasshoppers.' Layla was grinning now. 'I'll have to get him a cigar.'

'They might have chocolate ones in the gift shop. Come and have a look. That's why I'm here.' Chloe steered Layla across the lobby. 'I need to get a teddy bear or something before I go visiting and I've seen some really cute ones in our shop.'

'I've only got a minute. There's a queue of patients I need to catch up with this morning.'

'Must be a serious case amongst them.'

'Why do you say that?' Layla stopped beside a rack

of cards. She could get one and send it to Eleanor and Tyler with Chloe.

'You look like you're on the way to give somebody some very bad news.'

'Oh...' Layla bit her lip. 'I guess I have got a conversation coming up that I'm not looking forward to.'

Chloe had reached out to pick up a teddy bear from the shelf but her hand stopped in mid-air. 'I knew it. What's going on?'

Layla sighed. She picked up a card and pretended to read the message inside as she stepped closer to Chloe and lowered her voice enough to ensure she wasn't going to be overheard.

'You know how awkward it was seeing Brad at work after you two had slept together?'

'Do I ever. Oh, my God, Layla Woods.' Chloe's whisper became a gasp. 'Who *was* it?'

Layla was silent. Chloe's eyes widened.

'OK, you don't have to tell me because I can guess. It was Alex, wasn't it?'

It was Layla's turn to widen her eyes with shock.

'Don't worry.' Chloe touched her arm. 'It's not written all over your face or anything. I can guess because of the way I saw you two looking at each other when we had that girls' night out a while back.' She sucked in a deep breath. 'When did it happen?'

'Last night.' Layla felt the warmth of colour touching her cheeks. That was the only information she was about to share. Imagine if anybody heard about the actual circumstances? Oh...Lord...

'So what's the big deal?' Chloe picked up the bear and tested its cuddliness. 'You're single. So's he. He's *gorgeous*…and I'll bet the sex was…um…' she grinned mischievously '…memorable?'

'Oh, you have no idea,' Layla murmured. 'But it was a mistake. A big one.'

'Why?'

Why indeed?

Because they had to work together again now?

Because both of them were focussed so completely on their careers?

Because they had messed with each other's lives in the past so much they would never be able to trust each other?

That was more like it.

'Been there, done that,' Layla muttered. 'It wouldn't work.'

Chloe looked thoughtful. 'You can't know that for sure. If there's something there that's strong enough to pull you back together after…how many years?'

'Five.'

'Hmm. That's a pretty powerful something, if you ask me. Does Alex think it was a big mistake?'

'I don't know. We haven't talked about it.'

'Oh…' Chloe's grimace was sympathetic. 'No wonder it's awkward. Good luck with that.'

'Thanks. I think I'm going to need it.'

CHAPTER FIVE

It was later on that Saturday morning before Alex and Layla saw each other and when they did, it was so much like a stand-off in some old Western movie that Layla almost laughed aloud.

She'd stepped out of the elevator on the eighth floor with the intention of going into the neurology ward and finding Alex. She had expected to see him so she shouldn't have been so surprised. What she hadn't expected was to find him striding towards the elevators. That was why her breath caught in her throat and why her heart rate suddenly accelerated. Why her feet seemed to be glued to the floor.

Alex had stopped dead in his tracks with the double doors of the ward entrance still swinging gently behind him.

They were both frozen.

Who's going to reach for their gun first? Layla wondered. Her lips twitched at the ridiculousness of this and, with a determined inward shove she started moving. So did Alex.

Not exactly towards each other. By a kind of telepathic tacit consent they both moved in a V-shaped track that brought them together close to the big windows.

The view over Central Park from this height was spectacular. You could see from the park's southern border almost as far as the huge reservoir in the northern half of this massive area. Layla stared down at the park rather than directly at Alex.

'Gorgeous day, isn't it?'

'Mmm.' It felt like Alex was staring at her rather than the view. Layla's heart skipped a beat. She knew they needed to talk about what had happened last night but she wasn't ready. Nowhere near ready. She could feel her heart skip a beat and she had to dampen her suddenly dry lips.

'I love this end of the park,' she said brightly. 'It's got the best bits. I just love the bird sanctuary and the zoo and…and the sheep meadow.'

Oh, good grief…the sheep meadow? It was nothing more than a vast grassy space where people had picnics or threw Frisbees.

Alex cleared his throat. 'The lake would be a nice spot on a warm day like this.' His hesitation was almost imperceptible. 'Got time for a walk?'

'Um…yeah, I guess.' Layla risked a quick glance at Alex, wishing her heart rate would settle. It was crazy to be feeling this nervous. 'I've only got a bit of paperwork waiting for me and it'll still be waiting when I get back.'

'Same.' Alex met her glance briefly and Layla realised he was as nervous as she was about having this conversation. Was that why he was suggesting they have it well away from the place they both worked?

Oddly, the fact that Alex was nervous calmed Layla enough to make her smile. 'I could kill for a hot dog or something,' she said. 'I'm *starving*.'

A wash of surprise, or maybe relief, crossed Alex's features.

'Same.'

'Let's get out of here, then.' Layla led the way.

They had to share the elevator with a troupe of candy-stripers heading off to the cafeteria for lunch. If Alex was remotely aware of the increase in the amount of giggling and the eyelashes that got batted in his direction, he gave no indication of it.

The lobby was crowded with people. Weekends were a time when lots of visitors could get to Angel's and often there were special treats planned for the young patients. Today it looked as if a celebrity basketball player was making an appearance and he was being tailed by a television crew.

Alex and Layla still hadn't spoken another word to each other by the time they emerged from the front entrance of Angel's into the welcome fresh air and sunshine. Walking side by side, Layla turned her head as they passed the small statue.

Alex noticed the movement. 'You know who that is?' he asked.

'I got told by the taxi driver who dropped me here when I came for the job interview. It's Angel Mendez, a little boy who died of polio during the Great Depression. That's where the hospital got its name.'

'Did you know that his dad was a paediatrician?' Alex asked.

'No. I hadn't heard that bit. How tragic that he couldn't save his own son.'

'His name was Federico Mendez. He wanted to honour Angel's memory and try and make sure other parents didn't lose their kids. This was New York's first free children's hospital.'

'It's a great history.' Layla couldn't help reaching out to brush the statue with her fingers as she passed. She was by no means the only person who ever did that. The bronze of this much-loved statue had weathered to a greenish tinge but the hands of the small boy were shiny because they were on a level that could be touched. By adults like her, or by children being lifted up or climbing so that they could make contact with something they could identify with.

'Mmm.' Alcx was a littlc ahcad of her now. 'Kind of sums up what we're all about, doesn't it?'

The road in front of them was wide and busy. Ambulances were turning into the hospital grounds and yellow cabs were sprinkled thickly amongst the heavy traffic. A police car went by with its lights and siren blaring. Alex led the way as the lights changed. A horse-drawn carriage was turning into the park and open-topped, double-decker tourist buses were offloading passengers.

'Which way? Right to the bird sanctuary or left to the lake?'

'The lake,' Layla said. The draw of water in the middle of a late summer's day was irresistible.

So was the smell of hot food from the carts as they walked through the crowds in the shade of the big old trees. Layla shook her head at someone trying to sell her a balloon and at someone else who wanted her to buy a walking guide to the park but she couldn't go past a cart selling Mexican food.

'Nachos,' she breathed. 'My favourite. Even better

than a hot dog.' She smiled winningly up at Alex. 'Do you mind waiting?'

He didn't seem to mind. In fact, the corners of his eyes crinkled as he smiled back. 'Go right ahead. I'll go and grab a burger from that cart we just passed. Meet you back here in five minutes.'

They kept walking after buying their food and drink because it wasn't far to the lake now. And then they sat and ate under the shady trees, watching people in row-boats and elegant swans floating past. A group of hungry ducks emerged from the water to watch them eat.

'No way,' Layla told them. 'You wouldn't like corn chips, anyway.'

She scooped another mouthful of savoury beans and cheese into her mouth and closed her eyes from the sheer pleasure of it all. Then she opened them and blinked. She was enjoying this?

The cloud of the conversation she and Alex had to have was still there but, again by some unspoken agreement, they were putting it off until they'd eaten. For the moment this felt remarkably like…well…a *date.*

Here she was, in a gorgeous setting on a stunning day, having a meal in the company of the most attractive man she'd ever known.

What had Chloe said? He was single. So was she.

There was something between them that was clearly strong enough to pull them together again with the force of an overstretched rubber band being released.

Was it even remotely possible that they could make a fresh start?

Would she *want* to?

Layla found herself watching Alex as he broke a

piece off his hamburger bun and held it out. A brave duck was edging closer, gathering the courage to snatch the morsel from those long, surgeon's fingers. But Layla's gaze travelled up his arm to where his shirtsleeve was rolled up far enough to show the bulge of muscle in his upper arm.

The skin was dry now, of course, but Layla could still see it glistening with the drops of water from his shower last night. And she knew exactly what that bunch of muscle would feel like if she gripped it really tightly.

Oh…yes…

Shc would want to.

The duck who was brave enough to take bread from his fingers probably wasn't expecting his friends to turn on him the instant he succeeded. The cacophony of quacking and the violent flapping of so many wings broke the peaceful, summer picnic vibe that Alex had been enjoying more than he was prepared to acknowledge.

Late summer suited Layla. The sunlight made her blonde hair glow golden and she still managed to look smart in her light clothing. The skirt that swirled around her bare legs. The soft-looking shirt that had rolled-up sleeves fastened with a little tab and button and was unbuttoned down the front so it was like a jacket over a camisole top that clung to her curves and had an eye-catching bit of beadwork around that hint of cleavage.

Those bare legs were stuck out in front of her as she sat on the grass, licking melted cheese and salsa off her fingers with a totally unselfconscious enjoyment of her food. The skin on her calves looked tanned and smooth but Alex had been successfully resisting the urge to touch them because he knew that, however smooth the bits on show were, they couldn't compete with the skin hidden beneath the folds of that pretty skirt.

Yeah. It was just as well the duck fight broke the spell and reminded him of the intended purpose of this outing. It wasn't a date. Somehow they had to clear the air and sort out a way of being able to work together.

Alex sat up from where he'd been lounging on the grass propped up on one elbow. He took a deep breath and turned to look directly at Layla, wondering just how to start this conversation.

She caught his glance and he could see the way she caught her breath. She knew what was coming and she was nervous about it.

Why? Why was *he* so nervous, for that matter? They had a common goal here. They both wanted the same thing, didn't they? Maybe Layla simply wasn't ready to talk yet. Not about the big stuff, anyway.

'I saw Mike Jenner this morning,' she told him. 'Tommy's dad. He and Gina had brought Tommy in to get the pre-admission tests done. I didn't realise that Monday's the big day.'

Alex made a noncommittal sound. Why would she? Tommy Jenner was his patient, not Layla's.

Except that the little boy's case had captured the imagination of the entire staff at Angel's once the story had got round of how close a call it had been for his father to be accused of abuse. And of how serious Tommy's condition was. Any kid with a brain tumour was enough to tug at the heart strings but this one was definitely special.

'Mike's really stressed,' Layla continued. 'Which

was why he was so keen to talk, I think. There's so much riding on this.'

Alex could feel an unpleasant kind of pressure himself. Of course there was a lot riding on this. A little boy's life.

'He wants to ask Gina to marry him,' Layla said quietly into the silence. 'But it's not the right time. If things go well, then he can see it being part of the celebration later. A new future for Tommy. A new family. It's lovely, isn't it? That Mike and Gina found each other in the midst of all that worry and that they both love Tommy so much?'

Still Alex couldn't say anything. He didn't need to be hearing this. Didn't want the feeling of emotional blackmail that could colour the huge decision he had to make on Monday about whether or not to go ahead with the complicated surgery.

'It's just as well they have each other.' Layla sounded as if she was talking to herself as the soft words continued to spill out. 'How awful would it be when you have to pin the hopes for your future on a decision that would mean your baby had to undergo such a risky operation?'

And then, as though the implications of her words were only now sinking in, Layla ducked her head and bit her lip.

'Sorry…' she muttered. 'I…get a bit carried away, don't I?'

'No kidding.' Alex spoke more sharply than he'd intended. 'Surely you're experienced enough by now to know how unwise it is to get too emotionally involved in a case?'

'It's never unwise to *care*,' Layla retorted.

A bubble of something hot and nasty was expanding in his gut. Anger that was encased in a skin of confusion.

He didn't get it.

Layla had always become too emotionally involved. He'd seen that when they'd first met over Jamie Kirkpatrick's case—the little boy whose condition was eerily similar to Tommy's. She was so passionate about her job. Cared so intensely about her patients and their families.

And yet she could dump someone she was in a relationship with without so much as a second thought. Without even looking back to see what kind of damage she'd done.

Without *caring.*

'I'll make my decisions based on my professional expertise,' Alex said coldly. 'I'll look at the results of the MRI on Monday and judge whether the chemo has made enough of a difference to improve the odds of attempting a surgery that has the very real risk of ending Tommy's life immediately.'

The bubble was getting bigger. It wouldn't take much to burst it.

'I do not need anybody telling me just how much the future happiness of his father depends on the outcome,' he continued. 'I will make a rational, *professional* choice about the actions I take.'

'Oh…?' Layla's hands were curled into fists and her voice was laced with derision. 'Like you did last night, do you mean?'

OK, that did it. This might not be the way into that conversation that he'd anticipated but he wasn't about to hold back now. Except that Layla got in another barb first.

'Do you make a habit of having unprotected sex?'

'No.' Alex spoke through gritted teeth. 'Do *you*?'

Layla gave an incredulous huff. 'The last person I had sex with, other than my *husband*,' she hissed, 'was *you*.'

Alex had only just started to form a coherent train of thought through the mist of red-hot anger. Now he was stunned into silence again. How long had Layla been divorced? There hadn't been anyone since?

Why not?

'So you don't need to worry that you've caught anything unpleasant,' Layla went on scathingly. 'And I'm not pregnant. If I hadn't been right at the end of my cycle I would have taken a morning-after pill today.'

The clinical delivery of the information was chillingly impersonal. Alex couldn't meet the glare he knew was coming in his direction. He stared straight ahead. The ducks, realising that any prospect of food was gone, were filing back into the lake. In search of a more congenial atmosphere?

'You don't need to worry either,' he told Layla stiffly. 'The only relationship I've had in the last five years was way back when I first arrived in Brisbane. I've been tested and cleared of any transmittable diseases since then, thanks to having to work as a surgeon.'

He could actually feel Layla digesting that startling piece of information.

There was a long, long silence. He could feel her curiosity building. He might be wondering himself why Layla was still single but he wouldn't ask her straight out. Layla wouldn't shy away from something like that, though. She just wouldn't be able to help herself.

Sure enough, she asked, albeit a tad hesitantly.

'Why not?'

Alex shrugged. 'Too busy,' he said, with an attempt at lightness. 'You know how it is.'

'Yeah…' The agreement encompassed something a lot bigger than a busy career. She knew.

Alex shot her a glance. 'And maybe I'm too well aware of the damage that emotional involvement causes. Professional *and* personal.'

Another silence. And then Layla sighed and the sound was like an admission of defeat.

'I'm sorry,' she said quietly.

'What for?'

'The…way things ended. That whole mess. I didn't think for a moment that anything would go wrong with Jamie's operation and that made it all so much worse.'

'Not for you.' Alex didn't care what the bitter words might reveal. 'You just walked away without a backward glance. *I* was the one who got slapped with a malpractice suit. *I* was the one left wondering if my unprofessional involvement with a colleague had somehow undermined my ability to do my job well enough.'

'You think I didn't feel guilty?' Layla whispered. Her voice rose. 'I was *married*, for God's sake, Alex. My life was falling apart.'

Alex had to get to his feet. How dared she suggest that that black time had been just as bad for her as it had been for him? He jammed his hands in his pockets and took a few jerky steps towards the lake. Then he whirled back to face Layla.

'So why the hell did you get tangled up with me in the first place, then?'

She looked…anguished. Her voice came out sounding as though she might start crying.

Layla Woods crying? Unthinkable.

'Probably for the same reason that last night happened,' she said, jerking her head sideways as she stopped speaking, as though it was taking an enormous physical effort to break the eye contact with him.

So she hadn't wanted it to happen? Simply hadn't been able to resist, despite knowing that it was, somehow, so wrong? There was a world of unspoken pain hidden beneath those quiet words.

Alex had to exert the same kind of physical effort he'd seen Layla display. To stop himself moving forward. Reaching for Layla's hands to pull her to her feet. So that he could wrap his arms around her.

And hold her.

The silence around them was broken by the far-away sound of children laughing and the much closer sound of a rowboat near the shore of the lake, the oars dipping and splashing. The sound make Alex think of more than water.

Of wet skin.

The slide of bodies that couldn't get close enough fast enough.

Layla was getting to her feet but she didn't come any closer. She just stared at Alex.

'It happened,' she said steadily. 'The point is, what are we going to do about it?'

He swore softly, under his breath. She was right.

There was a physical attraction between them that was irresistible.

So powerful it had the potential to destroy them both.

'I don't know,' he said, his voice catching. 'I really don't know.'

Layla held his gaze. 'Neither do I.'

This was a standoff of a very different kind from the one Layla had been aware of when she'd stepped out of the elevator on the eighth floor of Angel's a couple of hours ago.

This one wasn't funny at all.

'Do we just walk away?' Alex suggested. 'Pretend it never happened?'

He still hadn't broken that intense gaze that was locked with her own. No. They both knew that wasn't going to happen.

'There's another way we could deal with it,' Layla heard herself saying cautiously.

A tiny flash of interest—hope, maybe—brightened the dark gaze in front of her. 'Which is?'

'Um… There's some kind of a spark between us, isn't there?'

A huff of breath from Alex. Something halfway between a snort of laughter and a groan.

'And being around each other is kind of like having a pile of fuel available.'

Alex was silent but he was listening. Carefully.

'Sometimes…' Layla swallowed hard '…if you throw the fuel onto the spark and make a fire, the fuel runs out and the fire just…goes out by itself.'

She could see Alex processing the idea. His face went very still.

What was he thinking? Did he feel the *shower* of sparks Layla could feel dancing in the air between them? And the certain knowledge that the tiniest bit of fuel, in the form of a kiss maybe, would ignite those sparks into the hottest flames imaginable. And that those flames could be healing. They could burn away the resentment and mistrust that lay between them after the way they'd parted five years ago.

'Is that what you want to do?' His voice was the rawest sound Layla had ever heard.

She couldn't say a word.

All she could do was hold his gaze, knowing that he would see her answer in her face.

She saw his chest expand as he sucked in a huge breath. Saw the way he dampened his bottom lip with his tongue and the sparks got so bright her vision blurred.

'It could work,' he added, as they both began moving, the spell that had held them so still now broken. 'But fire's a dangerous thing to play around with. There's a risk that someone could get badly burned.'

Layla nodded, far more slowly this time. It would probably be her, she thought.

Did she really want to put herself in such a vulnerable position?

Yes…

The tiny voice was remarkably decisive.

Because there was just a chance, wasn't there?

A chance that the fuel wouldn't run out completely. That the huge flames would burn with a blinding brightness but then settle and leave a glow that might…just *might*…be enough.

And if she didn't take that chance, she might regret it for the rest of her life.

CHAPTER SIX

LAYLA ARRIVED AT work on Monday morning as nervous as a long-tailed cat in a room full of rocking chairs.

Yesterday had to have been the longest day in her life.

The longest night, anyway.

What had she expected? That Alex would give it some thought, decide that it was a good idea to see if they could deal with their lingering attraction by indulging it and then be unable to wait another night until they could put the plan into action?

Yeah…maybe she had and that was why she'd been waiting for her phone to ring or, at least for a text message signal to sound.

Why her heart had leapt into her throat when her ringtone broke the increasingly tense silence of her Sunday evening.

Talking to her mother was the same as always. Gully-washing October rain had set in. Her father was planning to run for yet another term as mayor. Her ex-husband, Luke, was going to be a father again and there was even a whisper about town that it might be twins this time. Fortunately, the topic of conversation Celia Woods was most concerned about was how she was going to provide the best treats in town for the children who would come knocking on Halloween.

'I don't know, Momma.' If she was honest, Layla didn't actually care. Halloween traditions were the last thing on her mind right now but this was preferable to being reminded of the life she could have had if she'd stayed with Luke. 'Why don't you do some of those meringue ghosts or the cat-shaped cookies you did one year? They look pretty special when you wrap them up in Cellophane and ribbons. Can't you get food dye that makes things black now?'

'I do believe you can. That's a real good idea, honey. I'm gonna go and fix my shopping list right now.'

The silence seemed even heavier after that phone call.

Nothing changed in Swallow Creek and suddenly that was making Layla feel even more on edge about what was happening in her life. The new life she had come here to start. One that had been so full of promise.

One that she had just lobbed a grenade into and now she was waiting to see if Alex was going to pull the pin.

Maybe it would be better if he didn't.

And how long was she going to have to wait to find out? Mondays were always hectic. Surgery lists would be jam-packed and weekends had the habit of accumulating issues that could wait until somebody senior enough was available to make decisions.

Layla was caught up in meetings, one of which was with the committee dedicated to raising the funds for a new MRI machine. The meeting had barely started, however, before she received an urgent summons to the emergency department.

And that was when her day started to go downhill.

Not that she realised it at the time, but it took another dive when she sent someone to page Alex with an even more urgent summons than the one she'd received.

It should have been Ryan O'Doherty that Layla had summoned because the deputy head of the neurology department was on call for emergency cases today. Alex had arrived with the intention of telling Layla that but one look at the determined set of her mouth and he knew he wasn't going to be permitted to delegate.

'I need the very best surgeon we've got,' she said.

Was this some kind of play to weld something personal into the professional? Had Layla done her own thinking and second-guessed the decision Alex had come to last night? Was this was a clever counter-offensive to make him change his mind? Now certainly wasn't the time to set her straight but he couldn't leave it much longer.

Taking a closer look, Alex could see that the fierce passion making those blue eyes glow so brightly was purely professional. Layla had no head room for any kind of personal agenda right now. This was all about a six-year-old boy called Matthew.

Alex had perched one hip on the edge of the desk in the office Layla had commandeered in the ER. 'Fill me in.'

'I met Matthew four months ago. It was my first outpatient clinic day during my orientation week. He was in the waiting room with his mother, Dayna. She's a single mum. Matthew's father was killed in an industrial accident before she even knew she was pregnant.'

Alex was tempted to tell Layla to cut to the chase. The medical details. But the words were spilling out with wobbly edges and she was using her hands a lot while she talked. This was pure Layla. The story of any patient had to include a picture of the whole person. He needed to be patient and simply listen for a minute because she was going to tell him the story whether he liked it or not.

'He'd found a toy aeroplane in the basket. One of those double-winged ones, you know? Like Snoopy uses when he's being the Red Baron?'

Alex felt one side of his mouth curl upwards and his impatience faded as he listened to the lilt in Layla's voice that always got stronger when she was passionate about something. He watched the emotions that flitted across her face and was reminded of what an extraordinary woman she was. Unique. If he could somehow distance himself enough to become merely a good friend, her company would be a joy.

'There was a battle going on. The Red Baron was gaining height, ready to dive-bomb something. Possibly his mother's foot because she was busy reading a magazine and wasn't paying enough attention to the battle. Anyway…I came round the corner and there was a…a mid-air incident and the Red Baron crashed into my leg.'

Alex's lips twitched. He could imagine the scene.

'Fortunately there were no major injuries but poor Dayna was mortified when she found me sitting in with the consultant when she came in with Matthew for his appointment. I told her it was a real joy to see one of our cardiology patients looking so healthy. Matthew was in for a five-year check because he'd been a patient at Angel's when he was a baby to have a major vascular anomaly corrected.'

Alex finally frowned. 'This is a cardiology case? Why the hell have you called me down here? I'm in the middle of—'

Layla held up her hand, cutting him off.

'Dayna asked for me when she brought Matthew into Emergency this morning, maybe because she remembered the way we'd met. She'd found Mattie banging his head on the floor of the bathroom 'because it hurt so much'. He vomited twice and was found to have neck stiffness and photophobia on arrival.'

Alex's frown deepened. 'Sounds like meningitis.'

'Spinal tap was negative. We wondered about a head trauma after that so we got a CT scan done.'

'And?' Alex had closed his eyes for a moment. He did not need another case like Tommy Jenner. A brain lesion in a small child that Layla cared about a little too much. Then his eyes snapped open. This was worse, wasn't it?

'A major cardiac vascular anomaly as a baby? He's got a cerebral aneurysm, hasn't he?'

Layla nodded, her face now a picture of misery. 'Dayna's beside herself. She thought they'd got through the worst that life had to throw at both her and Mattie. He's started school now and he's such a happy kid. He...he told me he's going to be a fighter pilot when he grows up.'

Oh...*hell*...

'You'd better show me the CT.' Alex knew he sounded cool and distant but he'd been sucked in, hadn't he? Lulled by watching and listening to Layla and now he had more involvement on an emotional level than he was comfortable with before he'd even met the patient.

And there would be no luxury of time to consider a decision here, like he'd had with Tommy. The CT results were crystal clear. The damaged vessel in Matthew's brain was at risk of bursting at any moment and the results would be catastrophic. Severe brain injury. Or death. The surgery could be equally catastrophic but it was his only chance.

Could Ryan perform this surgery? Yes. Did Alex want to pass it on? He *could* use his position as head of department and say that Ryan needed the experience of this case.

Layla had remained silent while Alex studied the CT scan images. She stood back when he went to meet Dayna and Matthew. Small for his age, Matthew had a very pale face, big brown eyes and spiky black hair. He was in pain and terrified.

'Hey, buddy…' Alex could feel something squeeze hard in his chest when he smiled gently at the little boy. 'I hear you're going to be a fighter pilot when you grow up?'

Huge brown eyes were locked on his face. He heard the suppressed sob that came from Matthew's mother, who was sitting beside the bed, holding her son's hand. And he could feel Layla's watchful gaze from somewhere behind him. Could feel the *hope*.

'I've heard that there's a special airplane bed somewhere around here,' he told Matthew. 'What say I arrange for you to fly upstairs to come and have the operation to fix that nasty headache you've got?'

He had to brush close to Layla as he went ahead to set things up. He hadn't expected her to follow him. He didn't want to see the gratitude in her eyes when she touched his arm and forced him to stop just as he got to the internal double doors of the emergency room.

'Thanks,' she whispered.

'Don't thank me.' Alex knew he sounded curt but he couldn't let this go on. 'This isn't anything personal, Layla.' He held her gaze and had the odd sensation that he was trying to use his own to push her as far away as possible. 'I've thought about it,' he added, 'and the answer's no. We're colleagues now. And that's all we can be. Anything else is a recipe for disaster.'

He saw the shock of his words but he had to hand it to Layla. If she was disappointed she hid it completely.

'You're probably right,' was all she said. 'I'd better get back to Matthew. Maybe I can catch you later to follow up.' She turned away. 'On the surgery, I mean.'

Alex pushed the doors open with a little more force than necessary. *Probably* right? What did that mean? And had she really needed to underline that talking to him later would be purely professional?

Hell…maybe she wasn't disappointed at all.

Scrubbing in for Matthew's surgery a commendably short time later should have been the end of any personal undercurrents in Alex's thoughts. This was always a private time when he could centre himself and focus completely on what was going to happen when he had finished this intensive preparation.

Except it was taking a lot longer than usual to get to that focussed space. The suds being formed by the small soap-impregnated scrubbing brush foamed all over his hands but he wasn't ready to rinse them off.

He kept scrubbing. Under each fingernail. In the

webbing between each finger. In a world of his own during this automatic preparation for surgery.

When you looked back on your life, he found himself musing, sometimes it's easy to see a particular day that marked a turning point in your life.

He'd had quite a few of them.

Like that dreadful day when he'd been only ten years old, and his beloved mother had died of breast cancer.

The day he'd finally walked out on his abusive stepfather, when he'd been sixteen, having made the heartbreaking decision that it would be better for Cade if he removed himself from the picture.

The day he'd first set eyes on Layla Woods and had realised that, against all the odds, he *was* still capable of trusting someone else.

Of loving them.

The flow of warm water was like balm after all that scrubbing. Alex rinsed the foam off his hands and then changed the angle of his arms so that he could rinse from his wrists to his elbows without letting the foam touch the well-cleaned skin of his hands. He picked up the sterile towel to dry himself, still lost in his thoughts.

In a few seconds he knew he would be able to turn them off as decisively as the tap he'd just been using and focus with the same intensity on the job ahead of him, but he also knew that, to get to that point of focus, he needed to let this train of thought reach its conclusion.

None of those earlier, turning-point days had been clearly marked in advance so that you got the chance to think about it and weigh up the potential benefits and downsides. Like he had been able to do ever since he'd parted company from Layla after their time in Central

Park. Ever since he'd seen that willingness in Layla's eyes to start something between them again.

The history he had with both Callie and Cade would colour whatever advice they might give him. The history he had with Layla made it impossible to think rationally when he was close to her, let alone talk to her and hear that sweet Texan drawl that had been one of the first things that had attracted him to her.

By late Sunday night Alex had decided that getting back into any kind of a relationship with Layla would be a bad idea. He'd been quite confident that, with the calming distraction of a heavy day at work, that decision would seat itself so firmly he would be more than ready to talk to Layla later and find another way to deal with having to work together.

He was still confident that the decision was right. He just hadn't bargained on this turning out to be such a stressful day.

OK, he'd known that making a decision about Tommy Jenner would be a tough call and his heart had sunk as he'd watched the MRI images coming up on screen this morning. The call was too close to make one way or the other right now. A professional and emotional tightrope. The hardest thing had been to face Mike and Gina in his office and tell them he needed more time. That, despite their desperate pleas, he couldn't tell them his decision until he'd given it a lot more thought.

And it had been at the end of that interview that he'd received the summons to join Layla in the emergency department.

Well…he'd told her his decision now. And she'd accepted it.

The worst was over.

Now he could focus properly and move on. Do what he did best and go into Theatre to try and save a young life.

Layla slipped into the observation area above the operating theatre.

She saw the busy team preparing the theatre around the tiny, still form that was Matthew lying there under the bright lights. The television screen up here showed a close-up of Matthew's head. A large patch of his adorable, spiky hair had been shaved off and a nurse was painting the skin with iodine.

She saw the moment the star of the show arrived, hands held carefully crossed in front of his body, using his shoulder blade to bump open the swing doors that separated the theatre from the scrubbing-in area.

Alex…

He could do this. He could save Mattie. Layla's teeth sank into her bottom lip so hard it hurt. It didn't matter about the decision Alex had come to regarding what they did about the attraction they had for each other. All that mattered in this moment was the life of the child on the table.

Please…

As if he felt the force of her plea, Alex looked up as he took his position at the head of the operating table. Layla was by no means alone in the observation area but his gaze went unswervingly to where she was sitting.

Could he actually see her face behind the wall of glass when the lights down there were so much brighter?

Possibly not. But he was aware of her, that was for sure.

Layla's heart gave a painful thump. Maybe she

shouldn't be here. Could her presence, reminding him of the tension between them, distract him in any way? The way she'd always believed it had in Jamie Kirkpatrick's case?

She'd put pressure on him back then, ending their affair.

She'd put pressure on him again now, suggesting that they revisit that affair as a way of dealing with their unfinished business.

If anything bad happened to Matthew today, that would be the end. Alex would never want anything to do with her again.

Had she realised how much she was putting on the line by insisting that Alex get involved with this case? Had she even thought that he might take the opportunity to get what he wanted to say over with?

Of course she hadn't. She had followed her heart.

The disappointment of hearing his decision had been a body blow that she was still reeling from but Layla was fighting back. She *shouldn't* be this disappointed. She'd never expected to have Alex Rodriguez back in her professional environment, let alone her personal life.

Why couldn't she learn not to be so impulsive? To take the time to really weigh up the repercussions of making emotionally based decisions? She'd done this too many times in her life already.

Like when she'd fallen into Alex's arms in the first place, all those years ago.

When she'd ended things between them because she hadn't been able to stand the guilt and the way he had been making her feel.

When she'd practically thrown herself at Alex and suggested they kept seeing each other. Intimately.

The emotional overload was unbearable but, thankfully, it coalesced into only an imperceptible moment in time.

The subtle nod that came from Alex was probably just as imperceptible to anyone other than Layla. He seemed to be acknowledging her presence.

And reassuring her that it wouldn't distract him.

The whole team was poised as Alex turned his attention to the exposed patch of Matthew's head. He held out his hand.

'Scalpel.'

The critical point of this surgery came when the blood supply to the brain had to be compromised to allow a permanent repair to the damaged vessel, which was a major artery. There was only a small window of time—four minutes—before the blood flow had to be fully restored to avoid the certainty of brain damage. If the repair hadn't been done well enough by then, there would be no second chances.

'Start the clock.'

The order was delivered with crisp precision.

Alex was ready.

A small boy's life depended on what he was about to do. The child's desperate mother was sitting in a waiting room not far away. Layla was sitting in the observation area of this operating theatre.

Part of Alex's brain was aware of all these things and their implications but none of them could even begin to intrude on his intense focus on the job in hand. The intricate and challenging clipping of this defective blood vessel without allowing it to burst or cause any collateral damage through the technique.

The clock kept ticking.

'Two minutes,' the anaesthetist warned.

Beads of perspiration formed on Alex's forehead. A nurse patted them dry with a gauze swab. He had to blink and refocus his vision through the magnifying lenses of his eyewear.

The clip was so tiny. Slippery. So hard to slip into exactly the right position and keep it there long enough to secure it.

'Fifty-eight seconds,' the anaesthetist said quietly. 'Forty-five…thirty…'

It was there. In place. Alex squeezed it shut.

'Stop the clock.'

Another minute of complete silence as Alex inspected his handiwork in minute detail and finally he could give the verdict that created a collective release of breaths being held.

'Looking good. We can close up now.'

It was done and he knew it had been done well.

Only now could Alex allow himself a split second of satisfaction before focussing on the automatic protocols of closing. A moment to take a deeper breath and know that he had made a difference. Saved a life?

Quite possibly, although there was still plenty to be anxious about until he could measure the steps to recovery that Matthew would need to take.

Still, he could look forward to telling Dayna that the surgery had gone as well as they could have hoped for.

He could imagine what he would see in Layla's eyes when they next came face to face.

Gratitude, for sure. Far more than he'd seen when he'd agreed to take on this surgery in the first place.

Admiration as well?

The bone flap was back in place in Matthew's skull a short time later and the probe to measure intracranial pressure was secured and tested. The final stitches and bandaging were the only tasks to be completed. Alex could relax.

And it was then that the realisation hit him.

He had been aware of the undercurrent of emotional pressure of this surgery, not only for his patient and the family but from Layla's investment in this case. From having her right there, watching his every move.

And it hadn't made any difference. He had put it aside and done exactly what he'd needed to do, to the very best of his ability.

Maybe he could handle more than he'd thought he was capable of when it came to Layla.

If he was aware of the danger of real emotional involvement, he could overcome it. Just like he'd just demonstrated when he'd been concentrating on Matthew's operation.

If he heeded Callie's warning, he could make sure he didn't start trusting Layla too much. So that when the end came, as it would, he would be prepared for it and it wouldn't destroy him because he would have been in control all along.

Maybe Layla had been right all along.

If they threw fuel on the smouldering ashes of what

had once burned so brightly between them, it could burn itself out for once and for all.

It had worked with Callie Richards, hadn't it?

And if it could burn itself out, he wouldn't be left for the rest of his life wondering what if…?

No wonder last night's decision had been so hard won.

It had been the wrong choice.

But he'd already told Layla so it was too late to change his mind.

Or was it?

As the final stitch was cut, Alex dropped the curved needle and its holder onto the instrument trolley and looked up to where Layla had been sitting at the end of the row of seats. As soon as he saw her again, he might know the answer to that burning little question.

The seat was empty now. Layla wasn't there.

Layla had slipped out of the observation area with much the same stealth as she'd entered it, only this time she was having to swallow past a painful constriction in her throat.

She was just so darned *proud* of Alex.

Not that she could tell him that. She needed to clear her head and get back into a space where she could tell him how well he'd done on a strictly professional level without revealing such a personal response. He wouldn't want to see that. It would spell the end of being able to work together without the kind of tension that would inevitably become too poisonous to be tolerable.

Keeping herself busy, Layla waited a couple of hours before going to the PICU herself, where she found Matthew resting comfortably, still well sedated, and Dayna exhausted but with her eyes still bright with tears of relief.

'Dr Rodriguez is brilliant, isn't he?'

'He sure is.'

'He said we won't know if there's been any lasting damage until Mattie's properly awake again. That he might have some hurdles with his speech for a while, or a weakness on one side. But that he's young enough to recover completely from anything like that and that it was so lucky we found the problem in time.'

'I'm so happy we did.' Layla shared a hug with Dayna. 'I'll come by and see how you're both doing again tomorrow morning.' She stood back to cast a practised eye over the monitors surrounding Matthew's bed and Dayna followed the direction of her searching gaze.

'Dr Rodriguez said it's all looking real good. You just missed him. He said he had to go and check on another patient on the ward. That it seemed to be his day for special little boys who needed big operations.'

Layla caught her breath.

Tommy.

Alex must have gone to give his decision to Mike and Gina about whether or not he would operate. She knew how big a decision that would have been to make because she'd seen those MRI results.

The tumour had shrunk thanks to the chemotherapy but it was still a nasty one and it was in a very difficult spot. Uncannily like the one Jamie Kirkpatrick had had.

She could understand if that was enough to make Alex shy away from the challenge but would it have made any difference, having had the success with Matthew today?

Layla had to find out. This wasn't personal so she had no trouble justifying the need to see him. She didn't even give herself the time to question the wisdom of doing so.

She went straight from the PICU to the neurology ward. To Alex's office.

The door was very slightly ajar and she could see the screen on the wall with an image from an MRI being displayed. Tommy's MRI.

Did he still have Mike and Gina in the office? She couldn't hear the sound of any voices but could they be sitting in stunned silence trying to absorb some very bad news?

No. Alex would have closed his door before having a conversation like that.

Indecisiveness was not an option here. Layla tapped lightly on the door and went in, pushing the door shut quietly behind her.

Alex was alone in his office. Standing by the window, clearly lost in thought, tapping the end of the ballpoint pen he was holding against his bottom lip. Papers were strewn across his desk and some of them had rough-looking sketches. The kind you might make if you were talking someone through what was going to happen in a complex operation.

Alex turned slowly to watch Layla as she looked up from noting the sketches.

'You're going to do it?' she asked softly. 'Tommy's operation?'

The response was a curt nod. ‘Everybody understands the risks.’

‘But it’s worth a shot?’

Another nod. More considered this time. Alex was holding her gaze and Layla could see something that had nothing to do with any patient in his eyes. She had to take in a slow, steadying breath. What she was seeing now was very, very different from the way he’d looked at her when he’d told her his decision.

He looked as if…as if he’d changed his mind.

‘What about us, Alex?’ The words came out as a whisper. ‘Do you really think we’re not worth a shot too?’

For a long, long moment Alex didn’t move a muscle. Didn’t make a sound.

He took a step towards her. The ballpoint pen clattered onto the surface of his desk.

And then he took Layla in his arms and she closed her eyes as her head tilted back under the pressure of his lips on hers.

It seemed like she had her answer.

CHAPTER SEVEN

SOMETHING WAS VERY different this time.

Giving in to the overwhelming attraction between them had always been illicit. Tinged with the knowledge that it was dangerous. That somebody was going to get hurt.

That it was *wrong*.

Even the other night, when Alex had been blindsided by Layla appearing in the decontamination shower, the encounter had been just as illicit. It was dangerous to have unprotected sex. Wrong to be doing it in their place of employment.

Quite simply, any occasion that had involved physical contact between Alex and Layla had been…wild.

Snatched moments of time when nothing had mattered other than slaking a white-hot lust.

But this time it was different.

They had all the time in the world and that made them both oddly apprehensive about taking that next step. So, when Layla suggested they had dinner at the tapas bar where she'd gone with Chloe a while back, Alex agreed without hesitation. It was a reprieve from more than making a decision about where and when they would next be naked together. It was also a way of keeping this to themselves. If they went out together to O'Malley's, the grapevine at Angel's would have been buzzing with the news within hours.

Because this felt so different it seemed right to keep it private. This was their business. The unfinished kind, and whatever they were planning to do to see it through to its conclusion was not something anyone else needed to know about.

Except…wasn't this supposed to be about throwing fuel onto the smouldering physical attraction that had never died between them? All they needed for that was a room with a bed. A hotel or motel, preferably, so that things didn't intrude too far into their personal lives.

Why were they here, in a vibrant but softly lit bar, about to share food and drink and conversation instead of some nice, uncomplicated sex?

Alex sighed audibly. He really had no idea. It had seemed such a good idea at the time. A way to put a hard day's work behind him and catch his breath before facing this new turning point in his life.

'So…' He raised his glass of beer in a mock salute as Layla looked up from the menu she'd been studying. 'Here we are.'

'Mmm.' Layla's gaze slid away from his and she lifted her glass of wine to take a sip. 'We've come quite a long way to get here, haven't we?'

She wasn't talking about negotiating rush-hour New York traffic to get to the meatpacking district on the banks of the Hudson River. And it was an accurate statement. They had both taken very different routes through life to get to this point.

Funny that it felt like a huge circle all of a sudden.

'Head of Paediatrics in one of the country's most prestigious children's hospitals.' Alex tilted his head to show his respect for Layla's achievements. 'Well done, you.'

'Head of Paediatric Neurosurgery in the same hospital,' Laya responded. 'I think being sought after as the person most likely to save a child's life tops my ability to boss people around and keep things running smoothly.'

The sound Alex made was dismissive. 'I'm just doing my job. The best way I know how.'

'Dayna wouldn't say that. Neither would I. I…um…didn't get the chance to congratulate you earlier. That surgery today was amazing to watch.'

'Thanks.'

'You didn't mind having an audience?' There was an unspoken question in Layla's eyes. She wasn't talking about an audience in general. She was asking him whether it had bothered him to have *her* in the gallery. Whether it had brought back memories of the last surgery of his that she'd witnessed. The disaster that had been Jamie Kirkpatrick's case.

The very idea of talking about that was enough to send a chill down his spine. He'd factored in the way his past with Layla was so inextricably linked to Jamie's case but he hadn't bargained on having to talk about it.

How stupid was that? Jamie had been part of their story right from the get-go. The reason they had met in the first place. And Layla pulling the plug on that relationship the night before Jamie's surgery might not have been the end of things if that surgery had gone well. Alex might well have tried to find out what had gone wrong. Tried to fix things between them. But it hadn't gone well. His world had shattered and the shards had driven him and Layla as far apart as it was possible to get.

But here they were again.

A huge mistake?

Quite possibly. Alex could almost hear Callie's voice in his ear.

I told you so, mate. You should've listened.

At least he could try and avoid the subject. It was easy to pretend he hadn't picked up on the subtext of Layla's casual query.

'I'm used to having an audience,' he said lightly. 'Might close the gallery for Tommy's surgery, though.'

Layla toyed with her glass. 'Have you set a date?'

'Not before next week at the earliest. There's a lot of preparation needed.' Like there had been before Jamie's complex surgery. Alex ruthlessly squashed the comparison.

'Let me know if there's anything I can do to help.'

His nod was offhand as he opened his menu. Alex didn't intend involving Layla. 'Food looks good,' he said a moment later. 'What are you going to have?'

'Maybe *costillas.*' Layla looked up with a smile. 'The barbecued mini-ribs. Messy but so tasty. And some *pimentos rellenos*.'

Alex raised an eyebrow. Her accent was perfect. Odd from someone with blonde hair and blue eyes and the face of a prom queen. She hadn't aged at all in the last five years. She could still be someone's high-school sweetheart. The girl next door, if next door happened to be some vast Texan ranch.

'They're peppers stuffed with rice,' Layla told him. 'Do you like shrimp? Try the *gambas a la plancha*.'

But Alex wasn't thinking about food any more.

'You never used to speak Spanish.' The statement came out almost as an accusation. 'I've been meaning to ask you about that ever since you stepped in to interpret for Ramona.'

The night that had shown him the depth of the connection he still felt with Layla. The connection that had blazed into that astonishing encounter in the decontamination shower. Hell…even the hint of a memory of that night made Alex wonder afresh why they'd come here at all instead of locating the nearest available bed. He had to suck in a slightly ragged breath and focus on what Layla was saying.

'I got a job in Miami.' She sounded offhand. 'There was a huge immigrant Spanish community and I got frustrated at not being able to communicate properly.'

'So you did something about it.' The lopsided smile Alex could feel tugging at his lips was tinged with a mix of admiration and…sadness? This was pure Layla, as much as the way she hurled herself into an emotional involvement with small patients. Show her a challenge and she grabbed it with both hands.

Like the way she'd approached him when she'd been merely a baby doctor, working different rotations to see what she might want to specialise in. He'd already made a name for himself so it must have taken guts for her to approach him. To tell him about Jamie Kirkpatrick and the radical new neurological procedure she'd read about that could possibly cure the toddler.

What had pulled him in so decisively back then?

This cute woman who'd had the courage not only to suggest the procedure but intelligent enough to have done her homework and to be able to discuss it at a level well above what he would have expected from her years and experience?

Or had it been something far less conscious? The appeal of someone who could care so much about a patient? A person who had a heart as big as her home state?

The echoes of that first meeting were disturbing. Alex needed to get his head back to the present. Back to at least a semi-professional space.

'Why Miami?'

He was expecting the conversation to move into the medical merits of a large city hospital and the work-load and experience gained. But Layla looked at him in silence for a long moment and then dropped her gaze.

'It was as far away as I could get.'

'From L.A.?'

A brief nod. '*And* Texas.'

Had she gone alone, then? She certainly would have had the courage to do that. Suddenly it was important to Alex to know *when* she'd done it. How soon after their affair her marriage had ended. Whether he needed to shoulder some of the blame.

'How long did you spend in Miami?'

'A bit over five years. Until I came to Angel's.'

The same time frame that Alex had spent in his own self-imposed exile.

And the last person she'd slept with, other than him, had been her *husband*?

Oh...*hell*...

A waiter arrived with fresh drinks and a notepad to take their orders. Alex told Layla to order for both of them and then listened to her rattle off the Spanish names of dishes. She had a conversation with the waiter in Spanish that made them both laugh but Alex couldn't raise as much as a smile. He drank his beer and waited until the waiter had gone and the noise of the bar closed around them again to create an oddly private atmosphere.

'Was it our affair that ended your marriage?'

Layla's eyes widened. Then she shook her head. 'It was already dead in the water, Alex. The affair would never have happened if that hadn't been the case.'

He nodded slowly. She wasn't just saying that to absolve him of any guilt. He knew enough about Layla to know how focussed her passion for anything was. If she'd felt that passionate about a man, nobody would have been able to distract her.

How lucky would a man be, to have that kind of passionate commitment from Layla?

'I did think about trying again to make it work,' Layla continued quietly. 'When I talked to my mother about it, she told me to "stop being so ridiculous". That marriage is for life and if it wasn't working then that was only because I wasn't working hard enough at it.'

Alex snorted. 'So your parents had the perfect marriage, then?'

It was Layla's turn to snort. 'That's the thing. My parents' marriage was like my whole life growing up. It only had to *look* perfect. That was all that mattered. Daddy was the mayor of Swallow Creek. Everybody knew he cheated on Momma repeatedly but nothing was ever said. It's like the whole town was in some kind of movie and they all knew the part they had to play to get to the happy ending.'

Alex was appalled. 'And you? What was your part?'

'Oh, I just had to be the perfect daughter. The town's "golden girl". To do well at school and be the captain of the cheerleading team and the high school prom queen.'

'So you *were* a prom queen?'

'Yeah… Why'd you ask?'

'Never mind. Go on.'

'Well, I married my high-school sweetheart, of course. No prizes for guessing that Luke happened to have been the prom king.'

'Sure sounds like a movie script.' Alex's comment was light but something like anger was building. How could anyone have tried to put Layla into a box and keep her contained?

She was far too unique for that. Too…*special.*

She laughed at his comment but there was no amusement in the sound.

'Yeah…but I lost my lines somewhere along the way. I got ambitions past being a stay-at-home mum and parading the mayor's cute grandbabies at every community event. I got a bee in my bonnet about being a paediatrician instead.'

Alex was watching her face. She'd had to fight for that ambition?

'Luke wasn't happy about it but I wasn't going to let anyone stop me. I even dragged poor Luke to L.A. with me and he was like a fish out of water. I couldn't blame him for being so angry. He was miserable. *He* knew his lines and what's more, he was happy to be a part of that damned movie.'

'Where is he now?'

Layla smiled. 'Back in Swallow Creek, of course. Married to another girl from our school. Sally. They've got two cute kids already. Another one on the way. Maybe even twins this time.'

The first dishes of their meal arrived. The sticky ribs came with bowls of water that had lemon slices floating in them because the ribs had to eaten with fingers and they lived up to their name in stickiness.

They were delicious and, for some time, they both ate with enormous enjoyment. For Alex, there was more than the taste to savour. Watching the enthusiastic way that Layla could eat. The expression of bliss on her face. The way she sucked the sauce off her fingers before she dipped them in the lemon-scented water.

Man…it was getting hot in here.

The heat wasn't just being generated from physical attraction. There was a warmth coming from something much deeper. Something else that was very different this time.

It was as if Alex was meeting Layla for the first time. This wasn't the doctor he'd worked with. Neither was she the lover whose touch had driven anything else from his consciousness.

This was the real Layla. The woman who'd been a little girl growing up in Swallow Creek. Who'd had parents and a boyfriend and a husband. Who'd had a script laid out for her life and who'd chosen to rebel.

Who'd become a woman he'd fallen head over heels in love with once upon a time.

Who'd crushed him unmercifully at the worst possible time.

Alex's appetite deserted him but Layla didn't seem to notice. He shook his head when she offered him the last rib and she was happy to pick it up herself.

He waited until she finished it.

'Can I ask you a question?'

'Shoot.' Layla rinsed her fingers and dried them on her napkin. She reached for her wineglass.

'What was it that made you so sure we were over?' Alex hadn't planned the question. The pressure had built so fast he couldn't seem to prevent the words escaping from his mouth. From his heart. 'And why did you have to pick the night before Jamie's surgery?'

Oh…God…

Layla's hand shook so much she had to put the wineglass back on the table. Just when she really, really needed a rather large swallow of that wine, too.

She hadn't seen this coming. Not this fast, anyway.

The arrival of more food gave her a brief reprieve but it was obvious by the way they picked at the dishes after the waiter had gone that neither of them were hungry any longer.

Layla's head was a mess but she only had herself to blame for being put on the spot like this after being so open about her childhood. Telling Alex stuff she'd never told anyone.

It was because this felt so different.

She and Alex knew each other physically as intimately as any two people could know each other but they'd never really got acquainted on any other level, had they?

Five years ago Alex had known that her marriage had been in trouble. How could he not when he'd overheard that horrible row with Luke that night when she'd abandoned her husband yet again to work late on the preparation for Jamie Kirkpatrick's surgery?

All she'd known about Alex had been that he was a sinfully handsome and incredibly talented young neurosurgeon who had been well on his way to becoming a leader in his field. Nothing had prepared her for the sizzling chemistry between them and, with her emotions at breaking point in the wake of that row, she had done the unthinkable and made the first move on Alex.

She had started that affair.

She had ended it.

It must have been a new and unpleasant experience for Alex Rodriguez on both counts but Layla had been confident that he would be able to dismiss the effects in no time given his established reputation that would have scared any sensible woman off.

She hadn't been surprised by the information that he'd gone straight into the arms of another woman when he'd stepped off the plane in Australia. Par for the course. That the fling had been over quickly was also no surprise. But there had been nobody since then?

That was…disturbing.

Even more disturbing given the intensity in that dark gaze when he'd voiced a question that had clearly been haunting him.

What was it that made you so sure we were over?

Layla had been open with Alex tonight because this

situation felt so different. As though they were meeting each other on a new level. Not a professional one, as they had when they'd embarked on Jamie's case together.

Not a physical one either, as they'd had from the moment Layla had put her arms around Alex's neck, stood on tiptoe and touched her lips to his that very first time.

Could she stop now? Be less than honest with him?

No. Of course she couldn't. Not when the compulsion to stop being dishonest had been the real reason her life had fallen apart back then.

Layla pushed her food aside. It took courage to look up and meet Alex's brooding gaze.

'I was living a lie, Alex. I always had been so I should have been good at it but I'd added a new layer of deception into my life. I was a married woman and I was having an affair. I felt guilty and I also felt kind of sick about it because I was doing what my father had done so often and I knew how wrong it was. How hurtful.'

Alex said nothing but he was listening to every word. He didn't take his eyes off Layla, even when she had to drop her own gaze and focus on the table. Grains of rice had spilled from the spicy peppers and she moved each one back towards the platter with the tip of her finger, aware of the heaviness of being watched so intently. The expectation that she had more to say. And she did.

'The first time we...we were together,' Layla continued quietly, 'I knew there was no going back in my life. I thought I had something to go forward towards but then I wasn't so sure.'

'Why not?' The words had a bewildered edge.

'You shut yourself away, Alex. The closer we got to the date of Jamie's surgery, the more closed off you got. The case was the only thing that mattered. I was... just a distraction that you needed to avoid. It got to the point that I couldn't even see the man I had fallen for so hard.'

A swift upward glance in the wake of that revelation showed her that Alex had closed his eyes. Retreated inwards again?

'So I was stuck in the middle,' Layla said sadly. 'I couldn't go back to what I'd had because you'd shown me what there could be and...and I didn't think there was anything to go forward towards any more.' Her voice wobbled just a tiny bit. 'It was a really lonely place to be. A really scary place.'

Layla had to close her own eyes for a heartbeat. To gather another dose of courage to answer that second question.

'The night before Jamie's surgery? I was there, in the same room as you, but it felt like we were on different planets. I couldn't believe how thoroughly I'd managed to mess up my life and...I got angry. With myself. With you. With everything in my life that had led me to that moment.'

Layla sighed. 'When I get angry, I have to do something about it. So I snapped and did what my heart told me I needed to do. I'm hot-headed, I know that. Impulsive. I know that, too. I let my heart rule my head too often and I know it's not professional. You don't have to tell me that I get too emotionally involved with patients. I know that as well.

'But it's part of who I am and…even if I didn't know it at the time, I made the decision to stop being part of that movie the moment I met you. I want to live my own life and I want things to be true on the inside, not just look like they're true from the outside.'

Oh…God…if she said anything else, she was going to start crying. She pushed back her chair.

'Excuse me,' she muttered. 'I need to…to powder my nose.'

She pushed her way through the crowd of people in the bar, making for the ladies room.

'What's the hurry, sweetheart?' A young man laughed. 'Let me buy you a drink.'

Layla didn't even see his face. Barely registered the invitation. There were only two people in this scene right now and she'd just laid herself completely bare in front of the other one.

This kind of nakedness made her feel far more vulnerable than any physical exposure could have done. What would Alex be thinking at the moment? Would he realise that she'd offered her heart on a plate back there? That, if he felt in any way inclined to exact revenge on the way she'd treated him, he now had the opportunity to carve her heart up into tiny pieces?

Layla needed a few minutes here. She was quite capable of gathering every ounce of courage she possessed and wrapping it around herself like a force-field. She'd already proved she was a survivor so she could survive whatever Alex had to say when she returned to their table.

She just needed a minute or two, that was all.

* * *

Alex watched Layla threading her way through the crowd. He saw some young jerk try to catch her attention and he knew that Layla hadn't even seen him.

He couldn't move a muscle. Couldn't even blink for the longest time. Talk about being walloped with an emotional sledgehammer.

If only he'd *known*.

Oh, he knew he'd pulled away from Layla. It hadn't been an easy thing to do but he'd done it because Jamie's surgery was going to make or break his career. Success had represented the future and the way he'd felt about Layla had had the potential to undermine everything he'd thought was rock solid in his life up until then.

That his career was all that mattered.

That emotional entanglements had to be avoided at all costs.

And maybe part of him had been aware that success had a new connotation. That the future had to be good enough for Layla to want to be a part of it. But had he told her why he was pulling away and erecting barriers?

No.

Why not?

Because that would have meant admitting how important she had been to him. That she'd had the potential to change his entire life if he could bring himself to trust her completely.

And he hadn't been able to.

He'd proved himself correct in withholding that trust because Layla had proved herself untrustworthy. She'd hurt him.

But he'd brought it on himself, hadn't he?

If only he'd known about what made her tick. About the way she'd been raised.

About that lonely place between turning points that had scared the hell out of her.

And most of all about the way she'd felt about him. What had she said? *The man she'd fallen so hard for?*

Alex could see Layla coming back towards the table now. Her chin was held high but the vulnerability in her body language was heart-breaking.

You could never turn the clock back. But Layla had been so honest with him. If nothing else, she deserved as much in return.

She sat down, eyed the leftover food and grimaced and then, slowly, raised her gaze to meet his.

Alex swallowed carefully. 'There was a bright spot, you know.'

Those bright blue eyes clouded with confusion. 'Sorry?'

'In the whole disaster that was Jamie's case and what happened after it…there *was* a bright spot.'

'Oh?'

'That's how Cade and I reconnected. He saw my mug shot in the papers, read about the malpractice suit and it was enough to make him ready to talk to me again for the first time in nearly a decade.'

He could see the stream of questions that Layla was dying to ask. It must have taken a real effort for her to remain silent.

'Any dysfunction in your family was hidden under a pretty exterior,' Alex said quietly. 'The problems with mine were there for everybody to see. There's probably a fat file buried somewhere with photographs of all the injuries I turned up to the emergency department with.'

'Oh, my God…' Layla breathed. 'From your *parents*?'

'Not my mother,' Alex said swiftly. 'No way. The only thing she ever did wrong was to marry an alcoholic bastard after my dad died. Cade's father.' He paused for a moment. 'No, maybe the worst thing she did was to get breast cancer and die.'

Layla's eyes had already widened with shock. Now they took on a brightness that suggested tears. Alex had to look away. He wasn't doing this to try and garner sympathy. He just wanted things to be equally honest between them.

'How old were you?'

'Ten. Cade was seven. He was safe enough, being Tony's son. I was the unwanted burden. A stepkid he'd never wanted in the first place. Anyway…' Alex wasn't going to dwell on those dark years of abuse. 'I upped and left when I was sixteen because I couldn't take it any more. Cade thought I'd abandoned him and he got pretty angry. By the time I tried to talk to him on his eighteenth birthday he didn't want anything more to do with me. I thought I'd lost my only living relative for ever but, thanks to the case, he made the first move.

'I'll always be grateful that he stood up to be counted when I needed it so much. He was about the only person who did. We've cleared up a lot of stuff since then and…well, I feel like I've got my brother back. So, that was a bright spot.'

Alex's smile was tight. There was no flicker of a response from Layla's lips.

'I'm sorry.' Her voice was choked. 'I felt so guilty… about everything. Luke, you…Jamie… I had no idea what to do about any of it and so I took the coward's way out and did nothing.'

'You didn't have anything to feel guilty about as far as Jamie was concerned. If I hadn't always had the ability to separate my personal stuff from my professional duties I would never have become a surgeon in the first place. What happened was a complication that none of us could have foreseen and, even if we had, we wouldn't have been able to do anything about it.'

'But it was me who persuaded you to try that new procedure in the first place. Because I'd fallen in love with Jamie and had got too involved and I was so determined to grab at any straw.'

'He would have died within weeks without the surgery. Technology has got a whole heap better now and I've perfected that technique since then as well. I'll probably use it for Tommy's operation.' Alex wanted to erase the frown lines creasing Layla's forehead. 'So, that's another bright spot, isn't it?'

Layla stared at him.

'What?'

'I can't believe you're trying to put a positive spin on any of this. You have every reason to hate me. I thought—'

'I don't hate you, Layla,' Alex cut in as she struggled to find words.

It was true. He didn't.

He couldn't have said exactly how he felt about her now other than an overwhelming physical attraction because the trust he'd been prepared to give her had been shattered and Alex had no idea whether it was even possible to repair something like that.

Maybe it was just as well he didn't need to say anything else just then. The waiter came back and eyed the plates of food on their table.

'You guys all done?'

'Yeah…' When Layla nodded to back him up, Alex pulled out his wallet and produced a credit card. 'We're all done here.'

Outside the bar, it was immediately apparent that the only completed business between them was the meal.

'Time to head home?' Alex asked.

Layla nodded.

'I don't live too far from here,' Alex heard himself saying. 'Come home with me?'

Layla hadn't expected that invitation. He could see the surprise in her eyes followed by a glow of…what? Pleasure? *Hope?*

He didn't want to try and analyse whatever it was because if he did, he might be tempted to run for cover. What had happened to the idea of a hotel or motel and some nice, uncomplicated sex?

Alex had no idea. And when Layla's hand connected with his as they started walking, he laced his fingers through hers. When he felt the warmth of her hand and the responding pressure he was aware of a wash of relief that told him he was heading down the right track even if he had no idea of the destination.

Whatever was happening here had become about a lot more than simply sex.

Yes…things were very different.

CHAPTER EIGHT

ALEX'S APARTMENT IN the midtown suburb was tiny. No more than a single, ground-level room in an old brownstone terraced complex but it was cleverly designed, with a kitchen tucked into a back corner and a comfortable living space featuring a huge couch and a widescreen television taking up two-thirds of the entire floor area. Bare wooden steps led up to a sleeping loft and beneath that was a closed-off bathroom and an open office that was clearly well used. The desk around the computer, like the coffee table in the living area, was strewn with papers and reference books festooned with sticky notes.

There was only one window but it was huge and above the heavy rectangle of the sash windows was a semicircle of coloured glass that gave the whole window the appearance of an archway. The original character of the historic building could also be seen in the richly polished floorboards and the rough whitewash covering the old brickwork of the interior walls.

Layla fell in love on the spot. When she came out of the compact bathroom a few minutes after her arrival she stood for a moment, soaking it all in. Alex hadn't turned on any lights but he hadn't drawn the curtains either and the streetlight gave everything a soft golden glow. Through the window she could see the wide steps that led into the building and the intricate wrought-iron fence that shut them off from the rest of the world.

Them?

Layla looked over her shoulder, expecting to see Alex in the kitchen.

He wasn't there and she caught her breath and held it, aware of spinning sensation that had nothing to do with how much wine she'd had to drink at the tapas bar.

'Up here.'

He'd only spoken softly but the small space seemed to catch Alex's voice and bounce it so it felt like his mouth was right against her ear.

'Waiting for you,' he added.

Oh…my… Layla kicked off her shoes and moved to the wooden stairs. *Stairway to heaven*, she thought, and almost snorted with laughter. Except that this didn't feel at all funny.

It didn't feel anything like it usually did when she knew she was on the verge of having sex with Alex either. Where was the heat that fried her brain and made her aware of nothing more than his scent? His taste? His *touch*…?

She climbed slowly and when she got to the top there was nowhere to go other than the bed.

And the bed was filled with Alex.

There was more than enough light to see the sheen of the olive-brown skin of his bare chest, the copper discs of his nipples amongst the scattering of dark hair that arrowed down to the crumpled duvet covering his legs. There was even enough light to see the question in his dark eyes. A sudden doubt. Was he suddenly as unsure about this as she was?

'Layla?'

She couldn't say anything. Couldn't even hold Alex's gaze because the heat wasn't there to fry her brain and it felt, ridiculously, like it was the first time they were making love and Layla was aware of an extraordinary sensation.

For maybe the first time in her life Layla was overcome by crippling shyness and she had no idea what to do about it. She felt completely lost for a moment. For as long as it took to raise her eyes and meet that dark gaze again.

For a long, long moment they held eye contact. And then Alex was moving. He knelt on the bed and held out his hands and Layla took them. He pulled her gently and her legs buckled and then she was kneeling on the bed too. Still holding her hands, Alex leaned in and kissed her lips. A soft touch. A wordless question.

Did she want this?

Oh...*yes*...

Layla's lips parted beneath Alex's and he took the invitation to deepen the kiss. With the first, exquisitely slow stroke of his tongue Layla knew that the heat was still there. It was all around them. Inside them. But, instead of an overwhelming conflagration, this time it was under control. They could play with it. Luxuriate in it. Take all the time they wanted and revel in every moment.

Still locked in that first kiss, Alex loosened Layla's top and they broke the kiss so that she could lift her arms while he pulled it off. And then his head dipped and she felt his lips on the side of her neck and she tipped her head back with a sigh as his kisses trailed down. He pushed the straps of her bra over her shoulders as his mouth reached the top of her breasts and then he kissed her lips again as he unfastened her bra. A one-handed movement that advertised a skill he might not have practised for a while but which he certainly hadn't lost.

Still kneeling on the bed together, Layla pressed her bare breasts against his chest and felt Alex's hand slip beneath her waistband to cup her buttocks and draw her even closer.

Oh, yeah…the heat was there all right. Layla could feel herself slipping, deliciously slowly, into the mindless pleasure that only Alex had ever been able to give her. Her fingers skimmed over the hard planes of muscle on his back, over the soft skin on the sides of his neck and then they buried themselves in the soft silk of his hair.

Alex's hands mirrored hers. She could feel a trail of fire from each of the fingers on his hands as they covered her back, his palms dipping into the curve above her hipbones. Touching her ribs and then that sensitive skin beneath her breasts on their way up. His hands became completely lost in the tumble of her hair and Layla could actually feel the ends of her pale hair tangling with the dark hair on Alex's arms.

She'd never known that touch could be like this. That every cell in her body could be *this* connected. *This* sensitive. She breathed in the air that Alex was breathing out and it seemed to have more oxygen in it. She could taste the spice of Spanish food in his mouth. Or was that just the taste of Alex himself?

The kiss went on. And on. Until Layla felt herself being gently lowered onto the bed and Alex began peeling the rest of her clothing from her body. The process seemed unbearably slow and she tried to help but Alex caught her hands.

'I want to do this,' he murmured, and she could hear the smile in his voice. 'It's like Christmas.'

Unwrapping a gift?

He saw her body as a *gift*?

Oh… Layla couldn't have moved to help him now. Her head sank back into the pillow and she closed her eyes as a wave of an emotion she couldn't identify swept her away.

She had known how good it was to be touched by Alex. To touch him. Her body had never forgotten the ecstasy of ultimate closeness. But it had always had an edge of something frantic to it. An insane race to capture satisfaction before they could be discovered. Before something, or someone, in the outside world intervened and ripped them apart. It had never been like this.

Layla had never imagined someone honouring her body like this. Worshipping her with the touch of his hands. The tips of his fingers. The silky glide of his tongue. She wanted to do the same for him. To explore his whole body. Slowly. To touch and taste every inch of his skin. To elicit sounds from him like the tiny whimper of need she heard coming from her own throat.

But not yet. She couldn't wait that long. Alex might still have control over that burning desire but she was rapidly losing hers. She was on familiar ground now.

Wanting Alex so much that she felt she might die if it didn't happen. Now.

'Alex...please...' She writhed under the unbearably gentle onslaught of his lips and tongue as they touched the core of her being. 'I need you. Inside me. *Now...*'

He responded with the swiftness of a whip cracking. A few seconds' delay as he wrenched open the bedside cabinet and then ripped into a foil package and then he was there. Between her legs. Looking down at her and touching her face with his gaze as intensely as the hard heat she could feel touching the entrance to the place she desperately wanted him to fill.

Layla was drowning in his eyes. She reached up to pull him closer and couldn't recognise her own voice as she cried out his name.

Layla woke first, a little before dawn, knowing that she'd had nowhere near enough sleep to face a day at work, but she didn't care. The need to go downstairs to the bathroom had woken her but she let herself drift into consciousness without moving a muscle.

She let herself become aware of everything she could feel. The heavy weight of Alex's leg draped over one of hers. The ridge of his arm beneath her head. The rise and fall of his chest against her cheek. The heavy grunt of his breathing that was almost a snore because he was still so deeply asleep.

Layla hadn't intended staying here all night. She must have fallen asleep first, because if Alex had she would remember it. She would have agonised over whether to wake him up to tell him she was going or just slip away and leave him a note or something.

Shifting her head carefully so as not to wake him, Layla moved so that she could see his face. His lips were parted slightly. Long, dark lashes nestled on his cheeks. She had never seen Alex asleep before. He looked so peaceful.

So young.

Something huge squeezed in her chest as she remembered their conversation of the night before and put the pieces of the puzzle together. She knew now what Cade had meant when he'd said that Alex knew too much. That he was too quick to jump to conclusions about a small patient who might have been abused. She could understand why Alex had been so angry. So ready to deliver a brutal blow to Ramona's boyfriend.

It broke her heart to think of any child being abused. But to know that *Alex* had been injured so badly, physically and emotionally, went beyond heart-breaking.

Tears stung Layla's eyes. She wanted to wrap her arms around him and hold him to her heart. She couldn't fix the past but she could protect him now.

She could let him know that he hadn't deserved a childhood like that. That he should have been treasured and loved. She had to move more now. So that she could lift her hand and touch his face. Just with a single fingertip. A butterfly's kiss on his temple. To let him know that he was loveable. That he *was* loved.

By her.

Oh…God…

Those tangled, dark lashes flickered and Alex's eyes opened at the same instant that the realisation hit Layla that this wasn't only about physical attraction. And it never had been. Not for her.

So much for throwing fuel onto the ashes of a smouldering lust to let it burn itself out. What Layla was feeling now was burning so brightly that she knew it would never go out. She never had, and never could, love anybody other than Alex like this.

Maybe it was just as well it took as long as it did for Alex to surface completely. That he reached for her while he was still more than half-asleep and that their slow kiss reignited their earlier passion. He would never know how tenderly Layla had touched him. Or see the tears that had filled her eyes.

Talk about mind-blowing.

Alex had often wondered what it would have been like to have the luxury of spending a whole night with Layla.

Now he knew.

Had he really thought that a sleazy motel room would have been a good idea?

Or that the sex would have been satisfying but uncomplicated?

Layla was in the shower now. Alex had pulled jeans on but nothing else and he was making a pot of coffee while he waited for his turn to freshen up. He'd been invited to share the shower. Nobody could have missed the flash of disappointment—confusion, even—at his swift turning down of the offer.

God knew, he'd *wanted* to share that shower.

So why wasn't he in there? Soaping Layla's gorgeous body. Wrapping her in a towel and pulling her into a kiss as steamy as the bathroom, while they were both wet and slippery and smelling like the soap?

Because it would have been a step too far, that's why.

And last night hadn't been? Alex shook his head, emitting an incredulous huff as he spooned ground coffee into the jug.

It wasn't supposed to have been like that.

So...*tender.*

It had never been like that before so he hadn't expected it. Hadn't expected to feel like that. As though he wanted to make it up to Layla for having had to live a lie for most of her life.

To show her that *he* was real. That *this* was real.

And it wasn't, was it?

What was eating at his gut right now was the knowledge that they hadn't been having sex for half the night. They'd been making love.

And that was a kind of lie all on its own because if you made love like that you were making some kind of promise about the future, weren't you?

And he couldn't make that kind of promise to anyone. Especially not Layla. She'd proved she could turn her back and walk off if it suited her.

The kettle boiled and he poured the water over the coffee grounds. The smell hit him and he breathed in deeply as he fitted the plunger. Time to wake up, Rodriguez, he almost snarled inwardly. Don't even think of going there.

Trust nobody. Except yourself.

It was the only way to stay safe.

The rap on his door was unexpected. Alex crossed the room and opened it to find Cade, who held up a large paper bag.

'Breakfast, man.' Cade was grinning. 'I've got news.'

He entered the apartment with the ease of someone who knew they were welcome. 'Mmm. You've got coffee ready. Perfect timing.'

They both knew that the clunking sound advertised the shower being turned off. Cade was over by the kitchen bench now, depositing the bag. His head turned swiftly. He took in the fact that Alex was only wearing jeans and that the button was still unfastened. Then he turned to stare at the bathroom door.

'Oops. Sorry. Am I interrupting something?'

Alex shrugged, turning to push the door closed. He didn't see the bathroom door opening.

'Nothing important,' he said lightly. 'I got lucky last night, that's all.'

The shock of seeing Alex's half-brother standing directly in front of Layla as she came out of the bathroom was nothing compared to hearing the dismissive words that had just been spoken.

'Hey, Layla…' Cade looked embarrassed. On her behalf, perhaps, after hearing that she'd just been a playmate for the night? 'I should…um…head off and get to work or something.'

'Nah…stay and have some breakfast, now you're here.' Was that relief in Alex's tone? An escape route from the intimacy of sharing a meal after the night they'd had? 'Layla doesn't mind, do you, Layla?'

'Not at all. I'll just throw some clothes on.'

'And I'll jump into the shower. I'll only be two minutes.'

Layla dressed as quickly as she could. She was planning on skipping breakfast. Alex had company and, besides, she needed to get home and changed so she didn't turn up at Angel's wearing the same clothes she'd left in yesterday.

But Alex was coming out of the bathroom as she went back down the stairs. He had a towel knotted around his hips and an apology written across his features.

What was he sorry for? That they'd been busted or because he'd dismissed what had happened between them last night as 'nothing important'?

He watched her pick up her handbag and stepped closer.

'Don't go,' he said softly. 'Please? At least have a coffee?'

This was confusing. Maybe the intention of last night had simply been to indulge the physical attraction they shared in the hope that it would burn itself out, but they both knew that it had been bigger than simply sex. That something had changed.

That they hadn't picked up where they'd left off years ago.

They'd made a fresh start.

And this time it actually held the potential of going somewhere.

If they let it. If they wanted it to.

Layla felt a wash of that emotion she'd experienced watching Alex sleep. She knew how damaged this beautiful man had to be, whether he was aware of it or not. Did she really expect him to trust her straight off? To trust that what had happened last night was real?

Maybe she could take the first step. She could let him know that she wasn't about to run away if things got tough. That, this time, she was quite prepared to do whatever it might take to be with him.

She smiled at him. 'Coffee would be great. And some of whatever's in that bag, if there's enough, because it smells divine and I'm hungry enough to eat a horse.'

'Is that what they do in Texas?' Cade welcomed her into the kitchen with a grin. 'Eat horse for breakfast?'

'Only if there aren't any griddle cakes and black-eyed peas.' Layla eyed the bag he was ripping open. 'Bagels. Yum.'

'Help yourself.' Cade watched as Layla swiped a smear of cream cheese from the bag and licked it off her finger. 'You and Alex, huh? And there I was, telling people that those rumours were rubbish.'

Alex had dressed himself with impressive speed. He was buttoning his shirt as he joined them but he paused to drape his arm over Layla's shoulder.

'Layla and I go way back,' he told Cade. 'Pre-Brisbane days.'

'Ahh…' Cade looked as though he was retrieving some more of those rumours. The ones about Layla being married at the time, perhaps. Or maybe he was putting two and two together about the unpleasant legal repercussions of Jamie's disastrous surgery and coming up with a reason for them splitting up that nobody would want to talk about. He gave his head a tiny shake and cleared his throat.

'Speaking of Brisbane,' he said to Alex, 'I was busy myself last night. Having a long conversation with your friend Callie.'

Layla was trying not to watch as Alex tucked his shirt into his pants and did up his fly and belt buckle.

There was something about the inflection on the word 'friend' that sent a shaft of something nasty through her belly. Was Callie the one that Alex had had the fling with when he'd arrived on that side of the world?

Jealousy. That's what that nasty sensation was. Layla had no right to feel this possessive. Good grief…what was happening to her here?

'She's talked me into taking the job,' Cade continued. 'I'm heading off as soon as I can work out my notice. Couple of weeks, tops.'

'Wow…you don't muck around.' Leaving his top buttons undone and his tie hanging loose, Alex filled a mug with coffee and took a big swallow. 'You sure you want to do this?'

'I'm not a kid any more, Alex. I get to make my own choices and learn from them if they turn out to be mistakes.' His gaze flicked to Layla and then back to his brother.

Layla caught her breath. Was Cade actually saying that he thought Alex having anything to do with her was a big mistake?

No. The sudden tension between the brothers suggested that some button had been pushed that had nothing to do with her. There were probably all sorts of triggers buried in their shared, stormy backgrounds. A background that Layla needed to take into consideration for all sorts of things. Like being patient with Alex if it took him a long time to trust her. And understanding his passionate reaction to cases of child abuse. Accepting his need for his own space at times to focus completely on the career that had been his way forward from a horrible start to his adult life.

The comment led to an awkward silence that Layla felt compelled to break.

'I should get going,' she said. 'I've got a big meeting at nine a.m. We're trying to find sponsors to help with the fundraising to update our MRI machine and it's a biggie. We were supposed to do it yesterday but the meeting got derailed when I had to see someone in Emergency.'

'I thought that was already sorted,' Cade said.

'What?'

'The social committee put out a flyer last week. They're hoping everyone will attend the big Halloween party they've got planned. That's down as a fundraiser for the MRI.'

'Oh…I hadn't caught up with that.' Layla smiled at Cade. 'Thanks for the heads-up. It might help to encourage the sponsors. Any money from a hospital fundraiser will be great but we'll still need more. New technology doesn't come cheap.'

'It should raise heaps. Tickets are a hundred dollars and everyone's being asked to bring as many people as they can. It'll be Angel's staff and all the friends and relatives they can bring with them. The venue could hold a thousand people apparently.'

Layla blinked. That was some fundraiser. Why hadn't she heard about it already?

'You'll have to come,' Cade continued. He sent a crooked smile in Alex's direction and it looked like it was intended to be an olive branch. 'I'm heading out to a costume-hire place with a few others after work today. Want me to pick something out for you?'

'I don't do dress-ups.' The words were curt. And he was looking at Layla rather than Cade.

I'm not going to pretend to be someone I'm not, the silent message said.

Was he trying to tell her that he was real? That this—whatever was happening between them—was also real? On the inside as well as the outside?

'Neither do I,' Layla said, still holding Alex's gaze. Then she looked at Cade and smiled. 'I'll be happy to buy a ticket, though.'

Cade shrugged. 'Well, if it turns out to be my farewell gig from Angel's, you'll have to come, costume or not.' His glance slid from Alex to Layla and back again and a corner of his mouth lifted. '*Both* of you.'

Was he giving his blessing to the idea of them as a couple now? Encouraging Alex?

This was doing her head in. It didn't matter where she stood with Cade but how Alex felt right now was very, very important. Did he still see this reunion as a means of putting out an old flame so that they could both move on and be able to work together without it creating any personal tension?

Had it really been her suggestion?

Yes. But she'd known, deep down, that there was more than just a flicker of hope that it could be more than that.

What had she done? She'd learned so much more about Alex, that's what. She'd stirred the ashes and discovered that she'd been in love with him right from the get-go and she'd only fallen deeper last night.

Had she set herself up for a devastating blow?

The thought was terrifying but there was nothing

she could do about it. As far as she was concerned, the step they had taken now was irrevocable. It was Alex's call how it was going to play out because there was no way she could pull the plug on this.

Vulnerability was dangerous. It made you weak. Layla had learned very early in life that if you felt threatened you had to make yourself stronger. Take charge. Fake it till you made it and all that.

She lifted her chin. 'I really do have to go. Got a hospital to run. I'll see you boys later.'

At least with Cade there, the awkwardness of what to say or do in farewell was gone. There would be no lingering kiss. No promises of when they could be together again.

It was a good thing, Layla told herself firmly as she flagged down a taxi outside Alex's apartment.

A promise was only words and a promise could be broken.

Like hearts could?

CHAPTER NINE

IT WAS AMAZING how quickly you could get used to a new routine. How quickly you could become lulled into a false sense of security. Within days, almost, Alex and Layla both stopped worrying about the rumours that might be circulating through Angel's. Now they didn't even bother to try hiding the fact that they were arriving for work together.

Tyler Donaldson wasn't about to let a chance slide by when he saw them standing near the huge fish tank in Angel's lobby one morning.

'You guys look as happy as pigs in muck,' he announced. His grin widened. 'Life's good, huh?'

'Hey, Ty.' Layla seemed happy to greet her old friend but Alex had spotted another early arrival at the hospital.

'Jack! Hey…haven't seen you for ages.'

'Alex…'

The handshake between the two men instantly morphed into a typically male, one-armed hug that involved a bit of back thumping.

Jack Carter held his hand out to Tyler. 'I haven't had a chance to congratulate you on fatherhood. How's it going?'

'I'm lovin' every minute of it.' Tyler shook Jack's hand but raised an eyebrow at the same time. 'And didn't I hear a rumour that you're gonna join the sleepless nights and nappy brigade? How's Nina doing?'

'Glowing,' Jack said proudly. 'Nearly five months along now.'

'She certainly is glowing,' Layla put in. 'I only caught up on that news myself last week. You must be thrilled, Jack.'

'Oh…for sure.'

'She told me that you'd adopted Janey and Blake, too.'

Jack shook his head. 'I know. Single man one minute, father of three the next. Life's full of amazing surprises, isn't it?'

'Mmm…' Alex caught just the flicker of a glance in his direction. 'I wouldn't disagree with that.'

He made no attempt to join in the conversation, however, because he had the uncomfortable sensation that he had been left alone in a parallel universe here. He wasn't disinterested because Jack Carter was his oldest friend. They'd been through medical school together. It had been Jack who'd set up this job for him at Angel's. They hadn't seen so much of each other since Jack had left to take up a full-time position at the pro bono centre in Harlem. He'd been Jack's best man at the wedding, of course, but that had been a long time ago now. Jack still did the odd consult here at Angel's and Nina was still a social worker but their paths didn't cross often enough. Perhaps that was why he hadn't noticed Nina's shape changing. Not that he wasn't happy for Jack because Jack looked on top of the world.

He just couldn't imagine it for himself. In the wake of his childhood—and Cade's—the responsibility of bringing a child into the world was not something he would touch with the proverbial bargepole.

Layla seemed to be more than happy to be discussing the expected arrival date and how Nina's younger siblings were feeling about the addition to the new family. There was something about the animation in her face that rang a warning bell for Alex.

Layla would want children.

The conviction came from nowhere and it felt curiously…disturbing. She may not have wanted to settle down and produce grandbabies for the mayor of Swallow Creek to show off but…hell…she *loved* kids. Given the way she got so involved with her small patients, Alex could imagine how fiercely she would love her own children. And she'd be an amazing mother.

Why was the thought so disturbing?

Because it would have to be another man who would be the father of those children?

He should be fine with that. This new…fling with Layla was not going to be permanent. They were just burning off a lingering physical attraction and he had absolutely no desire for it to become anything more than that.

It *couldn't* because that would mean trusting Layla to the same extent he had mistakenly trusted her the first time round. And she'd betrayed that trust and left him to fall into such a dark place that he was determined he would never go anywhere near there again.

What the hell had he been thinking, playing with fire like this again?

Totally unintended factors were sneaking into the equation. Like the need to be with Layla as often as possible.

Like a flash of downright envy for the man who would be the father of her children.

Alex tuned back into the conversation between in time to hear Tyler excusing himself. Jack made an apologetic face as the big Texan doctor walked off with a wave.

'Sorry about that. Kids aren't really your thing, are they, Alex?'

Alex snorted, ignoring the odd glance that came his way from Layla. 'No. That's why I became a paediatric neurosurgeon. Speaking of which, I'm due at a ward round upstairs right about now. Maybe we can grab a beer at O'Malley's later?'

'Sounds good. But you don't get rid of me that easily. I'm heading upstairs myself.'

'Me too.' Layla stayed with them. 'How's it going at the centre, Jack?'

'It's great. I feel like I'm making a real difference.'

'I wouldn't mind getting involved myself. Would you have any use for a doctor who can speak Spanish?'

'Are you kidding? We'd snap up any free time you had.' Jack shot Alex a sideways glance. 'From what I hear, though, free time might be a bit thin on the ground.'

The reference to time prompted Layla to check her watch. 'Oh, help…I'm going to be late for that meeting.' She waved and someone moved to stop the elevator doors closing.

The elevator looked pretty full. 'I'm going to take the stairs,' Alex said. 'I'll catch you both later.'

'I'll join you.' Jack hung back as Layla raced off. 'I could do with the exercise.'

'You here on a consult?' Alex asked as they entered the stairwell.

'Not exactly. Nina's hoping to get a bit of free time so we can go visiting. She tells me that Tommy Jenner is on the ward.'

'Yep.' Alex didn't slow his stride as they climbed the first flights of stairs.

'And you're going ahead with the surgery?'

'Yep. Scheduled for Friday. We had to put it off because he picked up a bit of a bug last week.'

'I hope it goes well,' Jack said quietly. 'Nina's going to be holding her breath.'

'I might be, too.' Alex could feel his breathing now after three flights of stairs. He paused to take a quick glance through the window. You could see the end of the ambulance bay from here. And the line of rubbish skips. The basketball court was deserted. Maybe he could find Cade later and he could get a workout in. And maybe that would dispel this odd edginess that was building in the wake of those disturbing thoughts he'd just had about Layla's future family. No. Now that he thought about it, that edginess had had been building ever since that night with Layla.

That *first* night with Layla. They'd clocked up a few more since then.

And whatever it was between them didn't seem to be burning itself out. If anything, those flames were burning higher. Brighter. He'd issued the warning himself, hadn't he? If you played with fire, things could get out of hand. Somebody could get badly hurt.

Had he been so confident of his ability to stay detached that he'd assumed the person who got hurt wouldn't be him?

'It was your first day at Angel's, wasn't it?' Jack was looking out the window beside him. 'When you got caught up in Tommy's case?'

'Yeah… It was a memorable elevator ride with Nina in there, trying to calm Mike down when he was furious with people trying to take Tommy away for treatment.'

'Hardly surprising when you look back on it all. There he was, struggling to be a single dad to a kid who'd been so traumatised by being left in a house with his dead mother for days and everybody assumed he was abusing Tommy. It's no wonder he went off the edge but it did make it harder to see what was really going on.'

'Not for Nina.'

'No… But she's a woman in her own class of amazing.' Jack's smile held a tenderness that made Alex feel left out again. 'She loves Tommy to bits. She's taught me a thing or two about taking notice of more than the clinical picture we get from patients.'

'Hmm.' Alex watched an ambulance turning into the bay. Layla did that. Was it a female thing?

Or maybe Layla was in her own class of amazing, too.

'She's really excited about the prospect of him getting a new mother soon. Is it true that Mike got involved with one of the oncology nurses?'

'Yeah...Gina. She's lovely. He's planning to propose if the surgery goes well.'

Jack sucked in a breath. 'No pressure, then...?'

Alex grunted and turned away from the window. He was more than ready to tackle a few more flights of stairs. Jack was half a step behind him.

'So...how's it working out?'

'With Tommy? We'll have to wait and see.'

'No...I meant at Angel's. That first day was a while back now and I haven't been around for months. You happy here?'

'Yep.' Until Layla had arrived anyway. And now that they'd found a way to deal with the tension, Alex had to admit he was feeling happier than he had in a long time.

Years. More than five years, to be exact.

They climbed the rest of the way in silence but paused again after Alex had pushed open the fire-stop doors on the eighth floor.

'I heard about the Kirkpatrick case hitting the grapevine,' Jack said. 'How on earth did that happen? I was quite confident that it was going to be buried.'

'Cade didn't realise it was being kept quiet.'

'Oh...' Jack's glance conveyed his understanding of the turbulent relationship the brothers had had. 'Problem?'

'Could have been,' Alex admitted. 'In the end it turned out to be a good thing. Gave us the chance to resolve a few issues that needed airing. Our relationship is better than it's ever been now.'

Jack's nod was pleased. 'That's great.'

'Yes and no.'

'Why no?'

'He's planning to take off. Follow my footsteps and go for a new job in Australia. In my old hospital, no less.' Alex rubbed his forehead. 'I've only got myself to blame. I told him that an old friend there was on the hunt for a prenatal surgeon.'

They could have left the conversation there and gone their separate ways. Jack was here to visit Tommy and Alex was going to be late to start his ward round but that edginess was suddenly boiling to the surface. Alex stayed where he was, with the safety of the wall right behind him.

'Do you ever get the feeling that life goes in circles, Jack?'

If Jack was disconcerted by the subtext, he didn't show it. Like the good friend he was, he simply moved a bit closer, giving the impression that he had all the time in the world to talk. Two men having a bit of a yarn. Or two doctors having a quiet word about a patient.

'Circles?' he prompted gently.

'Yeah. I had Cade in my life and then out of it for too many years. Back in it again when he saw the publicity about the Kirkpatrick case and then out of it when I took off to Australia. Now he's back but he's planning to take off himself.'

'You won't lose touch. Email's great. Phone calls by computer even better. There's nothing to stop you taking a holiday either. I'll bet you miss all the sun and those fabulous beaches.'

But Alex wasn't finished. 'It's the same with my job. Has it occurred to you that Tommy's case is horribly similar to Jamie Kirkpatrick's? That I'm back where I was all those years ago, about to tackle a surgery that could go belly up and wreck more than one life?'

'It's a tough call.' Jack's face was creased with sympathy. 'But you can't think about it like that. Be proud that you are one of the few people that can offer any hope at all in a case like this. Mike's not going to sue you if it doesn't go well. From what Nina's told me, he's well aware of the risks. He's incredibly grateful that you're even prepared to try.'

Alex shook his head. 'I'm not sure I should be. I'm not sure I could live with myself if it doesn't go well.'

'If you don't try, he'll die,' Jack said bluntly. 'Could you live with that?'

Alex sighed. He started to rub his forehead again but, instead, ran stiff fingers through his hair. 'It's not just those circles,' he admitted quietly. 'There's also...'

No. He couldn't say her name. Talking about it might mean he'd hear something he really didn't want to hear. He might have to admit what was really going on deep in his own heart.

He didn't have to say her name. Jack's gaze held a sympathetic understanding.

'Layla?'

That heat at the sound of her name was anger. Something very private was being exposed. Something Alex had been avoiding looking at too closely himself until this morning. 'How the hell did you find out about that?'

Jack's smile was conciliatory. 'You forget that I'm still involved with Angel's. That Nina still works here. We...ah...hear things.'

'Like what?' Oh, God...had the grapevine somehow

got information about what had happened in the decontamination shower that night?

'Just that there's a certain vibe whenever you two are in the same room. A rumour that someone saw a stolen kiss somewhere. I wasn't sure I believed it until I saw you two together this morning. You may as well have a neon sign above your heads.'

'Oh…' Alex couldn't deny that vibe. It felt like the very air came alive with sparks whenever he was within sight of Layla. Hardly surprising that other people could feel the heat. Had he really been bothered a few weeks back that Layla was stalking him and that their paths seem to cross far too often? It couldn't be often enough now. He really was in trouble here, wasn't he?

'There you are…' The voice came from the nearby elevator as the doors slid open. 'I've been looking for you, Jack.' Nina came towards them, smiling.

Alex found himself staring at the elevator as the doors slid shut again. Stupid to be disappointed that Layla wasn't amongst the people left. Her elevator would have delivered her to the top floor long ago. About when he'd been staring out the window, thinking about shooting hoops.

'Hi, babe.' If Jack had looked happy discussing his impending fatherhood, it was nothing compared to the joy on his face now. 'How's it going?'

'Wonderful. I've got our tickets for the Halloween ball.' Nina laughed. 'The suggestion was made that I could go as a pumpkin and all I would need is an orange dress.' She patted her belly. 'What do you think, Alex?'

'I think you could go as something far more glamorous than a pumpkin.'

Nina was still grinning. 'A witch, maybe?' She pointed at Jack. 'Don't you dare say a word.'

Jack managed to look totally innocent and highly amused at the same time. He cleared his throat. 'You going to the ball, Alex?'

'Nah…though it looks like it's going to be Cade's farewell and he's got some idea of us going in matching costumes.'

'The Brothers Grimm?' Nina had clearly caught the excitement that seemed to be taking over Angel's. 'Tweedledee and Tweedledum?'

Jack shook his head. 'Come on. Time to take you away. Let's go and see if Tommy's up for a visit.'

'I'll catch you later.' Alex could see Ryan O'Doherty coming through the ward doors. Looking for his senior colleague, no doubt, in order to get the ward round under way.

'We'll grab that beer.' Jack raised an eyebrow and his smile was encouraging. 'And you know what?'

'What?'

'Circles can be good. Sometimes they can take you back to a place you didn't know you wanted to be.'

Tommy Jenner was getting a lot of visitors today.

Mike was there, of course. He had taken time off work to be with his son for the duration of this hospital admission. Gina was rostered on as Tommy's nurse whenever she was on shift in the ward but she had other patients to attend to as well. Jack and Nina had been in this morning and Tommy's surgeons, Alex and Ryan, were checking up on their young patient at frequent intervals. As chief paediatrician, it was only to be expected that Layla was taking a special interest in this case as well.

The irony that the medical problem Tommy was facing was so similar to the one Jamie Kirkpatrick had faced and that this surgery was happening when she and Alex were in the fragile new stages of another relationship was lying more heavily in the back of Layla's mind every day, but it still seemed like a bonus to find Alex in Tommy's room when she made her own visit in the afternoon.

It was always a bonus when their paths crossed during working hours these days. Layla could see him in the room before she tapped lightly on the door and pushed it open so she hesitated for a heartbeat, just to enjoy the moment.

It was kind of like when you were a kid and you'd been given the most amazing Christmas or birthday gift, she decided. It wasn't that you necessarily wanted to play with it all the time but it was very important to keep it somewhere where you could see it as often as possible.

So you knew it was real.

The reality of this new connection with Alex could be found in the most fleeting glance or the hint of a smile. During a professional conversation that had a subtext only the two of them were aware of. It was delicious.

Addictive.

So much so that Layla knew the instant it changed and that happened the second she walked into Tommy's room. Alex raised his gaze from the notes he was reading to nod and smile an acknowledgment of her presence and the smile was the same as always, but Layla still knew.

It was the abrupt way the eye contact had ended. A split second in time, maybe, but it was enough to let Layla know it was happening again.

Alex was pulling away.

'Hey, Tommy.' Layla smiled at both Tommy and his dad. 'How're y'all doing?'

'Me an' Dad are having haircuts tomorrow. We're getting it *all* shaved off.'

'Wow.' Layla hitched a hip on the end of the bed. Close to where Alex was standing, flipping pages on the chart, but he didn't look up. Was it her imagination or did he shift just a little further away? 'Both of you, huh?'

'Yeah…' Mike ran a hand through his own hair and then ruffled his son's. 'We're going to have a race to see who can grow hair the fastest after Tommy has his operation.'

Layla was quite confident she was the only person here who was aware of the tension emanating from Alex. Or that it had just increased a notch. Tommy would have to survive his surgery if his hair was going to grow back.

'I asked Gina if she wanted to shave her hair off too,' Tommy told her. 'But she said she didn't *really* want to.'

Layla laughed. 'I'm not surprised. It's a bit different for girls.'

'Why?'

'I guess we're not as brave as boys. And we like our hair too much.'

'Dad said he likes Gina's hair just the way it is.

She's got pretty hair, so I guess it's OK if she doesn't do the race.'

Alex was scribbling something onto the chart and even his writing sounded tense. Layla could hear the scratching and tapping against the clipboard holding the papers. She wished she'd never told Alex about Mike's plan to ask Gina to marry him if the surgery went well.

Of course he was pulling away. The pressure was building and he needed to focus. It wouldn't be like the last time this had happened because this time she understood. She could give him space if that's what he needed. She was older and wiser now and she wasn't going to have a hissy fit because she felt she wasn't getting enough attention.

She was starting to feel a bit tense about it all herself, in fact. It was kind of unfair that life was throwing a testing time like this at them so fast. They needed more time to build trust. They were making a fresh start and it had a promise that was precious.

She had way too much to lose if things went wrong.

Could Alex feel the reassurance she was trying to project? If he did, he didn't acknowledge it. When he finally looked up from the chart, he looked straight at Tommy.

'There's another doctor who's going to come and visit you tomorrow, buddy. Dr Jill. She's an anaesthetist. Do you know what that is?'

'No. What?'

'She's the one who's in charge of helping you go to sleep so you can have your operation. It's called having an anaesthetic.'

Tommy's bottom lip wobbled. 'But I'll wake up again, won't I?'

'You won't even know you've been asleep,' Alex promised. 'You'll close your eyes and then it'll feel like you just open them again straight away but it'll all be over.'

'Will my head hurt?'

'We'll give you medicine to stop it hurting.'

'Will I have a big bandage?'

'You sure will. And you'll be in a special place called Intensive Care for a few days.'

Layla could see the way Mike's throat moved as he swallowed hard.

'I'll be there, too,' he told Tommy, leaning down to give him a kiss. 'I'll be right beside you when you wake up.'

The tiny break in Mike's voice almost undid Layla and she could see a tiny muscle jumping in Alex's jaw. She forced herself to sound bright.

'You know what's going to happen next week?' she asked Tommy. 'What you've got to look forward to when you come back to the ward?'

'No.' Tommy was frowning deeply, as though trying to figure out how to respond to the charged atmosphere around him. 'What?'

'It's going to be Halloween. There'll be lots of decorations and some of the doctors and nurses put on silly costumes and have a parade. And there'll be all sorts of yummy treats for everybody to eat.'

'What sort of treats?'

'Candy,' Layla said confidently. 'And ice cream and...and...*spiders*.'

Tommy's jaw dropped. Then he giggled.

'I'll leave you to it,' Alex said, moving towards the door. 'I'll see you tomorrow, Tommy.'

Layla watched him leave.

And she had the horrible feeling that she was watching him walk away from *her*.

Which was ridiculous. Wasn't it?

They were in a better place than they'd ever been.

And she was going to do whatever it took to keep them there.

CHAPTER TEN

THERE WAS COMFORT to be found in a case that required going the extra mile.

It was a lesson Alex Rodriguez had learned long ago and he slipped into that totally focussed mode with practised ease.

By seven that night his office looked like a bomb-site. Open textbooks and journals lay scattered over his desk and parts of the floor with relevant passages marked by bright sticky notes. Illuminated wall screens had MRI scan images on display. A white board was covered with intricate diagrams and bulletpoint plans.

He was standing in front of the white board, tapping the end of the marker against his teeth, when Layla ventured into his office.

'Thought you might like a coffee,' she said. 'And some food.'

Alex turned slowly, wondering if her presence was about to pop this comforting bubble of concentration. To his relief, the skin of the bubble appeared to be thick enough to cope. Layla was on the outside. It was like seeing her from a different perspective. Through the eyes of a surgeon and not a lover?

Whatever. He could work with that.

'Great idea.' He nodded. 'I can only stop for a minute or two, though. I think I'm on a roll with planning this surgery.'

Layla was trying to find a space to put down the carry tray that held two Styrofoam cups. She gave up and offered the tray to Alex who took one. Then she handed him a bag. 'It's nothing flashy, I'm sorry. I got one of the chefs in the cafeteria to make some filled rolls with the roast beef they had on the menu.'

'Smells good to me.' Alex unwrapped the roll and took a huge bite, letting his gaze travel back to the white board as he chewed.

Layla followed his line of vision and then turned to take in the illuminated screens. 'This looks like absolutely meticulous planning. Want to talk me through it?'

Alex shook his head. 'Later, maybe. There's one bit I haven't quite worked through yet. A bit of distraction might be helpful. Unleash my subconscious or something.' He smiled at Layla. This was working. The bubble was being protected as a private space. 'Tell me what you've been up to since I saw you visiting Tommy.'

Layla swallowed the mouthful of her own roll. She was leaning her bottom, carefully, against the edge of his desk. Alex stayed standing, too wired to sit down.

'Long meeting,' Layla told him, 'with the dieticians and kitchen management. You wouldn't believe all the stuff they've got planned for Halloween. We had to make sure that nutritional guidelines were still being adhered to and that special diets could be catered for. It meant going through every item pretty much and deciding who could and couldn't get the treats.'

'Are there going to be spiders, like you promised Tommy?'

Layla nodded happily. 'Yep. Made out of chocolate-covered marshmallows with liquorice legs and eyes. There's gingerbread cookies, too, iced to have skeletons on them. And witch's hat cookies. Upside-down cupcakes with a pretzel handle that look like brooms. Ghosts made out of strawberries dipped in white icing. I got shown pictures of what they've done in past years. It's unbelievable what a big deal Halloween is around here.'

'It's a kids' hospital. It's a big thing if they're missing out on Halloween. Wait till you see what they do for Christmas.'

'It's certainly creating a lot of excitement. Good for some kids, I guess, but Matthew was crying because he's going to go home before it happens.'

Alex nodded. Matthew was due for discharge tomorrow if everybody was happy with his progress. His speech was still slightly slurred but it was improving every day.

'I saw Felix on the ward, too. Ramona was practically chasing him down the corridor. He can crawl amazingly fast.'

'He's overdue for discharge. Nina wanted him kept as long as possible to give Ramona time to sort out her domestic stuff.'

'She said that her boyfriend was in jail, waiting for the court appearance. She's planning to take the kids back to Mexico as soon as the case is over. Her mother's arriving tomorrow.'

Alex nodded but he'd finished eating the roll now and

his thoughts were drifting back to Tommy's case. He looked up at the screens. The lesion was in such a tricky place. Was he really confident of the planned route to expose it without doing too much collateral damage?

Layla's voice was soft. 'He'll be the third.'

'What?'

'Good things come in threes. Special cases this time. Felix and Matthew and…Tommy will be the third.'

'Only if I get things absolutely right. And luck's on our side.'

'The luck came when you agreed to take on the case. Nobody else could do this.'

Alex shook off the reassurance. He didn't need it. Or, rather, he did but he didn't want it to come from Layla. What if it became something he relied on, like a touchstone?

'I'm going to head home,' Layla told him then. 'You'd be more than welcome to come over when you're finished here. I don't care how late it is.'

There was a note in her voice that threatened to burst the bubble. She was offering him more than the distraction of great sex here. She was offering solace. More reassurance. The comfort of being close to someone who understood the kind of pressure he was facing. Of being *cared* for.

'Not tonight.' Alex knew he sounded curt. Knew he was pushing Layla away.

Repeating history because this was exactly what he'd done in the run-up to Jamie's surgery.

And Layla hadn't liked it. She'd wanted more attention and there'd been a showdown. Would that happen again? Would this finish, once and for all, the night before Tommy's surgery, maybe?

Alex could feel an odd prickle on the back of his neck. He had to rub at it.

But Layla seemed completely calm. She came up to him. Stood on tiptoe and planted a gentle kiss on his lips.

'I understand,' she said. 'And don't worry, Alex. I'm not going to throw some kind of hissy fit because you don't have any time or energy for me right now. It's different this time.'

The skin of his bubble was being seriously dented now. Alex pushed back, trying to restore its shape. He turned physically so that he was facing the screens and the white board. Facing his work.

'I'm not caught between a life I don't want to go back to and a future that has been taken out of reach,' Layla continued quietly. 'I think the future I want exists and that's enough for me at the moment. I'm not in any rush to get there.'

Alex had to turn back. To try and decipher exactly what Layla was saying.

Did she see *him* as part of that future she wanted?

'I know it's too soon.' Layla started gathering up the rubbish from their impromptu meal. Her movements looked jerky. Nervous, even. 'There's no pressure here, Alex. Not from me, anyway.' She looked up and caught his gaze. 'Let's just get through this week. You do whatever you need to do. I'm here if you need me but I understand completely if you don't.'

Her smile was so sweet. So genuine.

'I believe in you, Alex.'

She believed in *them*. He could see it in her eyes. Could feel the pull of it between their bodies.

He wanted so badly to submit to that pull. To burst his protective bubble himself and get so close it would feel as if they were part of the same person. Like it did when they made love. A person with the strength to get through anything. Not just to get through but to succeed. Together, they had a power that was nothing like anything he'd ever been conscious of as an individual.

But what if that connection got broken? Again?

He'd lose a lot of what he had already. The strength and power that had been painfully accumulated again piece by piece since the last time his trust in someone had been shattered.

His trust in Layla, no less.

He couldn't risk it again.

Not now. Especially not now. Who was it who said history never repeated itself? Alex had no faith in that sentiment. It only didn't repeat itself if people could stop themselves being stupid enough to step back into the same set of circumstances.

He couldn't find the words to communicate any of his thoughts to Layla. Even if he could have found the words, he wouldn't have used them because that would mean they'd talk about it and Layla would have more of those sweet, seductive words of reassurance.

And he might not be able to keep up the fight. The urge to trust those words.

To trust Layla. To imagine a future like none he had ever envisaged for himself. One that involved so much trust. Loving someone with all his heart and soul.

A family, even.

The internal struggle was fierce. He wanted it but the forces automatically there to fight back were still winning. As they always had, with the one exception of letting Layla too close back then.

So Alex didn't say anything. He nodded to show that he'd heard what Layla had said but then he simply turned back to his work. He could hear Layla behind him, quietly collecting the rest of the rubbish and letting herself out of his office.

For a moment it felt heartbreakingly lonely being by himself.

But the bubble was still intact, thank goodness, and Alex drew it more closely around himself.

The gallery was closed for Tommy Jenner's surgery.

Layla hadn't expected anything else.

It was Cade who came to find her, late in the day, to tell her that it had gone well. Even better than Alex had hoped for.

'He thinks he got it all, with a safety margin. And that any damage from the surgery will be minimal. Another course of chemo should mop up any other cancer cells that might be floating around due to the surgery.'

'Oh….' Layla felt absurdly close to tears. 'I'm so happy to hear that.' The wave of relief made her feel almost euphoric. If history really had repeated herself and the operation had been a disaster, it would have been the end of the road for her and Alex. No question about that. But now? There was hope. More than hope. Confidence almost. 'Where's Alex now?'

'In ICU. I expect he'll be there for a while yet. He

won't want to leave Tommy until he's confident he's completely stable.'

Layla nodded. She could visit, though, if things were going so well. It was too big an ask to stay away for much longer. She hadn't seen Alex since she'd taken him that food in his office the other night. When he'd pushed her away and she'd said she understood.

She did. But the surgery was over now. It had gone well.

That would have changed things, surely.

It certainly seemed to have, on first glance, when Layla made her way to the intensive care unit an hour or two later. There was a quiet satisfaction to Alex's body language as he stood there, scanning the information various monitors were producing. When he looked up to acknowledge Layla, she could see a gleam of relief in his eyes.

Mike was there. Looking absolutely shattered but peaceful, sitting very still beside his son. Tommy was in an induced coma and still on a ventilator. He would be kept like that for a day or two at least, to allow his doctors to control the potentially damaging pressure that any swelling of the brain tissues could produce. His head was heavily bandaged and he was surrounded by an impressive bank of high-tech monitors that could reveal what his blood pressure was beat by beat. And what the pressures were inside his small skull. Whether his kidneys were functioning normally and exactly what percentage of oxygen he was taking in.

Life support.

The bridge between winning and losing the kind of

battle that Alex, and Layla, and all the other staff here at Angel's had dedicated their lives to fighting.

Layla didn't stay long. She didn't say anything directly to Alex either, but as she left, she touched his arm. And when he looked at her she hoped she was conveying that she was with him every step of the way. That there might still be a way to go but even getting this far was a triumph that Alex should be very proud of.

He had done it.

Against some very heavy odds, Tommy had made it through the most complex surgery Alex had ever attempted.

Well…ever since Jamie's surgery, anyway.

And so far so good. By the time Alex finally left the ICU just before midnight, with strict instructions to the staff to call him if the slightest thing changed overnight, everything was looking as good as he could have possibly hoped for.

There was more than professional satisfaction to be found right now. Something almost like euphoria was trickling through Alex's veins as he strode through the lobby and out into the night. He had no intention of going home. He'd find something to eat and then use an on-call room to grab a few hours' sleep before he went back to check on Tommy again.

He needed to get out for a little while, though. To walk off this excess of energy. To come to terms with what had to have been the hardest day of his working life. Nobody could know just how hard it had been to pick up that scalpel and begin a surgery that had, at best, a fifty per cent chance of his patient being alive by the end of it.

Not that other surgeons didn't face that kind of difficult surgery but they hadn't been through what he'd been through in the wake of the Kirkpatrick case. The public disgrace of being accused of malpractice. Of being a failure. Of knowing that his career—the most important thing in his life—was hanging in the balance and could be totally destroyed.

Nobody could understand how big this was for him. Knowing that he'd done it. More than succeeded, because he'd exorcised a ghost that had threatened to haunt him for the rest of his life.

No. That wasn't quite true.

There was one person who could understand.

The person who knew him better than anyone else alive. The person who believed in him. Who was intimately acquainted with his demons and *still* believed in him.

Alex raised his hand and flagged down a cab, which wasn't hard at this time of night. He didn't give the driver his own address, however. He asked to be taken to Layla's apartment.

Would she be there? Would she understand that there was only one way that Alex could release the huge feelings that were choking him? That some of those feelings inextricably linked to the Kirkpatrick case were also about *her* and if he'd dealt with one of those ghosts today, he had to see what it meant in relation to the other one because...because it was so big. It felt like the picture of his future was changing. Getting brighter. But he couldn't separate those ghosts so it was also confusing.

And he felt wired. Would she understand that he felt proud and excited and incredibly nervous all at the same time?

He couldn't explain why, despite the huge success of today, he felt more vulnerable than he ever had, even as a child.

Would she understand that he just needed to be with her?

Layla hadn't expected to see Alex tonight, of all nights.

She had thought he wouldn't be able to tear himself away from the intensive care unit and the watch over Tommy. That if he needed a rest he would go no further than a nearby on-call room where he could put his head down for an hour or two.

But here he was. On her doorstep. Still wearing his scrubs, as though he hadn't had the head room to give what he was wearing a single thought. Looking…

Like she'd never seen him ever look.

As if every defence he'd ever perfected had been stripped away. He looked like…Alex. Pure Alex. As if his soul had seeped into his skin and filled his eyes.

Layla felt her heart split wide open.

And the crack was big enough to gather Alex in and wrap her heart around him.

So she didn't say anything at all in greeting. She merely opened her arms as well as her heart.

And Alex stepped right inside.

Layla's bed was rumpled because she'd got out of it to answer the tap on her door. She was wearing nothing more than silk boxer shorts and a camisole top and the scraps of clothing seemed to evaporate as easily as Alex's loose theatre gear.

The sex was as different as the way Alex had looked.

Fierce and urgent but so tender it broke her heart all over again.

There was no conversation between them at all but how many times had Alex said her name?

With the groan of desire as his lips covered hers. The almost reverent whisper as his hands stroked her clothing away. The cry of need as he entered her. The echo of something she couldn't define at the moment of ultimate satisfaction. And a whisper again, as they lay, still joined, waiting for their breathing to slow and their heart rates to get somewhere close to normal again.

A whisper that could have been the start of being able to talk but the intimate sound was drowned by the strident notes of Alex's pager.

He ripped himself away from Layla and was out of the bed in the same fluid motion.

'Rodriguez.' The greeting was almost a bark. He listened for only a few seconds. 'I'm on my way.'

And then he was pulling the scrubs back on and it took only seconds.

'What is it?' Layla had to ask, because Alex wasn't telling her. She felt like she was suddenly on another planet and the contrast to where they'd been such a short time ago was brutal.

This felt…like she didn't exist for Alex right now. Like she was back in that scary place right before Jamie's surgery. When she couldn't go back to her past life but the future she'd been dreaming of seemed to have been suddenly taken away.

No. She could cope with this. She could see the bigger picture. She could make allowances for this intense focus that had nothing to do with her.

'It's Tommy, isn't it?'

A terse nod from Alex. 'He's had a seizure.' The words were heavy. 'Intracranial pressure has spiked.'

There was nothing more to say. A headline proclaiming potential disaster and they were both too far away to gather any more information.

Layla heard her front door closing. She even heard Alex's shout seconds later as he demanded an urgent response from a cab driver.

The shivering started then. Hunched on her bed, Layla pulled the covers up to her shoulders but the chill wouldn't go away. A short time later she pushed them aside and went to find her clothes. There was no point trying to sleep so she may as well go into Angel's and find out for herself what was happening.

And it was then that the curious way Alex had said her name in that most unguarded moment came back to haunt her.

Maybe the undertone hadn't been indefinable at all.

As it echoed in her mind now, she could hear the clear notes of something that sounded horribly like despair.

Alex fought harder than he'd ever fought before.

He juggled drugs and ventilator settings and didn't leave Tommy's side until the rise in pressure that had caused the seizure was under control. It took a long time and there were more seizures before he was happy that Tommy's condition was stable.

Happy wasn't the word, of course. This was a major setback and he could see the fear in Mike's face. In Gina's, too, because she was there by his side, clinging to his hand. Sharing this horrible vigil.

A vigil that stretched and stretched. When things had been stable for thirty-six hours, Alex decided it was time to lighten the sedation and get Tommy off the ventilator.

The drugs were tailed off and the breathing tube finally removed and everyone breathed a sigh of relief when the monitors showed that Tommy was managing to breathe on his own and his condition didn't deteriorate. Mike and Gina couldn't be prised away from his bedside now because he might wake up at any moment.

Except he didn't. Hour after hour went by and there was no flicker of returning consciousness. Tommy wasn't in an induced coma now. He was in a genuine coma and things were starting to look bleak. They looked even bleaker two days later when Tommy still lay still on his bed, totally unresponsive.

'Is he going to wake up?'

Why had Layla chosen the moment that Mike voiced his worst fear to visit the intensive care unit?

Alex shook his head slowly. 'We just don't know what's really going on. We know that the cerebral blood flow is fine now but we don't know what it was like when he was so unstable. The intracranial pressure is the same deal. His level of oxygenation is good. So are his electrolytes and fluid balance. The EEG to look for brain activity was inconclusive. There's some activity. We just don't know if it's enough. Or whether the readings were accurate. We'll run the tests again tomorrow.'

'But you must have an opinion,' Mike pressed. 'You've had so many cases like this. You're the best there is and you must have a gut feeling for how this is going to go.'

Alex had to shake his head again. 'I'm sorry, Mike, but all I can say is that I really don't know. I wish I could say something else, I really do.'

'But it's not looking good, is it?'

'No.' He had a responsibility to prepare parents for the worst possible scenario when it was looking more and more likely, didn't he? 'I'm so sorry, Mike. We have to wait and see but…' It was too hard to finish the sentence. Alex's throat felt like it was closing up.

'But don't get my hopes up?' There were tears in Mike's eyes but he was trying so hard to hold it together. He knew Alex had done and was doing the best he possibly could and there was no blame in his gaze. Just despair.

Alex could only give a terse nod. He gripped Mike's arm in a gesture of sympathy but then he had to look away.

And Layla was there, dammit. With those big, blue eyes swimming with tears.

Looking as scared and grief-stricken as Mike.

He couldn't help remembering what she'd looked like just before Tommy's surgery. When she'd told him that she believed in him.

Where was that belief now?

Gone.

She was scared. Under emotional pressure. What would happen if Tommy died? Would she snap? Had she lost her belief in a future with him along with her belief in his abilities? There was no getting away from how she'd tried to take control the last time she'd been scared like this.

Would she dump him? Again?

No. He wouldn't let that happen. Couldn't afford to, if he was going to survive.

Alex excused himself from the unit. He really, really needed some time to himself.

Why did Layla choose to follow him?

Was it fate? Giving him the chance to take at least some control of this horrible situation? A way to jump before he got pushed?

'Alex…'

'Not now, Layla.' Even now he was fighting it. Postponing the inevitable despite the fact that they were out of the unit now and there was no one else around. It might be the only opportunity to have a private conversation all day.

Layla ignored his warning. How typical was that?

'I just wanted to say I'm sorry. I…feel awful that you were with me when things started to go wrong. And…and I wanted to say…don't give up on Tommy yet. There's—'

'Don't say there's still *hope*.' Alex kept his voice low to control his sudden anger. 'You and I both know what the likely outcome is.'

Layla had tears in her eyes again. Her bottom lip trembled. That fear was back in her eyes again, too, and Alex couldn't cope with that.

'Will I see you later?' The words were a whisper.

'No.' Somehow Alex found the strength he needed. And the words. 'It's over, Layla.'

She went very, very still.

'You mean…*us*?'

A single nod but Alex couldn't meet her eyes. 'You were right.' How on earth did he manage to keep his tone so light? Conversational almost. 'All it needed was to use up the fuel.' He risked a lightning-fast touch of eye contact. 'It was a pretty good fire the other night. Unfortunate that I'd decided to take a break from my professional responsibilities but there you go. It happened. And that was when I threw the last bits of fuel on.'

He managed a longer glance this time. 'I'm sorry if it's not what you want but it's all gone as far as I'm concerned, Layla. It's *over*.'

CHAPTER ELEVEN

IT WASN'T OVER.

It *couldn't* be.

Alex might think it was but he was having a knee-jerk reaction to an emotional situation and he was taking it out on her.

Taking it out on himself, too, but he probably didn't realise that.

It was Halloween today and Angel's was buzzing with the kind of excitement that came with a special day. It was always a bonus when you could distract sick and hurting children from the frightening circumstances they found themselves in and occasions like Halloween or Christmas were gold.

There were decorations to distract a child with when something painful or scary was about to happen to them. Treats to promise for when it was over. The anticipation of the staff parade that would build all day and would not only break the normal routine for longer-term patients but make being in hospital a special place to be.

Normally, Layla would have become enthusiastically involved. She would have found herself a great costume to wear all day and had a bag of treats she could distribute to small, excited children. She'd thought about it. Tossed up between turning herself into a cowgirl to amuse the children or a witch to amuse the staff, but any incentive to play had been lost in the awful tension of Tommy's case.

And it had gone out the window completely in the wake of getting dumped by Alex four days ago.

Her secretary had been busy adding the spirit of Halloween to her office. Layla had to brush past a soft, fabric spider web hanging from her doorframe that had a very cheerful-looking plastic spider attached to its centre. A large, bright orange Jack-o'-lantern sticker on her window obscured a good percentage of the view. Not that Layla was going to be distracted by gazing at Central Park any more than by the invitations to share the fun of Halloween.

She had been so afraid that something like this might happen to destroy what she'd found with Alex. That Tommy's case was too like Jamie's not to bring the ghosts of the past out to haunt and sabotage the present. Somewhere in Alex's mind, maybe Tommy *was* Jamie. And he was bailing because he could see nothing but the rocks their relationship was doomed to flounder on.

A mirthless snort of laughter escaped Layla. It was Halloween. How appropriate that it was ghosts that were responsible for this new low point in her life.

But how *unfair*.

It shouldn't be happening because Tommy's case was *different*. Nothing had gone wrong in the surgery. There was no obvious explanation for why he wasn't waking up now. Nobody could say that Alex hadn't done everything possible. Much more than anyone else might have even attempted.

And what she and Alex had together was just as different from what they'd had in the days of that illicit affair.

They hadn't thrown fuel onto the smouldering ashes of what they'd had together back then. They'd started a new fire the night they'd gone out together and talked. They'd revealed things to each other that made them *real* people. People with difficult, hurtful things in their histories. They'd found a connection that went far, far deeper than anything physical could have achieved.

She'd learned things about Alex that had shocked her but it had also shown her how good he was at hiding things like that. Yes, she'd been aware of the shadows but she could never have guessed how dark they really were. He'd had a lifetime of practice at hiding. At protecting himself from getting hurt again.

And that was what he was doing now.

Protecting himself by pushing her away, as hard and as far as he could.

Because he didn't trust her?

Did he really think she was going to end things between them? Ever?

She'd done it once, hadn't she?

Had it ever occurred to her to wonder how much that might have hurt him? What had happened so soon afterwards, with the horrible publicity and the shame of the malpractice suit had been enough of an explanation for everybody else for why Alex had been so miserable. Why he'd quit and gone to the other side of the world, but…but what if there'd been more to it than that? If the way she'd treated him had contributed to more than potentially affecting his concentration the day of Jamie's surgery?

Oh, *God…* Layla didn't think she could feel any worse than she had been feeling for the last two days but she'd been wrong.

Sitting down at her desk, she ignored the pile of memos that would remind her of what she had to fit into today's routine. Instead, she rubbed her forehead with the base of the palms of her hands.

She'd had a premonition of precisely this, hadn't she? When Alex had walked out of Tommy's room that time and it had felt like he was walking away from *her*? That despairing note in his voice as he'd cried out her name at the climax of that extraordinary time together in the wake of the successful surgery?

She'd been so afraid of losing him.

Standing there beside Tommy's bed when Alex had been warning Mike not to hold out too much hope, Layla had seen more than the heartbreak of losing a small child. She'd seen what it would be like to lose Alex from her life and she'd been so afraid.

He'd seen that fear in her face, surely?

And yet he'd chosen that moment to run. To wall himself off emotionally so convincingly that Layla had done her best to stay out of his way. Knowing that another blow like that and what was left of her strength might desert her completely.

What would her colleagues think of their new chief of Paediatrics if they saw her sliding down the wall somewhere, to crouch in a sobbing heap, overcome by grief?

Layla raised her head. Her eyes were still closed but she took a deep, deep breath.

Not going to happen.

What was going to happen was that she would come up with a plan to take control of her own life again.

Somehow.

As soon as she could catch whatever it was that was swirling elusively around in the back of her mind.

Something that wasn't ringing true about any of this. That was adding a note of confusion.

Shining a tiny light that might feel like hope if she could just catch hold of the danged thing.

Alex was running on autopilot. There were surgeries to perform. Ward rounds to conduct. Patients to treat and parents to talk to. Any free moments he had between his duties were spent in the intensive care unit.

Checking Tommy. Going through every note that had been made. Analysing every reading any of the monitors produced. Calling experts from anywhere in the world that he could discuss the case with as he desperately tried to find an answer. A way out of this dreadful dead end.

Ryan had come into the ICU to check on one of his patients, a head trauma from a car accident earlier that day. Alex knew that underneath the theatre gown his second-in-command was wearing a pirate costume. He'd probably left his hat in his office and when he was finished here he would be heading off like everybody else to go to the ball. Halloween didn't make it into any of the intensive care units. Or into any of the operating theatres, and that suited Alex just fine.

He'd never felt less like being part of a party.

He didn't deserve to be having fun. Not when Mike and Gina were sitting here beside Tommy's bed, as pale and still as Tommy was himself. There was nothing to even talk about any more. They just had to wait. Tommy was breathing perfectly well. All his organs were functioning normally. The pressure inside his skull was back to what it should be.

He just wouldn't wake up.

And maybe he never would.

Like part of *him* never would again either. A big part.

He'd told Layla that the fire was out and there was no more fuel to put on it. What a lie. How could you put out a fire that was actually burning in every cell of your body? If you did put it out, something vital would die.

Right now that part of him was in a coma. Like Tommy. And what he didn't know was what would happen if it did die. Was it a part of himself he couldn't live without?

Would he be on autopilot for the rest of his life?

The thought was unbearably bleak. It was a relief to feel a tap on his shoulder and Alex turned, expecting to see Ryan.

But it wasn't. Cade had come into the ICU at some point as he'd sat here at the nurses' station, poring over Tommy's case notes.

'You need to get out of here for a while, man.'

Alex shrugged. There was nowhere to go. He wasn't on call and the day's duties were long finished with. He didn't want to go home because he'd be faced with an apartment that was filled with memories of Layla's company. A bed that tortured him with its emptiness.

'Come with me,' Cade suggested.

To shoot hoops? Alex shook his head. He wasn't angry or wired enough for that to be an attractive diversion. He'd never felt so tired in his life. So…sad.

'I've got your costume. Come and be someone else for an hour or two.'

Now that was an attractive option. But a costume wasn't going to make it happen. Heading off to a new job or a new country, like Cade was about to, wasn't going to fix this either. Alex had already been there and done that. He had several T-shirts, come to think of it. And look at him now. Back to square one. Trying to figure out how he was going to get through the aftermath of a case going horribly wrong.

Of getting involved with Layla Woods.

'You have to come,' Cade said. 'It's my last night here. Might be the last time we get to have some time together for a while.' His hand gripped Alex's shoulder. 'There's nothing more you can do here for now and it'd mean a lot to me, bro.'

Alex closed the case notes. He looked over at Tommy's cubicle. A nurse was hovering, probably moistening the little boy's lips or adjusting his pillow or something. Gina had her head on Mike's shoulder and he had his arm wrapped tightly around her. His other arm was outstretched, his hand completely enclosing one of Tommy's. Cade was right. There *was* nothing more he could do here. Was he getting too emotionally involved with one of his patients? Like he'd accused Layla of being so often?

And then Alex looked up and caught the expression in his brother's face. Cade was leaving a lot behind him here as he gave up his position at Angel's to head for new horizons in Australia. Bad stuff, for sure, but he was also giving up the only family he had. For a moment he looked like the kid brother Alex had let down so badly in the past.

Stiffly, Alex pushed himself to his feet.

'OK. Just for an hour or two. And I'm not saying yes to the costume if it turns out to be the back end of a cow.'

'No.' Cade's face lit up. 'Jack Carter helped me choose. You'll love it, man. Come on, we can get changed in your office.'

New York Children's Hospital was so quiet tonight.

Everybody who possibly could go had gone to the huge fundraising ball in the nearby venue.

Not Layla, however.

She'd come to the intensive care unit to share the vigil that Mike and Gina were keeping at Tommy's bedside. Just for a while. To let them know they weren't alone. That other people cared.

Their whispered conversation had died some time ago. Now they were all sitting in a silence that was broken only by the soft beeping of the machines watching over Tommy.

Layla's thoughts inevitably turned inwards again. She was still trying to catch that elusive thought glowing, tantalisingly, just out of reach. Her gaze was on Tommy's face but she wasn't really seeing him or thinking about him. There was just a background sadness that a such a young, much-loved child could be in such a situation. Children were so vulnerable. So *trusting*…

That was it.

Layla dipped her head, closed her eyes and held her breath as she finally caught the thought. It was the way Alex had looked when she'd opened her door the other night. When she'd been able to see everything that was Alex Rodriguez. Everything about the man that she'd wanted to wrap her heart around. To love.

Had she seen the brilliant surgeon? The breathtakingly gorgeous man that turned every female head? Yes, of course, she had.

But she could see past that as well. To a frightened, lonely child who was afraid to love because people that he should have been able to trust had hurt him.

He hadn't even been trying to hide anything at all.

And that had to mean that he *did* trust her. Or could. Maybe all he needed was reassurance but what had Layla done when he'd told her it was over? Stayed out of his way. Like she had after Jamie had died because she'd felt so guilty and hadn't known what to say.

Well…she knew what to say this time.

And she'd been right. That elusive thought offered hope.

Letting her breath out slowly, Layla opened her eyes to find herself looking at Mike. And, weirdly, the warmth of hope that was seeping through her veins like a potent drug to reach every cell in her body seemed to be contagious. Mike still looked completely exhausted but his chin wasn't on his chest any more. He was looking straight ahead and he looked completely stunned. Blinded almost.

Gina had caught it, too. Her mouth was open and she was also staring straight ahead.

At Tommy? What were they looking at?

Very slowly, Layla turned her own head. Her heart missed a beat and then thumped so loudly she could swear she heard it.

Tommy's eyes were *open*.

The little boy blinked. Once…twice. His mouth opened and then closed. And then it opened again.

'Dad?' The whisper was a hoarse croak. 'Is it over now?'

Mike's outward breath was a barely controlled sob. He had to fight for control as he leaned down to kiss Tommy.

'Yes, buddy. It's over now.'

Staff came running as the monitors tripped alarms due to the unexpected increase in activity. Layla helped with the initial assessment but just as his coma had been inexplicable so was this return to consciousness. He was still very drowsy but could be roused easily now. There was no sign that he might slip back into the coma.

'Somebody needs to find Rodriguez,' one of the ICU doctors said. 'He'll want to know about this.'

'I'll page him,' a nurse offered. But she came back a short time later and shook her head. 'He's not answering his pager or his mobile. Apparently he left word that he was going to the ball for a while but would still be able to be contacted. I guess he can't hear his phone.'

'I know where it is.' Layla was already heading for the door. 'I'll find him.'

The venue was within walking distance and Layla got there within minutes. She couldn't wait to find Alex. To tell him about Tommy, of course, but more than that.

Much more than that, she had to find out if the hope she was feeling about her future had a real basis. If Alex could trust her.

Could love her as much as she knew she loved him.

She entered the huge space through a doorway draped with black curtains and guarded by ghosts that had been made by white sheets draped over helium balloons so that they floated convincingly overhead. It was only then that she realised that it wasn't going to be easy to locate Alex .

There were hundreds of people here and she couldn't even see anybody she recognised because they were all disguised in an astonishing array of costumes. Not only that, the only lighting was coming from Jack-o'-lanterns on the tables and the music was loud.

Layla stood still for a minute or two, getting accustomed to this very odd atmosphere. There were groups of people standing talking, lots of people dancing and some were grouped around tables that had black coverings cluttered with wineglasses and platters of snack food. She could see ghosts and devils, clowns and fairies, a Frankenstein and a skeleton. An extraordinary couple dressed as Adam and Eve walked past her, wearing pink skin-tight body suits with fig leaves attached in appropriate places.

'Wow,' Eve shouted with laughter. 'You've come as a doctor. Very cool.'

It took Layla a moment to click and then she groaned aloud. She'd rushed out of Angel's so fast on her quest to find Alex that she hadn't bothered to take off her white coat. In this dim lighting she probably stood out as much as that man in the flashy white suit who was coming towards her. He had cowboy boots on, too, and a white Stetson hat a mile wide.

'Hey, darlin'. You've come to join the party, then?'

'Ty…' It was a huge relief to recognise someone. 'Hey, you make a good Texan tycoon.'

'I'm just tryin' it on for size. Might use this for my weddin' outfit. You'll be coming, won't you?'

'Of course I will. Have you seen Alex tonight? I'm trying to find him.'

'Who's he come as?'

'He doesn't do dress-ups.' He'd said that, hadn't he? She'd thought he was trying to tell her that what was happening between them was real.

It was. It still could be.

'I *have* to find him, Ty. It's really important.'

'I saw Ryan a while back. He might know. He's a pirate.'

'*Layla*, hi…'

Chloe looked adorable as Wilma Flintstone in her ragged-hem dress, a necklace that looked like it was made of out golf balls and a bright orange wig that matched Brad's 'Fred' costume.

'Have either of you seen Alex?'

'He's right behind you. See?'

Layla whirled round. There were three men right behind her. Dressed identically.

The three musketeers were all roughly the same height. They all had the same black trousers tucked into boots, white shirts with flowing sleeves and tabards with a Celtic cross on the front and a cape attached at the back. They all had shoulder-length, curly black wigs, huge hats with ostrich feathers in them, masks and pencil-thin moustaches.

Three peas in a pod but only one of them was looking back at Layla with an intensity she could feel right down to her bones.

'Alex...' Layla couldn't tell if he could even hear her with this background noise. 'I need to talk to you.'

'Hey, Layla.' She recognised Cade's voice. 'This is some farewell party, isn't it? Glad you could make it.'

Layla nodded. Smiled, even, but she couldn't look away from Alex.

'You don't look like you're here to party.' The third musketeer turned out to be Jack Carter. 'Everything OK, Layla?'

'It will be.' Layla felt absurdly close to tears. 'Alex... Tommy's woken up.'

'What? *When?*' He didn't wait for a reply. Alex grabbed Layla's hand and pulled her after him, heading for the doors. Away from the crowds and crazy costumes and all the noise. Out into the night with the trees of Central Park casting huge shadows in the light from the streetlamps. They were heading back to Angel's, still hand in hand.

Suddenly Alex stopped. 'Tell me,' he commanded. 'Tell me everything.'

It took no time at all to bring Alex up to speed on Tommy. Layla expected him to take off again. To go and see for himself that what she was telling him was true.

But he didn't. He let out a long, slow breath, closed his eyes and pulled Layla into his arms to hold her very tightly.

'Thank God,' was all he said.

A car horn sounded loudly beside them and Layla could hear some ribald shouting. Even in New York it was probably an odd sight to see a musketeer embracing a doctor. Alex caught the gist of the comments and stepped back with a wry smile.

'You're lucky you're not in a stupid costume,' he said.

'I don't do dress-ups,' Layla reminded him quietly. 'I'm not into pretending to be someone that I'm not.'

She held his gaze. 'I'm not going to live a lie or follow a script. Things are different now, Alex.'

He was listening to her words but was he hearing what she was trying to tell him?

'It's not just that Tommy's woken up and he's going to be OK that I had to come and find you tonight. I know you think you can't trust me because of what I did last time but things *are* different now.'

Alex was still holding her hands. Did that mean something good?

'I'm not trapped any more. I'm not in a marriage that was never right. I'm not feeling guilty or scared. I'm free and I get to choose what I want and...and I want *you*, Alex. I...I love you.'

He was staring down at her. Frowning. 'But you *were* scared. I could see it when Mike was asking about Tommy. You looked like...you'd stopped believing in me.'

Layla shook her head sharply. 'Yes, I was scared. Scared of losing *you*. I can't imagine my life without you in it now.'

She still believed in him.

She *loved* him?

The news about Tommy was a huge relief but this… this was way bigger. So big that words had deserted Alex. It was Layla who broke the new silence between them.

'I thought you didn't do dress-ups, either.'

'I don't.' Alex wanted to rip the hat and wig off his head but that would mean letting go of Layla's hands. 'I thought I wanted to be someone else for a while, that's all.'

'Oh…' She understood that he'd wanted to step out of his own skin to get away from everything that was happening in his life. He could see the fear in her eyes again. Fear that she really was going to lose him?

'But I was wrong.' The words came easily now. From a place deep inside his heart. 'I don't want to be anyone else. Not even for a minute.'

'Because of Tommy?'

'No. Because of *you*.' Alex dipped his head so that he could kiss her and the soft, welcoming touch of her lips was all he needed to know that this was right. So right it felt like he'd been waiting his whole life for this moment. 'I love *you*, Layla. I always have. And if I was someone else I wouldn't have you in my life, and I'm not going to waste another single minute of that.'

'There's a lot of minutes in every day.' Layla was smiling. 'And in every night. Can we go and visit Tommy now and then maybe go home?'

'Oh, yeah…' But Alex didn't want to move quite yet. 'How many minutes in a week are there? In a month? In a *year*?'

'Not enough, I reckon.'

Alex had an odd lump in his throat. 'Would a lifetime of minutes be enough?'

Oh…he could drown in those eyes. In the love he could see. A love that he wanted to claim. To return. For ever.

'Marry me,' he whispered. 'Please?'

It seemed to be Layla's turn to be lost for words. But she was nodding. And crying?

Layla Woods didn't cry. Unless…

She was scrubbing her tears away. 'Don't mind me,' she told him. 'I'm just so happy…as happy as a clam at high tide. Yes, Alex. I would love to marry you. As long as you don't wear that outfit to our wedding.'

'I won't, I promise.'

'Or a white suit.'

'It's a deal.'

Laughing, and still hand in hand, Alex and Layla set off again. Walking towards Angel's.

Towards their future.

* * * * *

0413/MB409a

Join the NYC Angels online community...

Get all the gossip straight from the hospital on our NYC Angels Facebook app...

- Read exclusive bonus material from each story
- Enter our NYC Angels competition
- Introduce yourself to our Medical authors

You can find the app at our Facebook page

Facebook.com/romancehq

(Once on Facebook, simply click on the NYC Angels logo to visit the app!)